Heartbound

The Kingdom of Aetherlyn Series

K.T. Carpenter

Email: AuthorKTCarpenter@gmail.com

K.T. Carpenter

ISBN: 9798346236929

Cover Designed by: Morgan Burger (Images created by AI)

Edited by: Cynica Lango & Danny Burns

Interior Formatting & Header Art by: Danny Burns

Interior Art by: K.T. Carpenter (Images created by AI)

For the dreamers who long to fly and
the friends who make the journey magical-

this tale is for you.

Contents

Trigger Warnings

Heartbound Contains :

contain sensitive content:
violence
explicit sexual scenes
explicit language
threat of violence
anxiety
emotional & physical abuse
loss of autonomy (mind-control)
heartbreak, loss, & mental distress
alcohol consumption
knife, sword, & weapon violence
murder & attempted murder
Physical assault
blood, gore, & injury
battle scenes
death
mental and physical abuse
grief

Pronunciations

Character Names &
Powers

Evandor Firethorne– King of Aetherlyn :
(Eh-VAN-*dor*)
Zephyrion – Evandor's Dragon (Weather Manipulation) :
(*Zeh*-FY-*ree*-*uhn*)
Adelina Firethorne- Queen of Aetherlyn :
(Ah-*deh*-LEE-*nuh*)
Nagaara- Adelina's Dragon (Foresight) :
(N*ah*-GAH-*rah*)
General Alvar- General of Aetherlyn's Army:
(AHL-*var*)
Morphandor- General Alvar's Dragon :
(Shapeshifting) (MOR-*fan*-*dor*)
Helena- Handmaiden :
(Heh-LAY-*nuh*)
Clara- 2nd handmaiden :
(KLAH-*ruh*)
Ellissandra/Ellie Firethorne- Princess of Aetherlyn :
(El-*ih*-SAHN-*druh*)
Saphirixia- Ellie's Dragon (Telepathy) :
(*Sah*-FIHR-*ix*-*ee*-*uh*)
Kyla Blackwood- Warrior Friend :
(KYE-*luh*)
Kaida- Kyla's Dragon (Animal Telepathic) :
(KAY-*duh*)

Stella Ravenscroft- Court friend :
(S*TEL-uh*)
Sentiara- Stella's dragon (Empath) :
(*Sen-tee*-AHR-*uh*)
Tristan Mormont- Lord's son and Captain :
(TRIS-*tuhn*)
Terbius- Tristan's Dragon :
(Manipulate the elements)(*TER-bee-us*)
Jace Fairhaven- Baker's son :
(JAY-s)
Eleanora Fairhaven- Jace's Mother :
(*El-uh*-NOR-*uh*)
Lord Mormont- Tristan's Father :
(MOR-*mont*)
Rigmor- Lord Mormont's Dragon (Manipulate the mind :
(RIG-*mor*)
Breccan Aldenridge- Tristan's best friend :
(BREK-*an*)
Vespero- Breccan's Dragon (Teleportation) :
(VES-*per-oh*)

Play List

Heartbound by K.T. Playlist on Youtube Music

Can You Love Me?- Croixx_
I'll Be There For You- Silent Child
Half Life- Livingston
Lose Control- Teddy Swims
Up In Flames- Ruelle
Deep End- Spicyverse
Way Down We Go- KALEO
War Of Hearts- Ruelle
Just Pretend- Bad Omens
Dangerous Hands- Austin Giorgio
Play With Fire- Sam Tinnesz
Free Animal- Foreign Air
The Death Of Peace Of Mind- Bad Omens
Easy To Love- Bryce Savage
Quick Musical Doodles- Two Feet
Last First Kiss- Abe Parker
Super Villain- Stiletto, Silent Child, Kendyle Paige
Trouble- Camylio
No Love For A Sinner- Shaya Zamora
Half Of Forever- Henrik
I Found- Amber Run
Hey- Marissa
I Guess I'm In Love- Clinton Kane

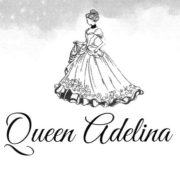

Queen Adelina

Prologue

Queen Adelina anticipates the pain coming before it begins to rage through her body so profoundly that it twists her bones, searing through her like dragon fire. She knows that the birth of her child will be excruciating. Her power of foresight often feels like a curse more than a gift for both her and her bonded. Nagaara isn't just her dragon, but the other half of her soul. They share thoughts, feelings, and pain.

"You can do this, my love," Evandor encourages. His words come out confident, but Adelina can see the fear he's trying to hide.

"I don't think I'm ready," the queen responds, clenching her teeth through the pain as it slowly starts to burn though her body. Tears stream down her face as the first wave of agony rips through her. Yet, her warrior heart doesn't allow her to give up.

Evandor brushes a tender kiss to her temple, tears lining his eyes as Adelina peers up at him. He has never looked so scared. She knows deep down that his fear of losing her is at the forefront of his mind. This is the sad reality of childbirth for fae females at her age of one hundred and sixty-six.

Adelina doesn't need her magic to know that he is her fated mate. Her love for Evandor consumes her, fulfills her, and outweighs every duty and responsibility she has- including the kingdom. She knows deep in her soul that he feels the same way.

"Where is Nagaara?!" the king yells over his shoulder, peering at his second in command with fury etched on his face.

“I'm not sure, Highness. No one has seen the dragon in days," General Alvar said softly, clearly fearing his response would unsettle them further.

“She needs Nagaara to keep her strong and talk her through this. I'm afraid her strength will waver otherwise," Evandor sighs, as he wipes his hand over his face.

"Shall I send patrols to find her?” General Alvar asked. The risk of entering a dragon's lair is potentially fatal. Even if the general or any soldiers did find her, they will never be able to command Nagaara to do anything she doesn't want, even if they tried. The only one who can command the enormous, strong-willed dragon is the queen and the queen alone.

Another wail rips from the queen's lips as she watches Evandor's limbs go utterly still, observing the anguish and fear in his eyes.

"Go, now!" The king orders and Alvar quickly exits the royal chambers, in search of a miracle.

"Push, Your Highness, push!" Helena encourages while gripping tightly to Adelina's other hand. Helena isn't just another handmaiden, but the queen's most respected and beloved friend.

With Adelina's strength stretching thin, she closes her eyes and reaches out to the one her soul needs. "*Please, I need you, my friend; I need your strength. I can't do this alone. Please don't abandon me.*" The only response she receives is utter, painful, silence.

With the king beside her, sharing his unwavering love, it gives her the strength she so desperately needs. Adelina closes her eyes tightly, and with one last deep breath, the agony tears through with her last push. The newborn's cries pierce the air, echoing through the bedchamber.

The royal healer exclaims joyfully, "Congratulations, Your Highnesses, you have a daughter!"

King Evandor releases a long sigh of relief; his eyes train on the royal healer who bundles his new heir in a cloth. He then looks down at his beloved, who peers up at him with a teary smile.

"You're remarkable, my love. She's finally here," the king says, unable to hold back the tears in his eyes.

The royal healer gracefully lays the bundled babe into Adelina's expecting arms, before slowly backing away with a bow and then silently leaving Helena and the other servants to clean the room.

Evandor sits beside her, one arm wrapped tightly around her and holding her close. She watches as he takes in their babe's precious little hand wrapped around his finger. She marvels at the tiny life they've created together. The living embodiment of their love and hope for the future.

"I have everything I could have ever wished for," Evandor whispers, his voice full of gratitude.

"We're truly blessed," she says softly, emotion filling her voice.

Evandor nods in silent agreement. At that moment, they both know that no matter what challenges they face in the future, their love and family will be the source of their strength. Their daughter is the future of Aetherlyn, the symbol of hope and renewal for the entire kingdom.

As the first rays of dawn filter through the windows, Adelina hears the clanging of bells throughout the kingdom from the open windows, accompanied by the joyous cheers of the people of Aetherlyn, welcoming the long-awaited arrival of their new heir.

.

1

Ellie

A heavy knocking pulls Ellie from the depths of her perfect dream. She buries her face in the pillow, letting out a low growl of frustration. Today is her twenty-fifth moon, her name day. *The dreadful twenty-fifth, kill me now*, Ellie thinks as she forces herself to sit up, rubbing her hands over her face.

"Good morning to you, too, your Highness. I see you are in a pleasant mood this morning," comes the familiar voice of Helena, her mother's handmaiden. A knowing smirk plays on her lips as she strides into the bedchamber and abruptly yanks the curtains open, flooding the space with bright morning light.

"I'll go draw your bath and lay out your dress. Your breakfast will be up shortly, along with your tea," Helena adds briskly before disappearing into the bathing chamber.

Ellie reluctantly slides out of bed, grabs her gloves, and quickly putting them on. A light knock sounds at her door as her other handmaiden enters. Her stomach grumbles from the scent of eggs, bacon, and honey biscuits as it permeates the room.

Clara smiles brightly as she greets Ellie, "Good morning, your Highness; here is your tea." Ellie wiggles her fingers with excitement and quickly takes the hot tea that Clara holds out to her, warming her hands almost instantly. The smell of citrus and honey makes her feel slightly better.

"Thank you so much, Clara. What would I do without you?" Ellie asks with a smile, making Clara chuckle lightly and shake her head.

“You would most likely go hungry and without ever having my special tea again, you would be incredibly miserable, your Highness,” her truthful words making both females chuckle. *She isn’t wrong. I do love her tea*, Ellie muses.

"Tell me, how does it look out there? Is my mother already ordering everyone around who is preparing the great hall for tonight?" Ellie twists her fingers, the question feeling heavy in the air. Clara busies herself by placing Ellie’s breakfast on a table by the fire.

Clara, the beautiful female with her auburn hair, chocolate brown eyes, and soft features, has been in Ellie’s service since she was sixteen. Over the years she’s become more of a friend than a handmaiden, given their close age. Ellie can always count on Clara, especially when it comes to the castle secrets that no one else will tell her. Everyone else seems to do their best not to speak to her.

Ellie figures it’s because she’s the princess, or the fear they all have of her gift. The thought used to bother her, but as she grew up, she started to find solace in being alone and the quiet peace it afforded her.

"The queen has been up since dawn making sure everything is pristine for your big day. I know you’re dreading it, Your Highness, but please try and have at least a little fun tonight. All you do is read, fly with your bonded, and shy away from everyone. You know the King and Queen just want you to feel special. So please, just try for me," Clara pleads. Ellie scoffs at that.

Even though she deeply appreciates Clara's concern, she has no interest in tonight's celebration, despite it being for her. She would much rather be hiding in her bedchambers reading a book, blissfully alone.

"For you, I'll try," Ellie promises with a smirk as she takes a sip of her tea. Placing the warm cup down, she walks to the bathroom where Helena is finishing drawing her bath.

Helena turns, "Is there anything else I can do for you?"

"No, that will be all. I would hate to monopolize your time when I know my mother *desperately* needs your services today." Helena chuckles and gently takes Ellie's gloved hands in hers and gives them a light squeeze.

"Today is your special day. Do try to make the most of it, will you?" Helena's voice carries a motherly tenderness. Her deep brown hair and soft, caring brown eyes adds to her warmth. Ellie truly respects and loves her deeply for serving her family all her life.

"Clara already gave me the speech; I promise to try." Helena wraps her in a warm embrace, and Ellie welcomes the comfort, inhaling her calming lavender scent.

Helena releases her slowly, and moves to leave the bathing chamber, pausing in the doorway. "Happy name day." Ellie gives her a soft smile, bowing her head slightly before Helena walks out of sight.

Ellie turns to the vanity mirror and hesitantly peers at her reflection. Her long blonde hair is messy and dark circles shadow her deep sapphire-blue eyes, a result of reading late last night. The slight glow of her skin reflects the time she's spent enjoying soaring through the sky and basking in the sun lately. The freckles that dot her nose and cheeks, becoming more prominent.

She brushes her teeth and puts her messy hair in a bun atop her head, knowing it will get dirty from training. Taking one last look in the mirror, she takes a deep breath at her appearance and begins to undress, then slowly steps into the large round porcelain bath.

The water is scalding hot and its heat rapidly soaks into her tense muscles, giving her the relief she didn't realize she desperately needed after her brutal training yesterday. She allows herself to soak in this moment of tranquility before the long day ahead.

After dressing, Ellie decides it's time to find her mother before she comes to find her, knowing full well that her lovely mother would be all too eager to scold her for not joining her for breakfast. She makes her way through the castle, passing many servants and guards. They all give her gracious smiles and a bow; a few even wishing her a happy name day. The urge to scowl at them tempts her, but she remains gracious, thanking them while she continues down the halls.

Ellie knew this day was coming and has prepared herself for the extravagant event that is expected of the next in line to the throne of Aetherlyn. Finally making it to the great hall, she can hear the queen ordering the servants around through the heavy wooden doors.

"No, no, no, the greenery should be higher. Oh, make sure all the candles are lit; I want it to be bright in here tonight," the queen demands.

Her mother's voice brings a smile to Ellie's face as she pushes the large door open, getting her first glimpse of the extravagant room. Her mother's dream seamlessly coming alive. The queen sure knows how to throw a party, thinking of every little detail from the drapes to the candlesticks.

But still, it all feels like too much for Ellie. It's not as if she's getting married, though, from the decor one might think otherwise. The thought alone sends dread pooling in the pit of her stomach. Shaking off the unease, Ellie says, "Good morning, Mother; I see you've been busy."

Adelina turns around, her face lighting up as her gaze meets Ellie's in the doorway. She swiftly walks over to her daughter, pulling her into a gentle embrace and whispers, "Happy name day, my dear," then kisses her on the cheek.

The queen smells of jasmine. Her stunning blonde curls flow freely over her shoulders, her gold crown perfectly placed atop her head. She wears a beautiful, full-length pale blue gown that perfectly matches her cornflower blue eyes. The gold of the earrings adorning her fae ears shine against the morning sun as it cascades through the large floor-to-ceiling windows. *She is truly breathtaking in every sense of the word*, Ellie thinks while she admires her.

"Thank you, Mother," Ellie smiles brightly. Her mother brushes her hair behind her ear and runs her thumb gently over her cheek, seeming to observe Ellie's features closely.

"You look tired, my dear. Were you up reading late again? Or was it flying this time?" She asks not in a scolding tone, but with concern.

Ellie quickly responds with a sigh, "I was reading and I simply lost track of time." The queen nods, understanding shines in her light blue eyes.

She has always supported her love for books and, of course, for flying. She assumes that's why her mother never scolds her too much for indulging in the things that bring the most joy into her life.

"I assume you're headed to training from your attire. Don't train too hard today; I want tonight to be perfect. Everyone will be here to celebrate you, so don't be late." Adelina commands in a regal tone.

"Yes, Mother, I promise not to be late. I have to go." She says hastily, wanting to escape to the training grounds. Ellie swiftly pulls her mother in for a brief hug, then turns around. Thankfully, a shattering noise echoes throughout the great hall, pulling the queen's attention from her before she can even say a word.

Breezing into the training grounds, Ellie starts scanning the soldier's that are training, she sees her best friend locked in a sparring match with another soldier.

Kyla is beautiful, with her auburn eyes and long brown hair tied in a ponytail atop her head that sways with each of her swift movements. She suddenly kicks out her right leg, making the soldier stumble and land hard on the unforgiving ground with a thud.

Ellie chuckles and claps her gloved hands, giving her a mock round of applause. Kyla instantly looks up, and her beaming smile indicates her triumph. She waves and yells over the training courtyard for everyone to hear, "Morning, El!"

Ellie chuckles again. Kyla is an incredible fighter, better than most. It's to be expected, considering she takes her training seriously and practices day and night. They met four years ago when Ellie first started her training and they bonded instantly. Kyla respects Ellie's need for solitude but she still finds ways to challenge her during training. It's one of the many things Ellie loves most about her friend.

Kyla quickly approaches and tilts her head, eyeing Ellie up and down. "You don't look any older," she teases. They both laugh and Ellie playfully shoves Kyla's shoulder.

"Let's just train, and not talk about tonight, yeah?" Kyla grabs another sword off the weapons rack a few feet to her right and hands one to Ellie.

With a wink and a slight bow, "With pleasure, Your Highness," Kyla mocks. Ellie hates it when she calls her that, and she knows i t.

"Don't mess up this pretty face, or the queen will have your head," Ellie quips back.

Before Kyla can react, Ellie swings her sword. Kyla blocks quickly, then steps back and giggles, "It seems you're not fighting fair today, El."

"You're the one who taught me that when it comes to a real fight, no one's going to fight fair." Then Ellie jabs with her sword, and Kyla blocks again.

Practicing with Kyla feels like a dance. They know each other's moves inside and out, after all these years of training together. Everything from their facial expressions to body movements. An hour later, they finish their training, dripping in sweat and muscles protesting.

"Have you spoken to Stella?" Ellie wonders while wiping her face with a towel and placing her sword on a nearby table.

"We talked yesterday. She did mention that she'd be out shopping this morning hunting for the perfect dress for your ball tonight. She's been excited about it for weeks! You know how Stella is..." Kyla smiles, and Ellie can't help but smile too. They both slightly nod towards each other, as if saying- *That's our Stella.*

Stella is beautiful and kind, and her father is a loyal lord to the king and his court. Ellie is thankful to have found a faithful friend in Stella. They met when they were only younglings. Honestly, she doesn't know what she would do without a friend like her. Stella also has her own bonded named Sentiara, however she has no desire to be a soldier; it's just not in her nature.

After Ellie turned ten and the first sign of her gift started showing, she had been terrified to confide in her best friend. Yet, she accepted her, wiped away her tears, and helped her pick out gloves the next day. To this day, Ellie still despises her gift, but at least her friends don't.

"I'm so glad I will have you both there with me; I don't think I could do this without you," Ellie holds Kyla's hand, giving her a gentle squeeze and an appreciative smile.

In return, Kyla squeezes her hand back and whispers, "Until death." It's been their promise to each other to be there until the very end, no matter what. It immediately makes Ellie's heart swell.

With a deep sigh, Ellie rolls her shoulders, attempting to ease the strain from her muscles, "I should get going; I need to go for a walk before the insanity of tonight."

Kyla replies, "You just want to go fly with your bonded. You don't need to lie to me, Princess," giggling and shaking her head slightly. *She knows me too well*, Ellie realizes.

She hugs Kyla tightly before quickly releasing her and sprinting towards the long stretch of beach that lays just beyond the forest. She yells over her shoulder, “I’ll see you tonight!”

2

Ellie

After a short walk through the trees, Ellie finally reaches the edge of the forest, where the trees meet the sand of the beach just beyond the castle walls. She finds herself instantly smiling as the ocean air softly brushes her face.

Ellie loves the soft ocean breeze, the smell of the sea, and the waves lapping against the shore. It instantly calms her racing mind. The sun is high in the sky as she catches sight of soldiers on their bonded dragons flying high above her. Most likely at her father's order, preparing for security tonight.

As her boots meet the water, Ellie takes a calming breath and tilts her head towards the sky. *I can do this; it's just a party*, she thinks to herself.

Moments later, with her eyes still closed, enjoying the soft breeze caressing her face. Ellie can hear the steady sound of wing beats in the sky. She knows those wingbeats nearly better than the beat of her own heart. Saphirixia, her bonded.

Turning around, she sees her sapphire blue scaled dragon peering down at her with a touch of concern. "*Saph, I've heard enough speeches today, so I don't need one from you. And yes, before you even ask, I'm all right*," glancing down and slowly kicking the sand underneath her boot, she attempts to hide her scowl.

"*I knew you would want to fly today. I wasn't going to say anything...*" Saphirixia replies nonchalantly, her deep voice resonating in Ellie's mind as she slides down into the sand, allowing Ellie to climb on.

Ellie smiles, feeling relief that her bonded won't be pushing the topic any further, "*Thank you, Saph, let's ride.*" Ellie quickly climbs up her bonded, and finds her favorite spot. She grips tightly, ready to feel the wind in her hair.

"*Your Highness?*" Saphirixia says slowly, almost hesitantly, "*Happy name day.*" Just as Ellie begins to grumble, Saphirixia shoots into the air like an arrow, the air whipping forcefully around her.

Ellie's gloved hands hold tightly onto Saphirixia's scales, feeling the deep rumble of her body underneath her. *Nothing could ever feel as good as this*, Ellie thought, knowing Saphirixia could hear her thoughts.

Once above the clouds, Saphirixia levels out her massive wings as Ellie opens her arms wide. Glancing down at the clouds below them, it's a breathtaking sight. Only the blue sky and white clouds surrounding them. She can't help but giggle as the freedom of the sky washing all her worries away.

They have been together since birth; no one knows her better than her bonded. Saph knows when she doesn't want to talk and when does. This is one of the moments that Ellie just simply wants to fly.

"*Hold on,*" is the only warning Saphirixia gives before diving down and then spinning in a circle with such force that she can feel herself lifting slightly off her bonded's back. Ellie tightens her grip and clamps her legs firmly around Saph's large form. She can't contain her squeals and giggles of excitement.

Sometime later, they reach the mountain peak just south of the castle, Saphirixia lands with a thud, slightly shaking the mountainside. Ellie gracefully slides down Saphirixia's leg, walking over to stand before her. Saphirixia remains silent. Ellie knows that it's for her sake. She places her gloved hand on her large snout, patting her lightly. Saphirixia practically purrs against her gentle, reassuring touch. Saphirixia then curls up in the grass as Ellie sits against her, staring at the vast ocean beyond, in blissful silence. An hour later, they finally land back on the beach closest to the castle; she can see Kyla and Stella striding towards them, smiling and laughing with one another. When Saphirixia lands, she slides off and lands lightly in the sand.

When Stella reaches her, she wraps her arms around Ellie and hugs her tightly while practically squealing, "Happy name day, El!"

"Stells, what are you doing here so early?" She asks in confusion. Wondering why her friend is there hours before the ball tonight.

"You didn't think I would let you get ready alone tonight, did you? I know you; you are undoubtedly dreading tonight, so I came to help lift your spirits." Stella brushes her short black hair behind her ear, giving Ellie a wicked grin.

Stella is so thoughtful, and Ellie knows that having her there throughout the evening will make it much more bearable. "You're the best Stells, but I hope you don't intend to keep my spirits lifted by manipulating my feelings," Ellie replies in a half-scolding, half-teasing tone.

"Me? Of course not; I wouldn't even dream of it," Stella replies mockingly, a playful glint in her eyes.

Rolling her eyes, she turns to say goodbye to Saphirixia, who pushes her large snout against her chest playfully, making her scowl fade and her smile brighten. "*Thank you, Saph, truly.*"

Saphirixia releases a soft rumble, "*El... remember, your life is worth celebrating. And for once... just have fun,*" then quickly turns around and shoots back into the sky, leaving a heavy gust of wind in her wake. Ellie assumes Saph is on her way to meet her mother back at the dragon's lair. Ellie always hates seeing her bonded leave, but tomorrow will be Saphirixia's name day, which is Ellie's favorite day out of the year.

Stella and Kyla come up alongside Ellie's once Saphirixia is flying high and link their arms on each side of her.

"Shall we?" Stella implores, practically bouncing on her toes with excitement.

They smile at each other and start walking back to the castle. When they reach the training grounds on the castle's north side, They observe the soldiers still training, the loud clattering of swords echoing through the courtyard.

Out of the corner of her eye, she notices a tall male with broad shoulders, and raven-hair holding a sword to another soldier's throat. Just beating him by the looks of it. His stance is solid and skilled, his presence dominating as he swings around, peering at the other soldiers in challenge.

"Who's next?" His voice is deep and commanding.

Kyla leans into Ellie's ear, "Isn't he the most beautiful male you've ever seen?" Nearly squealing her words.

As Ellie watches him closely, she has to admit he is a striking male, but another has already claimed her heart.

As if he can sense them staring, he turns to meet their gazes; his lips thinned into a curt line as he narrows his gaze, not just on her friends but on her. His piercing glare feels like daggers on her skin, slicing her to the bone. *What was that look for?* Ellie wonders. She doesn't even know this soldier, yet he looks at her with disdain. *Who in the bleeding stars are you?*

"Well, who is he?" Ellie wonders, trying to shrug off the intense feeling of his glare upon her skin.

"Oh, you don't know? That's Tristan Mormont, Lord Mormont's heir." Kyla whispers in Ellie's ear as she turns to see a blush on Kyla's cheeks and a bright smile on her face. "We got together a couple of weeks ago. Bleeding stars, El, he's incredible, in more ways than one, if you know what I mean." She says with a wink.

"Oh," confusion filling her voice. "Wait- that is the soldier you told me about?"

Kyla only giggles and nods with excitement as Kyla's gaze falls back to the soldier, tracking his every move.

Ellie looks at him again and can't help but think that, maybe, he doesn't know who she is or perhaps he just doesn't care. She is used to the occasional looks of disdain, but this is a look far more significant than disdain; it's hatred.

A moment later, his loud voice booms over the courtyard, "Soldiers! In formation!" Kyla goes rigid beside her, her arm wrapped around Ellie's side.

Kyla says softly, "I guess that means me too."

Then the raven-haired soldier yells, "NOW!" Louder than before, his voice fills with authority, power, and dominance.

Kyla jumps and quickly kisses Ellie on the cheek. "He can command me like that anytime," she whispers with a chuckle and a wink before she runs to get into formation, her long ponytail bouncing as she saunters over to the other soldiers.

Stella pulls her along, fanning herself, "Oh my! Me too... anytime." They laugh at that and continue into the castle. When they finally round the corner nearest her bedchamber, her heart slams in her chest as she sees who is waiting for her. *He's here*, Ellie thought, her heart racing harder at the sight of him. A smile instantly graces her face.

She turns to Stella, who is smirking at her in that knowing grin as they walk.

"I'll give you two a minute; but, don't take too long. You still need to get ready." She releases Ellie's arm and opens her bedchamber door, then closes it slowly with a light click of the latch.

Eyes pining on Jace's handsome face, she's struck again right in her heart. His eyes fill with desire, as if sensing her thoughts, he trails her body with his stare. He glances down the hall, quickly grabs her wrist, and pulls her down into an empty guest's chambers. He abruptly shuts the door with a thud, then laces his fingers into hers and pulls her against his chest. Without hesitation, he wraps his strong hand around the back of her neck and pulls her lips to his. She savors his hurried but gentle kiss; it was as if he had not seen her in ages, even though it had only been two days. He devours her lips, and Ellie can't help but release a soft moan in delight to feel his tongue against hers once again.

Jace hesitantly releases her lips and trails kisses down her neck, making her back arch, allowing him to consume her as he wishes. Then he brings his lips to her pointed fae ears, whispering against her skin, "Happy name day, Princess. Bleeding stars, I missed you."

Those words make her knees weak, her rapid heartbeat now beating more frantically in her chest. She runs her gloved hands through his short but shaggy blonde hair. She pulls him closer and looks into his sparkling emerald green eyes. He smells like freshly baked bread, which tells her that he has just been downstairs visiting or helping his mother in the kitchen.

She has known Jace since childhood when his mother, Eleanora, first came to work for them in their kitchen. She has been a shining light in their daily lives and bakes the most delicious bread and pastries. Ellie can almost smell and taste the food now.

When they were children, Eleanora taught her to cook until one day, when her beautiful emerald green-eyed, blonde-haired male faeling walked in. It was then that Ellie first believed in love at first sight. Never had a male taken her breath away.

The pair would spend their days running around the beach, playing games together, and riding horses. She loves that he's not scared of Saphirixia and has never been scared of Ellie. Even though Saphirixia never seems to accept him, she usually tries to stay away when he is around. It always makes her wonder if Saphirixia knows something that she doesn't. Shaking the thoughts from her head, she pulls him in for another deep, tantalizing kiss.

Reluctantly, she releases him. Trying not to sigh at his lack of contact, "Will I see you tonight?"

"I wouldn't miss your special day for anything." Jace places a soft kiss on her forehead that makes her eyes close, savoring this moment's intimacy.

"I need to start getting ready, and Stella is waiting," she grumbles.

Pulling her close and kissing her lips gently, Jace whispers, "You'll be a vision tonight."

Before releasing her, Jace grabs her hand and kisses it gently. Then, he gives her a devilish grin before he pulls at the chamber door, glancing down the halls to make sure not to alert anyone to their whereabouts, and strides away.

She sits in a nearby chair, her thoughts consumed by him. Then, her smile begins to fade; she feels a familiar pang in her chest. *He could never be my mate*, she realizes. The thought alone brings tears to her eyes, but she pushes them down.

The King and Queen undoubtedly know of her courtship with Jace, though they've never said anything about it. There is a general understanding that one day, hopefully far in the future, she will be expected to marry a titled male or one of royal blood.

One day, she would be the queen; even though that thought terrifies her, she knows what is expected of her. It's taken years to accept her fate, yet the sting of pain in her chest and knowing how her future would undoubtedly unfold, still lingers. *If only I could marry for love*, Ellie thinks to herself and then quietly snorts; *that will never happen*. With that, she decides it is time for her self-pity to cease.

Entering her bedchamber, she sees Stella sitting on her bed with a book. Stella lifts her brow and smirks at her. Ellie knows she can see her flushed cheeks and her swollen lips. She isn't ashamed of Jace; she never would be. He is honorable, loyal, and an incredibly handsome male. The stars would bless any female in the kingdom to have him as their mate. *There's that pain again*; she realizes as she subconsciously rubs at her chest as if it could ease that sting of reality away.

Unwilling to discuss their intimate moments, Ellie remains silent. Stella's power gives her the ability to read and manipulate others' emotions. Ellie knows just being near her will give her the knowledge of everything she's feeling.

"Spit it out, I know you want to Stells..." Ellie presses. Her emotions are already all over the place; she's sweaty, hungry, and desperately needs a bath and to hide away right now.

Giggling, Stella replies, "Me? I would never pry into your love life, Princess," and gives Ellie a wink before continuing. "Now, go clean up so I can do your hair." All Ellie can do is huff and walk into the bathroom.

Staring at herself in the mirror, she remembers this morning and how wonderful it felt to be soaring through the sky with Saphirixia. Then, her mind wanders to that moment in the training courtyard. She begins to question why that raven-haired soldier looked at her with such hatred. Ellie has never spoken to him before, let alone seen him. Perhaps she unknowingly disrespected him? Maybe knowledge of her gift makes him glare at her? *Why should I care?* Ellie thinks to herself.

After getting cleaned up again, Ellie sits at the vanity while Stella fixes her hair into a beautiful loose braid down her back with other little braids intertwining.

Stella goes as far as to add little jewels to her hair, which makes it sparkle in the firelight. She has to give her friend credit; she knows how to make her look beautiful. While doing her makeup, they talk about frivolous things. She can tell Stella is trying to keep it light, and not talk about topics such as the night ahead and events with Jace.

Ellie can't help but begin to wonder how Jace will look tonight.

Hope blossoms within her - hope for the chance to dance with him. Praying to the stars her parents will allow her just this one public moment with him. She doesn't want to upset her parents, but it is her name day, and she should be free to do as she pleases, at least for tonight.

As Ellie leaves the room, the falling sun paints the halls with a warm orange glow. A feeling of panic begins creeping into her chest as she notices that it's almost time. Then, a light knock sounds on her chamber door just before it flies open. Clara strides in, holding a beautiful, deep burgundy velvet box.

Clara's smile is bright as she holds out the box, bowing slightly, "Your Highness, the queen wishes you to wear this tonight." Ellie sighs and thanks Clara, forcing a small smile.

"Open it, open it! Your mother has exquisite taste. You know it will be stunning!" Stella is overly excited, and Ellie half considers allowing her to wear it to the ball. It was tempting, but she knew it would only hurt her mother's feelings, which wasn't her intention. "Okay, okay, calm down..." Ellie responds before forcing open the lid. A gasp breaks free from Ellie's red-stained lips.

Her mother isn't just giving her a beautiful piece of jewelry; she's giving her the most breathtaking blue sapphire necklace she has ever seen. Ellie delicately runs her silk-laced gloved hand over the oval-shaped sapphire, shimmering with diamonds around it. She can only imagine the mastery it must have taken to make something this exquisite.

Stella squeals with excitement, "allow me," and quickly grabs the box from Ellie to place the necklace around her neck. Stella is practically bouncing around excitedly, making it difficult for her to clasp it. That makes Ellie laugh because Stella has always appreciated the finer things in life, especially jewelry. With the stone resting just below Ellie's collarbone, she stares at her reflection and notices how the sapphire stone brings out the blazing blue of her eyes.

Stella bends down to place her hands on her shoulders. Peering at her in the vanity mirror, Stella whispers, "You will be the most beautiful princess at the ball." Smiling with adoration. Ellie snorts and looks at Stella, replying sarcastically, "I'll be the *only* princess at the ball."

Stella only laughs at that and lightly shoves her arm, "You know what I mean, El! Now, come on, I want to see this dress on you!" Ellie takes one last look in the mirror as she feels the night's pressure settles in. She gets up and gets dressed behind the partition in the corner of her chambers, Stella remaining silent.

When Ellie steps out, Stella is wearing a beautiful green ball gown with her short black hair curled to frame her face perfectly, hazel eyes shining, and an emerald diamond-studded pendant accentuating her pointed fae ears. She is uniquely beautiful.

Gasping, Stella places her hand over her mouth in surprise when she takes in Ellie's dress. "Do you not like it?" Ellie couldn't help but ask her, feeling self-conscious. She begins questioning her gown choice for the night.

Stella strides over to her with a lone tear streaming down her delicate face, and pulls her into a gentle but firm hug. "You couldn't have picked a more perfect gown."

The words sink into Ellie, and she finally lets out the breath she didn't know she's been holding. "Thank the stars for a friend like you, Stells".

3

Ellie

Walking towards the great hall with Stella's hand in hers, Ellie is nervous but pulls strength from her best friend. When they reach the large, elegant doors to the room, Stella halts her, "Wait!" She instructs the guards with their hands resting impatiently on the door. Turning, Ellie looks at Stella, her eyes softening before she speaks.

"This is your moment to shine, El. Show them who their future queen will be." With one last wink, she nods towards the guards, indicating for them to open the doors.

Ellie strides through with her head held high. The loud chattering of the guests ceases as everyone looks up to see her standing atop the grand staircase. Her breath catches as the overwhelmingly strong urge to bolt tugs at her.

Before she can turn, Stella whispers from a few feet behind her, "Don't even think about it. You can do this!" Ellie can't help hiding her smile at that.

Gathering all her courage, Ellie begins to descend the grand staircase. As she moves, she makes sure she doesn't look any of them in the eye.

Ellie's gaze finds the king and queen sitting on their thrones, looking up at her. The pride on their faces makes her heart swell. She can hear the guests begin whispering at what she hopes is their genuine awe of her stunning blue sapphire, iridescent silk, and tulle ball gown as it glitters in the light. Perhaps the silver crown adorning her head catches their attention as well.

As soon as her heels hit the floor, the usher announces with a deep voice that echoes throughout the hall, "Princess Ellissandra Lyria Firethorne of Aetherlyn."

Clapping and cheers fill the hall, like thunder rumbling throughout the grand room. Ellie searches for other familiar faces but only finds those of unfamiliar guests smiling gleefully at her and bowing their heads in congratulations.

In Aetherlyn, a fae female isn't considered to be of age until her twenty-fifth moon, making tonight uniquely special to her parents and the kingdom. Tonight, they wish to parade her in front of everyone in attendance and fully acknowledge her as the heir to the throne.

The king recently reached his one hundred and eighty-eighth name day this past moon, and the queen reached her one hundred and seventy-ninth name day. Even at their age, the two ruling fae are still considered to be middle-aged in their realm. It could be decades or even a century before Ellie would inherit the throne, but thankfully, for now and many years to come, she is just a princess. Which to her, is more than enough.

Ellie can see Kyla, with Stella standing with her. They gently push past the dispersing crowd. Both females have flutes lifted in their hands, clearly already celebrating. With bright smiles, they slip her a glass.

"You didn't run, congratulations! *Now* are you ready to have some fun, Princess?" Stella teases as she wiggles her brows in pure excitement.

Ellie takes a long drag of her champagne, nearly draining the glass, eager to use the alcohol to ease her nerves, she nods. Kyla only laughs at Ellie and lightly bumps her hip with hers, "I'm assuming you'll need more liquid courage tonight, eh?"

"I'll admit it definitely helps with being made into tonight's spectacle, grab me another?" Ellie responds bashfully. Kyla takes Ellie's glass from her hand and winks at her, before leaving to get more.

Males quickly begin flocking to Stella and Ellie, asking for a dance. Though they both anticipated having to participate in the festivities, they hesitantly obliged them. However, Ellie finds her gaze peering over the shoulders of her dance partners in search of the only male she wishes to dance with. The males are all kind, and most are even handsome, but she only has eyes for Jace. After a couple of turns around the dance floor, she is saved by her mother and father.

"You look ravishing, my dear." The queen reaches for Ellie's gloved hand and pulls her gently to kiss her cheek. Her father is beaming from ear to pointed ear. He's practically radiating with pride. Once the queen has released Ellie, he also pulls her in for a hug. His embrace practically swallows her. She breathes in his familiar scent of the forest and cigars, his hug calming and reassuring.

To the kingdom, he is a strong, fair, and empathetic king who rules for the good of the entire realm. Many still fear him and his massive armies, but to Ellie, he is just a loving and doting father. He wears a white doublet with gold embroidery, which makes his blonde hair appear almost white, and his full beard, strong jaw, and blue eyes are striking as ever.

The king whispers to Ellie so low no one can hear, "You're my pride and joy, El. I hope all your wishes come true tonight," then pulls back from her with a wink. *How could I possibly wish for more?* Ellie thinks to herself as she smiles brightly at her parents.

Kyla and Stella come up on both of her sides, quickly bowing their heads. Then Stella asked sweetly, "May we steal the princess for a moment, Your Highnesses?"

The king and queen smile at them, and the queen quickly responds, "Of course, go have fun my darling."

Ellie's friends steer her away, but when she turns, her gaze finds Jace eyeing her from across the room. Their eyes meet and he gives her a devilish smile. It makes her shiver in anticipation to see him.

He's dressed in a midnight black tailored doublet that fits his near six foot muscled frame perfectly, the deep color bringing out his emerald green eyes. He is even more beautiful than she could have imagined tonight. Seeing him dressed like this was so rare and it felt like a privilege to behold. His blonde hair swept back from his face, his eyes alight with affection as he took Ellie's hand in his. He places a gentle kiss upon it. "May I have this dance, my princess?" *My princess*, the subtle claim making her toes curl.

She feels heat warm her cheeks as she smiles gracefully and replies, "I'd love to."

Jace grabs her hand and sweeps her into the crowd of guests on the dance floor. With each graceful movement, Ellie feels herself being drawn deeper into the magic of this moment. All of her worries and cares start melting away as she loses herself in the music and warmth of Jace's embrace. To her surprise, he is a splendid dancer, and as they move, her senses become heightened, and she feels a profound connection to the world around her. She can feel the energy beneath her feet, the whispers of the guests dancing around them, and the pulse of life that flows through their veins. *What is that?* Ellie wonders to herself.

As the music reaches its crescendo, they spin faster and faster, their laughter ringing like bells in the night. As the final note fades away, they stop, breathless and exhilarated, their eyes lock. Utter silence pulls between them, neither Ellie nor Jace dares to say a word. There are so many desires on the tip of her tongue that she wishes she could speak to him but knows the guests crowded around them could hear.

She feels Jace's eyes move to her gown and the crown of silver atop her head. Ellie knows what this symbol of her royal lineage means to him, the piece of her life it puts on display. Jace's emerald, green eyes morph into a look of desperation, pain, and longing. He bows ever so slightly, then turns and walks into the crowd. All the guests are dancing blissfully unaware around them, to the heartache slowly building in Ellie. She paints on a smile as she just stands there, the pain in her chest makes her numb. *I can do this; I must do this*, she says to herself.

Ellie turns around, making her way toward the magnificent buffet that's piled high with an array of dishes from every corner of the fae realm. *Eleanora outdid herself*, Ellie thinks as she looks at the beautiful display and makes a mental note to thank her tomorrow.

Platters of roasted meats are glazed with honey and sprinkled with herbs. Towering pyramids of fruits and berries from their forests begging to be enjoyed, their sweetness tempting even the most discerning palate. She catches sight of her best friends at the dessert table, which is a remarkable sight in itself. There are mountains of pastries, cakes adorned with spun sugar and edible flowers beckoning those with sweet tooths, and trays of chocolate promising to delight the senses. She takes the opportunity to savor the delights of Eleanora's delicacies, grabbing a chocolate right next to Kyla and Stella. They both turn to her, laughing, knowing her sweet tooth.

Together, they drink and eat delicious treats and are, thankfully, only occasionally interrupted by guests giving her their congratulations and well wishes. As the other guests feast and drink, laughter and music fills the air, mingling with the tantalizing scents and flavors surrounding them.

As the night wears on and the stars dance in the sky through the massive floor-to-ceiling windows, guests raise their glasses in a toast to the princess, grateful for the bounty the fae realm and peace provided and the joy of sharing it with everyone in attendance.

Despite the joyous occasion, Ellie feels restlessness gnawing at her, longing for solitude amidst the chaos. Stealing away from the great hall, she makes her way to the castle's veranda, where the cool breeze brushes against her gown. She gazes out, observing the waves splashing onto the sand beyond, lit by the bright moon in the sky. Ellie takes a breath, seeking solace in the tranquil embrace of the night.

However, her stolen moment of solitude is suddenly interrupted by the sound of another nearby. Turning, Ellie beholds a tall, lone figure in the dark, nearly hidden from view by the plants and flowers gracing the veranda. She soon realizes that the figure standing in the shadows is the soldier she saw in the training courtyard this morning. His expression is brooding and obviously troubled.

With her curiosity piqued as to why he would be out here, she hesitantly decides to say something to him. He was scowling at her earlier and she deserved to know why.

She takes a deep breath, and then she breaks the silence with cautious grace, "Good evening."

The soldier's features are momentarily clouded with surprise, seeing who she is, before schooling his face back into a mask of indifference.

"What are you doing out here all alone, Princess?" He questions, his tone curt and guarded.

Undeterred by his rudeness, Ellie tilts her head, studying him with curiosity as she sighs, "I simply needed a moment of solace from the chaos."

For a heartbeat, the soldier remains silent, her response clearly surprising him. His gaze flits between the princess and the vast ocean beyond as he remains quiet and stoic. Then, with a resigned sigh, "Suit yourself."

Ellie watches him swallow down the last of the amber liquid in his glass and turn to walk back inside.

Ellie didn't expect his response. Words falter on her lips as he starts toward the open doors. "And perhaps... some company, if you'd care to share?"

The soldier halts, his boot scraping against the stone floor as he slowly turns to glance over his shoulder. Ellie feels his gaze travel up her body, his piercing ocean-blue eyes locking onto hers with an intensity that steals her breath. He gives a curt nod, then almost cautiously, moves to her side.

Standing on the veranda, Ellie stares at the star-strewn sky, wishing she could be soaring through the night with Saphirixia instead of standing here, vulnerable under the soldier's scrutinizing gaze. On nights like these, when the stars burn so brightly, she feels as if she could pluck them from the skies and hold their fiery light in her hands.

The warmth radiating from the soldier's body is palpable, seeping into Ellie's skin. His scent, fresh air tinged with sandalwood, invades her senses, grounding her. He towers over her, well over six feet two, his presence looming. Ellie struggles to find her voice again. "It's breathtaking, isn't it?" She murmurs, her eyes alight with wonder.

The soldier merely hums in response, his demeanor as guarded as ever, walls impenetrable. Yet Ellie, undeterred by his aloofness, presses on with gentle persistence. "What's your name?" She asks, her gaze drifting from the vast sky to meet his again.

He turns fully this time, his expression unreadable, though she catches a flicker of vulnerability crossing his features. "Tristan," he replies, his eyes scanning her face as if searching for something, perhaps trying to read her thoughts. *Can he read minds*? she wonders briefly.

Ellie nods, quickly diverting her eyes from his soul-piercing gaze, returning her attention to the view beyond. Silence hangs between them, thick with unspoken tension, and she can almost feel his clear disdain for her beginning to crack just a little.

To her surprise, he speaks again, his voice rough. "I don't need any company, especially not from the princess."

Ellie feels a pang of confusion at his hostility. "I mean no harm," she says softly. "I truly just want a moment of peace. Believe it or not, I don't love all the attention tonight is bringing."

The silence that follows is heavy, fraught with tension that neither of them acknowledges. But then, something in him seems to shift. He sighs, the hostility in his posture easing as if suddenly aware of how harsh he's been. Ellie sees the change and thinks to herself, *I guess I'll just kill him with kindness.*

"Forgive me," he says, his voice softer now, tinged with regret. "It's just been a rough day."

Ellie nods, her gaze softening as she senses the weight of his unspoken burdens. "I understand," she replies, her tone tender and full of empathy. "We all carry burdens, and it's easy to feel like we're alone in them." Ellie bites her lip and wonders why she's being so open with someone she doesn't know. "We have to remember that everyone is fighting their own battles, even when we can't see them."

She pauses, offering him a surprisingly gentle smile that radiates warmth and reassurance into the cool fall air. "Sometimes, just sharing what weighs us down can lighten the load, even if just a little." Her words are a balm, a quiet offering of solace. "There's a kind of strength in being vulnerable, in letting someone else in. It can make all the difference."

Tristan stares at the view, but his walls seem to crumble slightly in the face of her compassion. "Thank you," he murmurs, his voice quiet and hoarse. "For reminding me that even amidst the darkness, there is light to be found." He gestures toward the moon and stars shining above them. *It truly is a spectacular night, and perhaps,* Ellie thinks, *a spectacular moment.*

She turns to face him once again, and before any words leave her lips, she hears footsteps behind them. A stern and commanding voice piercing the stillness of the night, and it's one she knows well, "Tristan. A moment." The interruption sliced through the night with the sharpness of a sword.

Ellie notices Tristan tense before turning to see Lord Mormont standing in the doorway. Even by his tone, she could hear the mix of disapproval and annoyance.

With a heavy heart, Ellie's gaze falls upon him for one last fleeting moment. "Thank you for the company," her voice tinged with a hint of disappointment.

Tristan only nods, his expression unreadable, the weight of their unfinished conversation still hanging heavy in the air around them.

Ellie makes her way back to the ballroom. Feeling a little lighter after those stolen moments with Tristan. *I hope he found as much comfort under tonight's stars as I did.*

4

Ellie

Ellie reluctantly makes her way through the crowd of guests, making sure to say hello to all in attendance, knowing it will please her parents.

She spots her mother standing by the grand crystal chandelier, mingling with guests. Being as gracious as ever, she approaches with a small smile. "Mother," she greets, her voice soft and full of warmth. "May we speak?"

Queen Adelina turns to her daughter, her eyes bright with love. "Of course, my dear, are you troubled?" She asks with a gentle voice.

"No, no, of course not, Mother. I only wish to thank you for this spectacular ball." The queen smiles but almost seems relieved that Ellie hasn't said anything more.

"Are you troubled, Mother?" Her mother appears surprised and almost scared by her question and quickly forces her face to appear unphased by her question. *That's odd.* Ellie notices.

Ellie feels that for the past couple of months, her mother has wanted to confide in her about something troubling her but always seems to change her mind shortly after.

The queen sighs, "I'm just tired, my dear; it has been a long day and a night full of celebrating." Then she cups Ellie's face with a tender hand and smiles at her.

Before the queen can remove her hand from Ellie's face, a young female servant backs into them. With an overly apologetic bow, the servant tilts the tray in her hands and spills the goblets of rich red wine, splattering onto Queen Adelina's pristine gown and drenching Elle's silk protective gloves.

The Queen's serene expression flickers momentarily, her eyes betraying a hint of annoyance before she masks it. Ellie takes in her stained gown and then feels the wine soak into her gloves down to her skin, making her hands sticky and wet.

She quickly begins to peel her glove off and is about to tell her mother she is going to go to her chambers to grab another pair when another servant comes rushing up to them with a towel in hand. The servant attempts to hand it to Ellie, as she profusely apologizes. Ellie thanks the servant and takes the towel. She drys her hands, then hands it to her mother to try and clean her seemingly ruined gown.

Ellie feels her power tingle underneath her fingertips as their hands touch, inadvertently breaching the barriers she has meticulously erected. A heartbeat later, the queen's thoughts flood Ellie's mind as her blue eyes glow. "Look at this mess... *I was about to tell her... Why have I waited this long? If I had told her months ago or even days ago, she could've prepared herself... I must tell her that she and Saphirixia are the prophesized... I can't keep this secret from her any longer. She could be in danger*".

Ellie's heart races wildly, her eyes widen, and she is unable to form words. She simply stares at her mother in incomprehensible shock. *Did she just say... the prophesized?* As *in the prophesized bonded? This can't be*, Ellie contemplates.

She can't help but shake her head as if she is trying to shake herself out of delirium. The queen gives her a confused expression, but before she can ask what's wrong, her mother looks down at Ellie's hand resting on hers.

Her mother's gaze slowly meets Ellie's shocked and bewildered expression, noticing her eyes glowing with the flood of power consuming her. She watches her closely as the realization dawns on her that Ellie now knows her deepest, darkest secret with that touch. Their eyes lock in a silent exchange, a moment full of unspoken words. In that fleeting instant, her mother's mask slips, revealing a vulnerability few have ever witnessed.

Ellie can feel the anger bubbling within her; all she wants to do is run away. She looks around, trying to find her father, Kyla, Stella, or Jace. Her eyes finally land on Kyla and Tristan smiling at each other—the two dance to the melodic strains of the music. Ellie feels an overwhelming pain in her chest as if she's drowning in the thrum of the music and there is no one around to save her.

Before Ellie can turn around, her mother begs, "Wait." Her words are full of desperation as Ellie turns, ignoring her plea, and strides toward the doors.

As she enters the hallway, she can hear her mother's footsteps not far behind her.

"Ellie, please stop. We need to talk about this." Her voice is rushed, and her breaths are frantic. Ellie feels as if this secret is a knife to the chest, ripping her apart. *This can't be happening; we can't be the prophesized*, Ellie's mind reels.

As she continues her way down the halls to escape into the solitude of her bedchamber, her mother continues to follow her unrelentingly.

Ellie whirls around, allowing the words to finally fly out of her mouth. "How could you keep this from me!" Hurt laced her tone, her eyes glowing brighter as her anger rose.

Her mother covers her mouth, attempting to hold back the tears pooling in her deep blue eyes. The queen shakes her head as if trying to find the words to console Ellie and explain why she had kept such a secret.

Before Queen Adelina can speak, Ellie raises her hand at her, "Just... don't." A lone tear streamed down her face.

At that, Ellie turns and runs down the hall until she reaches her bedchamber. She walks towards her balcony as she slams the heavy wooden door behind her. Ellie stands alone, the weight of her mother's secret pressing heavily upon her heart as her breaths come in uneven and ragged heaves.

Ellie doesn't consider her power to be a gift because every time she peers into the veil of another's thoughts, she has always heard far too much. Tonight, was yet another example as to why she despises her gift.

As tears begin welling in her eyes, a soft rustle of wings draws her attention skyward. With a rush of air whipping, Ellie's long blonde hair swirls from her face, her faithful bonded, landing with her long talons on the balcony, her sapphire scales shimmering in the moonlight.

Without a word spoken aloud, Ellie reaches out to Saphirixia with her mind, her thoughts intertwining with those of her beloved dragon. In the silent language they shared, she conveys her pain of betrayal and longing for escape from the suffocation of the castle.

"*How did you know?*" Ellie questions.

"*I felt your pain, heard your thoughts...then spoke with* Naagara*...*" Saphirixia said gruffly, clearly just as upset and confused as she was.

"*How did that go?*" Ellie peers into her deep sapphire blue eyes, who only gazed at her back as a tear streamed down Ellie's face.

"*The same way I imagine yours did with your mother*", she replies with hurt and anger lacing her tone.

They both gaze out into the night, each sighing in unison, attempting to let the moonlit sky and soft ocean breeze calm their heightened emotions. With a gentle nudge of Saphirixia's snout, she urges her to climb onto her back so they can escape the castle. Ellie sniffles and wipes the tears off her face, trying to push away the pain aching in her heart. Plus, Ellie knows if they say anything else on the subject, it's best to do it away from the castle to ensure no one else hears.

Saphirixia unfurls her wings in readiness for flight. Ellie takes a deep, steadying breath and mounts her dragon, eager to leave the castle and soar into the night sky. As soon as they shoot into the sky and fly towards the ocean and along the coast, liberation washes over Ellie, she can feel the same coming from Saphirixia.

Together, flying in the moonlit sky, their bond is unbreakable, and their spirits free. Ellie knows that wherever their journey may lead them, they will both face it with courage, guided by the unwavering strength of her loyal bonded dragon by her side.

5

Ellie

As they reach the mountain peak, reality begins to sink in about the conversation they will need to have. Ellie is hesitant and weary due to the late hour. They both nestle into the tall grass of their favorite place in Aetherlyn, and Ellie slowly began to speak.

“So... *we are the prophesized bonded that’s foretold by the Enchantress, who are meant to break the curse on fae magic.*” Ellie is hardly able to believe the words she is speaking.

"*It's the secret Nagaara and Queen Adelina have kept hidden for twenty-five years,*" Saphirixia begins,"*Nagaara claims no other soul knows, and the reason they kept it from us was due to their fear for our fate.*"

"*If this is fate, do we truly have a choice?*" Ellie asks, her voice steady but laced with conviction. "*I’ve always believed that every fae deserves to have their own magic. It’s unfair that only those who are bonded possess power. And if magic is restored everyone has their chance at finding their fated mates. Don’t we all deserve that connection? I can’t even imagine finding my mate let alone having them know my feelings.*" She shakes her head, unable to believe the possibility.

She lets her thoughts flow, trusting Saphirixia, her soul's confidante, to understand.

“*You’re right,*” Saphirixia murmurs, her voice soft but firm. “*All fae should have their magic—it’s their birthright.*”

Ellie hesitates for a moment, then with a vulnerability she rarely shows, asks, "*If this is our fate, and we're truly meant to walk this path... will you be with me?*" She holds her breath, almost too scared to hear the response.

"*There is nowhere you could go that I wouldn't follow. Even if death claims you, I will follow you, for my heart does not beat without yours.*" Saphirixia's words bring tears to her eyes because she feels the same. She can't bear to live without her bonded, and if it were her choice, she would willingly follow her to the afterlife, to be by her side forever.

Even though many bondeds continue to live on without the other, Ellie knows in her soul that she would choose not to, that her heart couldn't take the grief.

Ellie nods silently, allowing the tears to fall down her beautiful face. Memories of their life together flood her mind but the memory of when they were ten years old makes her smile most.

"We shouldn't Saph, my mother said I'm not ready and that I must wait until I'm older." Little Ellie said building a sandcastle in the sand.

"You know I will always protect you; if you fall, I will catch you." Little Saphirixia replied.

Their mothers had told them countless times that they couldn't fly together until they were older and better trained.

Saphirixia was larger than many other dragons her age in Aetherlyn. Ellie was proud to call Saphirixia her bonded. They were born only a day apart and have been together since birth. Their mothers were also bonded and had the power of precognition.

Knowing their luck, their mothers already knew that they were going to have this conversation, or better yet know they were going to fly if Ellie conceded to Saphirixia's request.

Who was she kidding? Ellie has been waiting ten years to ride her bonded and today felt like the perfect day. The sun was bright, the ocean breeze was cool against her skin. And tomorrow is her name day, Saphirixia's following the day after. How mad would her mother even be at her?

Ellie pushed her hands into the sand, forcing herself to stand. She looked at her bonded and said, "Let's do it," nodding to Saphirixia.

With excitement bubbling in their hearts, her bonded got low to the sand allowing her to climb up her scales onto her back. Ellie's heart began to race widely and she could already tell that holding on would be challenging. Once she was on her neck, wrapped as tightly as she could, Saphirixia shifted beneath her and started flapping her large wings. They quickly began to take flight.

Nerves ran through Ellie's entire body as their laughter mingled with the breeze. As they soared higher and higher, the world she knew stretched out beneath them, she felt truly invincible. It's no wonder her bonded had been trying for so long to get Ellie to join her in the sky, she felt this was the best moment of her life. The anticipation for this moment was worth it in Ellie's mind. This moment with her bonded, alone, soaring high together as one with the sky.

As Saphirixia flew only feet above the ocean, the wind started picking up, her long blonde hair blowing in her face covering her eyes. A sudden gust caught her off guard as she tried to brush her hair off her face.

With a startled cry, Ellie lost her grip with her one hand and hurtled towards the ocean below. Panic gripped Ellie as she hit the warm ocean water.

She quickly swam back up to the surface and sputtered water from her mouth. Frantically, Ellie looked for Saphirixia in the sky. Once she caught sight of her bonded, she waved both arms in the air wildly hoping she could grab her. Saphirixia swooped down at lightning speed, gripped her with her talons, and pulled her out of the water, her mighty wings beating against the wind, forcing her skyward again.

Ellie could feel tears of relief welling up as she realized she wasn't seriously hurt by the fall. She felt sore from landing hard in the water, but looking down at her body as Saphirixia held her in the air, she knew she would be all right.

When they finally reached the dry land of the beach, Saphirixia set her down softly in the sand. She let out the breath she had been holding and wiped her wet hair from her brow. As she looked up to see Saphirixia's so she could thank her for saving her, she noticed the dread in her bonded's wide eyes.

As Ellie shifted her head, she saw their mothers waiting for them, worry and anger etched upon them. She knew right then that they were in a heap of trouble but, in Ellie's mind, it was worth it because she had never felt so fulfilled or free in her entire life.

Even amidst the scolding they received, there was still a hint of pride shining in their mother's eyes, for they had faced danger together and emerged mostly unscathed.

As the sun started to dip below the horizon, casting a golden glow upon the sand, they both knew that their bond would carry them through any adventure they would encounter together.

As Ellie wipes the tears from her cheek, Saphirixia nearly purrs in response to the precious memory flooding their minds. As she gazes into the night sky, Ellie can make out dragons flying towards them. *Did my mother seriously send soldiers after me?* she wonders.

As she and Saphirixia start to stand, Ellie counts six dragons and riders landing before them on the mountain's edge. Surprise sweeps through Ellie as her eyes fall upon Kyla, Kaida, and Tristan. She doesn't recognize the other soldiers, but their faces shone with worry, making her instantly feel uneasy. *Did I miss something? They couldn't possibly be here for us*, Ellie thinks to herself.

Kyla runs to her and envelops her in a tight hug, her heartbeat thumping against her chest. As Ellie pulls away, the words escaping Kyla's lips fade to a hum as she notices Tristan standing behind her. His ocean-blue eyes seem to pierce Ellie where she stands.

Kyla's voice drifts in and snaps her mind back into focus. "El, I'm so sorry that I must be the one to tell you this... but there was an assassination attempt on the king and queen, your father was injured."

Kyla looks down, quickly noticing Ellie's ungloved hands, her gaze quickly jerking back to her surprised expression.

Tristan then interjects, oblivious as to why Kyla has yet to explain more. As Ellie and Kyla stare at one another, Ellie begins to read her thoughts about what happened.

Tristan's words begin to cut through the fog, "The King will survive but a servant stabbed him during the celebration. The queen is with him now and they have asked for you to return to the castle immediately." His words are stern but gentle.

All the air leaves Ellie's lungs as she blankly watches him.

She tries to push down on the silent panic flooding through every cell of her body as Saphirixia's voice floods her mind. "*We should go, now.*" Her voice is uneasy. Her bonded seems equally as concerned for the King as she is.

She nods slowly, letting Kyla's hands fall to her side. Before she can turn, she sees Tristan grab Kyla's hand and return to their dragons to fly back to the castle. *Are they together, together?*

Ellie turns and swiftly climbs onto Saphirixia who wastes no time before urging, "*Hold on tight*," and shoots into the air without hesitation. Ellie turns around to look at Kyla, Tristan, and the other soldiers behind them preparing to follow their lead back to the castle.

They leave the other dragons far behind due to Saphirixia's speed. Ellie's heart races, as concern for her mother and father takes complete hold of her every thought.

As they finally land in the training courtyard, Ellie dismounts and runs inside to her parents' bedchamber hoping to find them there. She stills in the doorway as she pushes through the heavy wooden door. The royal healer is bending over her father, who rests in his bed with bandages wrapping around his middle. She sees her mother with her head resting on her father's shoulder watching the healer work closely, then peering back up at her father with immense concern in her beautiful eyes. Ellie feels her heart tighten in her chest and finally lets out a small sigh of relief after seeing that her father is awake.

She strides over to her father's bedside and her mother jumps up, pulling her into a tight embrace just before a choking sob racks her body. Ellie holds her mother tightly through her heart wrenching cries and somehow manages to hold back her tears. She realizes then that she still doesn't have gloves on as her mother's thoughts flood through her once again. The grief and pain invading Ellie, consuming her.

Then Ellie sees her father looking at her. He nods slowly at her with love in his eyes. *He's here, he's not gone. Breathe, just breathe.*

The queen slowly releases her, "I'm so sorry, I should have told you sooner. I just told your father; he didn't know either." Pain laces her tone as her gaze falls back onto the king, he lifts his hand, indicating for her to come closer. Ellie releases her mother and drops to her knees at her father's bedside, her hand clasping his tightly in hers. Ellie notices the quick acknowledgement of her ungloved hands, yet he freely gives his to her while smiling ever so softly.

The king's thoughts start to flow into her, and she hears him say wordlessly, "*Forgive her, you do not understand the love of a mother or the choices she felt forced to make to protect you, both of you.*"

His face begins to fall with sadness in his eyes. It's clear from his other thoughts that he was also angry, and rightfully so. Yet, his love for Ellie shines brighter than all his other emotions and thoughts.

Then the King begins to think back to what had happened during the ball, allowing her to see every moment of the attempts on their lives. All Ellie can do is close her eyes, and process the thoughts he's openly sharing with her.

Once his racing thoughts calm, Ellie lets her father's hand go to allow him the privacy of his thoughts again. Ellie asks him eagerly, but calmly, "Please tell me you'll be alright father?"

Unsure if he wants her mother to know what they just shared, Ellie waits with bated breath for her answer.

The king brushes his hand over his bandaged abdomen and winces at his touch. Ellie eyes his forced smile as he replies, "I will survive my daughter, do not fear for me, fear for the one who attempted to harm us, for the male will suffer far worse than I."

His voice is gentle with Ellie, though still the voice of a regal king. He manages to keep his commanding undertones, seemingly prepared to dole out severe and unimaginable punishments. His light blue eyes seem to dull with his increasing exhaustion.

Ellie nods in an understanding of his words and rises to her feet. As she looks down at her father, Ellie reaches for his hand once again, unable to hold back. Once their hands clasp, she hears him strongly proclaim into her mind, "*I love you.*"

Ellie allows the words to wash away her concern for him and feel grateful to know that his heart still beats. "I love you too, Father." With one last squeeze of his hand, Ellie turns towards the door.

Before Ellie can place her hand on the door, the queen speaks softly, almost hesitantly, "Ellie..."

She turns towards her mother, eyeing her cautiously, "It has been a long night Mother, we shall speak tomorrow." Ellie's response comes in a soft tone. She's too tired to fight for another moment tonight. Ellie quietly opens and shuts the door behind her without giving her mother a chance to respond.

As Ellie walks down the narrow hallway and turns towards the hall of her bedchamber, she sees Kyla, Stella, and Tristan waiting for her. Ellie's eyes immediately move to Tristan's arms wrapping around Kyla. As her friend's head drops to rest against his broad chest, all of Ellie's lingering anguish for her father suddenly goes numb.

Brushing off the odd feeling, Ellie takes in Stella as she sits on the floor with her knees to her chest. She looks utterly lost in thought. Ellie notes they all appear to be as exhausted as she feels, one that seeps into your bones.

As she strides towards them, the group turns to look at her. When she hears a familiar voice call her name down the hallway, Ellie turns to see Jace running towards her. He quickly reaches her and envelopes her in his welcoming embrace.

Ellie allows her hands to touch his muscular back and pulls him into her. As the ice that had just started to crawl over her skin starts to melt away, she allows herself to feel the comfort Jace brings her. Ellie rests her head on his chest as his thoughts begin to course through her while she holds him close. "*Thank the stars she's safe. She's safe and in my arms. She's still here with me.*"

Not noticing her intrusion, she removes her hands from his back. A moment later, she feels Jace being ripped from her arms with strength that surprises her.

Looking up, shock fills Ellie when she sees that Tristan is the cause of the interruption. With confusion crashing through her, Ellie's body stills in surprise.

She watches him point at Jace, "Keep your hands off of her!" With his rough, lethal tone bouncing off the walls, the promise of pain and death fills the hall.

Ellie starts blinking rapidly as she tries to process why Tristan would say such a thing, and before she can say anything to defend Jace, Kyla grabs Tristan's arm. Ellie watches as her friend yanks him back to her and scolds, "What's wrong with you Tristan?" Her words seem to drip with just as much surprise as Ellie feels. Tristan only looks back to Kyla and blinks slowly, as if he's trying to pull himself out of his thoughts.

Then he turns back to meet Ellie's confused gaze and mumbles, "My apologies, Princess, I'm on edge after the attempt on the King's life and wasn't sure in the moment if you were going to be harmed."

To Ellie's ears, Tristan seems to stumble over his words, but the others pay no mind to it. She watches him run a hand through his messy raven-black hair as she mentally recollects herself.

Ellie takes a deep breath, "I'm okay, soldier," not daring to say his name.

From behind her Jace practically yells over her shoulder to Tristan, "I would never harm her! How dare you question me!"

Ellie's shocked by his words, clearly forgetting his station. As she puts her hands up facing each of the males, not daring to touch them without her gloves she pleads, "Please, not now, not tonight."

They glare at each other in a silent standoff, and finally, they nod in unison. Ellie takes another deep breath and exhales loudly so they all can hear, "Thank you all for being here for me, but right now, I just wish to sleep. So I bid you all good night."

Each turns to look at the other and takes Ellie's words as the command that it is. Stella offers a sweet, understanding smile before gently rubbing Ellie's shoulder. She feels Stella's magic seep into her skin in that touch, a calming presence that soothes her soul.

Ellie watches Kyla grab Tristan's hand and pull him along to follow her down the same hall Stella went. Tristan looks at her with an apologetic, forced smile as they pass her. This entire night has been unpredictable; one strange incident to another, it's overwhelming.

Once they pass her, Jace's warm breath tickles her fae ears, sending a shiver down her spine, "Good night, Princess," then presses a soft kiss on her cheek. Even after he pulls away, Ellie can still feel the heat of his lips, a gentle reminder left on her skin. As Jace gives her one last soft smile, he strides down the other hallway leading towards the kitchen.

Ellie turns towards her bedroom door, but before she opens it, she looks over her left shoulder and sees Tristan and Kyla, hand in hand, still striding down the hall. To her surprise, he was also staring at her over his shoulder. His ocean-blue eyes are ablaze as they meet hers. The heat of his gaze seems to travel the length of her, lingering on her sapphire-sparking gown until she feels it practically to her toes.

As Tristan turns his head forward, he and Kyla veer around the corner. Ellie suddenly releases a breath she didn't know she was even holding. When she enters her bedroom, she's relieved to finally have a moment of solitude. The fire in the hearth illuminates her room in a soothing glow.

Ellie quickly slips into a nightgown and climbs into her four-poster bed with a white duvet enveloping her in calm serenity. Every time Ellie's mind wanders to the day, she tells herself - *that it is tomorrow's problem.*

Ellie's eyes feel heavy, she can feel sleep wanting to claim her. They finally begin to close and just as she succumbs to her exhaustion, Ellie hears the voice of her bonded clear in her mind, "*Goodnight, Ellie, we will figure this out together.*"

With a sigh, she replies, "*Happy name day, Saph. Goodnight...*"

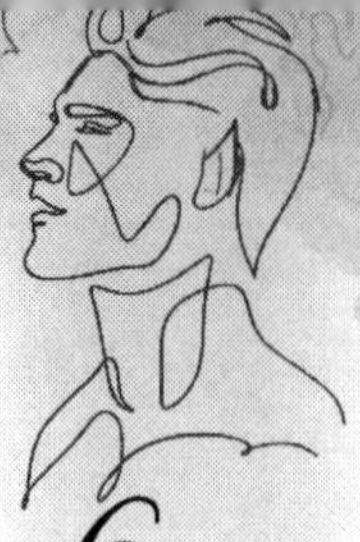

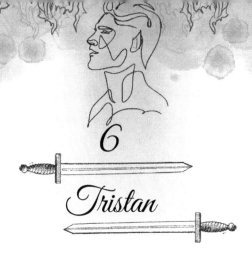

6

Tristan

Tristan finally arrives home, he hesitantly walks through the door and hopes his father is not within the walls. He's quickly hit with a wave of the familiar smell he knows all too well.

Before he can climb the stairs and sleep off the long day, he hears his father's voice echo through the entryway, "Tristan? In my office, please." He wants to laugh at the 'please.' There are no requests when it comes to his father.

After entering the Lord's office, Tristan's eyes sweep over his ornately decorated desk and throne like chair, which has intricate carvings embellished with gold. The room is painted crimson red, with black floor-to-ceiling curtains adding to the malevolent energy of the room. It's truly suffocating. On his desk itself, amidst scattered papers, rests an array of fae artifacts and relics of an age long forgotten. Tristan detests this room in his father's estate more than any other.

His father's voice pulls him from his thoughts. "Did you enjoy your evening at the ball?"

"Yes, my Lord."

A sour taste hits his tongue as the words leave his mouth. Tristan hates how his father demands that he address him.

"I saw you dancing with that little female soldier. Is there something you would like to tell me?" Lord Mormont demands with an smug look upon his chiseled yet ethereal face.

"No, she's just a dance partner. She's no concern of yours." Tristan answers quickly, hoping to divert the conversation away from Kyla.

Lord Mormont stands up from his desk, a glass full of amber liquid in one hand, his cigar in the other, and strides around his desk until he stands before Tristan. His father is tall, with black as night hair like his own only with streaks of gray, skin as pale as moonlight, and eyes gleaming like shards of obsidian.

"It truly is a shame what happened to the King, don't you agree?" Tristan can feel the dark insinuation within his father's tone.

"Let me guess, Father, you have absolutely nothing to do with what happened tonight?" he asks sarcastically and with a hint of annoyance.

When the King was stabbed, Tristan was only feet away, dancing with Kyla. The moment the blade sank into the king's flesh, time seemed to slow, and Tristan's eyes locked onto the male servant who had committed the act. The look on the servant's face once the soldiers subdued him was not hatred or satisfaction but utter bewilderment. His eyes were glazed, distant, as if he had just awoken from a nightmare, unaware of the horror he had unleashed.

Tristan's blood ran cold. He knew instantly who was truly behind the attack. The servant's vacant expression, the way he moved as though pulled by invisible strings—could only be his father's work. Lord Mormont's power was insidious and absolutely terrifying in its subtlety.

He could invade a mind with a single touch, bending it to his will without so much as a whisper. Worse still, he could erase the memory of his commands, leaving no trace of his influence. The realization struck Tristan with the force of a blow: his father could orchestrate the king's assassination. His control was so absolute that the servant himself wouldn't remember anything.

It was a chilling reminder of the darkness Tristan is up against, a dangerous power that could destabilize an entire kingdom.

Lord Mormont takes a long drag of his cigar, blowing the smoke in his direction, and filling the room. His father smirks at Tristan's disgust. He knows how conniving his father is, but attempting to murder the king during his daughter's name day celebration is diabolical. He shakes his head at the thought.

"The king is weak and far too... *empathetic*... to rule our great kingdom. Even his bonded's power is worthless. He is spineless, only caring about peace." Lord Mormont scoffs. Tristan has heard his father's rants about the king's weakness and all the qualities he lacks to properly rule the kingdom for many years. Quite frankly, the rantings are getting old.

"Getting into that servant's mind was far too easy," he mentions, grinning widely at Tristan.

His father's words confirmed his suspicions. Rolling his eyes, Tristan doesn't want to hear his father's ranting anymore. He's tired, tired from his father's scheming and, honestly, the whole damn day.

"You dare roll your eyes at me?! Do you need a reminder of whom you truly serve?" Lord Mormont threatens, spittle flying from his lips.

Tristan knows that tone is a promise of another beating. The memory is so vivid that, for a moment, he can still feel the dull ache from the last time, the sharp crack of his father's fist against his face, the way he loomed over him, demanding submission. The reminder is like an ever-present shadow casting over his life.

Tristan swallows every retort that burns on his tongue, forcing down the defiance threatening to rise. His father's hand clamps down on his shoulder, making him flinch, the grip crushing, paralyzing him where he stands. The familiar icy wave of power crashes through Tristan once again, oppressive and relentless, sending a shiver down his spine.

His father's voice follows, low and venomous, slipping into his mind like a toxic whisper. "Tristan," he hisses, each word dripping with menace, "you will obey me and you will never speak of my secrets to anyone."

Tristan grits his teeth, the echo of those words burning in his mind as his father finally releases him. He feels the cool remnants from his father's magic leaving his body, leaving him feeling drained and angry at himself for showing weakness.

After all of these years, his fathers magic and constant commands to obey him, to submit, to never question, has worn him down and has chipped away at his spirit. The chains of his fathers influence may be invisible, but he feels the weight with every fiber of his being.

Without another word, his father turns and strides to the door, pausing only to add, "Stay away from the princess. We can't have her filthy power anywhere near you."

He swings the door open with a force that makes the walls tremble. "You may go, I have somewhere to be."

With fists clenched and jaw tight, Tristan retreats to his bedchamber, the weight of his father's command pressing down like a lead shroud.

Stepping inside his bedchamber, Tristan releases a heavy sigh, the weight of his frustrations echoing into the quiet room. Fatigue tugs at his limbs, but a burning desire to unleash his pent-up anger simmers in him, overshadowing everything else. As he surveys the dying embers in the hearth, his fist clenches, and a surge of power courses through him, igniting the hearth into a blazing inferno.

Beneath his skin, the restless energy of his magic pulses, yearning to be unleashed with fury.

Shaking his head at the momentary loss of control, he hears Terbius's gruff voice, "*Do you want to talk about it, or do you plan to brood like a petulant child?*" The surge of power must have alerted his dragon.

"*I'd rather brood,*" Tristan replies, his voice laced with irritation.

"*Ah, yes well, I asked purely out of courtesy. I don't feel like talking either—it's been a long night,*" Terbius grumbles.

"*What happened?*" Tristan's curiosity piques, wondering what his bonded has been up to since the ball.

"*Dragon business,*" Terbius replies, the words sharp and clipped. "*Nothing a young fae would comprehend.*" His tone makes it clear that no further explanation will be given.

"*Well thanks for checking in, we both need sleep. I have training in the morning, then we're going to need to fly.*" Tristan hopes Terbius will take his words as a plea, not a demand.

"*Understood. Now, go get your beauty sleep, you need it.*" Terbius quips before Tristan feels their mental connection slip away.

Tristan cherishes the bond he shares with his dragon. They are both fiercely stubborn, their emotions often hidden beneath a veil of silence and understanding of the other. An understanding that can only happen between two halves of the same soul.

From his earliest childhood memories, he understood the relationship with his bonded was his most significant connection. To this day, Terbius is all he truly has.

As Tristan undresses and lays in his bed, he stares at the fire in the hearth as it pops and crackles, recalling each moment from his evening. He had genuinely enjoyed Kyla's company. She had caught his eye training many times and he admires her strength, beauty, and kindness. Even though it hurts to admit, her qualities reminded him of his mother.

It has been seven years since her passing, and his father insisted that he finally come to live with him. Tristan didn't want to but he felt like he had no other choice. He was a child born out of wedlock. That is frowned upon in this kingdom due to his father's station in the king's court. However, he was still granted the opportunity to have a bonded at birth, though many bastards aren't. It's the only good thing his father has ever done for him.

After coming to live with his father, he was provided an extensive education with a private tutor for years. Two years ago, when he turned twenty-five, he was forced to join Aetherlyn's armies alongside Terbius. Since then, he was named his father's heir and promoted in the army's ranks to captain.

He sometimes dreams of flying away on Terbius and never coming back. When he thinks of the shame it would bring his father, a smirk pulls at Tristan's face. *Maybe one day*, he hopes.

He closes his eyes, attempting to drift into sleep, but the image of the princess's face lingered in his mind. Tonight, she was a vision. Radiant in her silk and tulle sapphire gown, she possessed a kindness that Tristan had not expected. When he tried to walk away, he felt almost relieved that she had asked him to stay. The look in her eyes pierced him to his soul.

Realizing that he had no desire to leave. He would have rather stood quietly at her side within her peaceful aura and wrapped it around himself like a warm blanket. He can't help but feel a pang of regret for the cold demeanor he had shown her earlier that evening. Considering all his father's warnings about the royal family, how could he have acted any differently?

The time he and Ellie spent together on the veranda tonight has stirred something within him, causing him to question the validity of his father's words. The princess is seemingly genuine, casting doubt on his previous perceptions of her. When he witnessed another male embrace her, a surge of protective instinct raged within him, though he couldn't quite decipher its origin.

He suddenly feels like a fool for how he lashed out. It was as if someone had taken hold of his body as he ripped the other male off her. All he knows for sure is that such a scene can't ever happen again. His father's advice held some truth—he should keep his distance from her. *I need to, I should, I must*, Tristan tells himself.

Pushing aside further contemplation on the matter, he surrenders to a restless night's sleep; the last image in his mind is of her smiling at the moon and stars in the sky.

7

Ellie

The knock on the door in the morning comes too early for Ellie. She groans into her pillow and wishes she could sleep away the memories of the day before. After a brief moment, Helena and Clara walk in. Helena gives her a small smile, and Clara sets her breakfast and tea down at the table nearest the dwindling fire.

Helena walks to her bedside, "Good morning, Princess, there was a note at your doorway," she holds the small envelope in her hand and puts it out to Ellie.

She quickly flips off her duvet and jumps up to grab it from her hands, trying not to touch Helena with her bare fingertips. Ellie immediately sees the handwriting on the front of the envelope, and her heart begins to race knowing precisely who wrote it.

Ellie smiles sheepishly at Helena as she begs with her eyes for privacy. Helena slightly bows her head, "I'll leave you to it. If you need anything else this morning, simply just send for me." Before she turns away, she begins to speak again. "The queen wishes to speak with you this morning in the gardens after breakfast."

Ellie tries her best to hide her grumble, but as soon as the noise leaves her mouth Clara gives her an inquisitive look, clearly unaware of last night's events for which she is thankful.

Ellie forces a smile on her face as she tries to hide the pain flooding in as she thinks of her mother. Rising from her bed in her white silk nightgown, Ellie strides over to her vanity. Clara asks, "Would you like any help with your hair or makeup today,

Princess?"

"No, thank you, Clara, I will do it today," she wants to say yes but also knows she needs complete privacy to read the letter.

Though, she may come to regret those words later because she isn't good at fixing her hair and makeup, especially not like Clara does. Ellie has a fae's natural beauty with her glowing sun-kissed skin, long bright blonde hair, and deep blue, sapphire- like eyes. She doesn't feel inclined to wear makeup except on special occasions.

The moment Ellie hears the click of the door latch, indicating Helena and Clara left, she swiftly rips the envelope open to read the contents inside.

My Dearest Ellie,

As the moon rises and casts its gentle glow upon the world, my heart yearns for the warmth of your presence. In the quiet moments of the night, when the stars twinkle like diamonds in the sky, it's your radiance that illuminates my thoughts. With each passing day, my admiration for you deepens, like the roots of ancient trees intertwining in the depths of the forest. Your grace, your kindness, and the light that emanates from your very being enchants me beyond words. Tonight, as the world sleeps and the whispers of the night embraces us, I wish to steal away with you to our secret spot. Meet me there at nightfall, I long to hold you again.

Love, Jace

Ellie reads and re-reads the note, holding it to her chest, her heart melting at his words. Jace has always been passionate about the written word, much like herself. Ellie always felt a rush of excitement each time a letter came, even when they were young passing each other's letters. The servants still believe they are only childhood friends, but over the past two years, things between them have changed.

She can easily recall the day she felt that flutter in her heart for him. She has always seen how handsome of a male he is, how kind, and how easy it is for them to talk to each other openly and honestly. Quite frankly, if she is being honest with herself, she has had these feelings for him from the moment she saw him. He has always seemed impervious to her advances, causing her to cease her efforts—until that fateful day when everything finally shifted.

"Slow down Ellie or you'll get us both in trouble!" Jace yelled from behind her trying to keep pace with her on his horse. Ellie just laughed loudly, smirking at him as they raced through the trees. They had been riding for an hour down the beach and through the forest. She loved days like this when she was able to sneak away from the castle and feel completely and utterly free. Her mother always told her she was so much like her in the sense that she always longed for the feeling of freedom.

As they raced through the canopy of trees around them, they both heard a loud crash but before Ellie could turn to face where the noise came from, she was flung from her startled horse. She could hear Jace yelling from behind her as she hit the ground with a thud.

The panic in his voice was palpable but all she felt was shockwaves of pain down her back. Everything hurt as she looked up at the trees above her, rays of sunshine breaking through the canopy. As she lay on the ground, she slowly began to look around trying to find what had spooked her horse, Lightning, who was a gift from her father.

She groaned in pain, but she could hear the hoof steps of Jace's horse stop and his footfalls coming closer to her. He fell to his knees above her frantically and asked her where her pain was. As she looked up at him, seeing his beautiful emerald, green eyes, she couldn't help but hide her smile.

Quickly, he placed a delicate hand behind her head and grasped her other hand, pulling her up slowly, his gaze never leaving her. A sigh of relief escaped him, a tinge of concern evident in his eyes, his care for her palpable. Her heart swelled at the sight, causing her heartbeat to beat wildly against her chest.

Then, something shifted in the air between them, and she felt it—almost as if he finally recognized the depth of her feelings mirrored in her own eyes. With her head still cradled in his hand and her other hand in his, his grip unintentionally tightening, he blinked and then drew her lips to his.

Her breath caught in her throat, scarcely believing he was kissing her. In the next instant, she responded eagerly, allowing their tongues to intertwine in a dance. He felt so right, his touch sending shivers down her spine. His grip around her neck tightened, pulling her closer, while his other hand released her hand and slid up her back, drawing her into him as the kiss deepened.

She had waited years for this, and she wasn't about to let him slip away. With fervor, she kissed him back, feeling her heart racing in her chest, as she gripped his tunic tighter in her fist. Her other gloved hand slid into his blonde tousled hair cradling his head in return.

Slowly, he began to pull away, and she allowed him to release her gradually, already missing his lips on hers. Their breaths were ragged, their eyes still closed with their foreheads resting together, both attempting to steady their breathing.

After a moment of silence, he finally spoke, his voice strained. "I have wanted to do that for years."

Blinking rapidly, she processed his words. "What took you so long?" she replied, a hint of smugness in her tone, bolstered by the confidence his confession instilled.

"I was waiting for you, Ellie. You are the princess. I wouldn't dare

try to kiss you unless you kissed me first. But seeing you hurt... I couldn't hold back anymore."

The memory of that day brings a smile to Ellie's face. Since then, his notes have become a steady stream of sweet words that never fail to brighten her day. They have been meeting at the cabin nestled in the forest just beyond the castle grounds. It is their sanctuary—a place to talk, be alone, and escape the watchful eyes of the castle.

Peering at her reflection in the mirror with a smile, she can't help but think about how much she's been missing him over the past few days. Due to everything with her name day, they have been busy and never found much time alone, except for a couple of stolen moments. She aches to see him; all she has to do is get through the day, confront her mother, and check on her father.

With a deep sigh, she makes her way to the bathroom, brushing her teeth and splashing chilly water on her face, a refreshing wake-up call.

Emerging from the bathing chamber, and reaching for her steaming cup of tea, Ellie abandons all thoughts of breakfast and settles down at her vanity to tackle her unruly hair. After achieving some semblance of presentability, she slips into a casual light blue dress, accentuating her curves. Reluctantly, deciding to wear the sapphire necklace her mother had gifted her just the day before. The gem sparkling in the warm morning sunlight flooding through the open balcony doors, the gentle ocean breeze dances around her.

She always celebrates today with Saphirixia, because she's always been told that today is her bonded's name day. But of course, yesterday's events proved everything Ellie used to believe, otherwise. The feeling of betrayal courses through her rapidly, dampening her mood before she steps out to find her mother. Ellie doesn't feel even the slightest bit prepared for this conversation, yet she needs to have it today. Ellie needs the answers that only her mother can give.

8

Ellie

Slow and steady, Ellie strides down the hall in search of her mother. As she goes, the guards on post along the way give her a slight bow of their heads in acknowledgment.

Reaching the lush castle garden, Ellie spots her mother sitting on the edge of the water fountain. She is staring blankly into its calm crystal waters. She can't help but wonder if her mother feels regret for the secrets she's kept hidden for all of these years.

Ellie examines her mother as she stares into the water. "How is father this morning?" Ellie presses, startling her out of her thoughts.

The queen abruptly turns to her, and Ellie instantly notices the tears lingering in her mother's eyes. The queen quickly wipes her tears, offering a genuine, almost hopeful smile. However, Ellie can see the exhaustion in her eyes. Her mother clearly had not slept much the night prior. Ellie wants her mother to endure some regret and maybe even a little pain for lying to her. Yet, with her father's attempted assassination, Ellie is afraid it may all be too much for the queen.

Ellie tries to remember her father's words, how he insists she forgive her. She knows it will be an arduous task because, quite frankly, she is furious beyond words with her mother. However, Ellie knows her anger isn't going to help the situation, nor will it get her the answers she so desperately desires.

Wiping her tears, the queen responds softly, "He's much better.

He's still in some pain, but the healer believes he'll be back on his feet in a day or so. He was truly fortunate."

Her mother still avoids meeting her gaze for too long, but Ellie is persistent as she tries to communicate with her. "I'm relieved to hear he will be alright," she offers softly. The queen merely nods in response, fresh tears trailing down her cheeks.

Ellie picks at her fingernails as she speaks with a gentle determination. "Mother... I'm trying to forgive you, but there are many things we need to discuss. I need answers before I can move onto understanding you."

"I understand. I'm willing to address all your questions", her mother replies, finally meeting Ellie's eyes. The queen draws a deep breath, exhaling slowly, clearly trying to steady herself. "Ask whatever you wish, my dear. I'm prepared."

Ellie closes her eyes, steadying herself before speaking. Flicking them open, she questions, "Why did you keep this from me?" Ellie's voice trembles despite her best efforts to mask the hurt beneath her words.

"I intended to tell you this years ago, but the timing never seemed right. Nagaara and I made a standing agreement to wait until you were both of age and emotionally prepared to receive this information," she explains with a heavy sigh.

"I never meant to deceive you, only to shield you and Saphirixia from harm. The path ahead will be fraught with challenges, and I confess, I was selfish in my desire to keep you by my side," the queen admits. Ellie reaches out, her gloved hand finding her mother's and offers a reassuring squeeze.

Ellie tries to empathize with her mother's perspective, as her father encouraged her too. She recognizes her mother's immense challenge in keeping such a profound secret from everyone, including her husband for all these years. She closes her eyes briefly, suppressing any lingering anger or resentment towards her mother, and presses forward.

"May I share a memory with you?" With a hint of hesitation, Ellie nods and removes a glove, placing her hand in her mother's. Instantly, the familiar spark of magic tingles at her fingertips as her mother's memories unfold within her mind.

Adelina's strength returns a few days later than she had hoped. She was still terribly weak, and every muscle in her body ached. I cannot sit in this bed for one more moment, or I'll go insane, Adelina thought as she peers out the window.

"Is there anything else I can get you, your Highness?" Helena questioned with a smile. A moment alone would be marvelous. Adelina thought.

Even though the past days had been the best of her life, everyone fussing and doting over her had become irritating. She knows their intentions are good, but Evandor's overprotectiveness, as sweet as it is, starts to become frustrating.

Despite everyone's protests, she decided to seek out Nagaara. It had been days since they had spoken mind to mind, and she had begun to feel a hollowness in her chest that could only be eased by her bonded.

"Thank you, but I'm well, Helena. Please, I beg you to stop fussing over me. We couldn't be better." Adelina said with a smile, peering back down to her child resting peacefully in her arms.

She couldn't be more perfect, Adelina thought with a smile as she ran a gentle finger over her baby's face.

"I'll try, but make no promises, my Queen." She replied with a

smirk that always makes her chuckle. "His Highness wanted me to pass along his apologies; he is in a council meeting with the Lords and will join you later tonight."

"Thank you, Helena, you may go." With that Helena bowed and slipped quietly out of her bedchambers. Adelina took a moment to enjoy being alone, but couldn't stop her thoughts as they drifted back to Nagaara.

Fifteen minutes later, Adelina had dressed and tiptoed through the castle as she peered down each corridor and passageway before sneaking down to make sure not to alert any nearby guards. If she were to be seen, it would only be minutes until Evandor was warned, and she would have no hope of sneaking away to see Niagara. He would have guards stationed at every door and tailing her every moment of every day if caught. She couldn't have that. She truly adores his protectiveness and cares for her well-being and their precious child. However, Adelina is and always has been a free spirit. Locked up for the past few days makes the castle feel like a prison. A prison she is eager to escape from.

Adelina strode through the halls, concealed in her burgundy velvet cloak with her baby tucked safely in her arms. The queen softly shushed her baby, and placed a gentle kisses upon her forehead in hopes of soothing her back to sleep as she began to fuss.

"You're okay, my little love; we're just going on a little walk," she comforted in a whispering breath. Continuing through the castle down to the kitchens, where she knew no one would be at this late hour, the queen slipped out of the door into the moonlit night. Knowing her time is limited if she wanted to beat Evandor back to their bedchamber.

The night's chill seeped into her as she held her child close to her chest to keep her warm. Walking as swiftly as she could to the ocean's edge, she walked down the beach until she entered the dragon's lair. The night was dark, and the smell of the sea and stars above usually calmed her, but tonight, it did nothing to ease her nerves.

Torches can be seen at the cave entrance, flickering like fireflies in the blackness. With a deep breath, Adelina made one last attempt to seek out Nagaara, reaching out telepathically.

No more waiting, Adelina said to herself; as she stepped into the cave, the faint snores and rumbles of the dragons within made the sounds echo off the cavern's walls like distant thunder. The sound alone would make anyone tuck and run with fear, but not her.

"I'm here," she confessed as she rocked her peaceful, slumbering child in her arms. "Stop hiding from me when I call upon you. Come out now," Adelina said firmly, quickly realizing she could've been more pleasant with her demand.

Within moments, she could hear heavy footfalls making the ground quake underneath her feet, signaling Nagaara heard her. Squinting against the darkness, she sees Nagaara's golden scales shine against the torchlight, and then her eyes meet with the golden eyes she knew as well as her own. Nagaara gave a light huff of smoke in her direction. It indicated she wasn't pleased with her showing up here.

"You know me better than to think I wouldn't show up here since you have completely disregarded me for days. So, why did you ignore me when I reached out to you?" Adelina demands, trying to hide the hurt in her tone.

The child in her arms begins to stir as Adelina opens her cloak, concealing her child, and shushes her softly. Nagaara steps closer to Adelina, getting a better look at the child in the dim light, her gold eyes reflecting the firelight.

"She's perfect, my Queen," Nagaara said with a deep timber in her voice that holds a softness she has never heard from her bonded. It swelled her heart with the happiness she had longed for her entire life.

"She truly is," Adelina replied as she peered down, unable to con-

ceal the happiness on her face. After a silent moment of contemplation and contentment of having her bonded with her precious daughter together for the first time, she turned back to Nagaara and pressed, "Why?"

A flicker of pain shone in Nagaara's eyes, made her feel a shred of guilt, but she couldn't help the pain she felt by her bonded's actions.

"I'm sorry I couldn't be there with you. I heard your calls and wished I could've been with you. If I had been there, the truth would have been known." Nagaara replied with a light shake of her head.

"What truth?" Adelina asked curiously.

Nagaara remained silent until light footfalls could be heard throughout the cave's darkness, which forced Adelina to peer around her. Nagaara slowly turns her long golden scaled neck around to peer at the small figure coming up from behind her. A small dragon with scales as blue as sapphires shone in the dim light as it nuzzled against Nagaara's leg.

Adelina couldn't help but gasp in surprise at seeing the small dragon, who appeared to be days old by its size. "Is... is that...?" were the only words Adelina could muster.

Nagaara turned back to her and gave her a shallow nod; with one word, she felt the air pulled from her lungs. "Yes."

"You said your child wouldn't hatch until winter. I don't understand; you said you had another month." She couldn't help the confusion that laced her tone.

"Ade..." Her voice was soft in her mind, almost hesitant. "This is Saphirixia."

Adelina looked over the small blue dragon with deep, piercing sapphire eyes, watching her every move. The small dragon is undeniably magnificent.

"If I would've known she'd hatched, I would've been there with you. Why would you hide her? We have always said we would do this together." Adelina still couldn't grasp the reason for all the secrecy.

"Because Ade, our children were born at the same time." It's as if time stands still while she attempts to grasp what her bonded is saying.

"There is no way because if that were true then... then our children would be... the prophesized. It cannot be true," Adelina thought to her bonded.

"It is true, do you recall the vision I shared with you?" Nagaara asks, studying the queen's expression closely.

"I remember. You said our children would change the world." Shaking her head, trying to process before she dared to peer into her bonded's golden eyes and asked, "Are our children the prophesized bonded?"

"Yes", was all Nagaara replied.

Adeline took her slumbering child in her arms and strode out of the cave without another word. We have spent our entire lives together, and yet she kept something like this from me? This would change everything... Adelina thought to herself as she left the cave and walked into the night.

As the memory fades from her mind, Ellie is left reeling, the revelation her mother shared with her striking like a bolt of lightning. It feels like a missing puzzle piece falling into place, completing a picture she hadn't even realized was incomplete. The weight of this new found knowledge settles heavily on her shoulders, as she processes what she's just seen.

"If we're truly the prophesized bonded, destined to break the curse... how do we go about it? If we succeed, does that mean all fae will inherit powers?" She inquires, her voice lacing with curiosity and uncertainty.

The queen chews on her lip, contemplating Ellie's questions before responding, "I don't possess all the details of the curse. What I do know is that we have awaited the simultaneous birth of a fae and their bonded for centuries. And when you both came into this world, I understood that revealing your identities would burden you with expectations. I wanted you to experience some semblance of normalcy until you were ready to make a choice—until both of you were ready to decide if you wished to break the curse that has plagued our lands, or not."

Ellie gently squeezes her mother's hand, gratitude warming her heart. "You have granted me a beautiful life, Mother. I do understand why you made such a choice; however, it still hurts that I'm just now finding out the truth. If our identities had been revealed from the start, our lives would undoubtedly look a lot different than they do now."

The queen nods in affirmation, then shifts the conversation to a more crucial matter. "To break the curse, you must seek out the enchantress. Though I suspect there is only one way to find her."

Ellie's heart quickens with apprehension, bracing for her mother's next revelation. To her surprise, her mother continues with more unexpected news. "The necklace I gave you for your name day..." Ellie instinctively reaches for the pendant nestled against her chest, the queen goes on - "It arrived at the castle the day following your birth. It bore no indication of its sender, merely a note stating it was a gift for your twenty-fifth name day. It was bestowed upon you by the enchantress herself."

Her hands tremble around the necklace as her mind reels from the weight of the newfound information. Before Ellie can utter another word, Helena emerges, walking into the garden. Her presence interrupts their moment of reflection. With a hurried breath, she addresses them, "I apologize for the intrusion, but the king requests your presence, both of you." Ellie and Adelina exchange a glance, a silent understanding passing between them. They will revisit this conversation later, but they need to be by the king's side for now.

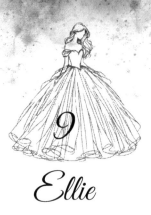

9

Ellie

As they reach the king's bedchamber, general Alvar exits the room grimly, appearing more tired than Ellie had ever seen him. The queen abruptly asks, "Is he alright Alvar?"

The general responds quickly, "Yes, of course, My Queen, His Highness has just updated me."

Then he looks at them both with understanding eyes. He peers back at Ellie and gives her a knowing smile as he bows his head before saying, "I know he wishes to see you both now. I'll be out riding Morphandor, should you need anything just call upon me." Then he holds the door open for them.

As they enter the room, Ellie takes in the king lying in bed, fresh bandages wrapping around his abdomen. Despite his injuries, he appears stronger after a night of rest, a sight that fills her with immediate gratitude.

Ellie watches as the queen approaches his bedside and kneels beside him, pressing a tender kiss to his hand and resting her cheek against it, whispering words Ellie can't discern. She stands silently, observing the depth of love between her parents. Her father tenderly brushes his wife's hair away from her forehead before gazing at Ellie. Relief floods her as their eyes meet, and she approaches her father's bedside, slipping in beside him and resting her head on his shoulder.

"I'm so relieved you're alright, Father," Ellie murmurs.

The king responds gruffly, "As am I." After a moment of silence, he speaks again. "Have you two had a chance to talk?

Queen Adelina and Ellie exchange a knowing glance, sharing a gentle smile before turning back to the king and nodding in unison.

"Good. We have much to talk about." The king winces as he adjusts himself in a sitting position.

As they exchange looks, he proceeds, his tone shifting to one of authority. "I have spoken with general Alvar, and he has assured me that our secret will remain known only to us until we deem it appropriate to reveal. Until then, we shall refrain from discussing this matter further. At least until we have more information. Do you both understand what I'm saying?" His words carry the weight of a king's decree rather than a father's gentle guidance.

Ellie has no other words to say; she only knows this would be their secret to keep. After a while, she excuses herself and allows her parents some time alone.

Leaving their chambers, she makes her way down to the kitchens, her thoughts turning to Eleanora, whom she has not seen in days. She was eager to express her gratitude for the exquisite desserts at the ball lingering in her memory.

As she strolls down the narrow corridor towards the castle's rear, the tantalizing aroma of prepared food wafting through the air, heightening her anticipation. She is looking forward to seeing what culinary delights Eleanora has concocted and, perhaps, by some stroke of luck, catching a glimpse of Jace before the evening falls. The mere prospect tightened her insides with a sense of eager anticipation.

As Ellie walks in, Eleanora is rolling out dough with her rolling pin. Ellie catches her attention, and Eleanora beams brightly at her. Her blonde hair is messy from cooking, she has flour on her cheek and her apron, and her wrinkle-lined smile lights up the room and brightens Ellie's heart.

Ellie feels that Eleanora knows about her and Jace but has never spoken of it and genuinely appreciates her silence. She is not ashamed of her feelings for Jace but doesn't feel comfortable talking to his mother about such things. Frankly, she doesn't like talking to anyone about her feelings.

"Good morning, Princess Ellie," Eleanora greets sweetly, her hands deftly rolling dough on the counter.

"How many times must I tell you, Eleanora? Please, call me Ellie," she insists, a hint of exasperation in her voice.

Eleanora shakes her head, her expression unchanging. "You will always be Princess Ellie, my dear," she replies, resolute.

"Fine, fine, Ms. Eleanora," she says sarcastically.

The warmth from the room and Eleanora's smile, make Ellie smile in return as she tosses some of the flour from her hands towards Ellie, making them both laugh.

"There are some strawberry pastries in the basket over there, go ahead and grab some for yourself." Ellie practically skips to the basket, eager to try the mouth-watering pastries.

With a small bite in hand, Ellie offers her gratitude. "I just wanted to thank you for the incredible food you prepared for the ball," she expresses with genuine appreciation. "Everything looked and tasted remarkable. If you had magic, I would swear you used it in your cooking." Once the words leave her mouth, Ellie's face begins to fall as she realizes what she said. *You could be the one to break the curse*, Ellie realizes.

She shakes her head slightly, pushing the thoughts intruding on her mind. Eleanora, ever observant, notices the expression on Ellie's face, "Are you alright, my dear?"

Ellie forces a smile, "I think I'm just tired. It was a long night."

Eleanora nods understandingly before continuing, "The poor king. I cannot believe a servant would dare to try to harm him. Your father is a wonderful king. It shows how many evil people there are in this world. Give him my best, would you, dear? I will make sure to send him up some pastries as well," she adds with a playful wink.

"Thank you, Eleanora, I best be going, I'm hoping to catch Kyla while she's still here training. These pastries are delicious!" She gushes with a full mouth. Grinning at her brightly, Ellie walks out of the kitchen doors and heads to the training courtyard.

Ellie hears swords clanging as she swings the large door open to the courtyard. She surveys the soldiers training and she can see that they are training in full uniform today. They appear to be training harder than usual. She can only guess it was due to the assassination attempt on her father last night. Ellie can't hold back her wince at the ache in her chest. She takes a deep breath to ease the heaviness and glances around for Kyla.

She finds her in a small group of other soldiers, chatting and laughing with each other. As she studies the soldiers around her, she sees Tristan smirking at another soldier who is making some joke. Kyla beams brightly at Tristan, who then looks at her and returns her smile.

Ellie feels a foreign pang of jealousy in her chest. She lifts her right gloved hand to hover over her heart, and wonders why she would feel such a thing. She has Jace and truly felt glad that her friend had someone in her life. The stars know that Kyla deserves to find love. If she does decide to figure out how to break this curse on the fae, Kyla and Tristan may be mates. Wincing at the thought and quickly shakes it off, forcing a smile on her face.

Kyla whispers something in Tristan's ear, then jogs to meet Ellie.

Kyla immediately grabs Ellie, pulling her into a gentle hug. "How are you feeling today, El? I was so worried about you last night."

Ellie releases her and smiles, happy to see her friend again. Being around Kyla always makes her feel more at ease and less alone.

"I'm alright, I just came from seeing my father. He seems better today."

"I'm so glad!" Kyla exclaims, hugging her tightly once more.

As Ellie lifts her gaze, still wrapped in Kyla's embrace, she finds Tristan's eyes fixed on her. Her heart seems to pause in her chest, and she can't resist returning his gaze with a curious expression.

Tristan blinks as if suddenly snapping out of a trance before quickly diverting his attention and refocusing on the other soldiers. Ellie realizes he's acting as though he had never glanced her way, making her wonder, *was he looking at me like that, or Kyla?*

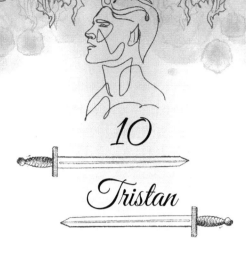

10

Tristan

“You look like shit today. Did you sleep at all last night?” Breccan comments.

Tristan knows his best friend is messing with him, but he can’t help the anger flooding his senses. He shakes his head, replying sarcastically, “I slept a little. Thanks for your concern.”

"You know me, always keeping an eye on you," Breccan grins widely while clapping Tristan on the shoulder.

Tristan swiftly shrugs him off, suggesting, "Let’s get out of here and go for a ride."

He watches Breccan's face light up at the prospect. " Stars, yes, Let’s go!"

As they turn away to summon their dragons, Tristan casts one more glance over his shoulder and sees Kyla and Ellie engrossed in conversation, likely discussing matters concerning the king.

He finds himself gazing at Ellie as she stands in the courtyard, her beautiful blonde locks cascade around her and her light blue dress sways with her movements. She seems to radiate with an ethereal glow, the sight of her leaving a hollow ache to form in his chest. Even though Tristan knows Ellie must be hurting right now with concern for the king, the longer his eyes linger, the brighter she seems to shine. The light surrounding her rivals the sun’s as a soft smile pulls her face. *What strength it must take*, he wonders.

Feeling foolish for his fleeting thoughts, especially as he grows fond of Kyla, he pushes aside his momentary lapse in judgment.

"*Terbius, ready to ride?*" Tristan asks as he reaches out to his bonded.

"*I suppose I can make the time. Vespero and I are on the way.*" Terbius responds, his voice filling the bond with rumbling sarcasm.

Minutes later, Terbius descends onto the beach, making the sand beneath Tristan's feet shutter. Beside him lands Vespero.

Terbius's scales, a deep crimson hue, gleamed like molten lava, while Vespero's scales shimmer a rich forest green against the sunlight. Though Terbius boasts a slightly larger stature, Vespero's strength is equally formidable.

Tristan reaches his bonded, he looks at Vespero, "Good to see you, Vespero." Vespero chuffs in response; Breccan turns to face Tristan, laughing, "He says hello to you, too."

Within seconds of climbing onto their dragons, they are in the air. As they soar higher and higher, the wind whips through their hair. Tristan can't resist the mischievous grin widening his face. He quickly dives into his power, and with a flick of his wrist, he unleashes a burst of wind to attempt to knock Breccan off balance. Breccan, ever agile, anticipates the maneuver and skillfully steers Vespero out of the way.

Undeterred, Tristan urges Terbius to soar even higher, his laughter echoing across the sky. Meanwhile, Breccan, utilizing Vespero's teleportation, falls back and then silently closes in again on his friend from behind. With a swift movement, he materializes beside Tristan, startling him with a playful nudge. Both of their dragons roar in response.

Together, Tristan and Breccan revel in the freedom of the skies; their bond is as unbreakable as the wings of their dragons.

Breccan has been his most loyal friend for years. He always looks forward to days like this when they can take to the skies and train. Tristan always enjoys the little fun testing games they play with their powers on one another. It is up here in the sky where all the thoughts of his father and his manipulative schemes can finally disappear.

The sun is starting to beat down on them, and sweat is already dripping down his back. He feels his flight leathers sticking to his skin. As Breccan catches his gaze, Tristan gestures towards the castle, indicating to head back. Breccan nods in agreement back as they fly over the ocean and back toward the castle.

As they near the beaches of the castle, Tristan's thoughts wander. A part of him hopes that Ellie will be meeting her bonded at this very moment, giving him another chance to glimpse her. He didn't mean to stare earlier, and he knew she must have noticed his gaze.

Ellissandra Firethorne is more than just beautiful—she is mesmerizing. Her long, silken blonde hair, captivating sapphire eyes, and timid smile holds a unique charm that leaves him yearning to see her smile as she did at the stars the night before.

Tristan attempts to divert his attention elsewhere, but each time he tears his gaze away, it feels like it gets pulled back toward her. It's infuriating, and he can't comprehend why. "*Yes, she's captivating and kind, but she is also the Princess of Aetherlyn—not to mention the best friend of the girl I'm courting.* "Stupid fool," Tristan mutters under his breath.

"*Yes, you are a stupid fool. Glad you've finally figured it out.*" Terbius snaps as he huffs a small puff of smoke from his snout. Tristan drops his chin and shakes his head. These are the moments he wishes his bonded was unable to read his thoughts.

As Terbius and Vespero finally land, Tristan glances around on the beach but sees no sign of her. He notices about a dozen soldiers a little further down the coast. They must be preparing to take to the air to practice as well.

After the morning briefing with General Alvar and the captains, the orders were clear: push their ranks harder, sharpen their skills.

Tristan had been doing just that, drilling relentlessly until sweat dripped down his back, his muscles aching with each strike. Now, as he slides off Terbius's flank, fatigue sets in, but he's focused, ready to return to his men.

Just as he turns away, Terbius's voice echoes through his mind like a rumble of thunder. "*There is something you should know.*"

Tristan freezes, slowly looking over his shoulder. Terbius's crimson eyes lock on him, glowing faintly in the midday light, an unsettling intensity behind them.

"*What did you do?*" Tristan's voice is sharp, his heart already hammering in his chest. *This can't be good*, Tristan thinks.

Terbius snorts, smoke curling from his nostrils, and glances toward Vespero and Breccan. Tristan follows the gaze, his gut twists as he sees them deep in conversation, their expressions light and causal.

"*My queen knows of your father's schemes,*" Terbius says, his tone low and grave.

Tristan's breath catches. The words hit him like a blow to the chest. His mind races, caught between anger and fear. "*You told her?*" he snarls, fists clenching at his sides.

"*I do not bend to your father's petty parlor tricks,*" Terbius growls, his voice vibrating with power. "*I kept my vow to you. No soul knows of your suffering by his hand, not from me. But I will not sit idly by and let Nagaara's bonded or Zephyrion's bonded be slaughtered. She is my queen.*"

Tristan's mouth goes dry, his pulse thundering in his ears. The weight of Terbius's words settles over him, thick and suffocating. Silence stretches between them, but it's anything but calm.

"*What did your queen say?*" Tristan's voice is a tight whisper in his mind, dread coiling around his heart like a vice.

"*She commanded Rigmor to rein in his bonded,*" Terbius replies, his tone lethal, like the calm before a storm. "*All dragons are sworn to silence, vigilance, and protection of their bonded. Should Rigmor fail, my queen will handle him and Lord Mormont herself.*"

The menace in Terbius's words sends a shiver down Tristan's spine. *My father... facing the wrath of a queen dragon? I'd love to see that.* The thought is terrifying, yet intriguing. "So... *My father knows that you said something? That I told you of his plans*?" Tristan's voice trembles despite himself, fear crawling through his veins.

"No," Terbius answers, eyes narrowing. "*Nagaara commanded Rigmor to say nothing to his bonded. No dragon can disobey their queen. You are safe... for now.*" His words offer little comfort, and the unspoken warning lingers in the air.

Tristan nods, though his mind reels, the terror of what could happen gnawing at him. A queen's command is absolute, binding dragons in unbreakable magic. He bites down on his lip, the coppery taste of blood grounding him for a moment.

"*Stay out of trouble. Keep your head down. Avoid Rigmor... and stay far from the princess.*" Terbius's gaze darkens, his voice dropping to a dangerous growl. "*The last thing you need is to be dragged into that... mess.*"

The way Terbius halts, the weight of his unsaid words, makes Tristan's heart pound harder.

"*What mess?*" Tristan's voice sharpens, suspicion flaring. But Terbius's eyes blaze, a warning flashing in their depths.

"*I mean it, Tristan. Do not make me repeat myself,*" Terbius snarls, his massive body vibrating with a barely restrained fury. His red eyes glow, dangerous and wise, the heat of his power suffocating.

Tristan swallows hard. "*Fine,*" he mutters, not because he's intimidated, but because he wants this conversation over. Yet the fear still lingers, curling in the pit of his stomach, whispering of the dangers yet to come.

With a final huff, Terbius launches himself into the sky. Tristan watches his bonded dragon ascend alongside Vespero, a hand running through his raven-black hair that got tousled from their time spent soaring through the air. Despite the ocean breeze, the blistering sun beat down relentlessly, offering little relief.

Tristan turns to Breccan. “I'm going to head home and clean up. I’ll see you later.”

Before Breccan can respond, they hear General Alvar’s voice. “Mormont, Aldenridge, a moment, please.” Tristan immediately looks at Breccan, concern evident on his face.

General Alvar strides over to them, his face stoic and devoid of emotion. The General is in his usual tailored uniform, his broad, muscular frame intimidating—a clear indication of decades of training. When he stops in front of them, the General’s brows pinch together as he considers his next words before speaking.

“I had a council meeting with your fathers, and Lord Ravenscroft this morning, and I have an assignment for you two. Your fathers have informed me that you both can be trusted and discreet,” Alvar comments sternly.

This must be another one of my father’s schemes, Tristan thinks.

It is Breccan who speaks up first. “It would be our honor, General. How may we serve?”

Tristan wants to laugh at his friend for sucking up to the General, but he can’t blame him. Even though Breccan’s father, Lord Aldenridge, is in the king’s court, he wasn't born a lord.

Lord Aldenridge works for everything he has and so has Breccan. He is a fine soldier and an even more loyal friend.

Tristan is eager to find out what the general has to request of them. Before he knows it, the general hands them both two letters each. “I would like you two to go to the four Archives and Scriptorium in the kingdom and gather the books the scroll masters will give you, then immediately bring them back to me. Do not ask any questions, just retrieve the books.”

"Absolutely, General. We will not let you down," Breccan responds enthusiastically.

"I expect you both to return as soon as possible," the General commands, nodding once before walking back towards the castle.

As Tristan watches the General walk away, confused by the task they've just been assigned, he glances at Breccan, who grins from ear to ear.

"Are you ready to hit the skies again?" Breccan asks with a devilish smile.

Tristan shrugs. "Let's get to it, then."

They each go to their respective estates to gather their belongings and food rations. They take to the skies within an hour.

11

Ellie

After her brief conversation with Kyla, she heads to the forest and reaches out to her bonded. “*How about we go flying, Saph*?” Ellie hopes Saphirixia will say yes.

“*With you, anytime*, Saphirixia replies, making Ellie smile.

As she strolls through the forest, the melodic chirping of birds fills the air. With a content sigh, she breathes in deeply, savoring the natural symphony around her. Eagerness to see her bonded fills her, she can’t wait to tell her everything she learned from her conversation with her mother.

Once she reaches the beach, she sits down on the sand, allowing the afternoon sun to shine on her face. Ellie closes her eyes, allowing herself to process what her mother has told her. As her gaze lingers on the endless expanse of the ocean, she gently nestles her gloved hands into the soft grains of sand, a sudden urge prompting her to peel off her gloves.

With a decisive motion, she sets them aside, allowing her bare fingers to sink into the warmth of the earthy sand. A prickling sensation envelopes her fingers. The very essence of the shore seems to pulse beneath her touch, pulling her deeper into the sand. *How curious*, she ponders, feeling an inexplicable connection to the mysterious energy dancing beneath her fingertips.

Then, as if on cue, she hears the familiar flapping of wings whipping the air around her; her eyes fall on Saphirixia landing before her. She sits up, grabs her gloves, and strides over to her bonded.

"*Hi Saph...*," Ellie greets with a broad smile, then starts stroking her under her snout, soliciting a deep purr from her bonded. She smiles up at her blue sapphire eyes, then leans her forehead to rest on her face. Ellie can feel her hot breath along her side, giving her a sense of comfort.

"*I spoke to my mother this morning; I have so much to tell you.*" Ellie releases Saphirixia and glances up at her before adding, "*Not here though, let's get out of here.*" Saphirixia only nods, then crouches down into the sand to allow her the ability to climb on. Once Ellie finds her seat on her back, Saphirixia shoots into the air.

Rather than soaring to their usual spot on the side of the mountain, Saphirixia veers towards one of the secluded islands scattered around the kingdom. These islands, often uninhabited, provide the ideal retreat when they seek solitude. As they approached the island, the white sand and lush forest with greenery, sparkling like a paradise, calling to them both.

After landing, Ellie swiftly dismounts, her gaze sweeping over the tranquil surroundings. A mischievous smirk plays upon her lips as she kicks off her boots, places her gloves on top, and ties up the hem of her long dress, baring her knees. With bubbling excitement, she dashes towards the water's edge, shrieking with laughter as she immerses her bare feet in the cool, crystal-clear waters.

Though their visits to this secluded spot were infrequent, her favorite ritual remains the same: immersing herself in the refreshing embrace of the pristine crystal-clear waters of the ocean here.

Saphirixia follows her into the water, her enormous form causing rippling waves to soak her dress from the waist down. Ellie can't help but burst into laughter again as she watches her bonded move through the water enjoying the moment as much as she is.

Finally, they retreat from the cool waters, and find a cozy spot under the shade of the lush trees, resting against Saphirixia.

"*Mother told me that in order for us to restore magic to the fae, we must seek out the enchantress*," weariness in the tone.

"*How will we find her?*" Saphirixia asks gruffly.

"*The necklace mother gifted me yesterday; she said it was received after our births with a note saying to give it to me on our twenty-fifth moon. She believes it came from the enchantress herself*," turning her head to look at Saphirixia.

Saphirixia cranes her neck to look back at her, "So, *we're supposed to use the necklace to find her?*"

"*That's what mother believes...*" Ellie feels silly even saying the words. *How could a necklace possibly help us find the Enchantress? It's just a necklace*, Ellie wonders more to herself, knowing Saphirixia hears every word.

"*Nagaara once told me the tale of the enchantress, known many centuries ago as the most formidable witch in existence. Amidst the tumultuous wars that ravaged our kingdoms and claimed countless fae and dragon lives, she cast a curse upon our realms, stripping away the very essence of fae magic until a bonded pair, hearts that must beat as one and be deemed worthy, could one day restore fae magic. Since the casting of her curse, the enchantress vanished, her whereabouts shrouded in mystery, and her name seldom uttered among the fae. It's as though the passage of these centuries has wrought a collective amnesia upon your kind, erasing the memory of fae magic from many minds. Yet, for us dragons, the memory remains etched in our very beings, we never forget our ancestors or their sacrifices....*" Saphirixia narrows her eyes with her last words.

Ellie leans in closer to Saphirixia, trying to give her comfort. "So *we use the necklace, find the Enchantress, find out how we're to break the curse, and then restore fae magic? It sounds like we have an adventure ahead of us, Saph.*"

Saphirixia let out a puff of stifling smoke, releasing a rumbling chuckle. "*An adventure it shall be.*"

"*I think I should start combing through the castle library to gather more information about the curse so we can make a plan.*"

"*That's a good plan. However, I think you should try using the necklace first...*" Saphirixia said cautiously. Ellie quickly looks at her bonded, noticing a hint of fear in her eyes.

She reaches her bare hand to her neck, traces the chain, and grasps the pendant. It's the first time she's touched it without gloves, and she notices how cold it is against her palm. As her hand closes tightly around the stone, she feels it begin to warm, suddenly becoming nearly too hot to touch. Startled, Ellie quickly drops the necklace back onto her chest, her eyes widening in surprise.

Saphirixia's eyes brim with concern, yet she offers a subtle nod of encouragement. With determination, Ellie reaches out and clasps the sapphire stone in her bare hand, feeling its temperature slowly rise and pulsate beneath her touch once again. Surprisingly, the stone's heat doesn't scorch her skin—an anomaly that gives her pause as its warmth intensifies beneath her grasp.

Closing her eyes, Ellie tentatively delves into her thoughts, knowing Saphirixia will accompany her every step of the way. A shroud of darkness envelops her mind, its presence ominous and tinged with malevolence. The power coursing through her feels like needles pricking her skin, eliciting a grimace of discomfort. Yet, with gritted teeth, Ellie maintains her grip on the necklace, embracing the encroaching shadows surrounding her.

Fear gnawed at her insides, a sensation unfamiliar and unsettling. Amidst the darkness, a soft whisper echoed—a feminine voice that seemed to materialize from the shadows.

"*I have waited a very long time for you, Ellissandra Firethorne,*" the voice purrs, words dripping with sinister sweetness, each syllable laced with chilling anticipation.

Ellie tried to form words but only managed to stumble out, "*Are you... the enchantress?*"

The voice purred again, "*I am, my dear.*"

Ellie's breath caught in her throat. She squeezed her eyes shut tighter, afraid to disrupt the connection. Behind her, she sensed Saphirixia's large form stiffen.

"*If we're the prophesized ones meant to break the curse, how do we find you?*" Ellie asked with a shaky breath.

"*Oh, you both are the prophesized ones, my dear. You shall use the stone to find me,*" the voice continued to purr sweetly.

"*But, how? I don't know how to use it...*"

"*You already have, my dear. I greatly look forward to seeing you and Saphirixia very, very soon.*" With that, the shadows around her dispersed, and the Enchantress disappeared with them.

A chill raced up Ellie's spine as the aftershock of fear began to take hold. She felt the necklace cooling down again and quickly released it, allowing it to fall back onto her chest. They both sit in silence on the beach, gazing out at the vast expanse of the ocean, trying to make sense of all that has just transpired.

Saphirixia is the first to speak, her voice laced with concern. "*Are you alright, El?*"

Ellie's response is soft but direct. "*Are you?*"

"*Whatever our fate may be, we'll face it together.*" The conviction in Saphirixia's voice immediately soothes Ellie's troubled mind, offering a comfort that words alone could never convey.

"*Until death, right, Saph?*" Ellie asks, her voice barely audible in her mind.

Saphirixia simply nods, their matching blue eyes meeting in a silent exchange, a promise unspoken but understood.

12

Ellie

As they return to the castle, a heavy silence hangs between them, unbroken since their time on the island. With dusk approaching, Ellie feels a sense of urgency creeping in. Saphirixia departs for her den without a word while Ellie hurries to her bedchamber, still damp from the ocean waters. Hastily, she begins going through her clothes to change, eager to prepare to see Jace.

A knock on the door startles Ellie, and as it opens, Helena walks in. “Good evening, Princess; your mother wished me to ask you if you'll join her for dinner tonight?”

Ellie tries to produce an excuse as quickly as possible, “Would you please tell her I'm tired from the long day and wish to go to bed early tonight?”

Helena gives her an amusing look as if she knows what she is up to but doesn't say a word. Helena asks, “Are you sure you are alright?” Ellie nods and forces a small smile on her face that doesn't reach her eyes.

“Alright, I’ll have Clara bring you some food shortly,” She then walks out her door.

As Ellie finishes touching up her hair and putting on a little makeup, she picks out the perfect dress for tonight. She chose a simple green cotton dress loose around her thighs but accentuates her thin waist perfectly.

Ellie hears her bedchamber door open again and knows Clara is delivering her dinner. She stays in her bathing chamber, and she calls Clara so she can hear her. "You can leave the food there, Clara. Thank you."

"Of course. Do you need any assistance before bed?" Clara asks sweetly.

"I'm fine, Clara. Thank you. Enjoy your evening," hoping her words didn't come off rude, but she was in a hurry wanting to make the most of her time with Jace tonight.

"Thank you, Your Highness. Sleep well," comes the gentle voice, followed by the soft click of the door closing. With a final glance at her reflection in the mirror, she can't help but smile. Her long blonde hair in a delicate braid, framing her face in a radiant halo. She feels a surge of confidence and beauty wash over her.

Ellie takes a moment and admires her reflection; anticipation bubbles within her. She hopes Jace will appreciate the effort she has put into her appearance, savoring the fleeting moment of excitement before their reunion tonight. Ellie quickly sneaks around each hallway and corridor before she reaches the forest just beyond the castle.

An abandoned cabin stands in the heart of the dense woods amidst the whispering trees and the moonlight filtering through the canopy. They stumbled across the cabin many years ago during one of their rides. Over the years, they have cleaned it up and made it their little secret spot.

As she nears the cabin, she quickly recognizes Jace's tall, shadowy frame sitting in the darkness. She runs to him, wrapping her arms around him as he pulls her in, his familiar scent cascading around her.

"I cannot express how happy I am to see you, Princess," Jace murmurs, reluctantly releasing her from his embrace. His gaze lingered on her in the moonlight, filled with a tenderness that spoke volumes. With a gentle hand, he cups her cheek, his touch sending shivers down her spine. His other hand grips her waist, pulling her closer as if unwilling to let her slip away.

As if unable to resist any longer, he leans down, capturing her lips in a fervent kiss. Ellie gasps softly at the sudden intensity, but quickly gives way to a warmth that floods her senses. His lips are soft against hers, igniting a fire that blazes with every tender caress. Each kiss leaves her trembling, yearning for more, as their embrace envelopes them in a world of their own making.

She can't help but think she could kiss him forever like this, but she realizes that they are still in the open, needing to get inside. Pulling away from him, her smile beaming, she grabs his hand, tugging him towards the entrance to the abandoned cabin.

As they enter the dilapidated home, the air crackles with an electric tension, a palpable anticipation of what will come. Moonlight filtered through the broken windows, casting ethereal patterns on the dusty floorboards.

Their eyes meet in the soft glow of the moon, a silent exchange of affection and desire. He draws closer to her with hesitant steps, their hearts pounding in unison.

Jace stands before her, intertwining their fingers together. Ellie wishes to touch him with her bare hands, yet she refuses to read Jace's private thoughts.

Jace releases her hands, and slowly begins tracing invisible patterns up her arm, igniting a fire that burns with an intensity unmatched by any flame.

"Have I told you how much I have missed you?" He asks softly. Feeling herself smiling, Ellie eagerly kisses him again.

Once their mouths collide again, they surrender to the passion that's consuming them. The tender kiss speaks volumes of their unspoken longing. The worries of the world fade to insignificance the deeper the kiss takes them.

Jace's lips left hers, asking with trembling breaths, "Is this alright?" His tone is tender and loving. They have been intimate many times over the years; he was her first. Even though she was not his, it didn't matter to Ellie. It was still the most magical night of her life.

Her heart racing, she replies, "Yes," smiling at him and pulling his lips back to her.

Jace moves them slowly back towards the cot behind them, as his fingers trail down her thighs, they reach the hem of her dress. Ellie's breath catches in her throat, his touch leaving sparks on her skin as a soft moan leaves her lips.

Jace grabs the hem of her green dress and slowly brings it over Ellie's head. She feels self-conscious at the thought of allowing a male to see her nearly bare, but with Jace, it feels liberating. As he lays her dress at the end of the cot, his gaze skates over her, admiring every curve of her body.

"You're so beautiful, El," he murmurs, as he places a hand over his heart. Ellie only smiles in return; her heart swells in her chest at his admission.

He grabs her hand, twisting them around as he lays her down on the cot. Jace hovers over her, placing gentle kisses along her neck and collarbone. He slowly pulls down the straps of her shift and bares her breasts to him. His lips leave a warm trail down the curve of her breasts before finding her peaking nipple. A moan pours from Ellie's lips as he gently sucks. She runs her gloved hands through his hair and along his back, pulling him harder into her as she relishes the feeling of his mouth.

She feels Jace's hand slide down her waist as he slips up her shift, exposing her to him. He slides a finger over her already wet center, instantly making her yearn for him again. Jace continues to kiss slowly down her stomach, until he is positioned perfectly between her legs, before bending her knees on the edge of the cot. He lifts his eyes to her, giving her his most charming, devilish smile, making her knees quake with anticipation. Ellie can't believe how truly handsome he is, not in the most prominent kind of beauty, but in his soul. At this moment, he is hers.

Jace doesn't hesitate as he traces his warm tongue up her center, making Ellie bite her lip as her back arches off the cot. He adds a finger, amplifying the sweet, torturous movements of his tongue. She knows it won't take long for her to find her release as she writhes under him, craving for him to push her over.

"Bleeding stars, you're so wet for me," his words make her shiver. He groans with pleasure as he licks her again, She can feel the tightness forming within her core, fervent for release. Adding another finger, he slowly pumps in and out of her. Curling his fingers, Jace brushes against the apex of her pleasure. Ellie's head grows fuzzy, then she shatters, his name spilling from her lips. He doesn't stop his onslaught of her clit until her body slacks against the cot.

Jace kisses her body as she tries her best to catch her breath, "You taste so good, El," as his lips find hers again, Ellie can taste herself on his lips, her only cohesive thought is - "I want more." Not realizing she said it aloud, Jace softly chuckles before sitting up and removing his tunic with one hand by grasping it behind his neck. With one swift movement, his chest is bare to her. His lean, sun kissed body drowns Ellie in a new wave of need.

He is truly a beautiful fae male, Ellie thinks. As he removes his trousers, he smirks at her as though he can read her mind; then, he unsheathes himself.

Ellie looks at his solid form, licking her lips with want, whispering, "Please." Jace leans over her again and kisses her with fervor, deepening it impossibly more. She is lost in him, lost in this immense pleasure.

He positions himself over her core before asking with a hint of concern in his tone, "Are you still taking your tonic?"

"Clara puts it in my tea every morning," She replies with ragged breaths. Jace only kisses her again, then pushes himself inside of her, eliciting a low groan from his lips. Ellie gasps at the intrusion, clutching onto him tightly. Giving her a moment to acclimate to his size, he slowly begins to push in and out of her with delightful strokes. Ellie's head falls back onto the cot, savoring the feeling of him inside of her. As his movements quicken, she can feel the familiar tension inside of her, aching for another release. Jace trails tender kisses up her neck, finding her sensitive, pointed ears.

Ellie's hands roam across his back and feel his taut muscles beneath her gloves. She grips desperately onto his shoulders as he thrusts harder into her. She moans, enjoying the euphoria only he gives to her. He claims Ellie's lips as he thrusts one final time, looking into each other's eyes, they delve together into pure ecstasy.

Once Ellie's heart rate slows to a steady rhythm, they stay nestled beside each other on the small cot for a few more moments. There is so much Ellie wants to say but she refrains from speaking a word. She chooses to enjoy the serenity of his arms around her. She lifts her face to meet his gaze, and he stares down at her. Jace kisses her with so much passion that Ellie can feel her heart swell in her chest.

In the intimate space of the cabin, Ellie releases a long sigh, "It's getting late, and I need to get back to the castle before anyone comes looking for me." She feels herself pouting at her own words. She always hates this part after they are together; saying goodbye to him and leaving their secret cabin feels like torture.

Jace rises from the cot and stands at the edge, holding out a hand to help her up. He leans down to kiss her sweetly, then grabs her dress and hands it to her with a smirk.

After they dress, Jace grabs her hand and tugs her outside. He pulls her into his arms and presses a gentle kiss to her temple. Ellie takes a deep breath and inhales the scent of sandalwood and pine.

She grips his tunic with her fists, holding him there as if she has the ability to keep him forever.

"Come, I'll walk you back," he whispers against her temple.

He clasps her hand once again and she smiles at him before they walk through the moonlit forest.

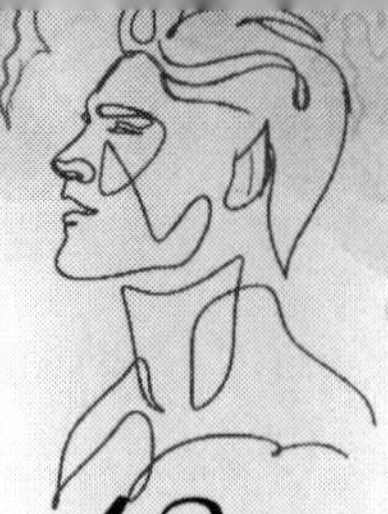

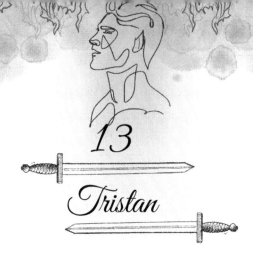

13

Tristan

As they soar through the skies toward the Royal Scriptorium, Breccan yells, “My ass is starting to hurt! Are we almost there?”

Tristan can’t help chuckling at his friend. “We’ll be there soon. You whine far too much!”

“We’re hungry too,” Breccan adds.

“You and your sky lizard are both younglings! You’ll survive.” Tristan jokes, smirking at them both.

In an instant, Vespero’s large teeth snap just feet from Tristan’s face, causing Terbius to twist sideways, roaring back in response abruptly.

“Vespero says don’t call him that,” Breccan shares, his laugh echoing across the skies. As Terbius levels out, Tristan shakes his head at them, enjoying the moment.

Within twenty minutes, they land on the expansive grounds of the Scriptorium. Tristan and Breccan slide off their dragons and immediately stretch their limbs to ease the tightness from their long flight. Vespero and Terbius, suddenly and without a word, quickly fly off. *They must be eager to hunt for their next meal*, Tristan realizes.

Tristan and Breccan nod towards each other before walking towards the entrance of the scriptorium. Tristan is eager to accomplish their first mission.

The scriptorium comes to life as the sun filters through stained glass windows, casting colorful hues across the worn wooden desks and parchment scrolls. Rows of monks, clad in simple cream robes, leaning over their work with focused diligence. Quills scratch rhythmically against the vellum, the ink flowing in intricate patterns gives life to their words of wisdom and tales long forgotten.

Tristan takes a steadying breath in. Tall candles stand illuminating the room, casting flickering shadows upon the stone walls adorned with faded frescoes depicting saints and scribes. The room is simple and clean, unlike the elaborate estates he's become accustomed to.

Tristan sweeps his gaze over the expansive room. Amidst the quiet hum of scholarly activity, a lone monk sits in contemplative silence, his eyes fixed upon the illuminated pages before him. With steady hands and a focused expression, he traces delicate swirling patterns, breathing life into the sacred text with strokes of vibrant color.

"Should we say anything?" Breccan whispers to Tristan, a smirk on his face.

They were instructed to gather the books, but the general had not told him who to ask. Tristan only shrugs, looking around once more before sighing heavily and walking toward the lone monk.

The male draped in simple robes looks up from the text, giving them both a stoic expression. Tristan clears his throat, still unsure of what to say. He holds out the folded note from the general and hands it to the male.

"General Alvar sent us to retrieve some texts." The monk's eyes bore into him, the intense stare making him shift on his feet.

The monk opens the letter, reads it attentively, and then looks them both over, nodding slowly. He gets out of his chair and, without a word, calmly walks away. Tristan and Breccan stand there, unsure of what to do next.

"This place gives me the creeps. It's too quiet..." Breccan whispers, observing the other monks at their tables and walking down the aisles.

"Just keep quiet. We'll be out of here soon," Tristan replies, unable to hide his annoyance at his friend.

About fifteen minutes later, the monk returns with a large leather satchel in tow. He then offers the bag to them and bows his head. They both thank the monk, then walk as swiftly as they can without drawing any more attention to themselves. Once they reach the expansive grounds outside the stone walls, they both exhale.

"Let's camp out for the night and finish the other stops tomorrow," Tristan suggests, his stomach rumbling in response.

"Good, I'm starved, and I don't think my ass can manage much more riding today, I'm going to lose my best attribute at this rate," Breccan chuckles at himself as he runs his hand through his red tousled hair.

By sundown, they have set up camp, have food in their bellies, and are sitting by the fire to keep warm from the chilled wind blowing through the trees.

Sitting on a tree stump with his hands on his knees, staring at the fire, Tristan is consumed with his thoughts. He wonders how the king is faring and if his father is planning another scheme. He even found himself thinking of Kyla, and though he hated to admit it, he thought of Ellie too.

Breccan walks up behind him, pulling him from his thoughts. He drops a handful of chopped logs next to the fire before sitting on the ground across from him.

"So, what do you think is in the bag?" Breccan asks, clearly curious.

"I don't know, nor do I care. General said for us not to look, so we will not. Leave it be, as a matter of fact do us both a favor and don't even breathe by it." Tristan replies, scolding Breccan. He knows his friend and he knew he was curious but there is no chance he was going to screw up his first mission because his friend couldn't control his wandering nose.

"Come on, you know you're curious too! Just open the bag and peek at the books; you don't have to read them!" Breccan pushes.

"No! Now drop it!' Tristan growls with frustration.

"What is going on with you? Why are you being such an ass lately?"

Truthfully, he didn't know how to respond. How can he tell his friend about his father, Kyla, or even Ellie? He simply couldn't.

"I can't talk about it...." Tristan replies, his words barely above a whisper as he runs his hands through his hair.

"Even with me?" Breccan presses almost jokingly.

"Even with you," Tristan replies, finally meeting Breccan's face.

Breccan stares at him, clearly seeing the pain Tristan knows is reflecting in his eyes.

"You know I'm always here for you, right?" Breccan says softly as Tristan stares into his friends' green eyes. Tristan nods and gives his friend the best reassuring smile he can muster.

A fierce wind begins to whip around them blowing the leaves around, and nearly snuffing out their fire. He can hear his bonded's wings momentarily, just before the ground shakes around them. He doesn't need to turn around because he can feel that Terbius is close. As the fire begins to die out from the gusts, Tristan lifts his hand, clenching a fist as the fire springs to life again.

"Let's get some sleep; tomorrow will be a long day," Tristan sighs.

Moments later, they crowd around the fire, allowing the heat to warm their bones as they try to get as comfortable as possible for a night of camping on the hard ground.

However, the moment before Tristan closes his eyes, he is met with the reminder of the stars shining brightly on the veranda that night with Ellie by his side.

Why do the stars alone have to remind me of her? Tristan wonders to himself while gazing up into the sky watching the twinkling of the bright stars above. He can't help the small smile that graces his face.

"*Don't even go there, you stupid fae fool*," Terbius interrupts his thoughts with his gruff voice. Rolling his eyes, Tristan forces himself to sleep.

The following day, they are all up and in the air before sunrise, eager to finish their mission today and return to the castle before nightfall.

A new ritual unfolds with their visit to each Archive. The monks, shrouded in the solemnity of their duties, exchanged no words, instead moving with purposeful grace, retrieving texts and scrolls with a reverence that spoke volumes. With each new Archive they visit, their curiosity blossoms into a consuming desire to unravel the mystery hidden within the ancient tomes. The weight of the secrets they guard, the knowledge they contain, tantalizes his mind, fueling his imagination with endless possibilities.

Finally they reach the last Archive, which sits on the outskirts of their kingdom, Tristan's relief is palpable. The end of their journey is within sight, with only a three-hour flight back to the safety of the castle. Yet, amidst the anticipation of their return, his curiosity burns brighter than ever, his mind awash with questions that beg to be answered.

Tristan eyes Breccan as he clutches the satchel tightly, and they walk back towards their dragons. He watches as Breccan trips, and with a gasp, he falls, the satchel slipping from his fingers and tumbling to the ground.

“Breccan! Seriously!” Tristan yells at Breccanas he places his satchel on Terbius’s back.

Tristan watches Breccan fumble to grab all the tomes and scrolls, attempting to place them back in the satchel as he freezes. He begins shifting through the scattered works, his eyes widening in disbelief.

He shoots him a warning glance, his eyes filling with concern. "Breccan, don’t. General specifically said not to look at the texts," he cautioned, his voice barely above a whisper.

Tristan watches as Breccan unfurls one of the scrolls with trembling hands. His friends' eyes scan the fading text with growing astonishment.

His hand falls to Breccan's shoulder, his grip firm yet gentle. Tristan’s curiosity takes over as he looks at what he is reading. "Breccan, this is dangerous," Tristan warns in an urgent tone.

Tristan hears Breccan’s breath catch in his throat, “Tristan, we *have* to read these. Only a handful of fae’s alive have had the opportunity to read this. You cannot tell me you aren't curious.”

They look at each other, Tristan can see the plea in Breccan’s eyes and his determination.

“No one can know, Brec. I'm serious.” Tristan replies hoarsely.

They both look around, luckily, there are no monks in sight. Tristan continues, “Not here.” They nod at each other, quickly putting all the texts back in the satchel and getting on their bondeds to head into the skies.

Once they finally find a private place to land, they quickly get off their dragons and place their respective satchels in the grass.

“Let’s unravel the mysteries hidden within these tomes, shall we?" Breccan declares with a mischievous grin, his eyes alight with curiosity.

Though Tristan's unease lingers like a shadow in the depths of his mind, he can't deny the pull of curiosity tugging at his thoughts. There is something about these ancient texts that whispers of secrets waiting to be uncovered. With a reluctant nod, Tristan joins Breccan in their quest, knowing deep down that their journey will lead them down a path fraught with peril and possibility.

Breccan combs through the texts, "Check this out..." Then begins to read allowed - "*Legends wove a story of the enchantress wielding a mysterious stone, a relic imbued with the very essence of magic itself. With a flick of her wrist and an incantation upon her lips, she called upon the stone's ancient power to cast her fateful curse upon the realm. As the enchantress raised the sapphire stone high, its surface shimmered with ethereal light, pulsating with raw energy. With each word she chanted, the air crackled and hummed as if nature itself recoiled from her potent magic. In a decisive moment, she unleashed the curse upon the land, weaving threads of enchantment that bound the very fabric of reality. From that day forth, the realm was veiled in darkness, its once vibrant fae magic now twisted and subdued under the weight of the curse until a bonded pair, worthy with hearts that beat as one could one day break the curse. The enchantress vanished into the shadows, but her legacy endured, etched into the very stones and trees of the land. Tales whispered of her deeds and the cursed stone that had wrought such devastation upon the realm vanished, ever a reminder of the enduring power of magic and the consequences of their greed while war raged across the kingdoms.*"

"Why would the General want these tome's?" Tristan stares at Breccan, confusion-lining his face.

"I have no idea. But I want to find out..." Breccan replies with determination in his voice.

"Let's hurry back, General Alvar will be expecting us soon." Tristan adds before striding away without another word.

14

Ellie

The following day Ellie wakes up early, hoping to catch the sunrise with Saphirixia. She barely slept after her defining night with Jace, eagerly wanting to get out of the castle before a long day ahead.

Today is the start of the Dracofaerian Revelry, unfolding over the next three days. A vibrant celebration throughout the Kingdom to honor the sacred bond between fae and dragons. Which was established centuries ago after the curse.

"*Are you looking forward to tonight, Saph*"? Ellie questions excitedly as they fly high above the ocean.

"*Of course, it's the one time a year the fae celebrate us. Plus, the king and faefolk ensure we get fed well*," Saphirixia replies with a light rumbling chuckle. Ellie laughs alongside her, Saphirixia has always loved a delicious meal.

"*Remember last year, the large flower necklace I made you to wear during the bonded flying performance?*" Ellie smiles at the memory.

"*We weren't even in the air for a couple of minutes until all of the flowers flew off your neck and smacked me on the face!*" They both start laughing at the memory as they approach the castle's beach.

"*I'll meet you on the beach with the others tonight for the performance. And please for the love of the stars, El, no flower necklaces this year*," Saphirixia winks at her before flying away.

Ellie always eagerly anticipates the annual flying performance of the bonded pairs. An exciting spectacle that never fails to captivate her. Each year, the sky above the town and castle becomes a canvas for the bondeds to showcase their mastery of flight and powers, along with beautiful fireworks that paint the stars in vibrant color. However, following the flower necklace incident last year, they opted to observe the festivities from a celestial vantage point, high above the fray tonight.

Ellie returns to the castle and meanders through the halls adorned with flowers. It's energizing to see all of the bustling servants carrying decorations and bountiful amounts of food. Ellie can't hold back her smile. *Tonight will be wonderful.*

It's still early in the morning and she hopes to check on her mother and father. Her next order of business will be seeking out Kyla and Stella, so they can all head to the celebration together like they planned. As she rounds the corner of the royal dining hall, she can hear her parents hushedly talking to General Alvar.

Ellie stands in the doorway, hesitant to interrupt, but quickly decides to speak, "Good morning," she chirps, "Happy Dracofaerian." With a wide smile. She tries not to overanalyze what they have most likely been whispering about.

"Oh, good morning, my dear. You're up early, and look at you, you must have been with Saphirixia," Queen Adelina greets with a smile. Ellie gives a quick wink as her mother looks her up and down. She tries to comb her hands through her long blonde waves to work out the wind-blown snarls.

"Good morning, El," King Evandor waves his hand at General Alvar, dismissing him and their prior hushed conversation. General Alvar gives a curt nod and a bow before striding out of the room, clearly in a hurry.

Ellie notices that the color on her father's face is returning. Seeing his swift recovery fills her with relief. She could see that he was still in pain, one hand was resting upon his bandaged abdomen as he ate. The very thought of her father hurting even the tiniest bit, makes her inside recoil.

"How are you feeling, Father?" Ellie asks with evident concern in her tone.

"Bah, no need to fret over me, my dear; I will be just fine," King Evandor replies with a quick smile and continues eating his food.

Ellie approaches the table and loads her plate with fresh fruit and pastries. It instantly makes her mouth water at the sight. *Eleanora must have made them this morning*, she thinks and inhales the sweet air wafting from the strawberry tart pastry.

"Ellie, we would like to speak to you," Queen Adelina says hesitantly after taking a sip of her tea. She eyes Ellie cautiously as she delicately sets the cup down. Ellie only nods as she chews, curious if this is about the conversation she overheard earlier.

"After what happened with your father, we feel it would be best if you had a couple of guards join you at the revelry this evening. We're still trying to figure out if the assailant acted alone or they had conspirators, and we simply do not want to risk a chance of you being harmed." She glances over at her father, who only returns her nod of understanding with a solemn pleading eye for her to obey their request.

"I was planning to spend time with Kyla and Stella. Surely Kyla can guard me? She is *more* than capable." Ellie says, peering back at her mother.

"We're confident that Ravenscroft is indeed skilled and plenty adequate to fully protect you if need be, but to ease our minds, we are sending two castle guards with you," The Queen replies curtly.

Ellie concedes, not wanting to fight her mother and father over this. She knows it will ease their minds and they will be able to enjoy the celebration more if they don't have to worry about her.

"Additionally, tomorrow I would like for you to join us in my study after breakfast. We would like to discuss some things with you in private," King Evandor commands.

"Did something happen?", concern tangling in her voice.

"No, my dear. I endeavored to gather all of the scrolls and tomes from all the archives in the kingdom that mention the curse, and I would like for us to go through them together."

Ellie is unsurprised by her father's determination to unravel the mystery of the curse. His relentless pursuit of knowledge mirrors her thirst for understanding. She can't help but admire his commitment to involving her in the endeavor.

Her heart swells with gratitude, knowing they will embark on this journey together, as a family. The prospect of uncovering the truth behind the curse feels more like a shared quest, a testament to their bond. She begins to feel a renewed sense of hope and anticipation bloom within her, knowing that they will face whatever lies ahead as a united front.

Ellie smiles at him and gives them both a grateful nod of appreciation. They each continue eating breakfast, not discussing the curse again.

After breakfast, Ellie pens a letter to Kyla and Stella, informing them she will have additional shadows for the night and arranging to meet them in the town square at sundown. Handing the missives to Clara for delivery, Ellie settles into a cozy nook in her bedchamber with a book. Hoping to seek a bit of solace before the evening's preparations begin in earnest.

Despite the weariness lingering from the previous night's escapades, a content smile graces her face at the memory of Jace's tender embrace. Anticipation thrums within her as she looks forward to seeing him again, yearning for another sweet, stolen moment alone away from the prying eyes of the guards tonight.

Ellie can't shake the longing for Jace's touch nor the bittersweet awareness of their forbidden love. As a princess, she is tethered to a destiny dictated by her station, a reality she can't escape.

Ellie huffs in annoyance, seeking solace in the pages of her book, hoping to momentarily escape the weight of her troubles and lose herself in the world of fantasy.

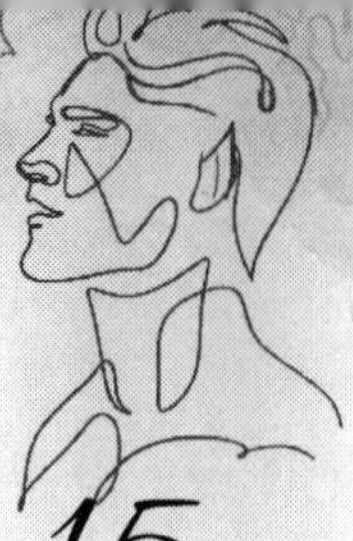

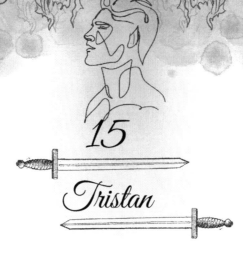

15

Tristan

Tristan and Breccan had returned late the night before and immediately handed off the large satchels to two of the general's most trusted guards. The pair of them then received orders to return this morning to speak with the general, so here they are.

Knocking on the general's study door the following day, Tristan feels the thrum of his nerves as he's unsure what to expect next. His eyes catch Breccan's worried glance as they await his response. *Does the general know we looked at the scrolls*? Tristan can't help but wonder.

"Come in," General Alvar's voice rumbles behind the large wooden door.

Walking in, Tristan and Breccan hold their collective breath as the general speaks, "Ah, Mormont, Aldenridge; sit."

The general sits behind his large wooden desk, gesturing to the chairs in front of his desk, his red tailored uniform pristine. They both sit without a word, hearts hammering in their chests.

"You both did very well on your mission, and I would like to thank you both for your discretion." General Alvar says appreciatively, "and because of that, I would like to assign you both a secondary order for tonight. It is imperative that I have both of you on board."

"Absolutely, sir. We're happy to help." Tristan says with more confidence than he feels.

General Alvars stares at them, "My most trusted guards unfortunately have other assignments tonight. This means that I am in need of two guards to protect the princess during the revelry. Following the incident with the king, we're not taking any chances with her safety. I am assigning the both of you to protect her."

"Us, sir? We would be honored to protect the princess; however, we are admittedly surprised by your assignment." Tristan admits, unbelieving. The magnitude of the task sinking in. Though, he can't help the slight tinge of excitement that ran through him. The unyielding need to stay with Ellie and protect her is at the forefront of his mind. Tristan knows that he has no business feeling this way. Especially considering that he should be spending the evening with Kyla at the revelry. However, there is a small, secret part of him that is even more excited for the evening and task ahead.

Tristan glances at Breccan, who remains silent. The only communication that passes between them is a nod toward Tristan in agreement at his comment.

As he peers back at the general, who is leaning on his desk, hands clasped over the scrolls that he had been reading before they walked in. "You both have proved to be strong and capable soldiers. I have watched the pair of you for a long time and I'm confident the two of you can keep her safe for the evening. If all goes well, then I'll be happy to consider you for other orders in the future."

He tries to blink back the surprise on his face as he nods, thanking the general. As Tristan and Breccan get up from their seats and head towards the door, the general speaks again.

"Mormont, Aldenridge, I would like to remind you both that the Princess's safety is paramount. This task requires you to guard her with your life. Is this understood?" He stares at them with an expectant gaze.

"Yes, General, we will not let you down," Breccan confidently declares. At that, the general returns back to the scrolls on his desk just before they leave the study.

Once they enter the grounds of the training courtyard, Breccan excitedly grabs Tristan's arm. "I can't believe this! This is incredible! An order directly from the general to watch the Princess! This is huge!" He gushes.

Despite Tristan's plan to keep his distance from Ellie, to simply be an unseen shadow, he can't help but feel deeply honored by the general's request. His shock lingers, leaving him reeling and unsure how to process this situation.

He hadn't been looking forward to returning to the estate this afternoon and seeing his father. Tristan simply didn't care what his father thought. He couldn't bear to listen to him drone on about it or, worse yet, get another beating.

"Why are you not more excited about this, Tristan?" Breccan demands.

Tristan didn't want to tell his friend about the night of the ball, on the veranda. He couldn't explain how that night, when Ellie looked at him, it felt like she was slowly trying to peel away every one of the protective layers. Layers he had carefully constructed around his ever present heartache, the ache he'd had ever since his mother died. He can't possibly tell his friend how remarkably beautiful he believes her to be or that he sometimes finds himself thinking of her. Or that, he finds himself looking for her anytime he is in or around the castle, wishing he could sneak just one peek, to know more about her.

Tristan shakes his head, trying to brush away all the thoughts infiltrating his mind about Ellie before he blurts them out to his buffoon of a friend.

"We're being ordered to guard the princess, not the king, Brec. Don't get too excited," Tristan stops in the middle of the courtyard and begins assessing the two dozen soldiers that are training today. No doubt, many of the soldiers have already been stationed throughout the kingdom to help watch over the faefolk in their preparation for the revelry.

"It's our start, Tristan; it's another chance for us to prove ourselves and hopefully it will give us both a chance to move up the ranks," Breccan replies with hopefulness. "I would rather earn my rank by doing my job and doing it damn well than just being moved up because my father is a lord in the king's court," Breccan admits. "Don't you agree?"

"You're right. Let's just get the job done," Tristan says as he lets out an exasperated exhale.

Breccan nods before saying, "I'm going to head home and get my uniform. I'll meet you here later and then we can head out."

"Don't be late. Bleeding stars," Tristan rolls his eyes, "I know how long it takes you to get ready, and don't stare at yourself in the mirror for too long," he teases, smirking as he gives Breccan a playful shove.

"I can't help it if all the females find me attractive," Breccan retorts, smirking. He brushes his shaggy red hair from his face and winks as he strides away.

Tristan stands in the training courtyard, taking in the soldier's training. *They are doing well enough*, he decides and begins his trek back to the estate instead of calling upon Terbius. While he makes his way through town, he takes in the banners bearing ancient dragons, fluttering proudly along the town streets. Each home has ornate flower displays on their doors as well as every pillar and archway marking the pathway of the festival—the air thrums with excitement by everyone in the kingdom.

Amidst the bustling marketplace, Tristan notices all of the artisans proudly displaying their dragon-themed crafts, from intricately carved amulets to shimmering tapestries woven with tales of legendary dragons. The tantalizing aroma of enchanting delicacies fills his senses. Food stalls offer delectable treats, enticing all who pass by to indulge in their delights.

The smells make Tristan's stomach growl, forcing him to grab a treat on his walk, making him feel lighter than he had in a while. That is until he makes it back to the estate. As he walks into the entry, he can already smell the cigar smoke coming from his father's study. The smell brings back memories brimming with the pain that is normally inflicted behind those doors.

Here goes nothing, he opens the large wooden door, his father sits in his chair with his back to him, peering out the floor-to-ceiling window.

"My Lord," Tristan acknowledges calmly, dreading the conversation undoubtedly about to unfold.

"Ah, I was wondering when I was going to see you. I presume the mission that General Alvar sent you on went well?" Lord Mormont presses smugly without turning to look at him. He takes another puff of his cigar, the smell lingering in Tristan's nose.

"Yes, of course," Tristan responds.

"Good. It took a good amount of persuasion on my end to get the General to entrust such a delicate task to you. I did so hope that you wouldn't fail me." His father adds as he finally turns around, his brow raised, taking Tristan in.

It takes a good amount of strength for Tristan not to roll his eyes at his father. *Pompous prick*,Tristan distains. Instead, he forces a curt nod and then decides to turn away before he says anything his father would make him regret.

"And Tristan? Did you happen to see what the monks from the

Archives gave you?", his father inquires.

There it is. Tristan knew this question would come but prepared himself for it. He takes a deep breath and replies, "No, My Lord, we were instructed not to look into the bags and to bring them directly back to the General, we did as we were ordered."

A devious smile spreads across his father's face, "Good knave," waving his hand in dismissal. Tristan walks out of his father's study and up to his bedchamber.

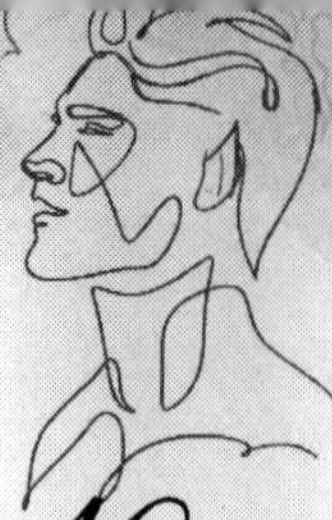

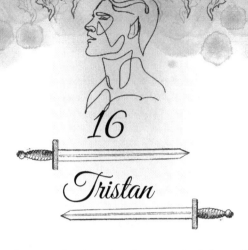

16

Tristan

That afternoon, he meticulously dresses in his uniform and is fully outfitted with his broadsword and dagger on his belt. He meanders across the grounds and stands in the hallway just down from the princess's bedchamber. Tristan taps his foot impatiently, waiting for Breccan's arrival.

He's late, again. Why am I not surprised? Tristan muses as he glances down at his timepiece, shaking his head. He ultimately decides to collect the princess himself, hoping to the stars above that he shows soon.

Reaching Ellie's bedchamber door, he knocks lightly. After a couple of moments, her soft steps grow closer just before Ellie swings the door open. When their eyes meet, he immediately notices the look of utter confusion written across her beautiful face.

"What are you doing here?" Ellie demands, puzzled by his presence.

Tristan tries to form words but finds himself speechless, entirely captivated by her. *Bleeding stars, she is devastatingly stunning in that light ocean-blue dress*. His mind runs wild as his eyes take in every ornate silver flower-adorning her dress, as they shimmer in the light. Her curled hair cascades over her bare shoulders in soft waves. His gaze suddenly catches on her full, inviting mouth. The princess shifts and she nervously sucks in her bottom lip.

Her mouth is.... Tristan realizes that she's searching his face for a response as he's been mentally memorizing hers. He tries to recall her question, but Ellie's scent of lavender and vanilla invades his senses.

His limbs grow numb, leaving him paralyzed while his mind spirals to places he can't even begin to comprehend. Tristan can't help but stare enraptured into her sparkling, sapphire eyes as they roam his inquiringly.

"Tristan... are you alright?" Ellie's concerned voice barrels through his haze. "You look as though you might be sick."

"I, um, I'm fine... It was a long day." Tristan replies as he places his fist over his mouth and coughs to clear his throat. "We're here to guard you this evening for the revelry, you know, to keep you safe."

"We?" Ellie asks, tilting her head to look around him, seemingly puzzled by his words.

As if on a cue, Breccan comes running down the hallway. He abruptly halts right next to Tristan. He turns to stare daggers at him as Breccan shrugs, Tristan presumes he's insinuating that he already knows he is glaring at him for being late.

"Hello Princess, you can call me, Breccan; we'll be guarding you, this evening. It's our honor," Breccan puffs in exhaustion, giving a slight bow and a gleaming smile.

Ellie glances at Tristan briefly, then returns her gaze to Breccan and gives him a sweet smile. "Thank you, Breccan; it's nice to meet you as well. I guess since you're both here now, we can go."

Wasting no time, Ellie elegantly strides past them, her lavender and vanilla scent enveloping Tristan, bewitching him entirely.

Breccan playfully shoves him, wiggling his eyebrows at him and begins following a couple of steps behind the Princess, Tristan follows beside him. Tristan can feel his insides as they recoil; he urgently needs to see Kyla so he can get Ellie out of his mind once and for all.

"She looks stunning tonight, eh?" Breccan questions with a wink.

Breccan's words make Tristan's steps falter. He holds back the response that he desperately wants to say: *Don't even think about it.*

They remain silent as they follow Ellie to the castle gates and into the town. The trio walks along the cobblestone streets observing the faefolk as they smile and bow their heads to her. Ellie smiles at each of them in return, wishing them well. Tristan can clearly see her discomfort, noticing how she plays with her hands nervously.

A group of younglings run giggling up to the princess yelling in excitement, "Princess Ellie! Princess Ellie! Happy Dracofaerian!" Ellie smiles warmly, returning their sentiment. Realization hits him in that moment, just how much the faefolk genuinely adore her.

Tristan is quite taken back, considering all he knows of the shy and demanding princess and the information he has been given by his father. Lord Mormont always complained that Ellie is too entitled, beyond naive, and her power is insignificant but, *Could he be wrong? Could I be wrong?* He wonders.

As they enter the square, his gaze immediately falls upon Kyla, who runs towards them, her thick braid swinging wildly behind her with a smile gracing her beautiful face. When her gaze first finds Ellie and then suddenly falls upon him. She gives him an inquisitive look, clearly surprised by his presence.

"El!" Kyla hugs Ellie swiftly, releases her, and then eyes him, "Tristan, I didn't expect to see you here tonight."

Tristan clears his throat, "The general has assigned me, well us, to guard the princess." He isn't sure why he feels the need to explain, but he does anyway, hoping to ease some of the burning he suddenly feels in his chest.

"Oh, well, that's wonderful. Congratulations on such a large assignment," she adds almost hesitantly.

As she peers back at Ellie she continues, "Sadly, I have been assigned tonight as well. I'm so sorry El, I'm so upset that I can't join you in the festivities." Kyla's whines, her eyes meeting his again, slightly frowning.

"I really need to get to my post. Have some fun tonight though!" Kyla says.

"Oh, that's alright, I understand, Ky," Ellie hugs her again, and then Kyla walks away, winking at him, "I will see *you* later tonight."

Once Kyla makes her way through the throngs of faefolk, Tristan can see Ellie's shoulders tense being in the labyrinth of teeming crowds around her. She gives a small sigh and looks at him and Breccan, "You know, actually, I'm not quite feeling up to it tonight; let's return to the castle."

Tristan feels his heartache at the disappointment on Ellie's face. The Dracofaerian Revelry is clearly one of her favorite holidays, as is evident by the sparkle that had been in her eyes. Her eyes practically lit up at the sight of the town adorned with her family's colors for the celebration. Tristan can't help but think about how much he wants to see her smile like that again.

"As you wish, Your Highness," Breccan says, clearly eager to finish his assignment and be able to celebrate tonight's festivities.

They turn to start walking back to the castle, but a voice calls behind them, stopping them. "Ellie! Wait up!"

Turning around, they see Stella running up to them. "Where are you going? Please don't tell me you are trying to sneak out of the festivities already?"

Tristan watches Ellie offer a weak smile as she replies, "Of course not."

"Of course you were; I know you, El. But tonight is a night of celebration, so we are going to have fun." Stella links her arm with Ellie's and pulls her through the throngs of townsfolk, Breccan and Tristan following quietly behind them.

Throughout the revelry, Tristan observes the fae performers

as they mesmerize audiences with graceful dances and haunting melodies, weaving enchantments that stir the soul. As night falls, ceremonial bonfires blaze to life. He takes a moment to revel in the warm feeling as they glow upon the gathered crowds. Amidst the flickering flames, he can sense the hope for unity and harmony echo through the town.

Tristan remains silent alongside Breccan throughout the evening, protecting the princess without a word, just like he told himself that he would. He can't stop himself from studying Ellie as she participates jovially in the celebration, eating delicious food and laughing hand-in-hand with Stella. He can't hold back his own smile a couple of times seeing her laugh, her joy infections. Something about her laughter pulls him in as though it is a tidal wave pulling him under.

Breccan catches him smiling at Ellie and Stella while they whisper and laugh with one another. Breccan gives him a cocky, questioning look, forcing Tristan to return his features to neutrality.

Covering his mouth and clearing his throat before speaking to the Princess, "It's almost time for the bonded performance. Shall we head back to the training courtyard?"

"Oh yes, thank you," she says to Tristan excitedly. She apparently is as anxious to be with her bonded as he is for the performance.

"Thank you so much for accompanying me, Stels, I must get going. I'll see you later?" Quickly, hugging Stella tightly.

"It was my pleasure, *Your Highness*," Stella's sarcastic tone makes Ellie roll her eyes.

Does she not like being called 'Your Highness,' Tristan wonders to himself; you *would think a princess such as herself would enjoy the royal acknowledgment.*

When they reach the training courtyard back at the castle grounds, his gaze immediately falls upon the crimson-red scales of his bonded. Terbius must have been waiting for him. Next to him, Vespero is also waiting, and a few paces behind them is the eloquent blue-scaled dragon he knows to be Ellie's bonded, Saphirixia.

Tristan takes a moment, as they walk up to their dragons, to appreciate her dragon's shining sapphire-like scales. Tristan can't help but notice how similar the scales are to Ellie's shining eyes. She is large in size, though not quite as huge as his own bonded.

"Uh, Your Highness?" Tristan winces at his words, realizing now that she hates the term. Ellie turns to look at him, her lips pursed and eyes squinting at him in clear discomfort.

"Breccan and I will be... um... behind you in case you need us." Tristan's words nearly stutter as he says them.

"Thank you, Captain, however, I'll be well protected with Saphirixia. You both should go and enjoy yourselves. I will see you both after the performance." Ellie's eyes pierced him where he stands, smirking at him, then quickly climbing onto her dragon without another word.

I want to hear my name from her lips, not 'Captain', he realizes then immediately scolds himself at the unwelcome thought. *Stars! Pull yourself together*, Tristan groans to himself, turning away and stomping toward Terbius.

"Since when do you get tongue-tied over a beautiful female?" Breccan asks, clearly finding amusement in his discomfort.

"Shut up, Brec, let's go," Tristan growls. Breccan's laughter follows him before he and Vespero shoot into the sky.

Climbing onto Terbius, he huffs, "*You're right, pull yourself together, we have a job to do and you are acting like a faeling who's never encountered a female. Now mount.*" Seconds later, they bolt into the air, following Ellie and Breccan into the skies among the other riders.

The skies are full of riders and their bondeds performing aerial twists, dives, and other skills. The drums beating loudly and the cheers of the faefolk below, echo throughout the night sky.

Breccan is already showing off his teleportation skills as he and Vespero speed as fast as lightning through the skies. The pair seems to disappear before reappearing somewhere else, eliciting "Oohs" and "ahhs" from the crowd below. Dragons roar and screech throughout the skies, blazing their dragon fire and lighting up the night with their infernos.

Casting his gaze around to find Ellie, Tristan notices her hovering high above all of the other dragons and their riders. She appears to be watching the spectacle. Her posture seemingly relaxed, the peace and contentment shining off her in the moonlight.

Tristan takes a deep breath and flies toward her. He levels Terbius next to Saphirixia and they hover in the air, their dragon's heavy wingbeats steady. Ellie glances at him only once, before giving him a small smile in acknowledgment.

"Are you going to simply watch, or would you care to join?" Tristan asks curiously.

"I prefer to watch," she replies sweetly. Tristan can't help but study her, memorizing each angle and dimple on her beautiful face in the moonlight. Her attention is on the spectacle below.

Tristan tears his gaze away from her, maneuvering his bonded clear of Saphirixia and Ellie. "Suit yourself," he shrugs, patting Terbius's thick neck. "Let's give them a show, shall we?" He says with a determined grin.

They swiftly dive, barreling towards the sea below in a breathtaking nosedive. During their descent, Tristan gathers his power, feeling the familiar tingle in his hands as his eyes begin to glow crimson red. With a swift motion, he swirls his hands, conjuring a towering cyclone of water that reaches high into the sky. The funnel explodes with a flick of his wrist, raining mist over the town below. The crowd of faefolk erupt in cheers, their excitement mirrored by the rhythmic beat of the drums growing louder and more fervent.

After enjoying the demonstrations for a while, he flies back towards Ellie where she's perched high in the sky with Saphirixia.

"Impressive," Ellie gives him a knowing smile; he knows she can see how much he enjoys using his gift.

"I'm glad you liked it," giving her a devilish grin, allowing his eyes to glow crimson red with the flood of magic igniting in his veins. *Did she just blush*? he wonders.

"*In your dreams*", Terbius says with a huff making him scoff.

"Shall we head back? I believe the fireworks should start soon," Tristan asks. Ellie appears hesitant but nods as they fly back to the castle side by side.

17

Ellie

Saphirixia and Terbius land in the training courtyard where Ellie and Tristan both dismount. Ellie goes to stand before her bonded, "*Thank you Saph.*"

"*For what El?*" Saphirixia questions as Ellie begins stroking her scaled face, leaning into her and feeling the soft rumbling of her breaths. The feeling is so comforting that she smiles.

"*For making me never feel alone,*" Ellie admits.

Saphirixia nuzzles into her, almost knocking her over which elicits a giggle from Ellie.

"You will never be alone as long as I am breathing. Now, go watch the fireworks and I'll see you tomorrow," Saphirixia replied, stepping back. Within seconds, she shoots into the air.

Ellie turns around just as Terbius shoots in the air also, leaving her and Tristan alone in the courtyard. She glances around, starting to feel uncomfortable. Ellie is unsure what to say to him though he calmly stares at her.

"I would like to watch the fireworks from the veranda if that's alright." Ellie manages to say softly.

"As you wish, Ellie," Tristan replies in a husky tone that she feels reverberating through her as she realizes, *Ellie, not Your Highness.* She forces her gaze from his, smiling as she strides into the castle, Tristan close behind.

Once they reach the veranda, Ellie sits on the edge, holding her breath as she waits eagerly for the fireworks.

"You know, you don't actually have to guard me; I won't be leaving the castle anymore tonight," she remarks, looking over her shoulder at Tristan who tenses ever so slightly at her words. He walks over to her slowly and stops a few feet behind her.

"If it's alright with you, I would like to stay a little while longer. I'm not in a hurry and I would like to see the fireworks as well," he replies. His deep timbre sends a tingling sensation across her skin.

Ellie turns to gaze back at the sky, anxious for the fireworks. She can't help but smile a little, though she tries to hide it. *I wish he didn't have such an effect on me. You're being ridiculous*, Ellie scolds herself.

Fireworks suddenly begin exploding across the skies, illuminating the kingdom with cascades of shimmering colors again. Ellie watches the bursts of light in wonder, wishing she were with Saphirixia right now, soaring through the sky. However, when Tristan had offered to take her back to the castle, she felt strangely compelled to follow him.

As she stares at the beautiful display, seeing him in her peripheral before Tristan sits beside her. The two of them watch the fireworks in continued silence and contemplation. Something about his quiet presence gives her a sense of peace, which she finds deeply soothing. She realizes that she has to keep reminding herself that he wasn't her friend; he's her guard.

She could sense his stare. Smiling toward the sky, she watches the fireworks blasting overhead in mesmorizing colors, nearly transfixed. When she finally finds the courage she turns to meet his gaze, it pins her in place. His captivating ocean-blue eyes seem to peer into her soul, analyzing her, taking her in. The look in his eyes is surprisingly gentle; yet so intense. His expression seems to carry immense weight, though he doesn't smile or say a single word.

Ellie can feel the shift in his energy, the icy exterior he wears cracking and giving way to something deeper, something raw. For the first time, she sees a completely different male than she had first imagined.

Tristan lifts his hand and gently sweeps a stray hair behind her ear and Ellie's breath catches. The world seems to pause as his fingers linger on her face, his thumb brushes softly against her cheek. The contact sends a jolt through her, rooting her in place. Her heart begins to pound against her chest, each beat a chaotic rhythm that seems to match the tension crackling between them.

I can't move. I can't even breathe, she thinks, feeling the weight of the moment settle around them. *What's happening*? Her mind races, but her body refuses to respond. She's paralyzed by the soft intensity of his touch. She's terrified that even the smallest movement will steal away the captivating look in his eyes, or could shatter the fragile moment.

"*I think the stars must have created you just to torment me*," Tristan whispers, his voice soft, filling with awe.

His eyes trace her features slowly, it's as if he is memorizing each line and curve with a reverence that takes her breath away. Wonder shines in his gaze, and for a moment, Ellie feels like she's the only thing in his world.

His words force her heart to a stutter. She wasn't expecting something so raw, so honest, so... unexpected.

Does he even realize what he just said? She wonders, her throat tight with emotion.

Tristan slowly blinks and clears his throat. Ellie notes he looks as if he's breaking a spell, or perhaps he's just now realizing the words that came out of his mouth. Each of them quickly return their gazes to the sky as they watch in silence once again while her thoughts run wild.

The night air is full of the scent of blooming flowers and the distant echo of sweet laughter from the faefolk and younglings in the town below, warming her heart. Ellie feels a shiver run down her spine as Tristan's touch lingers on her skin. The fireworks continue to burst overhead, casting fleeting shadows and light across their faces.

As the final burst of light fades into the darkness, they sit in silence, listening to the cheer of the faefolk slowly beginning to fade.

Ellie begins to stand up when Tristan places his hand atop hers, holding her in place. Warmth from his seeps into hers. Tristan begins to speak, "Ellie, I, um..."

"Please don't tell me that I missed it?" Kyla pouts, eyeing the pair as she walks through the grand doors to the veranda "I was trying to reach you both before the big finale but-"

Tristan quickly snatches his hand from Ellie's, acting as though her touch had burned him. He stands so abruptly, a planting pot tips over, loudly shattering on the ground.

Ellie slowly slides to her feet, trying to steer her gaze away from reading Tristan's expression. "Yes, it just finished. But it's alright, Ky. I appreciate you making a valiant effort to join me." Kyla looks at them, clearly trying to assess what she walked into.

"Would you mind walking me back to my room, Ky? I'm exhausted from the celebration and would love nothing more than my bed right now," Ellie asks, trying her best to lighten the moment.

Kyla only smiles at her in return and nods. Ellie strides past Tristan, her shoes crunching on the pot's remains. She makes sure not to make eye contact with him, and grabs Kyla's hand as they walk towards her bedchamber.

Ellie can feel a small amount of tension radiating off Kyla, so Ellie begins to speak again, "Thank you for coming once again. I know you're on assignment, but I'm glad I got to wish you a good night." Though guilt still lingered for the stolen moment between herself and Tristan, Ellie gives her friend a genuine smile. One she hopes truly conveys her appreciation to her best friend for thinking of her.

"I didn't want to just leave you alone, and then when I saw Saphirixia and Terbius fly away, I assumed you went to the veranda to watch the display," Kyla said, glancing back to Tristan behind them, eyes pinned to the ground, hands shoved deep in his trouser pockets, as he follows them.

As they reach her door, Ellie pulls Kyla in for a tight hug and kisses her on the cheek. Releasing her friend, Ellie finally finds the strength to look at Tristan again. "Thank you for guarding me tonight, Captain. I will ensure that General Alvar knows you *both* fulfilled your duty honorably and without fault. Please give Breccan my thanks as well."

"Your highness," Tristan bows, still avoiding meeting her gaze.

With that, Ellie smiles at Kyla one last time and enters her bedchamber, softly closing the door behind her.

Once inside, she walks to her bed and collapses onto it, releasing an exasperated sigh. She places her gloved hand upon her cheek, she is still able to feel the warmth of Tristan's thumb. Almost as if his touch had left a blazing imprint on her skin. His touch ignited something within her—a feeling almost like longing but more intense than anything she had ever experienced before, even with Jace.

She closes her eyes, trying to push the memory out of her mind. *How could I be such a fool? My heart belongs to Jace.* She wants to scold herself for thinking such things about Tristan Mormont. She has Jace, and Tristan is with Kyla. Now, if only her heart would understand that it belongs to another.

The moment she shared with Tristan continues lingering in her thoughts, making her question everything she believes about her desires. The way his gaze had pierced through her, the tenderness in his touch—it all felt too significant to dismiss.

How can I be so drawn to someone else? And why now when everything seemed so clear before? Ellie thinks, wishing she could turn back time and erase the moments that have led her to this turmoil. Deep down, she knows that something has irrevocably changed. Her connection with Tristan, however fleeting, has awakened a part of her heart she had not yet known to exist.

She takes a deep breath, attempting to steady her racing heart and remind herself to focus on what is real and true—her love for Jace. But as she lays there, the memory of Tristan's touch and the intensity of his gaze refuse to move to the back of her mind, leaving her to wonder what her heart truly desires.

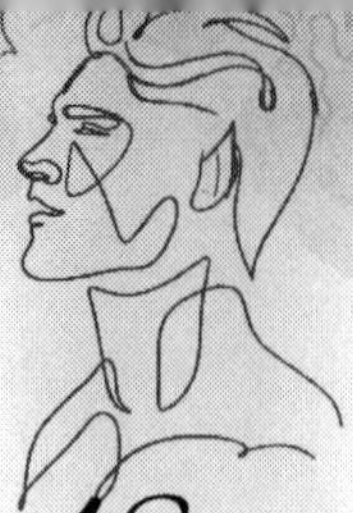

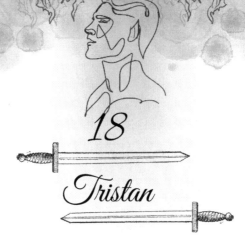

18

Tristan

As soon as Ellie shuts the door behind her, Kyla whirls and focuses on Tristan as if studying him. He can see the anger that he's certain from seeing his hand on Ellie's, etched across her features.

He feels like a fool and knows he shouldn't have sat with her; he should have stayed hidden in the shadows and simply allowed her to watch the fireworks display alone. But as he watched her, he felt compelled to be near her, like being drawn by an invisible cord. He tried to stay away for as long as he could stand it, inevitably he caved and had walked closer to her.

Standing before him, Kyla takes a deep breath. "Just tell me one thing..." Tristan looks into Kyla's auburn eyes, pinning him with a glare.

"Do you have feelings for Ellie?" Kyla demands abruptly, startling Tristan.

"Don't be ridiculous, Kyla. I was guarding her because the general ordered me to," Tristan replies, hoping his words sound more convincing than he feels.

"I do hope you're telling the truth, Tristan." She sighs. "Because now is your chance to tell me if you don't want to pursue this, pursue us," Kyla gestures between them and then glances down at her boots.

Tristan steps towards her and lifts her chin with his finger, gazing at her until her eyes hesitantly meets his.

"You, Kyla Blackwood, are the female that I desire to be with,"

Tristan claims, her mouth with his, willing all of his emotions and feelings into the kiss. It is near impossible to think of anything other than her and her sweet eucalyptus and pine scent as it rapidly invades his senses. He pulls her closer into his muscled chest, drawing out their kiss. Tristan allows himself to get lost in the feel of the kind, beautiful female in his arms.

Even though they have only been together for a short time, Tristan feels like she could be someone that he could be happy with. Tristan admires her as a female and as a skilled soldier. She respects him and his role, especially during duty rounds, which he appreciates and definitely needs in a mate. Her gift for speaking to animals is remarkable and highly valued within the kingdom's army. She will undoubtedly move high up in the ranks on her own accord and will be worthy of the honor.

Tristan pulls away and looks into her eyes, "I'm glad I got the chance to see you again tonight. Might I walk you home?" Kyla nods and smiles as they turn to walk down the hall. As Tristan glances one last time over his shoulder at Ellie's bedchamber door, he notices the light shining beneath her door flicker out.

After walking Kyla home and kissing her goodnight, he walks through the town where the faefolk are still celebrating by dancing in the streets and drinking ale and wine.

When Tristan reaches his father's estate, a sudden gust of wind lashes his face, bringing with it a deafening thud that shakes the ground. He barely has time to react as he instinctively grips the hilt of his sword, his heart pounds as he spins. Tristan finds himself staring into the blazing eyes of Rigmor, Lord Mormont's dragon.

The beast's massive form looms above him, obsidian-black scales gleam ominously in the flickering torch light from the estate walls. Rigmor's teeth are bared in a vicious snarl with his lips pulled back to reveal rows of razor-sharp fangs. He lowers his head dangerously close to Tristan. His hot breath is rank, almost sulfur like.

Tristan takes an involuntary step back, his muscles tensing though he forces himself to stand his ground. The force of Rigmor's presence is overwhelming like a mix of raw power and feral rage. The air seems to crackle with his fury. Tristan knows there is nothing he can do if Rigmor decides to attack him. If he called upon Terbius now, there is no way that he would make it in time.

"Rigmor," Tristan murmurs, his voice barely audible over the dragon's low, menacing growl. The tension is unbearable, and Tristan knows in this moment that his life is hanging by a thread.

Before Tristan can react, his father descends from Rigmor's back with a casual grace, as though the dragon's foul temper is of no concern. Lord Mormont's boot hits the ground with a light thud, and he adjusts his coat with a deliberate slowness, his eyes never leaving Tristan's.

"Do not mind him," Lord Mormont says, his voice smooth and detached. "He's in *quite* a foul mood today." His lips curl into a nasty smirk as though he finds the situation amusing.

Rigmor growls again, the sound low and threatening as the ground beneath him rumbles; smoke billowing dangerously from the dragon's nostrils. Tristan can feel the heat as it radiates from the beast's body, the weight of his presence pressing down like a suffocating blanket.

Lord Mormont walks toward Tristan, his steps slow and measured, his eyes cold. "Come inside now. We have much to discuss," he says, his voice taking on a commanding edge. Without waiting for a response, he turns on his heel and strides up stairs.

Tristan hesitates, feeling Rigmor's gaze still burning into him, the dragon's snarl lingering in the air. With a final glance at the beast, he forces his feet to move, following his father up the steps.

Walking inside, his father shuts the door and abruptly turns towards him, a wicked gleam in his gaze. "I saw you walking that soldier home. I thought you said she was of no concern?" Lord Mormont sneers, his predatory eyes burning holes into Tristan.

"She isn't," he replies sternly. "We had both just gotten off duty and happened to be walking home. Don't make this into something it's not" Tristan said snidely.

"And how was your assignment guarding our *precious* princess?" His father asks as he walks towards the living room pouring a glass of amber liquid into his glass.

Grinding his teeth together, Tristan holds back a retort. He knows what he wishes to say would undoubtedly make his father angry. "It was fine," he replied sternly.

Lord Mormont eyes him for a moment, then drains his glass. "I will speak with General Alvar tomorrow. It is simply unacceptable for you to be anywhere near that... creature or her disgusting power."

"Please don't...," Tristan replies abruptly, immediately wishing that he hadn't.

"Oh? And why is that?" His father lifts his brow, studying him.

"I wish to earn favor with the general of my own accord. I ask that you don't interfere with my assignments, please My Lord."

Lord Mormont only studies his expression before nodding slowly, "As you wish. However, do remember this: you may guard her, parade around as the spectacle she yearns to be even, but do *not* talk to her. Nor allow her to touch you. Do you understand me, *Captain*?" His voice rises with each word and with an authoritative tone. A tone Tristan knows all too well.

Tristan bites the inside of his cheek, as the pompous prick narrows his eyes on him. "You will respond when I am speaking to you. Am I clear?"

Giving a sharp nod, Tristan replies, "Yes, My Lord." He is eager to leave his father's presence as swiftly as possible. He turns from the room and heads to his bedchamber.

Once he closes his door, a storm of emotions floods through him. Hatred for his father simmers within him, a dark, consuming fire he struggled to control. Anxiety for his future and his station gnawing at him, knowing that there was a chance the general would assign him to watch the princess again.

The ridiculous longing to be near Ellie begins gnawing at him. Shame for harboring such thoughts when he should be thinking of Kyla twists his insides. He begins to question the legitimacy of pursuing things with Kyla, pondering if it would be better to end it now before things become more complicated.

The torrent of emotions he feels slowly eats away at him, piece by piece. Tristan closes his eyes and takes a deep breath, trying to hold back the sudden title wave of power crashing through his veins. The last thing he wants is to lose control. Causing the fire in the hearth to explode or burn down the estate wouldn't do, though he desperately wishes that he could.

He feels like such a fool, feeling anything for the princess. Even worse, he feels like a fool for feeling anything at all for anyone. Since his mother died, he swore he would never care for another for fear of heartbreak again, yet here he was testing the fates.

Tristan recalls when his mother died, the anger and pure anguish boiled up within him and he nearly burned down all the crops on their land and nearly all of his mother's small cottage where he grew up. He let his anger take control. Ever since then, he refuses to allow himself to shatter like that ever again. Over the years, he had trained himself and his powers to be in control, however he sometimes felt the need to purge it all out of him.

Tristan knows he needs to rein in his temper, but he isn't sure how. Desperation starts clawing at him, realizing the only way he can find a moment of peace is to be with his bonded.

Determined, Tristan slips out into the night, the cool air calming his heated thoughts. Once clear of the estate, he calls upon Terbius.

Minutes later, he feels Terbius's wingbeat billowing the air around him. As he lands in the street, Tristan says, "*Terbius... I need to get out of here, now.*"

The dragon's deep, rumbling purr vibrates through him, grounding him in the present moment. Tristan climbs onto Terbius's back, and with a powerful burst of wings, they are airborne. The wind rushes past him, carrying away all of his worries and fears. High above the world, with the moonlight casting a silver glow on the landscape below, Tristan feels a sense of freedom and the clarity that eluded him on the ground.

For a while, he could forget his conflicting feelings for Ellie and Kyla, the hatred for his father, and the anxiety about his future. It is just him and Terbius, and the boundless sky stretching out before them. The dragon's steady, rhythmic flight soothes his mind, allowing him to think more clearly.

In the tranquility of the night sky, Tristan resolves to face his emotions head-on. He knows he has to be honest with himself. He couldn't continue to have these feelings, feelings that felt as if they were on the verge of consuming him whole. With Terbius's strength and companionship, he could find the courage to confront his feelings and the determination to find a path forward, no matter how difficult it might be.

Tristan unleashes his elemental powers upon the ocean waters below as they soar through the night sky. The cool night air whips past him, heightening his senses and fueling his energy. With each gust of wind, he summons, he feels the raw power coursing through his veins, a cathartic release for the turmoil within him. He manipulates the wind precisely, directing it to topple boulders and scattering rocks along the shoreline. The force of the elements responding to his will was exhilarating, a fierce display of control and strength.

The ocean roars in response, waves crashing violently against the shore as if bowing to his command. Tristan's mind is a whirlwind of emotion as he channels every ounce of his frustration, anger, and confusion into manipulating the elements. The sky above him seems to pulse with his energy, the stars flickering in harmony with his power. Each movement he makes is a testament to his skill, a dance with the very forces of nature that obey his every whim.

As Terbius flies steadily, Tristan continues pushing himself, testing his abilities' limits. He creates whirlpools in the ocean, swirling and churning like a frenzied dance. He directs gusts of wind to carve patterns into the sandy shore, the grains shifting and swirling in intricate designs. The more he exercises his power, the more he feels the tension within him begin to dissipate.

Despite the physical and mental strain, he revels in the sensation of being utterly spent, his muscles aching and his mind quiet. The world around him feels more vibrant and alive, each breath of the sea air revitalizing his spirit. The tumultuous emotions plaguing him earlier now seem distant, replaced by a sense of calm and clarity.

Tristan knows he can't avoid his problems forever, but for now, he allows himself this moment of freedom. It is already well past midnight, and he didn't want to sneak back into the estate and risk his father catching him.

They decide to camp tonight on one of the many deserted islands around the kingdom as they fly towards the island. Once they land on a beach, settling in the sand, Tristan leans against Terbius for comfort.

"*I saw Rigmor*," he admits, the words heavy on his tongue.

Instantly, Terbius's muscles tighten against him. Tristan can feel the way Terbius stiffens, as if bracing for something terrible.

"*And...?*" Terbius's voice is low, a dangerous edge creeping into his tone. The unspoken question lingers in the air, thick with tension.

"*He was furious. I thought he was going to kill me right there. He's unhinged.*" Tristan admits.

Terbius huffs, smoke curling from his nostrils, his body still rigid beneath Tristan. "*Rigmor has always been unpredictable. But he will submit to our queen's orders. Why did you not call upon me?*"

Tristan chuckles softly, "You wouldn't have made it in time."

Terbius turns his massive head to look at him, crimson eyes glowing in the twilight. Terbius rumbles softly, his voice filled with a mix of sorrow and resolve. "*Next time you call upon me immediately.*"

They remain silent as they sit on the beach for a long while before Terbius says gruffly, "*I can tell you feel much better now.*"

"*I do, thank you, by the way. I was afraid of what I might do if I stayed in that dungeon a moment longer,*" Tristan admits.

"*I could sense it. I can even sense what you feel for the princess, but you must keep your distance as much as possible. You cannot go down that road,*" Terbius huffs.

Tristan arches his head, peering at Terbius, "*You know something I don't. You must tell me.*"

Terbius only gives a light, unamusing chuckle and replies, "*I will not. It's dragon business, and this is something I cannot share, even with you.*"

Terbius's reply only angers him more. But Terbius continues, "*It has nothing to do with you, Tristan, and I'd like to keep it that way.*"

Tristan then realizes that Terbius is only trying to protect him and whatever the secret he keeps from him might be. If he says it has nothing to do with him, he believes him.

19

Ellie

The following day, Ellie wakes up to the sound of a knock on her bedchamber door. She grumbles as usual when Helena and Clara come in with her breakfast and help prepare her for the day.

"Good morning, Your Highness. Your mother asked me to remind you to meet her and the king in the library this morning," Helena says sweetly, clearly curious as to why. It was, afterall, unusual for them to meet in the library.

Nodding and thanking them both, Ellie goes into the bathroom to make herself presentable. As she braided her hair, memories of the evening washed over her. She couldn't help the frown that graced her face, remembering what she felt when Tristan was beside her. Mostly, his piercing gaze as he brushed her hair from her face and ran his finger along her cheek. A wave of heat raced through her core at the memory, which immediately made her grumble. The urge to smack herself out of it is strong; *you are with Jace; now stop thinking about him.*

After dressing, Ellie took a few bites of her breakfast, her thoughts consuming her, and she is eager to learn more about the curse today with her parents.

When she reaches the doors to the library, she takes a deep breath to prepare herself. Once she is content and as mentally prepared as she could be, she pushes open the double doors to find the king, queen, and General Alvar speaking between two tables covered in tomes and scrolls scattered across them.

The king spoke first, “Good morning, Ellie. Did you enjoy the celebration yesterday evening?”

“Yes, Father, I did. The fireworks were spectacular this year,” Ellie gives him a genuine smile.

“Were your guards suitable yesterday, Princess?” General Alvar asks.

“They both fulfilled their duty honorably and without fail; thank you, general,” Ellie answers, a part of her wanting to know if he might have Tristan and Breccan guard her again.

“I’m glad you are here, my dear; we have much to go through together. We agreed it would be better not to let anyone know of these tomes or scripts and to figure this out together.” Queen Adelina reaches for Ellie’s gloved hand and gives her a light squeeze and a mother’s smile.

Ellie no longer feels anger towards her mother for keeping her secret. She knows it would be far wiser to have her parents help her and support her rather than them arguing against her. They had always protected her; of course, she knew little of the extent of that protection, but she was beginning to see it now.

“Shall we?” Queen Adelina waves towards a table with two awaiting chairs and tomes ready to be combed through while a chair for her father is at the table across from them.

“I will leave you to it, then, Your Highnesses. Please let me know if I can be of assistance,” General Alvar bows his head at the king.

“You have already been a huge help, Alvar. Your honor and discretion are deeply appreciated,” King Evandor replies, bowing his head slightly with respect.

“Thank you, Sire,” Alvar responds, nodding before exiting the doors and shutting them behind him.

“Well, it’s going to be a long day; I hope you both are ready,” King Evandor winks at them, making them both chuckle as they start going through the tomes.

After hours of searching, they still had not found any more than what they already knew. Multiple times, Ellie almost confided in her parents and told them how she used the sapphire necklace to speak to the enchantress. However, her fear of her parents' potential outburst at her for not telling them earlier prevented her from revealing that secret.

"I found something," King Evandor says as he peers down at the scroll before him. Ellie and Queen Adelina look at each other, quickly getting up to stand by the king's side.

"What does it say, my love?" Adelina asks anxiously.

Then her father begins to read, "Legends wove a story of the enchantress wielding a mystical stone, a relic imbued with the very essence of magic itself. With a flick of her wrist and an incantation upon her lips, she called upon the stone's ancient power to cast her fateful curse upon the realm. As the enchantress raised the stone high, its surface shimmered with ethereal light, pulsating with raw energy."

"Wait, my necklace?" Ellie asks, interrupting her father who nods and continues to read.

"With each word she chanted, the air crackled and hummed as if nature itself recoiled from her potent magic. In a decisive moment, she unleashed the curse upon the land, weaving threads of enchantment that bound the very fabric of reality. From that day forth, the realm was veiled in darkness, its once vibrant fae magic now twisted and subdued under the weight of the curse until a bonded pair, worthy and hearts that beat as one could one day break the curse. The enchantress vanished into the shadows, but her legacy endured, etched into the very stones and trees of the land. Tales whispered of her deeds and the cursed stone that had wrought such devastation upon the realm, a reminder of the enduring power of magic and the consequences of their greed and war raged across the kingdoms." sighing heavily the king sits back in his chair.

"So, we know why, but we still have not found out how Ellie is to break the curse besides having to find the enchantress," Queen Adelina wraps her arm around the king's shoulders.

"I'm afraid Ellie will have to use the stone you gave her to find the enchantress," The king said tiredly.

"When she does find her, what then? Will she even tell Ellie what she is to do to break the curse? We have been searching for hours, and nowhere does it state how," Queen Adelina said, fear lacing her every word.

"It's alright Mother, we will figure it out. If the prophecy is correct, then I'll find her," Ellie says confidently, trying to ease her parents' worry.

The king looks at Ellie, giving her a grim look, and implores nervously, "Are you sure you are ready for this, my dear? When you seek her out, you will be doing so completely blind."

"Honestly… no. If Saphirixia and I are the prophesied pair, then we will be ready," forcing a smile upon her face.

"You make us so proud, dear. I wish your future were one that I could foresee, so I could better guide you," Queen Adelina walks over to her side, pulling her into a warm embrace.

King Evandor stands up and places his hands on the table, staring at the scrolls before him. "It's time I speak with Alvar and plan for our journey. I refuse to let you go alone and unguarded."

Queen Adelina releases a startled gasp, "My love, you cannot leave. You are the king. You cannot just leave the kingdom unprotected." Ellie can feel her pain and fear creeping up her throat as her mother pleads with the king.

"Father, I believe this is a journey I must venture with Saphirixia alone," Ellie admits hesitantly.

"Absolutely not. You will not go unprotected!" The king's voice rang out, ringing through the library.

Queen Adelina pats his shoulder, saying to the both of them, "We have a lot to figure out before you journey to find the enchantress. Let us speak with General Alvar on how best to prepare and see how many soldiers we can spare to accompany Ellie. But you, my love...," the queen says, looking into the king's eyes, "will not be leaving this kingdom. As much as it pains me to see Ellie leave, I have always known it was her destiny to do so. It is time you accepted it as well."

Ellie found her mother's words surprising, even more so that her father wishes to accompany her on this journey. She still didn't know where she would have to go or how long she would be gone. Her father is king, and he couldn't leave the kingdom without their ruler, even for her sake.

King Evandor only gave them both a reluctant nod in agreement. His features were tight, his eyes were weary, but most of all, love shone through them as he gazed at them both.

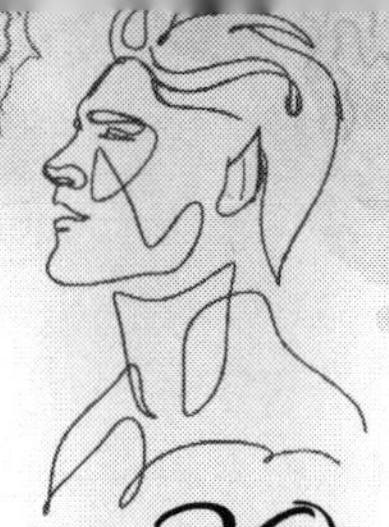

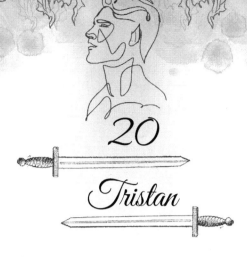

20

Tristan

The first light of dawn began to creep over the horizon, casting a gentle glow across the landscape. Tristan awoke feeling a renewed sense of purpose as he sat on the beach, gazing over the water with a newfound determination to face his challenges head-on. With Terbius by his side, he felt ready to confront whatever lay ahead, armed with the strength of his powers and the clarity of his heart.

As Tristan stood up, shaking off the sand, Terbius stirred and awoke.

"*We need to head back; I should be at training right now*," Tristan said, realizing how late he probably is and hoping that General Alvar wouldn't be there today.

Terbius stood, shaking sand from his scales, huffing a cloud of smoke right into Tristan's face.

"*I nearly forgot you're not fond of mornings*," Tristan chuckles, though Terbius is clearly unamused.

"*If you dare interrupt my slumber tonight or tomorrow morning, I'll rip your leg off*," Terbius grumbles.

Tristan laughs, his voice bright and carefree. "*You would never do such a thing; you care for me far too much, you big softie!*"

Terbius's growl only made Tristan laugh harder. Within minutes, they were airborne, flying back towards the castle and the training courtyard.

Entering the courtyard, Tristan took in the soldiers sparring, catching a glimpse of Breccan, who only gave him a grim look and shook his head in silent warning.

"You're late Mormont!" General Alvars authoritative tone booms through the courtyard, making Tristan flinch.

"My apologies, General, I got caught up doing additional training this morning," Tristan hoped his voice didn't waver.

General Alvar stood a foot in front of him, eyes drifting over the uniform he had worn the evening before, wrinkled and unkempt.

"Hmmmm... Well, I suggest you do better, not just for me but as an example to the other soldiers," the general said, voice lower as he spoke.

"The princess claimed this morning you and Aldenridge fulfilled your duties honorably yesterday evening. It's because of that I will allow your lateness to be excused, this once."

"Thank you, General. I assure you it will not happen again," Tristan said as he stood tall, his hands behind his back.

"Good, I should hope not because you and Aldenridge will guard the princess throughout the Revelry. If you guard her well, I just might assign you both to guard her permanently."

Tristan's insides tighten at the thought of being Ellie's permanent guard. *Can I do it? Can I handle it?* He thought as he swallowed the tightness in his throat, replying to the general, "Us, Sir?"

General Alvar nods at him, shocking Tristan with an uncharacteristic smirk; he wasn't sure if the general even knew how to smirk. The male is as hard as a stone, a true general in every sense of the word. His gift of shapeshifting made him invaluable to the kingdom, and his bonded dragon, Morphandor, was one of the fiercest in the realm.

Tristan's father secretly despises the general, often whispering words of disdain in Tristan's ear over the years. Despite this, Tristan has come to respect him. He admires Alvar's unwavering dedication and the silent strength that commands respect from everyone in the kingdom.

As Tristan stands there, the reality of his new assignment begins to sink in. Yet, despite his nerves, Tristan could feel a spark of excitement. He wasn't sure if it was for the chance to protect Ellie or because this was his chance to prove himself, to show that he was worthy of his trust. The weight of responsibility felt heavy, but the potential for honor and the chance to protect the princess fueled his determination.

The general's smirk faded into a stern expression. "Remember, this is not just an honor but a duty. You must be prepared for anything. The safety of the princess is paramount."

"Yes, General," Tristan replies, his voice steady.

General Alvar's gaze lingers on Tristan for a moment longer before he turns to leave. As he walks away, Tristan couldn't help but feel a sense of pride mixed with apprehension. He looks over at Aldenridge, who strides over to him and places his hand on his shoulder, offering a reassuring nod.

"We've got this," Breccan gives him a confident grin.

Tristan nods, feeling a surge of confidence. With his best friend by his side and the general's guidance, he felt ready to take on the challenge ahead. As they prepare for the Revelry, Tristan couldn't shake the feeling that this was the beginning of something monumental, a turning point in his life that would shape his destiny.

As Tristan takes a deep breath, he and Breccan stand side by side, observing the soldiers during their sparring. His mind begins to wander back to Ellie. Tristan knows the only way for him to fulfill his duty is to forget about any feelings he was harboring for Ellie and make things work with Kyla. *That is my decision, and I'm sticking to it. I refuse to be the fool who falls for the princess.*

Tristan takes a deep breath, turning to Breccan, "So where did you go last night?"

Breccan laughs, "I was in the skies while you both were on

the terrace," Breccan shrugs. "You didn't look like you needed me standing behind you, so I just guarded you from the sky."

Tristan honestly thought for a moment that Breccan had abandoned his assignment, but he should have known better; his friend would never abandon him or his post.

Breccan leans in to whisper in his ear, making Tristan go rigid, afraid of what his friend is about to say, "I hope you know what you are doing."

"It was nothing," Tristan shrugs his friend away from him and tightens his jaw.

"It sure didn't look like 'nothing' as you claim," Breccan said, smirking, which made Tristan grind his teeth together, watching the soldiers before them.

Tristan looks Breccan right in the eyes, saying, "It'll never happen again."

"Good," Breccan replies, "Glad to hear it."

Tristan hears wing beats making him turn, his gaze catches on Kyla on the back of her large orange scaled bonded, Kaida. Kyla smiles brightly at him, making him smile in return. As she dismounts, she strides over to him with a devious grin. Other soldiers and their bondeds followed behind her, landing in the courtyard behind her, clearly just completing a mission or training.

"I'm glad I caught you," Kyla says as she stands before them, "Are you fighting in the games this evening? I heard many of the soldiers entered this year."

Tristan clears his throat. "I was planning to, but Breccan and I were just assigned by the general to guard the princess this evening."

"Oh," a hint of disappointment shining in her eyes. She quickly looked down at her boots, her long brown hair falling to cover her face. Looking back up, she continues, "That's an honor. Well, I'm off duty this evening and was planning to watch the games with

Ellie and Stella. It seems I'll get to see you after all." She smiles again, giving him a little wink before striding away.

"Well, this is going to be a fun evening," Breccan grumbles.

Tristan elbows him in the stomach, making him bend over and cough. "Shut up, Brec, or I'll cut off your beloved ears," Tristan growls.

"Relax, I was just messing with you," Breccan replies, still rubbing his stomach where Tristan had hit him, probably harder than he should have.

"I have something to do before duty tonight. I will see you later," Tristan strides off without looking back at Breccan.

As Tristan walks away, his thoughts are racing. The weight of the evening's responsibility pressing heavily on his shoulders, and he knows the best way to manage this evening is to remain quiet and not talk to Ellie, only protect her.

He walks through the bustling town, full of faefolk and soldiers preparing for the evening's festivities and setting up the fighting rings for tonight's games. The air was thick with anticipation; Tristan couldn't help but feel a surge of pride as he looked around at all the laughing and smiling faefolk. The Kingdom of Aetherlyn is thriving under King Firethorne's rule. The faefolk of the realm were fed, businesses thriving, and families growing; even crime was low in the kingdom. Which made him wish his father wasn't so power-hungry and vile that he couldn't see that.

Arriving back at his father's estate, he notices his father isn't home. Tristan takes advantage of the peace and quiet, deciding to catch up on some sleep before his duty tonight, knowing how much he needs it.

He wakes feeling far more rested than earlier that morning; Tristan quickly eats, cleans up, and is dressed in a new uniform. Using his weapons belt, he places his sword in the sheath and two daggers at his hip. Tonight, they would be in the town longer than the night before, and there would be fighting everywhere during the games. He knows he must remain vigilant and clear-minded.

Stepping back onto the streets in front of his father's estate, Tristan takes a deep breath, the cool evening air filling his lungs. He glances up at the sky, where the sun begins to descend. Tonight would be a test of his skills, his resolve, and his loyalty. He was ready.

With a final nod, he set off toward the castle, ready to fulfill his duty and protect the princess. The night was young, and the Revelry Games were awaiting.

Arriving at the castle, he ascends the stairs to the princesses corridor and immediately notices Breccan posted outside her door dressed in his full uniform and gear.

"I see someone is early this time," Tristan smirks.

"Ready and reporting for duty," Breccan says with a mock salute.

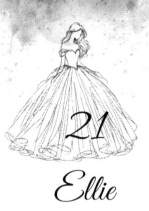

21

Ellie

Ellie stands in front of her mirror to assess the forest green dress she's chosen for the evening. The rich fabric complements and hugs all of her curves while her loose blonde curls flow freely down her back.

Hope fills her at the chance to see Jace again. It has been days since their evening together, and she has not received any letters from him, making her worry about what's to come. Despite the looming feeling, hope still flickers within her. *Perhaps he's just been busy, maybe I'll get to see him at the Dracofaerian Games tonight.* She knows how much Jace enjoys the fights and she can't imagine him missing them this year.

It's already been a dreadfully long day. Ellie spent many hours in the library with her parents, pouring over ancient texts and discussing their plans. Afterward, they all decided to have an early dinner together. The meal was quiet, each lost in their thoughts, feeling the weight of their worries and the nervous anticipation of what lay ahead. Once dinner was over, Ellie wished her parents a good evening and hurried to her chambers to dress with Clara's help.

She stands before the mirror, when a knocking at the door pulls her out of her thoughts. Since neither Helena nor Clara enters her room, she assumes it must be her assigned guards for the evening. *Please don't be Tristan; please don't be Tristan*, Ellie contemplates, her heart pounding. "Be out in a moment," she calls.

She takes a deep breath, trying to calm her nerves. The idea of seeing Tristan again stirs a confusing mix of emotions within her. She wishes she could forget how his touch ignited something deep within her, a feeling she had never experienced before, not even with Jace, that thought alone makes her feel guilty.

She gives herself one last look in the mirror, straightening her dress and smoothing her curls. Ellie squares her shoulders and walks to the door bracing herself for whoever awaits her on the other side. The anticipation of the evening, the hope of seeing Jace, and the dread of encountering Tristan all swirl within her, making her heart race as she opens the door.

Tristan and Breccan turn to face her as she holds the door open. Ellie releases a deep sigh, "Well, good evening."

Tristan and Breccan straighten up before saying, "Good evening, Your Highness," in unison, giving her a slight bow of their heads. Ellie nods in return and walks with her head held high through the castle halls.

As soon as she exits and heads toward the castle gardens, her eyes lock on Kyla and Stella, laughing and talking while they wait for her. As soon as they both see her, their smiles brighten. Ellie feels lighter and more eager than ever for a night with her friends watching the games.

Looking absolutely stunning, Stella is wearing a teal dress that shimmers like the ocean under moonlight. Her short, straight black hair perfectly frames her face while her hazel eyes shine with joy and excitement. Adorning her sharp, pointed ears is beautiful, ornate jewelry with hoops of varying sizes lining them, adding elegance to her appearance.

On the other hand, Kyla is wearing a forest green dress that is remarkably similar to Ellie's. Although far less modest. Her dress has a plunging neckline that showcases her lean, strong figure; Kyla seemingly exudes confidence. Her brown hair is elegantly tied up, and she has used a green eyeshadow that accentuates her striking auburn eyes. Ellie can't help but assume that Kyla's choice of such a revealing dress has everything to do with Tristan. The anticipation of the evening's events and the hope of seeing Jace adds a layer of excitement and nervous energy to the atmosphere.

Looking over to Tristan and Breccan, she notices that Tristan isn't looking at her or any of them. His eyes scan the gardens as if he is trying to avoid eye contact with her altogether. *He's just doing his duty. Stop overthinking it*, Ellie reminds herself.

When her gaze leaves Tristan's they land on Breccan who's watching her intently. He gives her a knowing wink before quickly turning away. *He is a strange one, but I think I like him*, Ellie thinks to herself.

When she returns to the conversation with her friends, Kyla says, "We should get going if we want to make it to the first fight of the night."

As her eyes meet Stella's, she notices her eyes glowing light blue before quickly flickering out. Stella gives Ellie an inquisitive look, and all Ellie can do is give her a hesitant smile. She is reading her emotions and Ellie desperately doesn't want to talk about it, especially not around Kyla or Tristan.

"Yes, let's go. I don't want to miss a thing," Ellie chirps, hoping Stella senses her excitement instead of her mixed emotions.

They begin to make their way out of the castle gates, laughing and talking as they make their way to the town square, where the celebration is about to begin. Even though the fights are often brutal, the use of powers, if bonded, is both accepted and encouraged. The result of these types of fight pairings always made the games very entertaining.

The town square is alive with anticipation, filled with townsfolk eager for the evening's fights to commence. Flowers are strewn everywhere, their vibrant colors adding a festive touch to the atmosphere. Twinkling lights intertwined with garlands and torches illuminate the square, casting a warm, enchanting glow over everything. The air is buzzing with excitement, and the faint scent of blossoms mingles with the crisp night air.

In the center of the square stands the fighting ring, that's surrounded by rows of seats which were quickly filling up with spectators.

Tristan and Breccan stay close behind Ellie and her friends, vigilant yet unobtrusive. Ellie can't help but notice Kyla wink at Tristan when she turns back to look at him. Tristan responds with a small, subtle smile, a sight that makes Ellie curse herself for caring. The playful exchange between Kyla and Tristan feels like a tiny dagger to her heart, a reminder of the confusing feelings she is desperately trying to suppress.

As they find their seats, Ellie tries to push aside the conflicting emotions, focusing instead on the vibrant scene before her. The town square was a picturesque tapestry of light, color, and anticipation. The faefolk clearly ready to witness the thrilling contest that is about to unfold.

Horns begin blaring throughout the square, their resonant notes echoing off of the stone buildings, signaling the arrival of the king and queen. Ellie turns her gaze toward the raised dais near the fighting ring, where her parents were making their entrance. As they walk out with regal grace, the King and Queen wave to the crowd, bestowing kind smiles upon their subjects.

Her father, dressed in an elegant golden doublet that shimmers in the torchlight, exuded an air of majestic authority. The queen, equally resplendent in a stunning gown of matching gold, stood beside him. Their crowns are incredible masterpieces of intricate design and precious gems. They catch the light and cast dazzling reflections, adding to their already mesmerizing presence.

The crowd erupts in cheers, a wave of adoration and respect

sweeping through the square and their beloved royals take their seats. The faefolk's faces light up with admiration, their voices a jubilant chorus of welcome. Ellie's heart swells with pride at the sight of her parents, their regal bearing a testament to the strength and unity of Aetherlyn.

As the King raises his hand, the cacophony of cheers gradually subsides, the crowd falling into a hushed silence. Every fae in the square leans forward in eager anticipation, waiting to hear the King's words.

"Welcome to this year's Dracofaerian Revelry Games! We celebrate this evening by honoring the sacred bond between fae and dragons established centuries ago. I look forward to tonight's event and seeing the masterful fighters duel to be crowned this year's fighting champion."

Cheers erupt through the square once again, making her father and mother smile at the crowd. "I know you all are as eager as I am, so let the games begin!" the King exclaims, gesturing to the first two fighters of the night in the ring.

The fights were captivating and brutal. Many soldiers enter the ring and use their gifts against other faes without gifts, which many of the bonded faes won. It almost didn't seem fair to Ellie as she watched the fights. She couldn't help but think about what gifts the fae would have if she broke the curse. Pushing the thoughts from her mind, she glances around, looking for Jace. Her eyes caught on Tristan and Breccan standing just a couple of yards to the side, watching the fights and the fae's crowding the square.

As Ellie peers back at the fighting ring, her eyes catch on a tall, broad-shouldered male with shaggy blonde hair near the ring. She feels her heart leap into her throat. Without even seeing his face, Ellie knows it's her Jace. When the fight finishes and the winner is announced, she watches as Jace removes his tunic and enters the ring alongside another fae male equal in size and stature. Ellie feels the breath being pulled from her lungs with fear for him. *Will* he be okay? *Can he fight? I've never actually seen him fight before,* Ellie realizes.

"Oh, this should be good!" Kyla exclaims, utterly oblivious to the rush of emotions flooding through her. Stella's hand comes up to rest upon Ellie's shoulder and gives her a tight squeeze of reassurance. Ellie's gaze meets Stella's, and she nods, noting the look of fear etched on her face.

The fae male lunges first, his speed astonishing. Jace barely dodges the blow, countering with a swift punch to the male's ribs. The impact barely fazes the male, who retaliates with a powerful kick, sending Jace sprawling to the ground. Ellie gasps, her hands flying to her mouth.

Jace quickly recovers, rolling to his feet. The fae male charges again, delivering a series of rapid, brutal strikes. Jace blocks and parries as best he could, but the male's strength is relentless. Ellie's concern deepens, her heart aching with every blow Jace took.

Summoning his remaining strength, Jace delivers a series of rapid strikes, each blow landing with precision. The fae male staggers, visibly shaken. As if sensing an opening, Jace lands a powerful punch, sending his opponent crashing to the ground. The crowd erupts in cheers as the announcer declares Jace the victor.

Ellie's eyes never leave Jace, relief flooding through her as he stands in the middle of the ring, breathing heavily but victorious. The fight had been brutal, but Jace had proven his strength and resilience. As he exits the ring, Ellie's concern lingers, her heart still pounding from the intensity of the match.

"He's okay," Stella whispers in her ear, trying to reassure her as she gives her gloved hand another squeeze.

Ellie continues to watch him from afar as he speaks with other contestants, who pats him on the back and congratulates him on his win. The fights continue as the King and Queen exit the revelry and wave at the crowd as they leave.

Kyla and Stella continue talking around her, but Ellie barely hears a word they say as her thoughts drift to Jace, her eyes never leaving him.

During the next fight, a fighter gets so severely injured he can not continue, which makes the match uneven. The game's announcer stands on the dais and addresses the eager crowd.

"Due to a fighter being unable to continue in the games, would anyone like to join in on the games?" The crowd remains silent; everyone glances around to look at one another and is eager to see who might volunteer.

"I'll volunteer," a deep voice says, echoing through the crowd.

Ellie freezes, she knows that voice but can't believe it. As she peers around to find Tristan, his eyes locking on hers, he smiles as the crowd erupts with cheers.

Tristan then begins walking towards the ring as Kyla says, "I thought he wasn't going to fight tonight?" clearly as confused as she is.

Tristan is preparing to fight as he nears the ring. He begins removing his weapons and tunic, handing everything to Breccan. Ellie isn't sure if she was even breathing anymore. She is almost too afraid even to blink. *This can't be happening*, she thinks, completely unbelieving.

22

Ellie

The town square erupts in cheers, Tristan and Jace enter the ring, and the crowd is eager to watch Aetherlyn's soldier fight against the town's bladesmith. Ellie's eyes lock on the fighting ring where Tristan and Jace walk inside the ring, ready to face off.

Tristan, standing tall and composed, radiates confidence. His raven black hair is damp with sweat and is clinging to his forehead. His muscles are tense, clearly ready for the fight. Across from him, Jace's emerald-green eyes glint with determination, his stance equally poised. The air between them seems to spark with unspoken tension.

The horn blares, signaling the beginning of the fight. Tristan wastes no time, summoning a gust of wind that knocks Jace off balance. He stumbles with the force but quickly regains his footing and charges at Tristan. Jace swings a powerful fist, which Tristan deftly dodges and retaliates with a secondary blast of air that sends Jace spirling backward and away from him.

The crowd roars as Jace straightens, determination etched on his face. He darts forward, weaving deftly through Tristan's elemental assaults. Jace lands a solid punch to Tristan's side, followed by another to his jaw. Tristan staggers but quickly recovers, he raises his hands to summon a wall of water from the nearby fountain in the square. He directs the torrent at Jace, who braces himself and pushes through the deluge with sheer willpower.

Ellie's heart races as she watches Jace struggle against Tristan's elemental onslaught. Tristan shifts tactics, calling forth a flurry of small rocks from the arena floor and causing the ground to quake. They hurtle toward Jace, who dodges and blocks as many as possible, his movements swift and calculated despite the rumbling beneath his feet. A stone grazes his arm, drawing blood, but Jace pressed on, closing the distance between them.

With a fierce yell, Jace launches himself at Tristan, tackling him to the ground. The impact breaks Tristan's concentration, causing the elemental attacks to cease. The two males grapple, rolling across the ring in a fierce struggle. Tristan's eyes flash with determination as he attempts to summon another elemental attack.

He manages to summon a burst of wind, dislodging Jace's grip and sending him tumbling. Using the moment to his advantage, Tristan calls forth a whirlwind, which lifts Jace off his feet and hurls him across the ring. Jace lands hard; the wind knocks out of him. Struggling to rise, he looks up just in time to see Tristan summoning another elemental attack.

Tristan brought his hands together and a jet of water surged from the fountain, slamming into Jace like a battering ram. Jace tries to stand, but the relentless force of the water keeps him pinned. With one final surge, Tristan sends a gust of wind that knocks Jace back, leaving him sprawled and defeated on the ground.

The crowd erupts in cheers, but Ellie's concern deepens as she watches Jace struggle to rise. Tristan, though victorious, extends a hand to his fallen opponent. Jace, bruised and exhausted, accepts the gesture with apparent disdain all over his face.

As they exit the ring, Ellie's eyes meet Tristan's, who pins her to her seat. He only smirks at her, then grabs his weapons and tunic and strides back towards them. He stands once again next to Breccan, who stares at him with wide eyes, clearly as shocked as she is.

Her eyes meet Jace who is clearly struggling to walk. She jumps up from her chair, uncaring who sees her as she pushes through the crowd towards Jace. When she is only a couple of yards away, she can see the pain in Jace's expression as he wipes his face with a towel.

A female pushes through the crowd and falls to her knees next to Jace lovingly wrapping her arms around him. Ellie freezes in place, observing the beautiful, young fae female with flowing, rich brown hair that cascades down her back in soft waves. Her eyes are a deep, enchanting shade of green, overflowing with concern for Jace. The two speak in hushed tones but she reluctantly releases him. He smiles at her in return, the kind of smile Ellie knows all too well.

"Please tell me you're alright!" the female begs.

"Of course, I'll be alright, I'm just a little battered and I have a few bruises," Jace says to her with a smile that makes Ellie feel like she is the one who got punched in the gut.

The realization dawns on Ellie as she watches Jace take the female's hand in his and bring it to his lips, kissing it softly. Ellie feels as though the ground below her would swallow her whole. Her limbs begin to tremble, and she could feel tears pricking behind her eyes, desperate to be released.

As if sensing her nearness, Jace looks up, his eyes widening in shock, his smile falters, and then a look of guilt washes over his face.

"Ellie," his voice is thick with desperation, "Please, let me explain. It's not what it looks like."

Ellie holds up a hand, her body quaking as the anger from the burning betrayal begins to fill her veins. She forces herself to stay calm and not let the tears fall in front of him. Her throat feels tight, she knows if she speaks right now, she will break. Instead, she says nothing, her silence more powerful than any words.

"Your Highness, are you alright? If you'll forgive my forwardness, you look as though you may vomit." The female says, her eyes wide with concern. Confusion begins to slide across her face, probably wondering why the princess is in front of them.

Jace takes a step toward her, but a shadow moves between them before he can reach her. Tristan, tall and imposing, blocks Jace from Ellie. She steps to the side, watching him, his eyes are cold and hard as they remain locked on Jace.

"Stay away from her," Tristan's voice is unusually low and menacing. "If you so much as lay a finger on her, I assure you it will be the last thing that you will ever do."

Jace's face pales as he steps back, his gaze darting between Ellie and Tristan. Standing a bit taller than before, Jace says, "That isn't your choice, *soldier*," the last word comes out as a sneer as he steps closer to Tristan in clear defiance.

The fae female takes a step closer to Jace, her hand landing upon his arm, "Jace, what is going on?"

Jace and Tristan completely ignore her, acting as though she is not even there. They continue to glare daggers at each other. The female backs from between the males, clear discomfort written across her features.

"I dare you to challenge me, you little bladesmith peasant," Tristan says quietly, his voice a feral growl now, "you won't live long enough to regret it." He doesn't look at Ellie, his focus is entirely on Jace. Ellie can feel the protective energy radiating from him in invisible waves. His anger and magic pulsing wildly in the air around her.

Jace hesitates only for a moment, then nods reluctantly as his eyes sweep back to meet hers. "I'm so sorry, Ellie," he whispers, his voice breaking.

Jace returns his glances back to Tristan one last time before hesitantly turning and walking away, the fae female following him, casting one last curious look back at Ellie.

Ellie watches them go, her heart aching in her chest. She realizes she's barely breathing. Then she feels Tristan's hand as he places a gentle, reassuring pressure on her shoulder.

"Ellie," Tristan looks at her. "Are you alright?"

She shakes her head and swallows hard. "No," she chokes out, her heart feels like it's breaking all over again.

Ellie turns suddenly to Tristan, her voice rising in anger. "You shouldn't have done that! You should've stayed out of it!"

Tristan's anger flares, and his eyes glow fiercely. "I was trying to protect you!" he shouts, his outburst startling Ellie. She takes a step back, shocked by the intensity in his voice, his eyes glow crimson red with anger.

"Your duty, *Captain*, is to protect my *life*, *not* interfere in my private affairs!" Ellie sneers. She almost flinches as soon as the words leave her mouth, realizing they were harsher than she intended. Even though deep down she knows it isn't his fault, she can't hold back the anger raging inside of her, as it finally boils over.

"My apologies, *Your Highness*, I can assure you it'll *never* happen again" Tristan replies, his voice stone cold and controlled. His face hardens into an expression of neutrality, like forged steel.

Ellie turns around, feeling the urge to run from him. She wants to get as far away from everyone as she can. As soon as she turns to leave, Kyla, Stella, and Breccan stand there, mouths agape, clearly shocked at their hostile exchange.

Stella gives her a sad, worried expression as her eyes begin to glow a light blue shade, most likely sensing all of her pain. Stella quickly runs up to Ellie, wrapping her in a hug as Ellie begins to quiver, a few tears spill down her face.

As she looks past Kyla with tears in her eyes, She notices that Kyla is watching Tristan, jaw tense, clearly upset with their exchange. She shakes her head at him in warning. However, as soon as Kyla's gaze meets hers, her eyes soften and she strides over to them, wrapping her arms around them.

After a few moments, Stella lifts Ellie's chin and gazes into her eyes. "Let's get you back to the castle." Kyla and Stella wrap their arms around each side of her as they guide her out of the town square and back to the castle gates leaving Tristan and Breccan to trail behind.

When they return to the castle gardens, Ellie stops and looks at Stella and Kyla before saying, "Thank you, both of you. I'd really like to be alone right now though." Kyla nods at her in understanding. She brings her hand up to wipe the remaining tears from her tear-streaked face and tucks her blonde waves behind her ears. "If you need anything at all, you let us know. We'll be here for you, always," Kyla gives her a small smile.

When Ellie peers at Stella, she gives her a small smile and whispers, "Until death," making Ellie's lip quirk up.

"Until death," Ellie and Kyla say in unison, pulling a reluctant chuckle from them all.

As her friends leave the castle gardens, Ellie stands alone with Breccan and Tristan behind her; she closes her eyes, taking a deep breath, not allowing herself to break down again in front of them.

"Is there anything we can get you, Your Highness?" Breccan questions, words barely above a whisper, kind and sincere.

Ellie turns and gives him a small smile, shaking her head. She appreciates Breccan's silence and the tenderness in his voice as he spoke to her. However, she refuses to meet Tristan's gaze. Though there was no need to look because she could feel his eyes watching her closely.

"I'm going to go to bed. Thank you though. You can leave now," Ellie whispers, eyes unwavering from Breccan's.

Breccan bows and gives her a small smile, then nudges Tristan with his elbow. They both turn and walk away, leaving Ellie alone in the quiet, moonlit gardens.

Ellie hesitantly walks into the castle doors but decides to take a last second detour instead of heading straight to her bedroom.

Ellie descends the narrow stone steps that lead to the castle's wine cellar, her footsteps echoing softly in the dimly lit corridor. The air grows cooler as she goes deeper, the scent of aged oak barrels and the rich aroma of fermenting grapes fills her senses. The castle's cellar is a vast labyrinthine space, with rows of shelves stacked high. Each containing bottles of every shape and size.

Flickering torch lights cast a warm glow, highlighting the wine bottles' deep reds and shimmering golds. Some are ancient, their labels fading and curling, while others are newer, their glass gleaming in the soft light. She passes by bottles of velvety Merlot, robust Cabernet Sauvignon, crisp Chardonnay, and sweet Riesling. There are also exotic varieties from distant lands, which the Queen loves to have stocked in the castle.

Her eyes settle on a bottle of a deep red Bordeaux, its label marked with an elegant script and an intricate design. She pulls it from the shelf, the cool glass smooth under her silk gloves. Prying off the cork with a practiced hand, she lifts the bottle to her lips and takes a long, slow drink. The wine is rich and full-bodied, with notes of dark berries and a hint of spice. It warms her from the inside out, a comforting contrast to the cellar's chill.

Ellie sits on a red velvet settee in the middle of the cellar, pushing off her shoes while letting the wine's warmth and the cellar's quiet solitude wash over her. The weight of the day begins to lift slightly, the sting of Jace's betrayal and her harsh words to Tristan fading to a dull ache as the wine seeps into her system.

After a while, with the bottle in one hand and her shoes in the other, she makes her way back up the stairs, continuing to take large gulps as she reaches the heavy door creaking. She pushes it open. The castle is quiet, most of its inhabitants already asleep.

She moves silently through the dimly lit halls, her now bare feet whispering against the cold stone floors, as she swings her shoes in her other hand.

When she reaches the hall that leads to her bedchamber, her footsteps halt abruptly, making her sway on her unsteady feet. Blinking against the tears and fog clouding her mind, she sees Tristan through her water filled eyes, standing by her bedchamber with his hands stuffed in his pockets, pacing in front of the door.

Ellie shakes her head, hoping that her wine-induced state is playing tricks on her, quickly wiping away any remnants of tears from her face, the wine sloshing out onto the polished floor. "Shit." She grumbles. Her gaze meets his, realizing he is now looking at her. She gasps, covering her mouth, "shit! Oops, I definitely said that out loud." She giggles.

His mouth sets in a thin line, his eyes squint, clearly noting the wine in one hand and her shoes in the other.

She attempts to continue walking to her room but stumbles along the way. Before she can right herself, Tristan is in front of her. "Are you drunk, Ellie?" Tristan asks, studying her flushed face.

"Go away. I wish to be alone," Ellie whispers softly, trying to push past him, but his muscled frame blocks her path, making her stagger again. "Ugh! You weigh like a million pounds! Move, you beast!" *Stars, he's like a brick wall.*

Without a word, Tristan bends down and sweeps Ellie off her feet, softly cradling her against his chest, making her gasp in surprise. "Put me down," she slurs, making no attempt to escape his firm but gentle hold on her. She wants to fight him, but his warmth relaxes her instantly.

Tristan remains silent, his hold steady as he carries her into her bedchamber. He gently lays her atop her four-poster bed, his touch surprisingly tender. Ellie glares at him, but the wine makes her protests weak.

With a slight smirk and shake of his head, Tristan takes the bottle of wine from her hand and places it on the bedside table. Removing her shoes from her grasp, he sets them neatly on the floor. Ellie watches, confused as to why he's returned after she had dismissed him earlier.

Tristan's gaze softens, a trace of sadness flickering in his eyes then he suddenly flicks his gaze to her lips. His gaze heating. Ellie wonders what his thoughts could be, as he slowly leans forward, now just inches from her face, making her breath catch in her throat.Tristan pulls back the covers. "Get in," he instructs gently with a single nod.

Ellie hesitates, still dazed and dizzy from the wine. He nods towards the blankets again, silently urging her to comply. She hesitantly moves, slipping under the covers. She blushes as he tucks her in with her white duvet comforter, the gesture so gentle it makes her cold demeanor melt away. She nuzzles into her pillow, feeling comforted by the warmth of the heavy blanket.

Tristan's eyes roam over her face as if trying to memorize every line and dimple. "For what it's worth, El, he is an absolute fool. I'll gladly kill him or anyone who makes you cry if that is what you wish," his face stern and deathly serious. She knows she should be mad at him, but right now, she doesn't have the strength to be angry.

Ellie couldn't help the small smile that tugged at her lips. His words warmed her heart and gave her the comfort she so desperately needed. Seeing Tristan's caring, protective side was endearing. Part of her wishes to see more of it. She bites her lip and replies,"I'd rather you not kill anyone for me."

Tristan smirks, glancing briefly at his feet before meeting her eyes again. "I will most certainly kill for you one day. However, him I will spare. If that is your wish."

His words make her smile again, and she chuckles softly, feeling the warmth of the wine pinken her cheeks.

"Why did you come back?" Ellie presses, staring at him.

He hesitates before saying, "I needed to know if you were alright," Tristan admits, crossing his arms over his chest, his muscles going taut.

Ellie notes the way he is speaking to her, honest, yet incredibly gentle with his words.

"I'll be fine," Ellie forces herself to say, slightly slurred and unconfident.

"Get some sleep, Princess," Tristan turns to leave.

Before he gets to the door, Ellie forces herself to speak, "Can you...". Ellie stops herself as he turns around, noticing how his ocean-blue eyes sparkle against the firelight.

Tristan tilts to the side and places his hands in his pockets, "What do you need, El?" His voice is soothing, calm.

Ellie tries to form the words, *What do I need?* she ponders.

Taking a deep breath, she forces herself to admit the one thing she doesn't want to, "I need to not be alone right now".

She watches Tristan's chest rapidly rise and fall, as if his breaths are coming in as quickly as hers. Ellie knows what she is asking for is wrong, knows she should let him leave, but she refuses to consider the consequences.

Without saying a word, Tristan strides over to the table near the burning hearth, pulls out a chair, removes his sword, and silently puts it on the table beside him before sitting in the chair.

Ellie watches him, her gaze taking in his shadowed features against the firelight. His strong jaw and raven black hair is tousled as though he has been running his hands through his hair. When his piercing gaze meets her again, she notices his eyes are soft, and his brows are slightly furrowed.

"I will stay until you fall asleep," he says softly.

Ellie nods slowly before forcing herself to close her eyes. She lies there, wholly dizzy and unable to process what happened tonight. She pulls the soft blanket up to her neck, the evening's events swirling in her mind. The wine eases her shattering heart and calms her into a state of drowsiness. As she drifts off to sleep, she clings to the hope that tomorrow will bring the peace she so desperately needs.

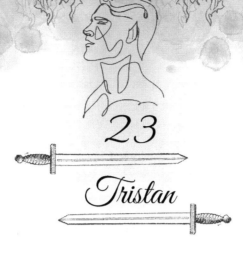

23

Tristan

Shutting Ellie's door behind him, Tristan stands outside of her door, unable to move, finding his hands tightening into fists.

The look in her eyes, as her heart shattered in front of him this evening, felt like daggers to his own heart as he watched her break. If he's being honest with himself, he was seconds away from killing Jace as he begged Ellie to listen to his pitiful lies and desperate pleas. *Over my dead body*, Tristan thought to himself.

Tristan watched Ellie closely throughout the fights, trying to hide his gaze though it kept finding its way back to her. He noticed immediately when her body stiffened, her eyes never leaving the bladesmith as he fought. Tristen's jaw tightened as the realization began to dawn on him. He could see the concern in her eyes for the foolish male who clearly, yet undeservedly, held her heart.

When the moment came, and the announcer asked for an opponent, he was more than happy for the chance to beat the bladesmith to a pulp in that ring. He honestly couldn't remember the last time he had fought someone, and it felt so good. He almost wished he would have beaten him harder after he saw Ellie's face watching Jace with that fae female.

The stupid male should have been counting his lucky stars that someone like Ellie, a *princess*, could care for a male like him. *Stupid, stupid fool, he's not worthy of her*, he chastised.

Tristan had been so close to heading back to his father's estate after Ellie had dismissed them. He had said goodnight to Breccan and had turned to leave, but a nagging feeling stopped him. He felt an intense need to apologize to Ellie. If he was honest with himself, he also wanted to ensure that she was okay. His instincts told him she needed someone, even if she wouldn't admit it.

When he arrived at her bedchamber, he figured she was just refusing to answer her door when he had knocked. That is, until he saw her in the hall with a nearly empty bottle of wine, swaying slightly as she stumbled towards him. The sight tugged at his heart, he simply couldn't leave her like that.

As he cradled her in his arms, he knew that he could claim it was to protect her from falling, but the truth was that the need to hold her close was too strong to deny any longer. Her warmth against his chest and the beat of her heart felt too right, too necessary. Of course she had fought him, but then she had quickly sunk into his body, which pulled a small smirk from him knowing she found a sliver of comfort in his arms.

When Tristan gently laid her on the bed, he watched her with a mixture of longing and sadness. He wanted to do more than tuck her in; he wanted to erase the pain the foolish male had caused, to be the one to tell her that she deserved far, far better.

I would love to show her what she's been missing, show her what being with a true male feels like, he thinks, but immediately dismisses the impulsive thought.

When he took the wine bottle from her hands, Tristan tried to steady his emotions. He looked at her, confused and vulnerable, all he felt was the urge to lean down, brush the hair from her beautiful face, and kiss her. The need was so strong that had he not stepped away when he did, he would have caved.

Instead of fleeing her bedchamber like he knew he should have, her plea for him to stay, crippled him. He didn't want to leave her alone, and she needed him to stay throughout the night and watch over her; so he did.

Hours had passed, and now he stood in the hall outside her door; Tristan ran his hands through his hair, cursing himself for being such a fool this evening. He had intended to keep his distance and guard her from afar, but all his plans had crumbled when she saw Jace. Seeing the hurt in her eyes had shattered his resolve completely.

Watching her sleep throughout the night made him realize that Ellie was more than just his duty; she had become someone that he had to admit to himself he cared for. Someone that he would go to great lengths to keep safe. He wasn't even sure when exactly things had changed for him, but he knew, beyond the shadow of a doubt, that it had. *Stars, what am I going to do now?*

Now, standing just outside her door, he vows to himself that he will do everything in his power to help her find that peace, even if it means putting his feelings aside. For now, knowing she is safe and resting is enough.

Tristan lingers there contemplating if he should head back to his father's estate. The thought of stepping into that house and talking with his father makes his stomach recoil. He decides then that he would much rather stand guard outside her door because the thought of leaving still didn't sit right with him.

Hours later, as the sun slowly peeks over the ocean and through the window in the hall. Servants begin bustling through the castle. Tristan finally decides to leave.

As he walks through the castle corridor, Tristan abruptly comes to a halt when he sees the king, General Alvar, Lord Ravenscroft, and his father standing in the hall, engaging in a conversation. His father's eyes meet his first, a vicious grin spreads across his face making Tristan's insides twist with unease. When the others turn to see who has caught the Lord's eye, Tristan quickly bows to the king. "Good morning, Your Highness, General, My Lords."

General Alvar speaks. "Ah, Captain Mormont, I didn't expect to see you here so early. What brings you to the castle at this hour?" His tone clearly conveys confusion about Tristan's presence.

The king's piercing gaze studies Tristan, echoing the same curiosity; his father glares at him cautiously. "I chose to stand guard over the princess, Your Highness," Tristan responds, noting their surprised expressions.

"Any particular reason why, Captain?" the king finally asks. The question makes Tristan stand a little straighter, feeling the weight of the question.

"I had a bad feeling, Your Highness," Tristan replies with as much confidence as he can muster.

"A bad feeling?" The king takes a step toward Tristan, his powerful presence making Tristan straighten his shoulders and lift his chin, deciding to commit fully to his statement.

"Yes, Your Highness. I trusted my intuition and I didn't wish to risk the princess's safety."

The king narrows his gaze upon him, as if picking him apart or studying him under a lorgnette, but Tristan doesn't waver. "I have heard many wonderful things about you, Captain. I am pleased to see that my daughter's guard is showing such dedication to his duty," the king gives him a slight smile.

"Great choice in guard assignment, Alvar. You seem to have chosen a good one this time," Lord Ravenscroft adds, smirking at the General.

As the king turns back to him, Tristan bows once again, attempting to leave before the king speaks again. "You keep her safe, Captain. Do you understand me?" the king's voice carrying a note of finality.

"I will, Your Highness. I'll protect her with my life," Tristan replies as genuinely as he can. The king seemed to relax slightly at his words.

"Shall we? Our bonded's are waiting," his father interrupts, pulling Tristan's attention back to the group of males.

With one last smile, the king strides out of the hall towards the training courtyard, followed by Alvar, Ravenscroft, and his father. Tristan stands there, taking a deep breath to collect himself, then walks home, hoping for a couple of hours of sleep before the ball tonight, where he will once again guard Ellie.

Tristan's mind replays the encounter as he walks through the castle grounds. The king's words are like an echo in his mind, the intensity of the exchange left a lingering tension. He couldn't shake the image of his father's sinister grin or the weight of the king's expectations.

Arriving at the estate, Tristan sinks onto his bed, exhaustion mingling with the whirlwind of emotions. He knows he needs to rest, but sleep seems distant. The evening's events replaying in his mind.

He found solace in knowing the king had acknowledged his commitment to her safety as he drifted into a restless slumber, thoughts of the ball and his role in protecting Ellie swirling in his mind, a reminder of the responsibilities and challenges ahead.

24

Ellie

Ellie woke with her head pounding from the wine she had ingested the night before as the golden morning sunlight shines in through the double doors of her balcony. She groans, almost wishing she hadn't headed down to the cellar last night and tries to drown her sorrows.

Realization hits her like a brick as the memory of Jace's face when she saw him with the beautiful female. A part of her desperately wanted to hear what he had to say as he begged her to listen to him. However, the way the female had her hands on him, how they spoke to each other, even how he touched her, it was apparent that Ellie wasn't the only female in his life anymore.

She had desperately wanted to flee when she saw them but then she remembered how her feet didn't cooperate. She was so utterly and devastatingly surprised, that her heart had crumbled in her chest and she just stared at them. Ellie had to summon every ounce of strength she had not to cry in front of him.

She knew that they could never truly be together because of her duty but she had always hoped that she had more time with him. Jace had also been her best friend, her first love, and now it seems her first heartbreak. Tears run down her face as memories bombard her.

A part of her is so angry with Jace, but another part can't help but think about what right she has to be mad. They both knew, and had spoken, of what their futures might hold. She had never expected him to lie to her though or withhold something like this from her. The emptiness in Ellie's chest feels like a hole has been carved out of her heart, a feeling she has never known before.

A knock on the door pulls Ellie from her thoughts as Helena strides in with her usual bright smile, "Good morning, Ellie. There was a letter by your door." Helena ceases her words as she sees the tears on her face.

"Are you alright, dear?" Helena's face saddens as she strides to her bedside, sits beside her, and begins rubbing circles over her back.

Ellie tries to form words, but none come out. She only shakes her head as Helena pulls her into a hug, allowing her to safely cry. It could've been minutes or even an hour as she sits there and lets her tears fall freely.

"Whoever did this to you surely does not deserve your tears," Helena says sweetly, trying to console her. "Is there anything I can do for you?"

Ellie shakes her head again, wipes the tears from her eyes, and tries to sniff away her now runny nose.

Helena gives her a slight nod, then places the letter in front of Ellie atop her white duvet. Ellie stares at the letter, believing it's going to catch fire any second, there is no doubt in her mind about who it's from.

"You go freshen up, and I'll make sure Clara has your breakfast ready for you when you come out," placing her hand on her back, she guides her out of bed and toward the bathroom.

"Thank you," Ellie's words are barely above a whisper as she sniffles again.

After brushing her teeth and hair, she puts on her flight trousers and jacket, then stares at her swollen eyes in the mirror. She closes her eyes, wishing the pain in her chest to ease as she walks back into her bedchamber.

"*Saph, I need you*," Ellie reaches out to her through their bond, and within seconds Saphirixia responds.

"*I'm already on my way*."

A sigh of relief escapes Ellie's lips, knowing her bonded will be there soon. She needs to get out of these stone walls and into the sky because if she doesn't, she isn't sure if she would leave her room.

Breakfast was already at her round, small table in front of the now-lit hearth in her chamber. Ellie grabs the letter off her bed and sits at the table, taking one last deep breath, she opens the letter.

"*My Dearest Ellie,*

I'm writing to you with a heavy heart, filled with regret. I feel a desperate need to explain myself. I know that recent events have caused you pain and confusion, and for that, I'm deeply sorry.

Ellie, I want you to know that I still care for you deeply. You have always held a special place in my heart, and it pains me to think that I might have caused you to doubt that. The female you saw with me is not what you think, and I can explain everything if you give me the chance.

Please, Ellie, I'm asking you to speak with me. Let me clarify the misunderstandings and show you that my feelings for you have not wavered. I value what we have more than words can express, and I believe that we can work through this together.

I understand if you need time, but I hope you'll consider meeting with me soon. You mean so much to me, and I don't want to lose you.

With all my heart,

Jace

As Ellie places the letter on the table, her mind races, replaying each word repeatedly. *What could he possibly need to explain*? Ellie wonders; part of her eagerly wants to know, but right now, she can only feel heartache and she doesn't wish to see him.

Ellie quickly eats breakfast, shoving one last piece of egg in her mouth as she hears Saphirixia's wings beating outside her window. She jumps from her chair and pulls open the double doors as Saphirixia lands on the balcony stone railings, her blue scales shining in the morning sunlight.

"*Please tell me you are giving me permission to bite off his limbs?*" Saphirixia demands gruffly.

Ellie can't help but hide the laugh that breaks from her lips. She knows Saphirixia would say precisely what she needed to hear to cheer her up. No one knows her like she does, and being with her right now was all she needs besides being in the sky.

Ellie shakes her head and quickly runs back into her room, grabs her boots, and walks back onto the balcony and then puts them on.

"*Right now, a part of me wants to say yes, but you know I'd never wish him harm even if he did hurt me*," Ellie replies quietly.

"*If you change your mind, just say the word*," Saphirixia says with a puff of smoke spewing from her nostrils, heating the air around them.

"*I know, Saph, thank you, truly. But right now, I just want to get out of here*," Ellie gives her a pleading smile.

Saphirixia wastes no time, crouching low onto the balcony, she gives Ellie room to climb up her leg and onto her back.

"*As you wish*," Saphirixia says, swiftly shooting into the sky.

Saphirixia flies gracefully over Aetherlyn as the town's folk wave at them high in the sky. The streets are full of faes, flowers are strewn about, and merchant tents are still lining the streets. It's sad to think today is the last of the Dracofaerian Revelry. She almost wishes the celebrations were longer, just so she could enjoy the beauty of the town more.

Saphirixia flies past the town and towards the forests outside the kingdom. The rhythmic beating of her wings ruffles the lush green trees below, lulling Ellie into the calm state she desperately needs after reading Jace's letter. The tranquility is short-lived, however, as an arrow shoots past Saphirixia's neck, jolting Ellie from her thoughts. Saphirixia abruptly maneuvers to avoid the projectile.

"What's going on?" Ellie exclaims, hoping it was just an accidental stray arrow.

Moments later, arrows burst from the canopy of trees, barreling straight towards them.

"*Hold on!*" Saphirixia's voice echoes in Ellie's mind as she swiftly dodges the barrage that is now very clearly aimed at them. Ellie clings tightly to Saphirixia's neck, her heart pounding wildly against her chest.

Sharp pain slices through Ellie's shoulder, making her scream in agony. She quickly glances down, to where a large gash cuts through her flight jacket. Blood drips down her arm and onto Saphirixia.

"*How bad is it?*" Saphirixia growls, anger seeping into her voice.

"*It's just my arm!*" Ellie shouts over the wind whipping past them as Saphirixia twists to avoid yet another wave of arrows.

To Ellie's surprise, Saphirixia turns back towards the trees below, to where the arrows are being shot from.

"*Why are we going back?*" Ellie asks, unable to hide the fear in her voice.

Seconds later, Saphirixia roars, sending a torrent of fire down into the forest, setting it ablaze. Ellie can hear screams rising from the inferno below, the arrows finally ceasing. Saphirixia's fiery rage is unrelenting as hundreds of trees are reduced to charred remains.

The blaze wipes out everything in its path, leaving nothing behind. Ellie's heart races, both from the pain in her arm and the shock of the sudden attack. She feels a mix of fear and awe at Saphirixia's intense blast.

As the last of the flames flicker out, Saphirixia finally veers away from the burning forest to head back towards the safety of the castle. Ellie is still clutching her dragon tightly as she tries to steady her breathing. The sudden danger shakes her, but she is grateful for Saphirixia's swift and fierce protection.

"*We're safe now*," Saphirixia assures her, the anger in her voice replaced by concern. "*Let's get you back to the castle and have that wound treated.*"

Ellie nods, still feeling the adrenaline coursing through her veins. She looks back at the scorched forest, a stark reminder of the threats that lurk even in the calmest moments. As they fly back toward the kingdom, Ellie can't help but wonder who would attack them and why. The beautiful day has turned into a harrowing ordeal, and the unanswered questions weigh heavily on her mind.

Within minutes, they land in the training courtyard as soldiers spring into action at the sight of Ellie's bleeding. The pain in her arm suddenly intensifies. Ellie slides off Saphirixia as quickly as she can. Her feet barely touch the ground before her knees buckle, sending her crumpling to the ground. Ellie grips her shoulder tightly and grinds her teeth to hold back a scream from the pulsing pain in her.

Soldiers rush to her side, checking her injuries and trying to help her up. Their voices blur into a cacophony as Ellie feels herself on the brink of passing out. The world around her spins, and her vision began to fade.

Through the haze of pain and confusion, a single voice pierced through the others. "I've got you, El," Tristan's tone is steady and reassuring. He scoops her into his arms, his eyes locking onto her wounded arm with a fierce, determined look.

Without hesitation, Tristan takes off running towards the medical wing of the castle, his grip on Ellie is firm yet gentle. She tries to hold on, focusing on the rhythmic pounding of his footsteps and the steady rise and fall of his chest.

"Stay with me, Princess," Tristan urges, his voice filled with a mixture of command and concern.

Ellie clings to the sound of his voice, fighting the darkness that threatens to consume her. She could feel his heartbeat through his chest, a comforting reminder that she wasn't alone. But despite her efforts, the pain was too much, and she could feel herself slipping further into unconsciousness.

Tristan's grip tightens as he sprints through the castle halls, his breaths coming in determined gasps. He barks orders to the soldiers they pass, ensuring the path to the medical wing is clear. The castle's torches cast flickering shadows on the stone walls, illuminating the urgency of their race against time.

The medical wing doors burst open as Tristan barrels through, shouting for the healer. Tristan gently lays her on a cot, his eyes never leaving her face.

"Stay with me, El. Please, just hold on," he repeats, his voice softer now but no less insistent.

As the healer works, Tristan stays by her side, his presence a steadfast anchor in the storm of her pain. Ellie's vision dims, but she holds onto the warmth of his hand in hers as she slips into darkness.

25

Ellie

Ellie's eyes snap open, and she finds herself standing in the heart of a dark, unfamiliar forest. The air clings to her skin, thick with moisture and the heavy scent of wet earth. Every breath feels dense, as if the very atmosphere is pressing in on her. A deep, unsettling silence blankets the forest, broken only by the faint rustling of leaves and the distant, constant rush of water. Above her, the canopy is so thick that it chokes out most of the light, casting the world below in oppressive shadows. The gnarled branches above her twist together like skeletal fingers, further blocking out the sky and making it impossible to tell the time of day.

She turns slowly, her heart pounding. She spots a decrepit cottage on the edge of a fast-moving river. Its crumbling stone walls are covered in thick moss and ivy. Smoke curls lazily from a crooked chimney, the smell of burning wood mingling with something sharper, more acrid. The faint flicker of candlelight from the small, grimy windows offers little comfort. The faint light from the candles flickers erratically, barely keeping the darkness at bay.

A deep sense of foreboding washes over Ellie, a feeling so strong, it seems as though the air itself is holding its breath, waiting for her to approach. The shadows around the cottage seem to shift and writhe as if alive, and despite the stillness, she can't shake the feeling that she's being watched.

"Where am I?" she whispers to herself, confusion and fear mingling in her voice.

"You are not supposed to be here yet," a cold female voice says behind her, making her yelp in surprise. Ellie whips around, her heart pounding wildly in her chest. Standing before her was a tall, slender female in a regal purple gown. Her long dark black hair frames a face of porcelain-white skin and piercing dark obsidian eyes that seem to peer into her soul.

Startled, Ellie takes a step back, nearly tripping over her own feet, knowing instantly who she is. The female's presence exuded an aura of power and dark menace.

"It's you...," Ellie stammers, her voice trembling.

The Enchantress responds with a vicious smirk, her lips curling in a way that sends chills down Ellie's spine.

"It is not your time, my dear," the Enchantress's voice is dripping with cold annoyance. She lifts her hand and reaches for Ellie, her fingers wrapping around the sapphire stone necklace around her neck. Ellie's body freezes in place, her wide eyes locking onto the Enchantress's malevolent gaze.

The Enchantress begins whispering soft, arcane words that Ellie doesn't understand. The incantation seems to reverberate through the air, and Ellie feels a powerful force tugging at her consciousness. The edges of her vision darken as a profound sense of helplessness overwhelms her.

Ellie tries to fight against the encroaching darkness, but it is far too strong. Her thoughts begin to blur, and the last thing she sees is the Enchantress's cold, triumphant smile. The world around her fading to black, utterly lost in the depths of the Enchantress's spell.

When she opens her eyes again, she is looking up at the ceiling of her bedchamber. She quickly tries to sit up, but a forceful hand lands on her shoulder and lays her back onto her bed. When she turns, she sees a healer, garbed in a white robe, "You need to rest, Your Highness. The arrow you took was laced with poison."

Ellie can only squint due to the bright light coming in through her window, but then she sees her parents at the end of her bed. They are holding each other as they watch her, concern written on their faces.

"You are going to be alright, El. You were most fortunate," King Evandor says softly. Her mother only nods at her as she brushes a tear from her face.

"Thank the stars, you're alright," Queen Adelina releases her husband and walks to Ellie's side, grabbing her ungloved hand and bringing it to her lips, placing a soft kiss atop it.

Scanning the room, she also sees General Alvar standing behind her father. Tristan is standing beside him, watching her intently. Ellie bites her lip when her gaze meets Tristan's, concern and relief shining brightly in his eyes.

General Alvar's voice breaks through the silence, ripping her gaze from Tristan's, "I have already had Morphandor speak with Saphirixia so she could inform us of what happened, and if you are up for it, I would like to find out from your perspective, what happened and what you saw."

Ellie knows the general to be a stern and authoritative male, unwaveringly loyal to her family, but she can see the concern in his eyes. She glances back at Tristan briefly as he gives her a nod of encouragement, realizing then how badly she needs that simple, yet, comforting gesture.

Queen Adelina squeezes her hand again, giving her the same kind of comfort and reassurance. “Unfortunately, I probably don’t have any more information than what Saph gave you. I didn't see any faces through the trees. One moment we were flying, and the next arrows were being shot toward us.” Ellie takes a deep breath before continuing. “After Saph scorched them, I saw nothing else before she flew us back here.”

The king and queen glance at each other, giving one another a weary look. Ellie couldn't help but ask, “Who tried to kill us?”

The king clears his throat and declares, “As of this moment, we do not know, but I assure you, we will discover who attempted this treachery,” his last words infused with a fierce resolve for vengeance. Turning to face Alvar and Tristan, he continues, “Thank you, Captain, for getting her to the healer so swiftly. Your quick thinking likely saved our daughter’s life.”

Tristan straightens up, bowing his head respectfully. “If I may, your highness, I would like to assist in finding the traitors who dared to harm Princess Ellie.” Tristan’s voice is brimming with promise of retribution. Ellie bites her lip as she studies him.

“Hmm...” the king muses, glancing back at Ellie with a small, affectionate smile. Then, he turns back to address Tristan and Alvar again, he commands, “General, I would like Mormont to be Ellie’s permanent guard until further notice.” The general’s eyes widen in surprise but he swiftly nods in agreement. “I will grant your request, Mormont. However, I would much prefer you to protect my daughter and ensure nothing like this *ever* happens again.”

Tristan’s eyes widen in shock at the king's command. “Do not be so surprised, Captain. You have protected her well, and I am confident that you will not let us down."

Ellie's heart races as she absorbs her father's words. Tristan clears his throat before finally speaking again, "It's an honor, Your Highness. I will not let you down."

"Good. Will you two please give us the room? I would like to speak with my daughter," the king says. Alvar and Tristan bow low, and then quickly exit her chambers, closing the door behind them.

King Evandor closes his eyes momentarily, releasing a long sigh as he runs his hands through his white, blonde hair. His tall, broad frame taut with tension. He moves to the queen's side, placing a comforting hand on her shoulder. Queen Adelina looks up at him, offering a weary smile as she gently strokes Ellie's hand.

"My dear, after today's events, I think it is best to prepare you to leave with some soldiers to seek out the enchantress in the next few days. It cannot be a mere coincidence that someone has tried to harm us since your name day," Queen Adelina says.

"There is something I need to tell you both," Ellie admits cautiously, knowing that revealing her encounters with the enchantress would undoubtedly increase their worry. She took a deep breath as her parents looked at her with concern etched on their loving faces.

"When I was at the beach a couple of days ago with Saphirixia, I used the necklace and spoke with the enchantress. And when I must have passed out due to the poison, I think she helped save me," Ellie watches her parents' faces turn to shock as her father begins pacing the room.

"What did she say?" the king asks harshly.

"She confirmed that I'm who she was waiting for, 'the prophesized.' When I was sleeping and I felt like I was going to die, she said that it wasn't my time yet and that I wasn't supposed to be there. Then somehow she sent me back here," Ellie explains, biting her bottom lip as she waits for her parents to respond. They remain silent for long minutes, processing all she's told them.

"It would see that someone else, besides the General, knows our secret. I will speak with Alvar immediately and have him prepare his best soldiers to escort you to find the enchantress. If we wait too long, someone might try to kill you to prevent you from restoring fae magic. I will not risk your safety any longer," her father says.

"When will I leave?" Ellie questions nervously.

"In the coming days, we should not delay. Until then, I will have Mormont and other guards protect you," he adds.

Ellie feels torn between the fear threatening to consume her and the duty to liberate and protect her people. She had thought she had more time, but now it seems she only had mere days. The thought of having soldiers escort her in her search for the enchantress makes her insides recoil. She knows the journey will be challenging and uncertain.

"Why don't you rest for a while? We will send Clara up soon to help you dress for the ball. Though I should ask, are you feeling up for it? If not, you may rest as much as you need," her mother says sweetly.

Ellie knows she doesn't have to attend the ball but she wants to. If she is truly leaving soon, she wishes to say goodbye and have a chance to speak to Jace. Despite his betrayal, which feels like a knife to her heart, she has things to say to him in case she never gets another chance.

"I'm feeling much better. I'll make an appearance this evening," Ellie smiles at both her parents.

"We'll let you rest then, my dear," her mother says, standing up and kissing her forehead before striding out of the room with her father, who gives her one last smile before closing the door behind him.

Ellie lays in her bed, staring out the window, formulating a plan. She wants to avoid being accompanied by soldiers. She knows her parents will never allow her to leave alone, so she decides she will have to sneak out in the middle of the night. The thought made her heart ache, but it is her only choice. She and Saphirixia are the prophesized ones, and this is their burden to bear alone.

Ellie knows her parents will be furious once they discover she has left without notice, but she will leave a letter for them. However, she feels the need to confide in her friends; she didn't want to leave without telling them. So, Ellie immediately decides to tell them her secret and say goodbye.

As she gets out of bed and walks to the bathroom to wash up, she feels lightheaded but pushes through the dizziness. She shakes off the drowsiness, quickly climbing into the large round bathtub and sighing as the heat soothes her aching muscles. Removing the bandages from her arm, she grimaces at the large gash. Thanks to the healer's gifts, it had already begun to close. The pain was minimal but still a tender ache.

Once dressed in her midnight blue robe, she returns to her bedroom just as Clara places a tray with steaming hot tea on her table.

"Just what I needed. Thank you, Clara," Ellie grabs the tea mug and gives her a gracious smile before heading towards her vanity in the corner.

"You're most welcome. I'm just grateful you're all right, Your Highness. You really scared us," Clara admits as she gently brushes Ellie's long blonde hair.

"I'll be alright, Clara. I promise," Ellie looks at Clara through the vanity mirror, offering a genuine smile.

"Good, because this kingdom desperately needs you. More needed than you know," Clara halts, her eyes filling with unshed tears.

Ellie turns around and pulls Clara into a hug. "I'm not going anywhere." As soon as the words leave her mouth, she immediately regrets them.

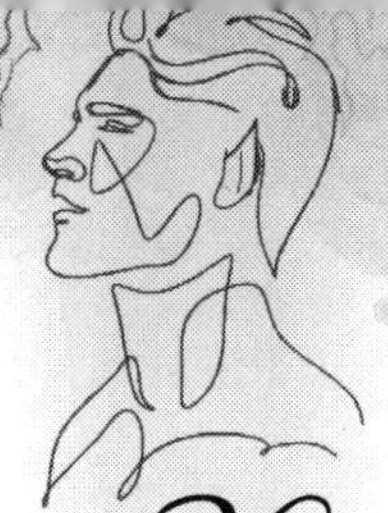

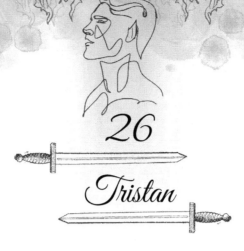

26

Tristan

Tristan paces his room at his father's estate, his mind reeling from the events that had transpired with Ellie. She had come perilously close to death, too close. She doesn't deserve such a fate, and deep down, he knows there is only one person who would dare to harm her: his father.

Running his hands through his raven-black hair, Tristan pulls at the ends, feeling the urge to scream and viciously tear something apart. The attempt to control his anger felt like an impossible task, his magic tingling at the ends of his fingertips, begging to be released.

Ellie had already passed out from her injuries, and though the healer had glanced at him as he held her hand, he couldn't care less who saw because he refused to leave her. However, when the king and queen entered, he quickly released her hand as though it had burned him and stepped away. The second his hand left hers, it felt like his skin was being flayed off; a stinging pain from the loss of her warmth seared through him.

While Ellie was asleep, she murmured a word that sent a chill up Tristan's spine, "enchantress." His breath caught in his throat, and he had clung to her hand even tighter when her sapphire stone necklace began to glow brightly around her neck. Tristan turned immediately, noting that the healer was too busy to notice. When he looked back, the stone's light had already dimmed.

Why would she say that name? Tristan wondered as he recalled the past few days' events, the mission to retrieve the tome's, the king's order to protect her with his life. And not to mention, the secret that he could sense she was keeping. The weight on her shoulders was evident, and now with the attempt on her life, it was even more apparent. Each piece slowly fell into place in his mind, leading him to one logical conclusion: Ellie and Saphirixia must be the prophesized. *Could it be true*? He asks himself.

Tristan stops pacing and reaches out to his bonded, seeking answers he had a gut feeling he knew. "*What do you know, Terbius? You warned me to stay away from her. Is this why*?" he demands gruffly.

A moment later, he feels his bonded's hesitant response, "*I warned you to stay out of this.*"

"*So, it's true then? This is the dragon business you referred to? The dragon's know that she and Saphirixia are the prophesized?*" Tristan urges, feeling a wave of betrayal wash over him.

Terbius grumbles, Tristan could feel his frustration in his bones. "*It's true. We're all sworn to keep this secret, and so must you. This isn't supposed to be your burden to bear,*" Terbius says hesitantly, his usual gruff demeanor replaced with concern and protectiveness.

Tristan stands frozen in shock. Ellie, his Ellie, would be the one to restore fae magic. *Not my Ellie*, he realizes as he shakes off the thought. It is his duty to protect her. His eyes flare with anger as he clenches his fists, using all his strength to keep from destroying everything around him.

The sound of the front door slamming shut yanks Tristan from his thoughts and he quickly puts on a clean uniform. He descends the staircase two steps at a time, heading straight for his father's study. Without knocking, he swings open the double doors to find his father behind his desk, a devious grin spreading across his face, a grin that sends a chill up Tristan's spine.

Tristan refuses to let his father intimidate him. The look on Lord

Mormont's face enrages him even more. "It was you, wasn't it?" Tristan growls as he stomps into the room, rage radiating off him in waves.

His father looks at him and smirks. He opens his desk drawer, retrieves a cigar, and lights it without a word. "I made sure you were not with her when it happened. You *should* be thanking me," his father said with a sneer, puffing his cigar.

"You tried to have the princess killed, and for what?" Tristan yells, but he knows the answer as soon as the words leave his mouth. His father knows who Ellie is.

"I have my reasons, and they are none of your concern!" His father shouts back, venom in his words.

Tristan suddenly realizes that he should pretend to be ignorant about Ellie's identity. Let his father think of him as a fool who knows nothing when, in reality, he now knows everything.

He steps back, shaking his head in disgust at his father's actions. His father's desperate need for power is undoubtedly the reason for his actions. If Ellie breaks the curse and restores fae magic, all fae would gain abilities, and his father would no longer be superior. Who knows what kinds of magic have been suppressed over the decades? Magic that can be wielded once Ellie breaks the curse. *If she breaks the curse*, he thinks.

Lord Mormont's voice pulls him from his enraged thoughts. "You'll be assigned a mission soon. I suggest that next time, you stay out of my way. Do you understand me?"

"So, there will be a next time?" Tristan retorts.

"Do your duty and guard her if you wish, but If I were you, I would stay out of the way because if you do not, I'll make sure *you* are the one who kills her," Lord Mormont threatens. Tristan freezes, knowing his father could easily manipulate his mind into killing Ellie if he wishes.

Grinding his teeth, Tristan bites back every retort that he wants to hurl at his father. He does the only thing he can: turn around and walk away.

He storms from the estate and makes his way down the street through the crowd of faefolk celebrating the last night of the Dracofaerian Revelry, his anger sears through him, burning him from the inside out. He takes a deep breath, trying to calm himself before he returns to Ellie, where he will guard her tonight at the ball.

Once he makes it through the castle gates and walks briskly through the halls near her corridor, he stops by a window, peering out at the ocean beyond as the sun begins descending. He knows he must find a way to protect Ellie and find out more about the mission his father had mentioned.

When he gets to Ellie's bedchamber door, he knocks softly, the sound of light feet pattering behind the door, and then the door swings open, revealing Ellie.

Her blonde hair is intricately curled and pinned into an elegant updo, with a few delicate tendrils framing her face, highlighting her ethereal beauty. Her breathtaking crimson gown hugs her curves and flows effortlessly to the floor.

Tristan studies every inch of her as she stands there, giving him a small smile in return. He feels his heart begin to race and all the anger from earlier completely dissipate, almost as though his anger were never there.

She's stunning; no, she's more than stunning; she's... captivating. He loves seeing her in blue, but now, seeing her draped in his color, he couldn't help thinking, *she could bring any male to their knees.*

"What? Is the dress that bad?" Ellie asks shyly, looking down at her gown and then nervously back at him.

Tristan clears his throat and shakes his head, not realizing how long he must have been staring at her.

"No, Princess, you're... exquisite," Tristan admits honestly, coughing lightly into his fist.

Ellie nods slowly as she glances down at the ground as a slight blush flushes her cheeks.

"Come in; I need to grab a couple of things, and then I'll be ready," Ellie says and then abruptly turns around, hurrying back into her room.

Tristan walks in and shuts the door behind him, taking the opportunity to absorb the details of her room. The space is charming and intimate, even though the fire in her hearth has dwindled to mere embers, leaving a chill in the air.

He watches Ellie retrieve her gloves from the table near the hearth. With a subtle gesture, he clenches his fist, reigniting the fire and casting a warm glow throughout the room. Ellie turns sharply at him, clearly startled by the blaze.

Tristan shrugs casually. "It's cold in here," he explains.

Ellie quirks her brow and smirks, slipping her other glove onto her hand. "Just warn me next time," she teases.

Tristan nods, then blurts out a question before he can stop himself. "Do you like wearing your gloves?"

Ellie glances up at him as she sits down to put on her red heels for the evening. She sighs softly, "The gloves reassure everyone that I won't pry into their thoughts. But no, I don't enjoy wearing them."

Tristan gives her a solemn nod as she stands and approaches him. He could only imagine the burden of having such a gift and not being able to use it freely. "Are you feeling better? Well enough to attend the ball?" he implores, still concerned for her well-being after the day's events.

"Honestly, I'm just tired. I promised my mother I would make an appearance, so don't worry, you won't have to guard me for long tonight," Ellie replies shyly.

Her words unsettle him. *Does she think I don't want to protect her*? He thought, knowing he needed to correct that misunderstanding immediately.

"It's my honor to guard you. I promise to protect you from harm, not because you are the princess but because you are *you*. If I've ever made you feel otherwise, I'm terribly sorry," he said earnestly.

Ellie stares at him, taking an unsteady breath. The tension between them is palpable. Without thinking, Tristan lifts his hand and gently tucks a strand of hair behind her pointed ear, revealing her stunning blue eyes. His gaze falls to her matching crimson-red stain lips, lips that are begging to be kissed.

They continue to gaze at each other, the moment's intimacy overwhelming him as her lavender and vanilla scent envelopes his senses.

Ellie is the first to break the spell, looking away with a sheepish smile. She walks past him towards the door, her crimson gown flowing elegantly behind her. Tristan can't help but admire how the fabric accentuated her graceful movements and the delicate curve of her open back, showcasing her flawless skin. The back of the dress is adorned with intricate lace detailing that adds an air of sophistication and allure.

She turns, catching his appreciative gaze, and with a radiant smile that nearly takes his breath away, she asks hesitantly, "Shall we?"

27

Ellie

The great hall for the Dracofaerian Revelry was transformed into a spectacle of enchanting beauty and grandeur. Crimson red drapes cascade along the stone walls, their rich fabric catching the flicker of torchlight that bathes the hall in a warm, golden glow. Suspended chandeliers adorned with crystals that shimmer like dragon scales cast a kaleidoscope of colors across the room.

The air is filled with the heady scent of exotic flowers that are meticulously arranged into breathtaking displays, no doubt the queen's doing. Blooms of every hue, some glowing faintly in the dim light, contribute to the hall's ethereal atmosphere. The floral arrangements, often intertwined with delicate vines, create an otherworldly canopy above the revelers.

Music, both haunting and joyous, drifts through the air, the small orchestra playing beautifully. The melodies weave a spell of their own, compelling guests to dance in graceful, mesmerizing patterns. The rhythm of the dance was a harmonious blend of power and elegance.

Laughter and the clinking of crystal goblets add to the symphony of sounds. Ellie walks through the crowd of guests throughout the hall looking for her parents or friends. She is captivated by the celebration of the unbreakable bond between dragons and fae in a dazzling display of light, color, and sound.

This has always been her favorite celebration because it recognizes her bond with Saphirixia. However, the more she observes the guests and the immense grandeur, the more she feels sadness sweeping over her, knowing that there is a chance this will be her last.

Looking over her shoulder, she sees Tristan a few footsteps behind her, giving her a silent nod as if to let her know she isn't alone.

"Ellie, my dear, there you are," Ellie turns to see her parents walking up to her, both looking quite regal. They wear matching crimson and gold crowns that sparkle elegantly in the torchlight from the chandeliers. The smile on their faces makes Ellie's heart clench tighter. She will truly miss them but can't risk telling them her plan.

Ellie can feel the tears sting behind her eyes as she takes a deep breath to calm her emotions, "You both look beautiful tonight." The king and queen notice her emotion and give her a concerned look, her father speaks this time.

"Are you all right, Ellie? Are you still not feeling well?" His face reflective of a father's love and concern.

"No, no, I feel much better. I'm simply just happy," Ellie realizes she truly is happy. Her heart feels on the verge of bursting from it shattering to pieces over Jace, the fear she still feels over seeing the enchantress, the terror she felt with Saphirixia earlier today, and the fact that they could have been killed. Ellie wants to be as happy as possible so she can make the most of the night that she has left.

Her parents glance at each other for a moment as though speaking to each other without words. When her father turns back to her, he releases the queen's hand and reaches for her, "May I have this dance?"

Ellie wants to laugh at her father as a bright smile lights up her face. She has loved dancing with him since she was little. He taught her how to dance as she stood on the tops of his feet.

Those memories were some of her favorite memories when she was youngling.

"I would be honored, *Your Highness*," Ellie replies, making them both burst out in a fit of laughter. The king takes her gloved hand in his and leads her onto the dance floor as their guests graciously make space for them. Once the tempo picks up, her father spins her around, dipping and twirling her around the dance floor as Ellie's smile only widens.

As the music slows and softer music begins to play from the orchestra, her father leans in and whispers in her ear. "I know you have an immense burden on your shoulders; just know that we love you and are so incredibly proud of you." When his gaze meets hers, she feels the tears prickling at her again, so she pulls him in for a hug and holds him tightly.

When the music stops, they release one another as she bows to her father. The king grabs her hand and leads her back toward her mother, who is standing on the side, lovingly watching every moment of their dancing with Tristan just a couple of feet behind, watching her.

"That was beautiful," the queen's voice is brimming with emotion and adoration.

"Let's allow Ellie some time with her friend while we go grab a drink, my love," the king nods towards Kyla and Stella who are walking through the crowd towards them, pulling Ellie's gaze towards them. They both give her a bright smile, bringing up their flutes. Ellie smiles at her parents one last time before her father directs her mother away to mingle with more guests.

Ellie takes one last moment to watch them walk away, whispering to each other with their arms wrapped around each other, smiling. She had always hoped for a love like theirs, a deep and unwavering love that stood the tests of time.

Tristan pulls her thoughts away as he says, "I will give you some time with your friends. I will be over there with Breccan." Ellie turns to see Breccan near the food tables, loading up a plate full of treats. He waves and gives her a silly grin that makes her smile.

Ellie only nods at Tristan, looking at him briefly before turning and walking towards Kyla and Stella. As soon as Ellie reaches them, they both pull her into a tight hug. "Thank the stars, you're all right! I cannot believe someone tried to kill you and Saphirixia!" Stella exclaims.

Kyla quickly speaks next, her soldier's voice taking front and center. "Do they know who the attackers were?" She gives an inquisitive look.

"No, General Alvar said he is still looking into it," Ellie replies quietly, hoping none of the guests are listening. "Actually, I could use some air and I would like to speak to you both in private. Can we go outside?"

Kyla and Stella exchange curious glances and nod in unison. Kyla leads the way out towards the veranda overlooking the castle gardens. Once outside, they scanned the area for lingering guests, but no one was in sight.

"What's going on, El? Are you finally going to tell us the secret you have been keeping?" Stella pressures.

"How did you know I have a secret?" Ellie challenges, seeing Stella's eyes begin to glow, providing a clear answer.

"Right... that," Ellie sighs, taking a deep breath to muster her courage. She had to tell them the truth; she didn't want them to find out from someone else and misunderstand. And if something happens on her journey, she wants the chance to say goodbye.

"I found out on my name day that Saphirixia and I were born on the same day... and at the same time," Ellie says softly, preparing for her following words.

"Wait. I thought Saphirixia's name day is the day after yours?" Kyla asks, confused.

"That is what we were always told. But I accidentally read my mother's mind at my name day celebration and discovered the truth. We were born at the exact same time," Ellie whispers.

"Hold on. Exactly the same time? Like the prophecy foretold?" Stella's eyebrows lift in surprise.

"I know this sounds crazy," Ellie glances at each of them. "But I have spoken to the enchantress twice now."

Kyla and Stella gasp and shake their heads, clearly struggling to believe her. Ellie waits to see if they will say anything, but they stand there, seemingly in shock.

"I'm sorry I had to keep this secret, but only the king, queen, and the general know. After what happened to me today, I wanted to tell you both everything," Ellie says cautiously.

"El, we're glad you are telling us. We're your friends, you can tell us anything. We're here for you," Stella steps forward and grabs her hand, nodding encouragement.

Kyla steps closer, grabbing her other hand with a reassuring smile, "We want to know everything. However, let's maybe go somewhere more private." Kyla takes another look around, ensuring they were alone. They agree and descend the veranda staircase into the gardens.

Ellie tells them everything, revealing her mother's secret, what she discovered about the necklace, her conversations with the enchantress, the discoveries in the tomes, and her plan to leave. Kyla and Stella listen intently, only giving small nods of encouragement.

"Wow. You have been keeping a big secret," Kyla shakes her head in disbelief. "This is incredible. You and Saph will be the ones to restore fae magic. You are the one we have been waiting for." Ellie swallows deeply, feeling the weight of Kyla's words.

"But how are you supposed to break the curse?" Stella questions curiously.

"I don't know. I assume I will find out when I find the enchantress," Ellie admits hesitantly. She wishes she knew more but hopes to learn once she finds the enchantress.

"If you go alone, Ellie, it will be extremely dangerous. You do not know where she is; any journey outside our kingdom could be treacherous. You cannot go alone," Kyla says.

"I will not risk anyone's life. This is our burden, our fate. My father wishes to send guards with us but I plan to leave before then," Ellie lifts her chin, showing her resolve.

"That is truly honorable, but bleeding stars, Ellie, there is no way I'm letting you go alone," Kyla urges.

"You have too. I'm leaving tomorrow night. I only wanted to tell you everything and say goodbye. I didn't want you both to worry," Ellie's voice shakes.

"I'm coming with you, El," Kyla says firmly.

"If you are both going, then I'm coming too," Stella smirks.

"Absolutely not," Ellie shakes her head defiantly.

Kyla and Stella laugh, saying in unison, "Yes, we are."

"And we're coming too," Tristan's voice booms from the darkness. They turn to see Tristan and Breccan emerging from the shadow, Ellie's brows rising in surprise.

"You two are not coming!" Ellie yells, glaring at them.

Tristan steps closer, his broad frame and ocean-blue eyes staring her down. "If we don't go with you, I'll gladly inform the king of your plan."

Ellie flinches, knowing she is cornered. Tristan continues, "I swore to protect you, so we," she gestures between himself and Breccan, "Are going."

Ellie looks at Breccan, who shrugs and winks. "No way, I'm not missing out on this adventure." His words make Tristan grin and Kyla and Stella try to muffle their laughter.

"Well, Princess, what's your decision?" Tristan asks, standing at ease, his arms folded over his chest.

Ellie turns to her friends, each smiles at her in return. Grateful for their loyalty but fearful for their safety, she knows she has no choice. It is either the five of them or a group of soldiers and the general.

Ellie sighs and looks back at Tristan. "We leave at midnight tomorrow night. We'll meet at the mountain peak. I'm assuming you know my spot," Ellie lifts one brow and glares at him.

Tristan only gives a curt nod, "I do. The king and queen are looking for you, which is why we overheard everything."

"Fine. Let's get back inside before they send a whole search party for us. Plus, I would very much like to enjoy the rest of the evening," Ellie replies.

"I could *definitely* use a drink after all that," Breccan admits, his words making everyone chuckle in agreement.

Once they each enter the great hall, Ellie feels more at ease and begins to enjoy the flowing wine and delicious foods on display as she speaks with numerous guests. Many ask how she is and thank the stars for her quick recovery from today's events.

"May I have this dance?" a familiar voice cut through, pulling her attention away from the guests that she is speaking with. Ellie's breath catches in her throat because she didn't need to turn around to know who was talking to her. She knows his voice as well as her own. She takes an unsteady breath and then she turns to see Jace standing there, his eyes laden with the same pain that she feels. She wants to say so much, but she bites down every word and nods.

Jace lifts his hand to her, and Ellie elegantly places her gloved hand in his. He leads her to the dance floor, his touch sending a familiar warmth through her. When they stop in the middle of the floor, he gazes down at her, placing his large hand on her bare back as they begin to dance. Serenading music envelopes them, creating a cocoon of melody and movement. Neither speaks for extended moments, then Jace finally breaks the silence.

"I'm so sorry, Ellie. So, incredibly sorry, for not telling you about her. I wanted to, so badly, but I didn't know how. Then everything got all jumbled up and I realized that I had missed my opportunity. I would give anything to have a long life with you and stand by your side, but we both know that isn't impossible. I'm a bladesmith, I'll never be of noble blood or even remotely worthy enough to have your hand. It will never be allowed, and I could never ask you to go against such odds for me," Jace said, taking another deep breath. "So, when my mother introduced me to Celeste and she pleaded with me to give her a chance, I agreed. She wants me to be with someone I can have a future with. And I can't deny my own mother's wishes for me. I still love you. I'm sure I will love you until my dying breath, but if we continue down this road, I'll be the one who is broken at the end."

Ellie listens to every word as tears line Jace's beautiful emerald-green eyes. "We could've talked about this. You could've fought for me. We could've gone to my parents, told them how we feel, how we could be fated mates..." Ellie's words are desperate, pleading with him.

"Ellie, you deserve so much more than me. I can never give you what a male of noble blood can. I'll never be wealthy, I'll never have magic, I'll never have a bonded, and I can never stand by your side as you sit on the throne," Jace's voice shakes with each word.

"You don't know that. It could be decades or a century until I sit on the throne. Yet, you just give up and decide not to fight for *me*, for *us*. What I want is a male who *will* fight for me, a male who would burn the world to stay by my side. You know actually, you're right. You're clearly not him," Ellie's voice sharpens with rising anger.

Thankfully, the other couples dancing around them are so immersed in their own joy that they barely notice the tension crackling between them.

Ellie glances around, her eyes catching sight of Tristan through the crowd. Her breath hitches in her throat as she meets his gaze—intense and unrelenting as if his eyes are burning holes into her, scrutinizing every emotion that flickers across her face.

She pulls her gaze from him when Jace's head falls in defeat, and instead of the pain she thought she would come, all she feels is anger when she looks at him. She takes a deep breath, realizing that this conversation didn't go as she had hoped, leaving her utterly hopeless.

Ellie allows herself one last glance into Jace's eyes before stepping back and walking away without another word. It takes every ounce of courage and strength within her not to cry as she distances herself from him and from what they had. As she weaves through the crowd of guests, holding her chin high, she hears the comforting voice of her bonded in her mind.

"*You did the right thing, El. If he were truly your fated mate, nothing and no one in the entire realm could keep him from you,*" Saphirixia says.

Walking up to the large grand doors, soldiers open them and bow to her. She lifts her chin higher as she strides into the empty corridor. Once she is alone, she replies, "*I know, Saph. Thank you.*"

Heavy footsteps echo behind her in the empty corridor; Ellie looks over her shoulder to see Tristan running up to her. "Are you trying to sneak away? You do know that I'm supposed to be guarding you, Princess," giving her a slight smirk as he keeps pace with her.

"I'm tired. Feel free to go back to the celebration," Ellie says quietly.

Tristan stops her and grabs her arm. "Are you sure you're alright?" he presses, concern lacing his tone.

"Ugh! I really wish everyone would stop asking me that," Ellie yanks her arm free and continues to her bedchamber. Tristan, still one step behind her, his footsteps echoing in the empty hallway.

When they reach her room, Tristan finally breaks the silence, "There is something that I would like to tell you. Can we speak in private, please?" he asks hesitantly.

Intrigued, she nods and walks into her room, allowing him to follow. Ellie strides to the table nearest the fireplace and sits down, removing her crimson-red heels and rubbing her sore feet. After shutting her bedchamber door, Tristan watches her for a moment before he strides to the table and drags the other chair closer to her, then sits down.

"Give me your feet," Tristan demands casually.

Ellie's eyes immediately widen as she shakes her head. "Absolutely not."

"Don't be stubborn, Princess." Ellie huffs but concedes, the ache in her feet too much to ignore. She lifts her feet to Tristan, who lays them on his knees and uses his masterful hands to massage her sore heels. Ellie feels the tension leaving her body. She sinks into the chair as the heat of the fire warms her skin.

"I think you made it too hot in here earlier," Ellie lightly chuckles, leaning her head back against the chair and closing her tired eyes.

A moment later, she hears her double doors to her balcony swinging open, and a cool breeze flows through the room. Ellie lifts her head and smirks at Tristan, who shrugs with a smile, eyes glowing crimson.

"Better?" Tristan asks coyly.

"Much." She sighs, "Now, what did you want to tell me?" Ellie presses, almost lost in the feel of his hands massaging her sore feet.

"I already knew who you were. Actually, I figured it out today when you were asleep from the poison. Your necklace glowed, and you murmured 'enchantress' in your sleep. Also, Breccan and I were the ones who were sent to gather the tomes and scrolls that mentioned the curse. We *might* have *accidentally* read a couple when they fell from one of the satchels on our way back," Tristan admits hesitantly.

Ellie took a steadying breath before saying, "Accidentally, huh?"

"Breccan is clumsy. You can ask him yourself," a smile spreads across his face.

Ellie sighs, feeling a mix of relief and frustration. "I suppose it was a secret that won't be hidden much longer anyway."

"Then let us help you. You don't need to be alone in this, Ellie," Tristan's voice is full of conviction.

Ellie nods, feeling a glimmer of hope. "Thank you, Tristan. It means a lot to me."

"Always, Princess. What are friends for?" continuing to massage her feet.

"Friends...," Ellie allows the words to roll off her tongue, testing the sound of it, "I think I'd very much like to be friends with you."

They both smile at each other as Tristan grabs her other foot and slumps down in his chair, getting more comfortable.

"Are you afraid of what is to come?" Tristan probes. Ellie can't help but feel relieved to have someone else to talk to about this. She sighs, turning her head to peer at the fire burning in the fireplace, "I'm terrified."

Tristan only hums as if he understood. They remain in comfortable silence for long minutes before Tristan breaks the silence again, "How are we going to find the enchantress?"

Ellie turns her head and meets Tristan's gaze, considering how much she should tell him. But something about him made her feel she could trust him. Plus, he has done nothing but protect her since they met.

"My hope is that when I use the necklace, it will guide us to her. If it doesn't, then we'll have to produce another plan," Ellie says and shrugs, her gaze turning back to the fire, lost in thought again.

"I would like for you to train with me in the morning," Tristan says, surprising her. That was the last thing she expected him to say.

Ellie abruptly turns to face him and gives him a confused look, which makes him laugh.

"If we do this, I want to see your fighting skills before leaving. We don't know what we're going to come across on this journey, and I would like to make sure you are prepared for anything."

She has been fighting since she was little, ever since her father had insisted she learn how to protect herself. Her years of training and sparring with Kyla have made her comparable to, if not better, than most of the soldiers. Instead of arguing, she concedes with a nod, stifling a yawn as she realizes how exhausted she is.

Tristan finally releases her feet and gently places them back on the ground. He stands up, peering down at her with a warm smile.

"Why don't you get some sleep? Tonight is your last night in your own bed before we leave, and you'll need the rest." Tristan's words surprise Ellie. His concern and care for her is a form of tenderness she has never experienced from a male before.

Ellie nods, standing up and walking him to the door. Opening it, Tristan pauses, looking at her once more before leaning in. Ellie freezes as his gentle lips press a single kiss to her forehead, sending a wave of warmth across her face.

"Good night, Ellie," Tristan says softly as he pulls away and turns to stride down the corridor, leaving Ellie frozen in place. She touches her forehead where his lips had been, a swirl of confusion, anticipation, and a flutter of excitement, she had not expected, mixes within her. With a deep breath, she closes the door and leans against it, realizing that tomorrow's training will be the least of her worries.

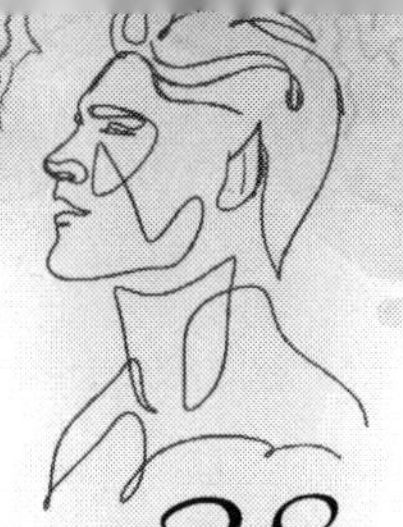

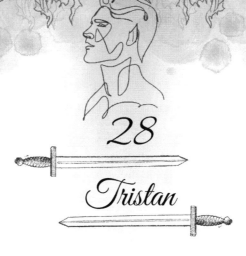

28

Tristan

The following day, as Tristan reaches the training courtyard, he begins warming up and sparring with the other soldiers. He feels oddly anxious, yet excited, about training with Ellie today.

Once he arrives back at his father's estate the night before, he has barely slept due to his thoughts wandering back to Kyla, Ellie, and the curse.

He feels nothing except for fear and panic as he and Breccan overheard her, saying that she will leave alone to find the enchantress. Before he can process the words on the tip of his tongue, he comes out of the shadows and tells her he is going to. *Bleeding stars, I am a fool*, he chastised himself.

There is no doubt when his father and the general find out that he left with the Princess, that he can easily be executed once they return, if they return at all. Tristan knows it will be worth the risk if he can protect her from his father and help break the curse on fae magic. The journey will undoubtedly be dangerous, but it would be worth the risk.

"Good morning, Tristan." Tristan looks up as he cleans his sword and sees Kyla standing before him. Tristan gives her a genuine smile as she beams at him in return. Seeing her smile at him, utterly oblivious to his internal war raging amongst himself over his feelings for Ellie and her, makes him feel utterly terrible. He knows he is a foolish male for having conflicting feelings for two females. He is tempted to let his next sparring partner beat him, hoping to knock some sense back into him.

"I must admit, I am surprised that you want to come with us." Kyla quickly looks around, making sure no soldiers are close enough to hear before she turns back to him, waiting for his reply.

"Did you honestly think I wouldn't want to come with you and help protect the Princess?" Tristan asks, almost annoyed by her question.

"I understand your duty to protect her; I do. However, I think only Ellie, Stella, and I should go," Kyla stutters as if she can sense his growing frustration.

Tristan feels the sting of her words. "Why would you not want Breccan and I to come?" Tristan's voice elicited anger with each word.

Kyla reaches for his arm and takes an unsteady breath, "It's not that I don't *want* you to come; I just feel like it would be better as just us three."

Tristan feels rage seeping into him. He tries his best to keep it at bay, but each time she speaks now, he is losing control.

"What would you have me do, Kyla? Stay here, and when the General asks me how the Princess disappeared under *my* guard, for me to say nothing?" Tristan shakes his head, unbelieving her words. "You know as well as I do that we all have a better chance of helping her if we stick together. All of our gifts and skills combined can help her succeed."

Kyla seems to be trying to process his words as she bites her bottom lip and stares at him. "You're right. I'm sorry. I shouldn't have said anything at all."

"Good morning," Ellie strides up to them, glancing between them both, clearly noticing the anger in his expression.

"Is everything alright?" Ellie questions cautiously.

"Everything is perfect. Let's see what you got, Princess," Tristan replies, quickly glancing at Kyla before walking past her without a word.

Tristan tries to calm his racing heart, reminding himself that he is about to swing a blade against Ellie. He takes a couple of deep breaths before stopping in a chalked-out circle in the grass farther away from the other training soldiers, wanting some privacy not just for himself but also for Ellie.

He never really paid attention when he would see her and Kyla train from afar. The couple of times he did glance their way, he noted their fighting skills. Today he is hoping to see what she could really do.

Once she stands before him, she wastes no time. She takes her stance, raises her sword, and gives him a small smirk.

“Ready?” Tristan raises his sword and assumes a defensive stance.

Ellie nods, her face set with determination. Without another word, she lunges forward, their swords clash as a metallic ring echoes through the courtyard. Tristan parries her strike effortlessly, but Ellie is quick, dancing around him with a fluidity that catches him off guard.

"Impressive," Tristan murmurs, blocking a flurry of blows. He retaliates with swift attacks, testing her reflexes and strength. Ellie meets each strike with a skill honed through years of training, her movements a blur of precision and grace.

As the fight progresses, Tristan can see Ellie’s confidence grow. She feigns left, then spins right, her blade slicing through the air with deadly accuracy. Tristan barely has time to counter, his eyes widening in surprise at her unexpected agility.

"You’ve been holding back," he admits, a hint of admiration in his voice.

Ellie grins, her breathing steady bursts, "You have *no* idea."

Determined to push her further, Tristan increases the intensity of his attacks, his strikes coming faster and harder. Ellie matches him blow for blow, her focus unwavering. She parries a particularly vicious swing and uses the momentum to spin around, her sword aiming for his unguarded side.

Tristan barely manages to deflect the strike, their swords locking together. For a moment, they stand face to face, the intensity of the fight mirrored in their eyes. With a powerful shove, Tristan pushes Ellie back, breaking the lock.

"You're good," Tristan encourages, a bead of sweat trickling down his forehead.

Ellie smirks, her chest heaving with exertion, "Better than you expected?"

"Much," he confesses. *Far better than I ever expected*, he admits only to himself.

With renewed vigor, they clash again, their swords a blur of silver in the morning light. Ellie moves with a ferocity that takes Tristan by surprise. She sidesteps a mighty swing and raises her sword, stopping just short of his throat.

Tristan freezes, his eyes widening in shock. Ellie holds her position, the tip of her blade trembling slightly against his throat as she struggles to catch her breath.

"Yield," she demands, her voice steady despite her apparent exhaustion. He sees it then, the fire burning in her eyes. *Now, that is the kind of fire I wouldn't mind being burned by*, Tristan admits to himself.

Tristan slowly raises his hands in surrender, a smirk tugging at his lips, "I yield."

Ellie lowers her sword, a triumphant smile spreading across her beautiful face. "Looks like I passed your test."

Tristan nods, genuine respect in his eyes for the beautiful princess he knows now he underestimated. "More than passed. You are remarkably skilled with a sword, Ellie."

As they step back, both catching their breath, Tristan can't help but feel a surge of pride. Ellie has not only matched him, but bested him.

The journey ahead is uncertain for them all, but now seeing how strong and capable Ellie is, he feels more confident than ever.

Tristan sheaths his sword, still processing the duel's intensity, "I underestimated you, Ellie. Your father trained you well."

Ellie smiles, the compliment seems to warm her cheeks. "I've had good teachers. And Kyla—she pushed me harder than anyone else."

"Remind me to thank her," Tristan says in a light but sincere tone. He glances around the courtyard, noticing Kyla is nowhere to be seen. "I'll feel a lot better knowing you can handle yourself," he says.

Ellie nods, a mix of pride and anticipation written across her bright face. Tristan feels an undeniable urge to grab and pull her into his arms. Her smile, shining brighter than the sun, making his heart tighten in his chest. But before he can act on his urges, she turns and walks away unknowingly, saving him from undoubtedly making a mistake.

As she walks away, Tristan stands there watching her leave, noting her graceful curves to memory as she heads towards the forest path to the beach beyond. A firm hand on his shoulder pulls him from his wandering thoughts as Breccan speaks, "She's much better than I thought she was. I'll give her that. You may have just met your match."

Breccan's word unknowingly hits a place in Tristan's chest he didn't expect. *My...match?* Tristan ponders to himself.

"She might just survive the journey after all," Tristan says, hoping to steer the conversation the best he could.

"Mormont, Aldenridge, the General wants to see you both in his study immediately."

Tristan turns and recognizes the soldier as one of the General's most trusted soldiers. Breccan and Tristan look at each other confused as they follow the soldier who has already turned to walk away.

They both remain silent the entire walk through the castle and as they enter the General's study. He stands staring out his window behind his large, with his hands behind his back, dressed in his full uniform.

Without turning around, the General says, "Sit," his voice curt and stern. After a brief silence, he speaks again, "We would like to speak with you both."

Tristan is immediately confused by the General's words, "We, sir?"

The door swings open behind Breccan and Tristan, making them turn to see who is entering. They both hold their breath and watch the king stride in. Clad in a white doublet with gold embroidering. His gold, jeweled crown shining in the light. The king is silent as he walks around the General's desk and sits down, staring at them both, his face devoid of any emotion.

General Alvar turns and stands beside the King as the King speaks, "Mormont, Aldenridge, we have a mission for you both that is of the utmost importance and secrecy. You have both shown yourself to be skilled and, most importantly, trustworthy. You both will be joining the General as well as twelve other soldiers. You depart tomorrow morning," his voice is unwavering and laden with authority.

Breccan asks, surprising Tristan, "Where will we be headed, Your Highness?"

The king nods at his question, clearly expecting it. However, it's the General who answers, "You'll be fully informed after we depart. We cannot risk any information about the mission getting out."

They both nod in understanding, Tristan clears his throat, "Understood. Thank you, Your Highness."

The king gives a brief smile and stands before adding, "Don't thank me yet, Mormont." Then he walks around the General's desk and walks out the door.

With that, the General sits down and releases an unsteady breath before saying, "You both are relieved of your duties today. Prepare your bonded, pack for days or possibly weeks of travel, and say goodbye to your families," his last words have a somber tone to them. They both nod in understanding as the General says, "You're excused."

Without hesitating, they both rise and stride out the door again, refusing to speak until they are alone. As they finally reach the castle garden, they observe around them anxiously. It is Breccan who breaks the silence, "We're going to be in such deep shit when we don't arrive tomorrow," shaking his head.

"I will understand if you don't want to go to Brec; we will most certainly be imprisoned, or worse, for leaving when we get back," Tristan silently hopes his friend won't change his mind. Knowing he has him by his side, he would feel much better on the journey.

"Are you kidding me? There is no way I'm letting you go alone or our princess. You know you need me. Plus, if we help her succeed, we will be heroes!" Breccan exclaims excitedly, making them both smile.

"*If* we make it back," Tristan admits with a little less enthusiasm but still smiling.

"You know we will. I'm more worried about how Vespero and Terbius will take the news," Breccan quivers at his words, knowing the tempers that both of their bondeds possess.

"Yeah, this should be interesting," Tristan admits hesitantly as he runs his hand through his raven black hair, the thought makes him want to cringe.

"I'll see you on the mountain," Breccan says as soon as they exit the castle gates, each going their own way.

Once Tristan makes it to his father's estate, he is thankful when he realizes his father isn't home. He hopes to escape him until he leaves. As he heads towards his bedchamber to pack, he reaches out to his bonded, hoping Terbius wouldn't burn him with dragon fire for this.

"*Terbius, I have something to ask of you,*" Tristan says as he feels the connection to his bonded.

"*You should've asked me last night before volunteering us both on this foolish and dangerous mission. Instead, I was informed by Saphirixia, Kaida, and Sentiara,*" Terbius responds with a growl.

"*I know, but I can't let them go alone. It's our duty to protect the princess,*" Tristan says, feeling his anger emanating through the bond.

"No, *it's* your *duty to protect the princess. I'm just the unlucky one chained to you. You're going to get us killed,*" Terbius responds.

"*Or she could break the curse,*" Tristan replies flatly. Taking a deep breath, he continues, "*please don't make me beg.*" Tristan feels Terbius's growl through the bond. After a brief silence, his bonded concedes, relief quickly flooding through him.

"*I'll see you tonight,*" Terbius says gruffly before the connection abruptly is cut off.

Tristan can't help the smirk that pulls. He knows his bonded will never let him down, and as long as he has Terbius by his side, they will conquer anything. He just hopes to the bleeding stars that he's right and not Terbius.

29

Ellie

Ellie walks from the training courtyard with her head held high, confidence soaring after her session with Tristan. He's an impeccable fighter, undoubtedly the best that she has ever faced. Ellie knows she got lucky when she pinned him with her blade, all thanks to Kyla's training.

Leaving Tristan standing there, she heads towards the beach to meet Saphirixia. She can't get Tristan's face out of her mind, the way he stared at her after their match. It was as if he radiated pride when he gazed at her, and his smile nearly brought her to her knees. She can still feel the spark of electricity between them, fighting the undeniable urge to touch him. Ellie shakes off the lingering warmth of his stare, which is still igniting her body. She desperately tries to snuff it out before it burns her from the inside out.

At the beach, she sits down in her black, soft leather training gear and watches the ocean beyond. The sea breeze brushes loose strands of her braid from her face. Taking in the scent of the seawater, she silently wishes to sit here in peace forever. Reality, however, is too hard to ignore. She has mere hours left, and now she must inform Saphirixia of her plan.

Ellie reaches out to her bonded friend, "*Saph, meet me at the beach.*" She instantly feels the familiar tingle of their connection, a comforting sensation.

"*On my way,*" Saphirixia quickly responds.

Less than ten minutes later, Ellie hears the familiar wingbeats above her. She looks up to see Saphirixia's blue scales shimmering in the sunlight as she lands in the sand. She smiles, knowing that Saphirixia will follow her anywhere despite the potential conflict.

"*I already know what you are going to say...*" Saphirixia's grumbles.

"*I'm assuming the other dragons are as pleased about our plan as you are,*" Ellie says with amusement, seeing Saphirixia's glare as confirmation, making Ellie chuckle lightly.

"*Kaida and Sentiara's loyalties are unwavering, so their decision to come was easy and without regret. However, Terbius and Vespero were quite angry with their bonded's abrupt decision. They will come nonetheless.*"

Ellie catches a hint of amusement when she speaks of Terbius and Vespero's anger. Ellie almost wishes she was a fly on the wall during *that* conversation.

"*I wasn't pleased with the idea either, but what choice do I have? I refuse to go with the General and his soldiers.* Ellie heavily sighs. *Plus, we stand a better chance of reaching the enchantress safely and much quieter with just the five of us and our gifts combined,*" Ellie said, hoping Saphirixia feels the same.

"*It makes no difference to me who goes; this is our fate. If having your friends and the soldier with the dark soul and his ridiculous bonded, makes you feel safer, I will not deny you this.*" Saphirixia crouches lower into the sand, nestling closer to Ellie. Ellie leans into her, resting her shoulder against Saphirixia's arm.

"*Thank you, Saph,*" Ellie releases a long breath as relief washes over her. She can feel Saphirixia's heartbeat thumping against her shoulder, lulling her into a tranquil space as she gazes at the ocean beyond.

"*My mother always told me stories of the creatures who live beyond our Kingdom. Do you think we will cross paths with any of them?*" Ellie asks nervously.

"*I have no doubt that we will encounter something dangerous, but do not fear; I will protect you, and your friends will, too,*" Saphirixia replies, bringing Ellie a slight sense of comfort against her rising anxiety regarding the journey ahead.

"*I wish my gift wasn't so useless. Why couldn't I be granted a more powerful gift that could be used in a fight?*" Ellie ponders desperately.

"*You are many things, Ellie, but you are not useless. Our gift may feel like a curse, but it can be precious and sometimes valuable,*" Saphirixia replies, her tone filling with bold truthfulness. "*Plus, your gift is more valuable than the soldier with the dark soul.*"

Ellie turns to look up at Saphirixia, giving her a confused look. "*Why do you say that about him?*"

"*He holds a quiet mask of control and unspoken deep secrets. There is always darkness in his kind of quiet.*" Saphirixia's voice brims with warning.

She can't formulate any response to that, and some of her agreed with Saphirixia. Tristan carries an aura of impenetrable darkness, a quiet and unsettling presence that lingers long after he leaves the room. His eyes, deep and shadowed, seem to hold a thousand unspoken secrets, glinting with a cold, calculating intensity.

His face's hard and unyielding lines speak of a past marred by pain and loss, yet he seldom lets his emotions surface. His demeanor is one of controlled stillness, like an undercurrent of chaos and anger simmering just beneath the surface, seemingly kept in check by sheer force of will.

There is a palpable weight to his presence, an invisible shroud hinting at his inner turmoil's depths. He moves with a lethal grace. He exudes a sense of danger and unpredictability.

Yet, Ellie has glimpsed something more from him in stolen moments when they were alone. She has seen brief moments of vulnerability that he has shown her and the fleeting softness in his eyes when he thinks no one is looking. In those rare instances, the hard mask slips, revealing a depth of pain and a potential desire for redemption that tugs at her heart.

Despite his dark aura, Tristan has shown her a protective kindness that she has become fond of despite his usual stern exterior. His actions speak of a fierce loyalty and a quiet strength. He's always watching over her, stepping in to shield her from harm with a gentleness that contrasts starkly with his usual demeanor. It is this complexity, this blend of darkness and light, that fascinates Ellie and draws her to him. It makes her wonder what lay beneath the surface of the male with the dark soul.

Saphirixia speaks, pulling Ellie from the fog of her wandering thoughts. "*You should head back and prepare, as should I.*" Ellie nods her agreement as she hesitantly stands, dusting off the sand from her leathers.

"*See you at midnight*," Ellie glances at Saphirixia, who stands and shakes off the sand. Saphirixia only nudges her with her snout before turning and shooting into the sky.

Once Ellie is back inside the castle, she searches for her parents. The castle was eerily quiet this morning, making her assume it was due to everyone being tired from the last night celebrations for the Dracofaerian Revelry.

A few servants wander the corridors, each giving her a slight bow of their heads as they pass. Ellie makes her way towards her parents' private parlor, hoping to find them there.

With each step she takes closer to the parlor, she hears her mother's joyous laugh echoing through the corridor. The sound makes Ellie's heart tighten in her chest for fear of when she might get the chance to hear the joyous noise again. Before opening the heavy wooden door, she takes a deep, steadying breath.

The king and queen sit on the plush velvet couch in the royal parlor, sipping their tea and smiling at one another lovingly. The parlor is a room of understated elegance, filled with rich tapestries, polished mahogany furniture, and the soft glow of morning light filtering through the lace curtains.

Their unwavering love was evident in their gazes and simple touches, sending a pang of jealousy creeping through Ellie. It's the kind of love and devotion she hopes to find one day if she's so fortunate.

The king notices her first, turning his head and giving her a kind smile. "Oh! Good morning, El. Come join us. We were hoping to speak with you."

Ellie takes a deep breath and crosses the room, sitting across them in a lone, ornate chair. Queen Adelina asks, "Tea, my dear?" Ellie nods, and her mother gracefully fills a delicate porcelain cup and hands it to her.

Her father shifts next to her mother, furrowing his brow in contemplation. Ellie knows his weary smile all too well; it's the look he always gives her before delivering unfortunate news.

"I have spoken to General Alvar, and we have handpicked the soldiers who will accompany you on your journey. To ensure our secret remains hidden, we feel it's best that you leave in the morning," his last words, cautious and broken.

Ellie couldn't hold back her shock as the words come stumbling out, "Tomorrow?"

The queen leans forward with her tea, giving Ellie a small, sad smile, "We know it's soon, but we do not want to risk another attempt on your life or our secret getting out."

"I understand," Ellie manages to say, her voice cracking. She knew this would be a goodbye, but now her parents know it too. Queen Adelina's face is somber, a lone tear streams down her beautiful face.

Ellie stands up and walks to the couch, sitting between them.

Her father wraps his large arms around each of them, pulling them in close. She allows his embrace to consume her entirely, drawing strength for the journey ahead.

Queen Adelina gently touches Ellie's cheek, her eyes overflowing with love and sorrow. "You are so strong, Ellie. We are proud of you, and we believe in you. If anyone could do this, it is you and Saphirixia."

The king kisses the top of her head, his voice thick with emotion. "Remember, no matter where you go, our love goes with you. You are never alone."

Ellie nods, tears brimming in her eyes as she feels the warmth and strength of their love envelop her. "I love you both so much," she whispers, her voice fills with emotion. "I'll make you proud, I promise."

As a family, they sit there in a shared embrace, the weight of the coming separation heavy in the air. Yet, in that intimate moment, their love and unity provides a brief respite for Ellie, a cherished memory that she will carry into the unknown.

The sun now sets when Ellie finally retires from the parlor, leaving her parents after hours filled with laughter and tears as they reminisce over cherished memories. They excused her from dinner, suggesting she get some extra sleep before her journey tomorrow, for which she was genuinely thankful. The thought of lying to them about her plans made her feel terribly guilty, but Ellie knows deep down that leaving is the best decision for her and Saphirixia.

Entering her bedchambers, a strange feeling washes over her.

The room, usually a sanctuary of comfort, now feels alien and cold. Her eyes fall on the neatly packed bag on her bed, clearly prepared by Clara or Helena, with everything she might need for her journey. A simple dinner sits on the table near the fire, untouched.

Ellie closes the door behind her and crosses the room slowly, each step echoing her mixed emotions. She slips off her gloves and feels the cool air against her skin, a stark contrast to the warmth of the fire before warming her slowly.

She touches the pendant, feeling its heat seep into her fingers. The warmth seemed to pulse with her heartbeat, a silent promise of guidance. Ellie knows that with the necklace, she can find the enchantress and, hopefully, break the curse that has plagued fae magic for too long.

Sitting on the edge of her bed, Ellie takes a deep breath, her resolve hardening. She gazes around her room, taking in every detail as if it were the last time. The familiar scent of lavender from the garden, the soft glow of the fire, the delicate tapestries on the walls to her bedspread. Everything holds a piece of her childhood, her innocence.

But she's no longer the child that she once was. She has a mission now, a purpose that goes beyond her own desires. She will find the enchantress and break the curse upon fae magic, no matter the cost.

I can do this, she thinks, feeling the weight of her decision settle firmly in her heart.

After eating her meal and washing up, Ellie lays on her bed, fully dressed in her riding gear. She tries to rest her eyes, knowing she has less than three hours until she has to meet her companions on the mountain. The weight of her mission and the anticipation of what lay ahead makes it difficult to find peace. It felt like she'd only slept for minutes before Saphirixia's voice startled her awake.

"*Time to go, El*," Saphirixia says down their bond, her voice a comforting yet urgent nudge.

With a deep breath, she pushes herself out of her bed, determination burning brighter in her eyes. She picks up her packed bag. Its weight is a physical reminder of her commitment.

Silently, she moves towards her balcony door. She opens it to see Saphirixia waiting, her dragon's blue scales shimmering under the moonlight.Climbing onto Saphirixia's back, Ellie feels a surge of exhilaration mixed with trepidation.

As they fly into the night, the ground quickly falls beneath them. She doesn't look back, her gaze fixed firmly on the moon shining brightly overhead. The wind whips through her hair, and the rhythmic beat of Saphirixia's wings is a steady, reassuring cadence. The stars above seem to shine a little brighter, lighting their path as they soar toward the mountain peak.

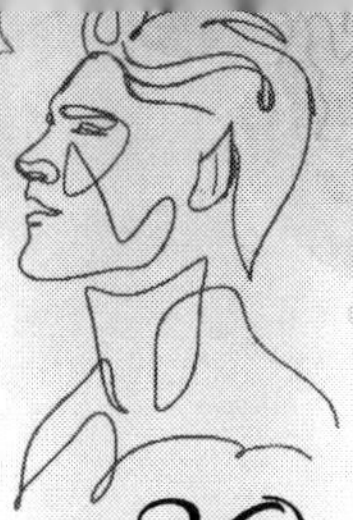

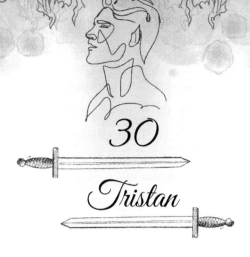

30

Tristan

Tristan feels as if his heart is going to beat out of his chest while he sneaks out of his father's estate. The decision to follow the princess weighs heavily upon him. The repercussions of her failure or his return without her is dire. The king will undoubtedly have him executed if anything happens to his heir. And if anything did, he would never be able to forgive himself.

He takes a deep breath as they fly towards the mountain peak. Terbius's words echo in his mind as they fly through the dark, moonlit sky. "*You do know how stupid this is, right*?"

Tristan can't help but chuckle softly. He knows how foolish this is, but every fiber of his being is telling him that this journey is where he's meant to be; even knowing it's unwise, something urges him to follow his gut.

"*I'm aware, and I have no doubt you'll remind me over the entire journey*," Tristan scolds.

Terbius growls in response, his body vibrating beneath Tristan. They still have about thirty minutes until they need to be at the peak, but Tristan left early to avoid his father, who thankfully wasn't home when he slipped out under the cover of darkness.

As they near the mountain peak, he can make out the sapphire blue scales shining in the moonlight. Tristan's heart pounds faster as they land. Ellie rests against Saphirixia casually, the only sign of her anxiousness is the tapping of her boots on the dirt.

"Well, princess, are you ready?" Tristan smiles. Ellie shrugs, remaining silent as she sits with Saphirixia. Tristan can nearly feel her weariness as he moves to sit close to her, getting a better look at her features in the dark.

Her eyes are glassy as she looks over at him with those deep blue eyes that make Tristan falter. Wearing black riding leathers, her long blonde hair braided over her shoulder, the sapphire stone necklace around her delicate neck, a sword hilt gleaming behind her back, two daggers on her belt, and a cross-body bag at her side. She looks like a true soldier ready for a mission. She's so stunning that Tristan finds it difficult to speak.

"Did you get any rest?" He asks.

"A little," she shrugs, gazing back at the ocean and stars above. Tristan slides to sit closer to her. Saphirixia immediately shifts her long neck and eyes him warily. He quickly raises his hands in surrender, making Saphirixia's glare relax slightly, clearly accepting his gesture. Tristan sits a foot away now, folding his hands together and resting his arms on his bent knees.

"Ellie… there's something I want to say," Tristan admits, drawing her gaze to meet his. She cocks an eyebrow at him, making him sigh as he struggles to find the right words. He didn't plan to tell her this here and now, but in case things went sideways, he wanted to make sure she knew.

"I wanted to apologize for how I spoke to you when we first met. You're nothing like what I presumed you to be, and for that, I'm sorry." Tristan peers at his fumbling hands before continuing. "Ever since that night on the veranda, I have come to care for you, admire your strength, kindness, and bravery even. I feel honored to be here with you, Ellie." Tristan nearly chokes on her name.

Ellie's face softens, and even though the darkness shadows her face, the sun might as well be shining because she lights up with a bright smile at his confession.

"I'm glad we've become friends, Tristan," Ellie says softly.

The word "friends" makes him wince slightly until realization dawns on him: *she said my name.*

Ellie has always called him "soldier," his name has never left her lips until now. He realizes then how much he eagerly wants to hear her say it again and again.

They sit in comfortable silence on the mountainside as Tristan's mind wanders to the princess at his side.

His gaze keeps falling onto her while she continues to stare at the stars, completely lost in her own thoughts; he allows his gaze to take in each detail of her moonlit face. *Why does she have to be so damn beautiful*? he wonders to himself.

The nagging urge to move closer to her, touch her to see what her skin feels like under his fingertips, consuming his thoughts. *I wonder what she would taste like on my tongue, how my name would sound coming from her lips as she moans for me*; Tristan immediately chastises himself for allowing his mind to go there. *Stop, you idiot; think of something else.*

Wingbeats echo in the distance; Ellie turns to peer towards the sound, "They're here."

She stands, dusting off the dirt. Tristan nods, thanking the stars for their impeccable timing. He stands and takes a deep breath, mentally preparing himself for the journey ahead.

Kyla, Stella, and Breccan all land within minutes, each dismounting their dragons and approaching them. Breccan speaks first, "Who's ready for an adventure?" in his usual comical manner.

Kyla and Stella are smiling brightly at Ellie. Tristan notices Stella in flight leathers for the first time, looking as much like a soldier as Kyla, who smiles sweetly at him. Ellie shifts uncomfortably next to him, clearly noticing Kyla's smile.

"So, do you know where we're going?" Stella inquires excitedly.

"Right, I guess it's time for us to find out," Ellie admits, removing her glove and placing her hand on her sapphire necklace. Once her fingers touch it, the stone begins to glow a bright, brilliant blue as if sensing her touch.

Ellie looks down at it nervously. "When I spoke to the enchantress, it warmed my hand. I'm hoping it will give me a sign again."

Ellie walks to the peak's edge, slowly turning to face North, South, East, and West. They all watched her silently, anxiously awaiting what would happen next. Ellie stops as she faces West, hissing and dropping the necklace from her grasp as it lies back upon her chest.

"West it is then," Ellie shrugs.

"Are you sure?" Kyla questions.

Ellie nods, "It was the only direction that nearly burnt me, so yeah, I'm assuming that is the right way."

"Well, let's get going then. We need to get as far from Aetherlyn as we can before daybreak," Tristan points out.

They all nod in agreement. Tristan eyes Ellie once more before instructing her, "Keep checking your necklace regularly to ensure we're heading in the right direction." Ellie nods again, and they all smile at each other.

"Lead the way, Princess," Tristan waves towards Saphirixia. Within minutes, they are all airborne in a strategic formation, with Ellie leading. Kyla and Stella are behind her, slightly off her outside shoulders. Tristan and Breccan complete the formation bringing up the center rear.

They fly over the vast ocean and islands for hours as the sun begins to crest the horizon. Tristan oversees everyone, staying alert. As the sun rises, they see a coast far ahead.

"*We're entering Aurelia*," Terbius alerts.

Tristan has never been this far west before. Aurelia, a green and lush kingdom under Aetherlyn's rule, is governed by high Lords loyal to the king. If they are recognized, the king will know their direction. By now, their families must know of their departure. It's too late to turn back; the only way is forward.

They stop briefly before continuing, Ellie following the warmth of the stone. As evening comes, Tristan feels sore and imagines how everyone else might feel after a full day in the air.

"*Terbius, can you tell Saphirixia to find a safe place to land? Let's camp and rest.*" After a few minutes, Saphirixia veers towards a heavily wooded area with a small clearing near a mountainside, far enough from the town to be safe.

Once they land, everyone gathers their food rations. Before the dragons take flight to find their own dinner.

Tristan urges, "Stay close. We don't know who might have seen us." Terbius nods before taking off with the other dragons. "Brec, why don't you find something a bit more substantial for dinner, that way we can save as much of the rations as possible?" Tristan asks.

Breccan smirks, pulling his bow from his back, and nods before teleporting away.

"I'll gather wood and prepare the fire," Stella offers, heading into the woods without waiting for a response. Tristan guesses she sought solace from all of the emotions she must have felt on their flight.

Kyla and Ellie speak in hushed tones before nodding at each other and turning to Tristan. "We'll gather water," Kyla says, grabbing water skins and handing a few to Ellie. Tristan watches them walk away, cursing himself for opening up to Ellie. He wished for more time to speak to her alone, but it seemed impossible now that they were all together.

He constantly finds himself worrying about her, wanting to ensure that she's okay. Despite his feelings for the female he is currently courting, Ellie's welfare seems to be his priority.

Tristan uses his magic to make a small hole and then finds stones to put around the fire. Shortly after he's done, Ellie and Kyla return with full water skins, the two females laughing together. Kyla gives Tristan a devious smile as she hands him his water skin, leaning in to kiss him.

Tristan quickly speaks, leaning back slightly, "Thank you," and drinks deeply. Kyla glares at him but remains silent. She then turns to sit with Ellie.

Stella returns with a stack of wood, looking rather winded. Tristan hurries to take it from her as she joins Kyla and Ellie. He arranges the wood, then clenches his fist, willing his gift to flood through him. A second later, the wood is set to blaze. Tristan smirks, finding his seat.

Breccan returns with two rabbits, holding them up proudly and grinning widely before saying, "Tada!"

"Rabbits? Seriously?" Kyla whines, making everyone laugh.

"Sorry, Ky. But we have to eat," Breccan shrugs. Tristan helps him prepare the food alongside Stella, watching Ellie and Kyla from the corner of his eye.

The sound of wingbeats draws his attention to the canopy as their dragons return. Each land and nestles near their bonded. "*Did you find dinner?*" Tristan ask,

Terbius rumbles, "*We found a herd of elk nearby.*"

Once they had all been fed and had cleaned up by the waterfall, they laid out their blankets by the fire. Breccan, Kyla, and Stella fell asleep quickly, their dragons' low rumbles providing a calm presence in the dark forest. Tristan noticed Ellie staring up through the tree canopy, a tear reflecting in the firelight.

As if drawn by his gaze, she looks at him, her eyes capturing his. There are so many words he wishes he could say but can't. Tristan gives her a firm nod as if to say, "It'll be alright. We got this." Ellie gives him a weak smile in return. She nods slowly before turning her back to the fire, facing Saphirixia, and away from him.

31

Ellie

Ellie wakes up to the soft rumbles of their bondeds and the faint chirping of birds. She slowly opens her eyes and finds herself surrounded by the dense woods. The early morning light filters through the canopy, casting dappled shadows on the forest floor. Nearby, she sees Kyla, Stella, Tristan, and their dragons all fast asleep, their faces peaceful in the dim light. Breccan stands guard, his posture alert and watchful as he scans the surroundings for any sign of danger.

Ellie carefully rises to her feet, trying not to disturb the others. She walks over to Breccan, who gives her a charming smile.

"I'm going to the waterfall to freshen up," she whispers, pointing toward the faint sound of rushing water.

Breccan's eyes narrow slightly with concern, but he nods. "Be careful, Ellie. Don't wander too far."

Ellie smiles and reassures him, "I'll be fine", as she taps the dagger on her belt.

She makes her way through the lush trees, following the sound of the waterfall. The forest is alive with the sounds of nature, and she feels a sense of calm washing over her as she walks. The waterfall comes into view, a stunning cascade of water tumbling into a clear pool below.

Ellie quickly undresses and steps into the cool, refreshing water, letting it wash away the grime and fatigue from their flight the day before.

As she bathes, Ellie hears a rustling sound behind her. She turns to see Tristan emerging from the trees, his eyes widening in surprise when he sees her.

"Ellie, I'm sorry. Brec only said you were at the waterfall," he quickly averts his gaze.

Ellie smiles and shakes her head as she sinks deeper into the water,so her chin rests on the water, trying to hide her bare chest. "It's alright. I'm almost done."

Tristan hesitates momentarily before nodding towards the trees, standing uncomfortably.

"Would you like to get in? Ellie asks hesitantly, her words stumbling a little as she speaks. *Bad idea, very bad idea. What are you thinking*? scolding herself.

Tristan nods again slowly, hesitantly. Ellie turns her back to him, giving him some privacy even though a part of her is dying to get a glimpse at his chiseled form. Once she turns, she can hear him undressing, and after a moment, he wades in finally joining her in the water. She turns around to look at him.

Ellie gives him a small smile when her eyes catch the lines of his muscles in his strong muscular arms and sculpted tan chest as he wades in the water.

Then Ellie's breath catches in her throat. It wasn't his broad shoulders or taut muscles that caught her attention but the red dragon tattoo covering the left side of his chest. Never has Ellie seen a tattoo so incredibly detailed as his; even the eyes of the dragon mirrored his bonded. On the other side of his chest was another tattoo, four beautifully drawn images- the four elements—a beautifully detailed symbol for earth, water, air, and fire.

She moves closer to him as she takes in each spectacular detail. It's a true masterpiece. Ellie lifts her hand out of the water, her fingers itching to touch each mesmerizing detail. But she halts before her fingers can touch him, refusing the contact before quickly pulling her hand away and back into the water.

She feels her mouth go dry, unconsciously licking her lips and staring at him. Tristan only watches her, unmoving, wordless, just following her movements, a knowing smirk gracing his face as his eyes flick to her lips, studying her intently.

This close, Ellie can feel the warmth of his body radiating off of him, setting her skin ablaze with a new kind of fire she has never felt before.

“That...” Ellie hesitates, her voice catching in her throat. “That’s truly beautiful.”

He smirks, a playful glint in his eyes. “Not nearly as beautiful as you,” he replies, his tone deep and sincere. His voice sends a shiver down her spine and makes her pulse race.

The pull towards him is so intense that the lack of air in her lungs makes it hard for her to breathe. *He’s with Kyla, you fool*, she reminds herself.

She quickly rubs her face with water, trying to hide the warmth in her cheeks. Tristan gives her another smirk as he submerges himself in the water, clearly noticing her discomfort but thankfully not saying a word about it.

Cresting the water’s surface again, he runs his hands through his raven hair. Ellie couldn't help but think that Tristan’s wet hair reminded her of midnight. So dark that even light didn't reflect off his dark hair.

The cool water feels invigorating as Ellie wades further in, allowing the water to shake off the last remnants of sleep while also trying not to look at him.

"How are you feeling?" Tristan’s tone is serious as he looks at her with concern, brows furrowing. "About finding the enchantress, I mean," A *subject change, thank the bleeding stars*, Ellie thought.

Ellie sighs and looks away, her expression thoughtful. "It's a lot to take in," she admits. "I don’t know what to expect or what we will find. But I'm determined to see this through. I want to do this for our people. For all the fae really, they deserve to have their magic and the chance to find their mate."

Tristan nods, understanding the weight of her words. "We will face whatever comes.... together," offering her a reassuring smile.

Ellie appreciates his support but finds herself lost in thought, her mind racing with the possibilities of their quest. The enchantress is a figure of great power and mystery, and the prospect of facing her is both daunting and terrifying.

"I'm glad you came, Tristan..." Ellie admits, staring into his piercing ocean blue eyes. She realizes then, she truly means it.

He only stares back as the air between them seems to electrify once again. His gaze feels like lightning sparks dancing along her skin, making her want to shiver at the sensation.

Her mind then wanders back to Jace, the male she once loved. The pang in her heart blossoms again at the thought of him and what they had. She has tried not to think of it for days, allowing everything else happening around her to take center stage. *It was over, so heartbreakingly over*, she reminds herself.

Ellie blinks as she again takes in Tristan and his devastatingly handsome face. From the first moment she looked at him, she knew he was an exceptionally attractive male, and yet he was Kyla's. The thought makes her heart ache more than she cares to admit to herself. *Kyla is your best friend. Forget about him*, she reminds herself.

There was something about his silence, the way his gaze bore into every fiber of her being without a single word—a silent understanding that pulled her in each time.

His unwavering support and mild overprotectiveness is sometimes aggravating but still so comforting. It is qualities like those Ellie thought, sending a silent hope to the stars, that she too may one day have.

"I came for a reason, Ellie," Tristan admits, making Ellie turn her gaze back to his eyes.

"The truth is that I have come to truly care for you. I find my thoughts wandering to you often, wondering if you are hurting, happy, or smiling."

Ellie's eyes widened as his words soaked into her. She takes an unsteady breath, shaking her head slowly. "Tristan...," she begins, but he pushes on.

"What I feel for you is not something I can turn off. The stars know that I've tried. Honestly, I'm not sure when it even happened. I don't wish to be the kind of male who feels for another while courting someone else. But *this*, I can't deny, I don't *want* to deny it. Yet something tells me that I shouldn't," his gaze pierces her as she tries to force herself to keep breathing.

Ellie remains silent, contemplating before finally speaking. "No matter how you or I feel, I will never betray my best friend. And I mean, *never*," her words were sincere and final.

"I know and I would never ask you too..." his brows furrowed in contemplation.

"Please... just tell me I'm not the only one who feels this way." His voice wavers with hesitancy, the words like a fragile lifeline.

Ellie's heart slams against her chest like dragon wings in a storm, each beat painfully loud in her ears. She sees the raw plea in his eyes, a silent longing for her to give him something, anything, to match the chaos stirring in his ocean eyes.

His vulnerability tears at her, but she hesitates, her mind racing to her best friend. Her loyalty tightens like a chain around her heart, holding her back from stepping over a line she never wants to cross.

She swallows hard, the air thick between them, her pulse thrumming with uncertainty.

Finally, she lets out a quiet sigh, the only sound breaking the tension. Her lips curve into the faintest, most reluctant smile she can muster, a mere flicker of warmth. She sees the instant it hits him. The flicker of hope that ignites in his eyes nearly breaks her resolve, and for a moment, his face softens, relief washing over his expression, pulling a genuine smile from his lips.

But it's bittersweet. She can already feel the ache of what she didn't say tightening in her chest.

Ellie quickly clears her throat before saying, "We should get back. Do you mind?" Tristan gives her a slight smirk as he nods and slowly turns around.

Ellie internally kicks herself for her lack of control as she wades back towards the water's edge. Quickly dressing and occasionally looking over her shoulder ever so often to make sure he isn't looking. Once she's dressed and ready, Tristan follows suit. Ellie keeps her gaze towards the forest while she waits.

Once they begin to walk back to the campsite, Ellie hears a faint whimpering sound nearby. She follows the noise and discovers a small wolf pup with black and white fur tangled in a bush. The tiny creature looks up at her with wide, frightened eyes.

"Tristan, look," Ellie calls softly. "It's a baby wolf."

Tristan approaches and gently untangles the pup from the bush, noticing the streaks of blood on its coat, where it clearly struggles to unravel itself. The little wolf is clinging to his hand, trembling with fear. "We should take it back to camp," he suggests. "Maybe Kyla can help."

Ellie reaches out, running her hand along the back of the small pup, "It'll be alright little one, we've got you."

They return to the campsite, where Kyla is already awake and tending to the fire. Stella is stirring from sleep as Kyla looks at them, her eyes widening in surprise when she sees the wolf pup.

"Oh, you poor thing," Kyla coos, reaching out to take the pup from Tristan's arms. She quickly cradles the pup in her arms when her eyes glow orange as she concentrates, using her gift to communicate with the little wolf. "The poor thing must be scared and lost," she says after a moment. "It must have wandered away from its family."

"*We have company*," Saphirixia observes as the other dragons quickly get up and quickly begin to move.

Suddenly, a chorus of growls echoing through the forest, startling them all. A pack of a dozen giant wolves emerges from the trees, their eyes fixed on the group with a mixture of anger and suspicion.

Ellie and the others instinctively move closer together, preparing for a possible confrontation. She quickly notices how Tristan and Breccan move behind her, both rigid, drawing their swords from their sheaths. The loud growls from their bonded nearly shook the earth beneath their feet in warning.

Kyla steps forward, raising her hands in a gesture of peace. "Wait," her calm and soothing voice says.

She focuses on the lead wolf, speaking to it with her gift as her eyes glow. "We mean no harm. We found your pup and brought it here to help."

The lead wolf's growls soften, as it steps forward, sniffing the air as its gaze sweeps over each of them, eyes clearly weary due to the five dragons behind them. Kyla gently places the wolf pup on the ground, and it scurries over to the lead wolf, nuzzling against its leg. The tension in the air slowly dissipates as the wolves recognize the pup as one of their own.

With a final, grateful look at Kyla, the lead wolf turns and leads the pack back into the forest, the pup safely in tow. Ellie released a breath she didn't realize she was holding, relieved that the situation had been resolved peacefully.

"That was impressive, Ky," Tristan admits, with admiration in his voice.

“I hate wolves; they scare the shit out of me,” Breccan says as he runs his hair through his red hair, shaking his head.

Kyla smiles, her eyes twinkling with satisfaction. "Just doing what I can to help," she replies modestly with a slight shrug.

Ellie feels pride and gratitude for her friends. They are strong and capable, each with their own unique gifts, and she knows that together, they can face whatever challenges lay ahead.

The group gathers around the fire for breakfast, the atmosphere lightening after the tense encounter. They share stories and plans for the day, the camaraderie among them growing stronger with each passing moment.

After breakfast, they pack up their camp and prepare to continue their journey. Ellie can’t shake the feeling of unease that has settled in her chest, but she pushes it aside, focusing on the task at hand. As Ellie strides over to Saphirixia, Tristan falls into step beside her.

"Are you sure you’re okay?" he presses quietly, his concern evident.

Ellie forces a smile and nods. "I’m fine, Tristan. Just a bit overwhelmed, I guess."

He looks at her for a moment as if weighing her words before nodding. "If you ever need to talk, I’m here."

Ellie appreciates his offer but wasn't ready to open up yet. The weight of their mission and the uncertainty of what lay ahead presses heavily on her mind. She glances around and sees everyone climbing onto their dragons, waiting for them.

Ellie’s eyes catch Stella’s light blue eyes glowing brightly, staring at her, and she tilts her head, clearly reading her emotions. Tristan caught Ellie’s stare, and when his eyes met Stella’s for the briefest of moments, he strides away to Terbius. Stella only lifts her brow as her hazel eyes return, then she smirks at her. Ellie rips her gaze from hers and quickly climbs onto Saphirixia.

Ellie wraps her ungloved hand around the stone as she turns her body, waiting for the warmth of the stone to help guide her way. It begins glowing faintly as she faces North. She glances at Kyla, Breccan, Stella, and Tristan, and with a collective nod, they take to the skies, their dragons' powerful wings lifting them into the air.

The landscape below them unfolds into a breathtaking panorama. They soar over dense forests, the trees stretching endlessly beneath them like a green ocean. Rivers snake through the terrain, reflecting the morning sunlight like ribbons of silver. As they fly further, the forests give way to rolling hills and vast plains dotted with wildflowers.

Ellie guides them with the stone, its glow growing stronger as they fly. Hours pass as the land below gradually changes. They cross over a range of rugged mountains, their peaks capped with snow even in the warmth of spring. Beyond the mountains lay an expansive desert, its sands shimmering under the midday sun.

The heat is intense, but the dragons press on, their endurance and strength carrying them through. As the afternoon wanes, the desert becomes lush, fertile land again. They pass over vibrant forests and sprawling meadows, the scenery starkly contrasting with the harsh desert they had just left behind.

As the day wears on, they fly over the vast expanse of the ocean, the deep blue water stretching out to the horizon, the waves crashing rhythmically against the shore. The sea breeze is a welcome relief from the heat of the desert, and Ellie feels a sense of peace as they soar above the open water.

The sun begins to set, casting a warm golden glow over the ocean. Just as twilight descends, they spot land in the distance. They realize they have reached Avernus, another fae kingdom known for its enchanting beauty and mystical aura and also under Aetherlyn's rule. The coastline is dotted with cliffs and coves, and beyond that lay a dense forest interspersed with clearings and small rivers.

They land near a small river, close to the edge of the forest. The surrounding area is tranquil, with the sound of water flowing gently over rocks and the rustling of leaves in the evening breeze. Mountains loom in the distance, their peaks shrouded in mist.

"This looks like a good place to camp for the night," Tristan observes, dismounting from his dragon. The others follow suit, and they begin setting up their campsite. As they work, claiming the same duties as the night prior, the last light of day fades, and the stars begin to twinkle in the night sky.

Ellie still can't shake the feeling of unease within her chest, but she pushes it aside, focusing on the task at hand. The stone's guidance has brought them this far; she trusts it will continue to lead them true.

Once their camp is set up, they gather around the fire for dinner. The camaraderie and shared purpose among them made the night feel less daunting despite the challenges they know lays ahead. After their meal, they discuss their plans for the next day and the best route to continue their journey.

Stella leans in closer to Ellie, her voice low and concerned. "All your worrying is giving me anxiety," her eyes glowing light blue.

“I know, I'm sorry, Stells, I can't help it,” Ellie admits as she rubs her gloved hands over her face.

“You don't need to wear those with us, not here,” Ellie turns her gaze back to Stella, who nods to her gloves. Realization hit her that she was right. With her friends here, she didn't need to conceal her gift or worry about anyone being fearful of her gift. A small smile graces her face, and she lets out a soft sigh before she peels off her gloves and tosses them into her bag at her feet. Ellie allows the warmth of the fire to soothe her now sensitive skin, feeling free for the first time in a long time.

“I already know what you are going to say, but I want you to know if you want to talk about it, we can," Stella's voice is cautious but supportive.

Ellie feels confused by her statement until Stella gives a short, curt nod to Tristan. She tries to school her expression into neutrality the best she can, but she knows with her friend's gift, there is no reason to hide it. "He's courting Kyla, so no matter what you are sensing, it doesn't matter. I would never betray her."

Stella cocks her head to the side, giving her a sad smile. Ellie quickly turns her gaze back to the fire, hoping to change the conversation. "The curse, the enchantress, our fate, it's so overwhelming, Stells. But I know we must do this. For our people, for our future. I refuse to get distracted by anything or anyone, not right now".

Stella nods, her expression thoughtful. "We'll face whatever comes together. You're not alone in this."

"Until death?" Kyla says as she strides out of the trees and sits beside them, smiling and full of confidence.

Ellie appreciates her support and feels a bit more at ease with his reassurance. They both know the road ahead will be difficult and together, they feel prepared for whatever challenges they might face.

Breccan and Tristan whisper in hushed tones with Terbius and Vespero as Ellie looks over her shoulder. Sentiara, Kaida, and Saphirixia are still out hunting. Ellie figures there must not be many large animals for them to eat since they have been gone a while now.

"I wonder how angry our parents are that we left," Stella remarks quietly, pulling Ellie from her thoughts. They look at each other with wide eyes, imaging it as they burst out in laughter. Ellie feels some of the incessant tightness in her chest release with each moment of laughter they share. She realizes then, just how long it has been since she laughed like this.

"Well, there's not much we can do about that right now, is there?" Kyla quips, grinning widely.

Suddenly, Terbius's head snaps up, his nostrils flaring as he sniffs the air. Vespero followed suit, a low growl rumbling from deep within his chest.

"*Saph, something is in the forest...*", Ellie relays down their bond, as she places her hand on her sword strapped to her back.

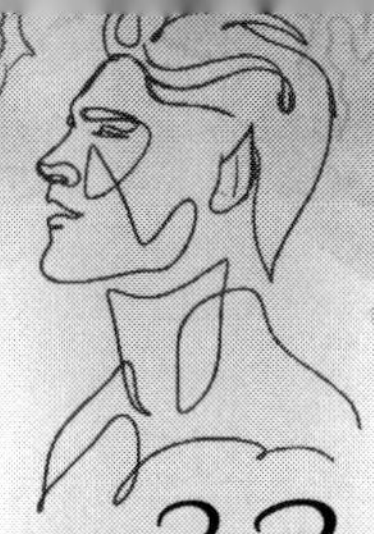

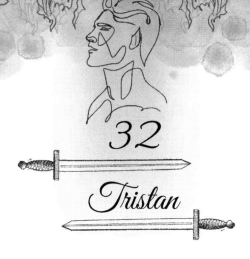

32

Tristan

Tristan and Breccan exchange a glance, their instincts immediately on high alert.

"What's wrong?" Breccan's voice is low and tense.

Terbius's eyes narrow, and he lets out a rumbling growl that resonates in Tristan's mind.

"*We have company...again*," Terbius communicates.

Tristan nods grimly. "Everyone, stay alert."

The females tense, their eyes darting around the dimly lit forest. The peaceful atmosphere of moments before is now replaced with a palpable tension.

The sound of rustling leaves and snapping twigs grow louder, and from the shadows, a group of thieves emerges, their swords and daggers glinting menacingly in the firelight. Ellie freezes, clearly counting the thieves, realizing, like himself, that they are severely outnumbered.

"Well, well, well, who do we have here?" a voice sneers from the shadows.

The leader of the thieves, a burly man with a scar running down his cheek, steps towards them. His eyes gleam with malicious intent as he looks them over and then draws his attention to their dragons. "*He's bold; I'll give him that. Very, very stupid but bold*," Tristan concludes.

"Hand over your weapons and any valuables you have. Then we *might* just let you and your dragons live," he demands, his voice cold and commanding.

His gaze settles on Ellie, noticing the sapphire necklace sparkling in the firelight that hangs around her neck. "Mmmm, look at that pretty little necklace. Hand it over."

Ellie instinctively clutches her necklace, her jaw clenching as she shakes her head. "Never."

The thief's eyes darken with anger. "Then I guess we'll just take it by force," he sneers.

"You can try", Ellie replies, her tone promising and lethal.

Tristan and Breccan move towards Ellie, their swords drawn, ready to fight. Kyla, though initially frightened, pulls her weapon, her face set with determination as her hand trembles. Terbius and Vespero rise to their full height, their eyes glowing as they prepare to defend their bondeds.

"Stay behind us," Tristan orders Ellie and Stella, his voice steady despite the chaos unfolding around them. Tristan notices Kyla's sword at the ready and he gives her a nod.

A dozen or more thieves lunge forward, their weapons flashing against the firelight as they attack. Tristan parries a blow aimed at his head, his sword clashing against one of the thieve's with a resounding clang. His muscles tense with the effort and the impact reverberates up his arm. While he is locked in one fight, he sees more thieves rushing towards them from his periphery, their faces twisted.

Tristan surges forward, knocking the thief off balance. He pulls back and thrusts, his blade finding its mark in his opponent's stomach. The thief's eyes widen in shock before he crumples to the ground.

Tristan sees that the approaching thieves have gained ground quickly and with a swift, practiced motion, Tristan waves his hand towards the campfire, directing the flames towards the advancing enemies. They shriek and flail wildly, as the fire engulfs them, the smell of burnt flesh quickly permeating the air.

Breccan engages another thief nearby, their blades dancing in a deadly duel. Each movement is calculated, and each strike is precise. Breccan expertly deflects blow after blow. Tristan admires his friend's skill, knowing they had trained for such moments.

One second, Breccan is swinging his sword in front of his enemy, and the next, he disappears and emerges behind his enemy, stabbing him in the back.

Still locked in a fight, Tristan steers his gaze to Kyla. She holds her ground close by, her weapon clutched tightly in her hands as she fights alongside them. Her blows have clear and precise aim, taking down several thieves that dared to approach. Terbius and Vespero roar, their powerful tails sweeping through the air and knocking several thieves off their feet. The two dragons' fiery breath illuminate the night, casting an eerie glow over the small open field. The thieves, though numerous, are no match for the combined might of their bondeds.

Terbius snaps his jaws, catching a thief by the leg, giving him a rough shake and then tossing him aside like a rag doll. Vespero's claws rake through another, leaving deep, fatal wounds.

Despite their best efforts, Ellie, Stella, and Kyla are struggling against the overwhelming number of thieves. Tristan's heart lurches when he hears Kyla cry out. He turns to see her stumble back, a thief's blade slashing across her arm, leaving a deep gash. She clutches her injured arm, her face contorted in pain.

Tristan is too far to reach Kyla in time, but he sees Ellie rushing to her aid. With a swift swipe of her sword, Ellie knocks Kyla's attacker to the ground and drives her blade into his chest, her eyes blazing with determination. Tristan feels a surge of pride at her bravery, but there is no time to dwell on it as he turns back and slashes his blade towards another opponent.

Despite her injury, Tristan can see out of the corner of his eye that Kyla continues to fight, her eyes burning with determination. Stella stays close to her, providing support and fending off any attackers who get too close. Tristan is still locked in his own fight with multiple attackers.

He hears Ellie scream and whips his head around to see her stumble back. Her hand is clutching her head while blood seeps through her fingers. Two of the thieves stand in front of her, grinning maliciously. One of them is clearly the leader and the other is a bulky fae male, probably one of the enforcers.

Tristan returns his attention to his opponent, desperate to finish him. The urge to help Ellie is so strong that he feels like his skin is on fire. Tristan swings his blade, cutting the male across his neck, he falls to his knees and drops his sword. He claws at his neck desperately, gasping for air.

When he finally turns to see Ellie again, she is facing off against the leader, a burly male

with a scar down his cheek. He lunges at her, his sword aiming for her heart. Ellie parries his attack, their swords clashing with a loud, metallic ring. They exchange blows, each strike more powerful than the last. Ellie persists, making it apparent that she is refusing to back down.

Suddenly, the sound of beating wings fills the air. Tristan looks up to see Saphirixia, Sentiara, and Kaida soaring toward them, their majestic forms silhouetted against the night sky. The dragons descend with deafening roars that shake the ground beneath their feet. Their breath scorches the ground as they unleash torrents of fire upon the thieves, who scatter in terror.

"You should've just given us the necklace," the leader sneers, his eyes filling with rage.

"It's not *yours* to take," Ellie shoots back, her voice steady despite the adrenaline that is surely coursing through her veins.

With a final, powerful swing, Ellie disarms the leader, sending his sword flying through the air. She follows up with a swift kick to his chest, knocking him to the ground. Before he can recover, Ellie places the tip of her sword against his throat, her eyes cold and unwavering, a side of her Tristan has never seen.

"Yield," she commands, her voice leaving no room for argument. She looks so fierce, like a true queen in her own right. Blood is dripping down her face and her eyes are locked on the male's shocked face.

The leader glares at her for a moment, then reluctantly nods, his face contorts with anger and defeat. Ellie steps back, keeping her sword trained on him as he slowly gets to his feet.

The dragons, sensing the ebbing resistance, redouble their efforts. Saphirixia's roar echoes through the clearing as she unleashes another wave of fire, driving the last of their assailants into a panicked retreat. Vespero and Terbius circle overhead, their watchful eyes ensuring no enemy escapes unscathed.

By now, the remaining thieves have either fled, been incapacitated, or killed. The campsite is littered with the bodies of the fallen, the air thick with the scent of sulfur and blood. Saphirixia, Sentiara, and Kaida land nearby, their massive forms casting long shadows over the small clearing.

Tristan sprints over to Ellie, his eyes keen as they scan her face. He finally settles on the fresh wound on her forehead. His expression darkens, a mix of fury and concern flashing across his features. Stepping closer, he gently tilts her chin up, examining the injury with a scrutinizing gaze.

"Which one of them did that to you?" Tristan demands, his voice as cold as ice, the warmth of his earlier words evaporating in an instant.

Ellie looks at him in surprise, and even some confusion just before her face softens into understanding. She lifts her blade and points towards a male sprinting towards the trees.

Tristan doesn't hesitate as he turns and sprints through the trees after the male. He's hot on his tail, running behind the male who peers over his shoulder, his face full of fear as he tries to outrun Tristan.

He goes for his dagger at his belt, and with trained precision, he lets his dagger fly. Hitting its mark, it lands right in the middle of the male's back. He crumples to the ground with a loud thud. Tristan thinks, *Pitiful.*

Tristan takes his time slowly striding up to him. He circles him slowly, his sword at the male's neck. "No one and I mean *no one* lays a hand on the princess," he snarls.

Leaning down he yanks his dagger out of the thieve's back. The male howls in pain and starts writhing in the dirt like a disgusting worm. Tristan takes a few steps back and reaches out to his bonded.

"*Terbius...*," Tristan communicates, calm and calculating.

A deep rumbling growl is Terbius' only reply as Tristan feels the wind from his strong wingbeats above him, rustling the leaves and tree branches around them.

"*Let him burn*," Tristan commands and turns away from the male, who's begging for his life in the dirt one last time. He walks away, refusing to acknowledge him.

A heartbeat later, Terbius lets out a scorching stream of fire, warming Tristan's back as he continues toward the campsite. The male's guttural scream echoes through the forest for a mere moment before falling utterly silent.

"No one touches the princess," Tristan says to himself as he walks away, smiling and without an ounce of regret.

Breaking through the trees, he sees Ellie holding onto Kyla's arm as Kyla winces from her touch. Ellie is inspecting her injured arm and seems to manage a small, determined smile.

"We need to get out of here." Tristan's voice cuts through the silence, "there might be more of them."

Breccan is standing in front of the now gagged and bound leader of the thieves, who's sitting against a nearby tree, thrashing against his restraints. Sentiara walks up to the male, her blue eyes glowing with fury. She releases a huff of smoke into the male's face, quickly silencing him as he stares at her in terror.

It is now that Tristan finally allows himself to breathe. He turns to Kyla, who's clutching her injured arm, blood seeps through her fingers. He rushes to her side, heart pounding with concern.

"Are you alright?" His every word laces with worry.

Kyla nods, though her face is pale. "I will be. It's just a scratch," she says, through the pain but her hazel eyes betray her every word.

"Let's patch you up, and get out of here." Tristan's tone is firm. She gives him a small smile in response.

As the others tend to Kyla and Ellie's wounds and gather their belongings, Tristan can't shake the feeling that this is only the beginning of their troubles. The night is calm, save for the occasional rustle of leaves and the distant call of nocturnal creatures, but Tristan knows better than to trust it.

"We need to move quickly," Tristan glances around at his companions. "Pack it up. We can't stay here any longer."

With determined nods, they pack up their camp swiftly, the dragons standing watchful guard. As they prepare to take flight once more, he strides over to Ellie, who's hunching over her bag near Saphirixia.

"How bad does it hurt?" he asks, his voice low and serious. She quickly glances up at him, her eyes piercing him and nodding slowly, hesitantly. When she stands, his eyes roam over her face, inspecting the blood now nearly dried on it. His hand instinctively approaches her face, but he abruptly returns it to his side before clearing his throat.

“You fought well, El, incredibly well,” Tristan admits, giving her a small smile. He hopes his words bring a smile to her face, but the only reaction Ellie gives him is another nod. Her eyes are distant and vacant, before turning back to packing her bag.

As they prepare to take off again, Tristan sees Ellie lift her stone necklace from under her jacket, its faint glow guiding their path. The moon casts the only light upon them as stars twinkle above them. The sight is almost enough to make Tristan forget the dangers that lay ahead.

They fly for hours, the wind whipping past them as they cross vast stretches of ocean. The water below sparkles against the moonlight, starkly contrasting against the chaos that they left behind. Tristan feels a sense of freedom in the open sky, though he remains alert, scanning the horizon for any signs of danger.

As time passes and the sun begins to rise, the landscape also changes. They pass over dense forests, their canopies a rich tapestry of green, and then over rugged mountains that rise like sentinels against the sky. Finally, as the sun sets, they cross the border into Avernus, a different fae kingdom that is nestled among the mountains.

They descend into a wooded area near a small river, the sound of the water a soothing backdrop to their landing. The location is heavily secluded, providing the perfect spot to set up camp for the night. As they dismount, Tristan can't help but feel a sense of relief. They have made it this far and he knows that they will continue to press on.

"Let’s set up camp here," Tristan's voice carries a note of resolve. "We’ll rest and then continue our journey at first light."

They all nod, everyone showing signs of both weariness and determination. They work quickly, setting up their tents and preparing to share dinner.

As night falls, the camp is bathed in the fire's soft glow, a beacon of warmth and safety in the dark. Their bonds remain close tonight; out of fear of another ambush.

Tristan sits by the fire, his thoughts racing as Breccan sits quietly beside him, reviewing the map in his lap. Ellie, Kyla, and Stella are sitting quietly eating, clearly all as tired as he is after their long day of flying.

Breccan's head pops up as he stares at them all, eyes wide. "What is it?" Ellie implores, concerned.

"If we continue on the path the necklace is guiding us, we could be crossing into the lands of Mystara," Breccan says with a gulp.

They have all heard of Mystara. It is known for its mists and the unknown creatures that lurk in the woods. Over the centuries, they had all heard stories of those who ventured into Mystara's woods and never returned.

Ellie's hand goes to her necklace almost instinctively, gripping it tightly in her hands. As if the thing could hear their every word, Ellie hisses and she quickly releases the necklace from her grasp, revealing the glowing sapphire stone against her chest.

"That's what I was afraid of," Breccan huffs as he tosses the map behind him.

Ellie looks at them all, "Mystara it is then."

33

Ellie

Ellie wakes, limbs feeling weightless as she peers into the frigid darkness. When did it get so cold? She wonders to herself.

She can see the warmth of her breath before her as the freezing air sends shivers over her skin. Ellie sits up and she can feel glass underneath her palms. To her shock, only a couple of yards in front of her, stands an old dark cottage hidden in the mists. Ellie sucks in a terrified breath knowing instantly where she is once again.

Fear makes its way up Ellie's spine the moment she hears the door of the cottage creak open. The slim figure of the enchantress, covered head to toe in her purple velvet cloak, strides her way. It is as if she is floating on air with an ominous darkness surrounding her.

She stops before Ellie and removes her hood. Her black hair falls freely around her shoulders. She smiles down at Ellie, a smile as venomous and cold as air around them. Once again, this female's presence exudes an aura of power and dark menace.

"What am I doing here?" Ellie asks unwaveringly, trying to express a confidence she didn't feel.

The enchantress's smile widens, a glint of amusement flickering in her eyes. "You know full well why you are here." She takes a step closer, her eyes locking onto the necklace around Ellie's neck. "My necklace that is now yours – will always call to me. Its power resonates through the very fabric of my vitality."

Ellie's hand instinctively goes to the jewelry, her fingers curling around its cool metal. "What do you mean, it will always call to you?"

"The necklace is a conduit, a gift I assure you. It is drawn to me because it is imbued with my magic. It wants to return to whence it was created. On the current matter at hand, however, the circumstance of you being here is a sign that your powers are beginning to manifest. Well done, I suppose."

Ellie's eyes widen, "My powers? Like, my own? But how?" She must be mistaken, Ellie speculates.

The enchantress's smile turns enigmatic. "Patience, my dear. All will be revealed in time. For now, you must wait until you return to my cottage. There, and only there, will you find the answers you seek."

Frustration wells up inside Ellie, "Why not tell me now? I'm already here. Why the secrecy?"

The enchantress's expression darkened. "There are rules, Little Princess. Rules that even I must follow. Speaking of such things as rules," her gaze shifts behind Ellie. "I do not approve of the company you keep on this journey. Your friends—they are a distraction. You are laying your weakness out on a platter for all to sample from."

Ellie's eyes narrow to slits, feeling anger surge within her, "They are my friends. They are with me to help."

The enchantress's eyes squint into a glare. "Help or hinder? Remember these words, Ellie. Trust is a precious commodity."

Ellie opens her mouth to protest, but the enchantress raises a hand, silencing her. "That is enough. Return to your slumber. We will speak once more when you arrive."

With that, the enchantress turns and glides back toward the cottage, her cloak billowing behind her. The door creaks open and she disappears into the darkness, leaving Ellie alone in the freezing night.

Ellie stirs from her uneasy sleep. She sits up, feeling the weight of the night's encounter pressing down on her. To her surprise she sees Kyla standing guard, her eyes sharp and vigilant.

"Kyla?" Ellie whispers, her voice hoarse.

Kyla turns, her expression softening. "Morning, El. Did you sleep all right?" She strides over and kneels at Ellie's side.

She shakes her head and begins rubbing her temples. Her thoughts still tangled with the very real dream. "Not really," she admits. "I had another... dream. Or whatever it is."

Kyla's brow furrows with what must be concern. "The enchantress again?"

Ellie continues as she nods. "She was talking about my necklace, saying that it was calling to her. She also said my powers are beginning to manifest."

Kyla's eyes grow wide with surprise. "Your powers? That is... that's huge, El! Did she tell you what our next step is?"

"Of course not," Ellie replies with a sigh. "She said that I have to wait until I reach her cottage. Oh, and she wasn't happy about you all being with me. She called you all a *distraction* and my *weakness*."

Kyla frowns, "A distraction? We're only here to help you. She clearly does *not* have any friends. Let alone know the first thing about friendship."

Ellie manages a small smile at that. "I told her the same thing. But she insisted that I be careful about whom I trust."

Kyla leans closer to Ellie, placing a reassuring hand on her shoulder. "We will figure this out together, El. No matter what that old coot says."

Ellie feels a surge of gratitude for her friend. "Thank you, Ky. I don't know what I would do without you, any of you, really."

Kyla squeezes her shoulder gently. "You're stronger than you think."

Ellie takes a deep breath, feeling a bit of her anxiety ebb away. "We should probably get moving. The sooner we arrive at the enchantress's cottage, the sooner we can get some answers from 'Miss Mystery'."

Kyla nods, "I'll wake the others and we should be ready to go in no time." Kyla strides off to rouse their companions.

Ellie takes a moment to center herself. Despite the fear and uncertainty that lingers from her encounter with the enchantress, she feels a flicker of determination. She will find out the truth about her powers, one way or another.

With the morning sun rising, casting a golden glow over the frosty landscape, the group gathers their belongings and sets off on their journey again. Ellie surveys each of her friends. She can see the weight of their journey on each of them. Everyone looks completely drained.

"*They are fine. They each chose to be here for you, for us,*" Saphirixia says into her mind.

"*I know, I just fear for them; they each have risked so much to come with us. I mean, for stars sake, they could have been killed yesterday,*" Ellie's shoulders sag as her mind brings her back to the fight with the thieves and how close they could have been to death.

"*This is a risk they are willing to take, El. If we succeed, your people's magic will be restored.*" Saphirixia's reassuring words rang true down to Ellies core.

She nods in agreement before continuing, "*I had a dream last night. The enchantress contacted me once again. She said my powers were manifesting...*"

"*Manifesting? You already grew into my power. I don't have any more gifts to share with you. That makes absolutely zero sense. Unless....*" Ellie's mind grows quiet, as her dragon seems to be processing the information.

"*Unless what?*" Ellie asks nervously.

"*Unless... you are manifesting your own magic, much like the fae's before the curse. That would only be possible if you are not restricted by the curse at all...*"

"*Well, that's an unnerving thought,*" Ellie contemplates that information and lets out an exasperated breath. After taking a couple of moments to soak in the possibility, she says, "*Let's not dwell on that too much, who knows... besides, we will find out soon enough when we make it to her.*"

Taking to the sky throughout the day, they fly over the vast forests. The group makes sure to stay clear of any towns or people. The dragons and riders remain mostly within Aetherlyn's territory. This way if anyone does happen to see them, they will immediately know who they are and where they fly from.

Once the mountains to the North are in sight, Ellie can make out the snow-covered peaks. Excitement builds within her as she takes in the towering beauty. It's so *high, they reach into the skies past the clouds.*

"*Once we pass them, we will be in* Mystara. *These mountains are impossible to navigate by foot. The only way to pass is by flying over them on a dragon.*" Saphirixia's voice startles Ellie, effectively breaking her focus from the view and moving her mind back to the task at hand.

She feels the bite of the frigid wind coming off the mountains as they climb higher, making her shiver and zip up her leather jacket to keep warm. She then tightens her grip around the necklace as it quickly warms underneath her fingertips.

"*It seems we're going the right way*," She states as her teeth chatter from the cold.

Peering down as they fly over the mountain peaks, the clouds make the view beyond them hard to see. After a couple of minutes, the clouds begin to disperse, and the view makes Ellie suck in a gasp.

The trees of the forest beyond are not lush like most of the kingdom, but a green so dark that they appear nearly black. Low hanging mist shrouds them, making the land look dark and ominous. Just like the enchantress's forest in her dreams.

"*We're close; I can feel it*," Ellie glances at her friends one by one, each giving her a weary and fearful glance in return. She nods at each of them, indicating that they are almost there. The sun is beginning to set, imitating a radiant glow as it descends past the mountains. "*Let's camp for the night, find somewhere to land, Saph*."

"*We're not safe here, El; there are strange creatures within this forest. I can smell them*," Saphirixia warns cautiously, going tense beneath her.

"*We don't have a choice; we'll find her tomorrow. For tonight, let's rest and regroup*."

Within minutes they find a clearing just large enough for them and their bondeds. They slide off their dragons and look around. Ellie squints, the thick mist making it nearly impossible to see past the surrounding trees.

"This place gives me the creeps," Breccan murmurs in a hushed tone as if too afraid to speak.

"I second that," Stella admits, walking over to Ellie.

"I third it," Kyla chimes in as she comes up next to Stella and grabs her hand in hers.

Tristan smiles briefly before saying, "Let's get a fire started and set up camp. The light will make it feel less foreboding. Tonight, two of us will guard and then rotate. There is no way only one of us will be left alone tonight. Stay vigilant, stay in pairs, and keep all your weapons on you."

They each nod in agreement as they get to work. Sentiara and Kaida fly off abruptly to scout for food for the dragons while Saphirixia stays behind. Tristan and Breccan leave for the woods to gather wood, while Vespero flies above with Terbius. Kyla and Stella remain at the camp alongside Ellie, going through their packs for food and laying out their blankets.

A sudden growl echoes through the clearing, snapping Ellie out of her reverie. She looks up, her heart pounding as two extraordinarily large creatures emerge from the woods. The monstrous cats are covered in dark fur. They have sharp-pointed ears, glowing dark eyes, and rows of sharp teeth gleaming in their massive mouths. Their sheer size is daunting.

"*Shadowfangs*," Saphirixia growls down their bond.

The creatures prowl slowly, their growls deep and menacing. Behind Ellie, Saphirixia slowly approaches, she seems much larger and is clearly readying for a fight.

Kyla steps forward, her voice steady. "I will try to speak with them."

She goes quiet, trying to communicate with the creatures. Kyla then turns to Ellie, her brows knitting in confusion. That's when Ellie knows that her friends' peaceful attempts are fruitless. Their growls grow louder and more threatening.

One of the creatures crouches, muscles tensing as it prepares to pounce. Its glowing red eyes fix on Ellie, clearly picking her as the target. Kyla turns back to them and raises her hands, trying once more to calm the beast, but it is useless. The Shadowfang is nearly the size of Saphirixia and equally as threatening.

Ellie watches as Tristan and Breccan emerge through the trees, their arms laden with wood. They freeze in place, eyes widening as they assess the Shadowfangs before them.

A sudden, strange surge of magic ripples through Ellie, sending electrifying sparks dancing across her skin. The world around her falls into an eerie silence, as if the air itself is being drained of all sound.

Every nerve in her body begins to hum with awareness, sensing the new magic around her. It's so close, so alive, almost as though it's reaching for her, beckoning, urging her to seize it. It feels terrifying and raw, yet somehow perfectly right, like a missing piece of her soul sliding into place.

A deep, primal instinct within her stirs, whispering for her to claim it, to weave it into her very being. Her heart races, and with a determined breath, she closes her eyes and allows the sensation to consume her.

Ellie reaches out, not with her hands but with her mind. She grasps onto the vibrant, pulsing thread of green magic that's flickering before her. The instant she touches it, the magic coils around her, clinging to her like a living thing.

A rush of energy surges through her body, igniting her veins with a fierce intensity. She inhales sharply, her chest expanding as the power floods her senses, filling her with an intoxicating, overwhelming strength. It's her strength now. Wild, untamed, and ready to be wielded.

Opening her eyes, she glares at the creature. Feeling more powerful than she ever has. Then, the creature lunges. Ellie focuses on it, and in an instant, she disappears, reappearing several yards away. She stumbles, trying to regain her balance. When she sees the beast land where she had been, it growls in frustration and turns to face her once more. Rows of teeth, sharp and ready to eat her alive.

Ellie feels a rush of exhilaration and a hint of fear. The creature prepares to attack again, so Ellie quickly grasps a pulsing red thread, *his power*, she realizes instantly. Warmth seeps into her, leaving tingles along her sensitive skin, strengthening her. She raises her hand, and a powerful gust of wind erupts, knocking thc creature off balance and sending it tumbling backward.

She stands there, eyes wide, in shock. She peers down at her hands feeling warmth radiating up her arms. She wills fire in her hands, much like she has seen Tristan do time and time again. Then, instantly flames engulf her hands. The warmth of the flame is like a warm comfort, not nearly as terrifying as she thought it would be. She peers back up at the Shadowfangs before her, eager and ready to wield his fire.

One of the Shadowfangs walks up beside the other, eye's assessing her. Ellie's heart thrashes in her chest like dark, mighty wings.

The creatures snarl, even angrier now, but before it can fully recover, Kaida and Sentiara land before her, shaking the ground beneath their feet, shielding and protecting her.

Without hesitation, the dragons unleash their own fire, streams of intense flames shooting towards the creatures. The fire cascades through the small clearing, a brilliant display of power that lights up the darkness around them. The creatures howl in pain and fear, scrambling to escape the searing heat. They turn back into the woods, their howls fading into the distance.

Frozen, her heart racing, Ellie's hands shake as the adrenaline slowly vanishes along with the flames. She looks to her friends, who are equally breathless and wide-eyed.

"Ellie," Tristan steps forward, his voice firm, "What did you just do?"

Ellie nods, eyes wide, still processing what had just happened.

"I... I felt each of your powers. I don't know how, but I just knew that I could wield it."

Breccan grins widely, "Looks like you are more powerful than any of us realized. Your eyes even glowed green, like mine! You are a badass, Princess!"

Saphirixia approaches her, her expression a mix of pride and concern. "*It seems the enchantress was correct. But be cautious when tapping into other's gifts, El. With great power also comes great danger.*"

Ellie takes a deep breath, feeling a newfound confidence, only nodding at Saphirixia in understanding.

Kyla wraps an arm around Ellie's shoulders. "That was incredible! I've never heard of anyone with the ability to wield other's magic."

"Me either...," Ellie admits cautiously as Kyla wraps her in her arms. Ellie's gaze finds Tristan's over Kyla's shoulder as he sheaths his blade across his back. As if drawn by her gaze, he lifts his head, peering back at her, eyes capturing hers. He only smiles briefly, pride shining in his eyes. Once he releases her gaze, he turns towards Terbius.

With the threat gone and the presence of everyone's gifts gone from within her, Ellie feels something she has never felt before with her magic: empty and utterly drained.

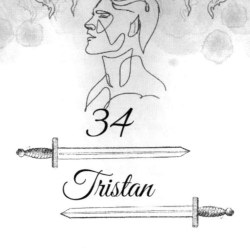

34

Tristan

"Can we speak? *Privately*," Kyla requests cocking an eyebrow and leveling her eyes at him.

"Of course," Tristan replies with a small smile. Kyla strides off into the woods and he reluctantly follows close behind.

With one last glance over his shoulder, he sees Breccan watching him as Ellie and Stella sit by the fire, talking and smiling. They seem to be wrapped in conversation with one another.

She stops and turns around to face him as she crosses her arms and takes a loud breath. "I know we rushed into things in the beginning, but you are the one who said you wanted to be with me." Kyla presses sternly, "What's changed?"

Her question freezes him in place. *She's nothing if not, brutally blunt*, he thinks. Tristan tries to find a response, any response, but comes up empty. He reaches for her hand. She notes his attempt, yet instead of taking his hand, She uncrosses her arms and pulls her hand behind her back. She keeps her inquiring stare on him.

"I like you, Ky. I really do. I just think that it would be better to discuss this once we return to Aetherlyn. Now isn't the time...," Tristan's voice is low yet cautious.

"It is the time actually. You have barely spoken to me in days. You're distant, quiet, and have made no attempt to show me any affection whatsoever," Kyla's voice is as sharp as daggers cutting into him. He can even see that her cheeks and the tips of her ears are getting red with her anger in the darkness.

Tristan internally winces at her words, knowing her observation is correct. He has made no attempt to show her care, check on her, or be alone with her while they have been gone... or really even before they left on this journey.

"I know, and I'm sorry. My concentration has been on this journey and my duty," Tristan says honestly.

"I see the way you look at her, you know. I saw how you ran after the thief who hurt her. You may care for me Tristan, but I'm not blind; I'm not the only one that you care for," unshed tears lining her eyes.

Tristan runs his hands through his hair, pulling at the ends while an internal battle rages within him. He knows he can't lie to her but he also feels that he can't tell her of his conflicting feelings. He shifts on his feet, knowing it is best to be honest.

"I don't know how I feel..." he admits softly, with an exasperated breath, as he glances at her again, noticing a lone tear on her cheek.

"I really am sorry, Ky. I don't wish to have feelings for anyone but you." Tristan's chin dips as he peers down at the ground, trying to find the words.

"Please don't say anymore. I don't wish to hear it," Kyla responds as his gaze meets hers once again. She shakes her head, more tears streaming down her face. "I think it would be best if you figure out how you feel. This is not fair to any of us, and I can't be with you while you do."

Kyla's words feel like a gut punch. She wipes the stray tear from her face, squaring her shoulders, then gives him a curt nod before striding past him back to the campsite without another word.

Tristan stands there as he runs his hands over his face, feeling like a complete and utter fool. He knows he must be the biggest idiot for allowing her to walk away. Yet, he didn't try to stop her. Kyla is kind, strong, beautiful, and he feels that he could be happy with her. She's the first female he's felt like he could be happy with in years. The problem is that he can't stop the voice inside of him telling him to allow her to walk away from him.

With a loud sigh, he strides back to the campsite where the group sits, still smiling and talking. Kyla's bright smile indicates no hint or sign of their previous conversation. Breccan meets Tristan's gaze. Standing, he walks over to Tristan, crossing his arms, unable to force even a fake smile onto his face.

"What was that about?" Breccan asks, voice full of concern as he jerks his chin towards Kyla.

"She told me to figure out how I feel and that she won't be with me while I do it," Tristan admits uncomfortably.

"You know, you can't blame her. We all see how you look at her, Tristan. You aren't as subtle as you may think," Breccan replies with a smile. He shoves Tristan, "I get it. She's a princess and beautiful, and with those new powers, she will be unstoppable. Sheesh!"

"*I told you not to even think about it*," Terbius gives him a low growl from behind Breccan, eyes narrowing in warning.

"*I know, I know, she's just...*" Tristan shakes his head, then stops before the words can fully form and turns his attention back to Breccan. "I don't want to talk about this; let's get back so that they can sleep."

When they reach the campfire, Ellie, Kyla, and Stella are still talking as he and Breccan sit across from them. Kyla only briefly lets her gaze meet his before returning to her friends.

Tristan's gaze finds Ellie's beautiful face, her smile genuine and bright with her friends. Reverting his eyes, he gazes into the fire in silence, allowing the conversation around him to wade on.

He stared into the fire, the dancing flames casting flickering shadows across his face. The warmth was a small comfort against the chill of the night, but his mind is far from the present moment. His thoughts run wild, carried away by the memories and emotions that are surging within him.

He remembers the first time he met Ellie. She had been curious and kind to him, a spark of determination that had intrigued him. Ellie had been braver, more inquisitive than any other female he had ever met. She had said things no one else had ever said to him before, and a fire in her matched the one before him now.

As the flames flicker, Tristan's thoughts drift to how they had come to be in this moment, surrounded by their friend and facing dangers that seem to grow with each passing day. It had been a journey fraught with challenges, but through it all, Ellie had remained a constant source of strength and inspiration. She had a way of making them believe that anything was possible, that she could indeed break the curse among their people.

Tristan's mind wanders to the moments they have shared together. There were times when he had seen her laugh, her eyes crinkling at the corners, and her laughter had been like music to his ears. He remembered the late-night conversations under the stars, where she slowly chipped away at the fortified walls he built around himself. Those moments have forged a connection between them, a connection he never wanted but knows that will not break easily.

He can't deny the feelings that have grown within him over time either. His heart clenches in his chest, realizing that his feelings for Ellie have deepened into something more dangerous than friendship. He craves her, his every instinct screaming at him to be near her, to be the one she turns to when the world gets too heavy. It's not just about caring for her anymore; it's the overwhelming need to touch her, to feel her warmth next to his, to claim a part of her that no one else can touch, her soul.

But then there was Kyla, too. Tristan's thoughts turn to her, to the memories that *they* have made together. She is strong and capable, and he admired her greatly. Their bond is considerably different from the one he shares with Ellie, but it's no less significant. Kyla has been there for him, made him happy at times, and their connection was growing.

The fire crackles and Tristan sighs, running a hand through his hair. It's impossible to ignore the conflict within him any longer. He cares deeply for Ellie and Kyla, but his feelings for Ellie are undeniable. A force he can't ignore or forget. It has grown and blossomed in ways he never expected, and he can't push them aside any longer.

As he sits there, lost in thought, Tristan makes a silent promise to himself. He will once again tell her how he feels, only this time he hopes that she reciprocates his feelings.

The journey ahead is uncertain, but one thing is clear, his feelings for Ellie are real, and they are not going away.

Tristan's gaze remains fixed on the fire, the warmth of the flames mirroring the warmth in his heart when her voice pulls him from his thoughts.

"Tristan are you okay?," Ellie asks sweetly as all of their friends turn to look at him.

He quickly clears his throat before saying, "Just tired."

Stella instructs, "You and Breccan get some sleep; we can stay awake for a while."

Tristan nods and gives her a small smile in thanks before getting up and lying on the cold bedroll. He wastes no time closing his eyes, hoping sleep will claim him soon.

35

Ellie

The forest is cold and Ellie finds it difficult to stay warm, shivering in her jacket and thin blanket. After the day they all had, she didn't really want to sleep. Honestly, she didn't think she could sleep even if she tried. Realizing that she now possesses a new gift had her mind reeling with possibilities and what this would mean for her and for Saphirixia.

Kyla fell asleep by Breccan, Tristan, and their dragons. She had noticed Kyla's fake façade after she returned from her conversation with Tristan. The thought of her friend hurting on top of the fact that she may be a reason for her friend's pain, made her sick to her stomach.

She kept reminding herself that she never intentionally tried to hurt her. She really did try to stay away from Tristan, but it's as if an invisible thread is tying them together, unrelenting and unwavering.

She refuses to put her happiness above Kyla's. A part of her hopes that she and Tristan can work through it. Maybe his feelings for Ellie were fleeting. Except, that thought makes Ellie wince unconsciously. When she peers over at Stella, her eyes are glowing brightly in the darkness, sensing every feeling flooding through her.

"Do you want to talk about it now?" Stella probes, voice barely above a whisper. Ellie only shakes her head, glancing at Kyla's sleeping form.

Ellie ultimately decides to get up and she strides over to the log that Stella is sitting on plopping down. Stella continues, whispering softly, “I have sensed how much he cares for you and you for him,” she takes a deep breath, “I will admit that I have never sensed emotions as strong as his are for you; it's quite… unnerving. I imagine that he would have gladly sacrificed himself to protect you if he could.”

“Okay, but that is literally his duty, Stella…,” Ellie explains with a shrug, trying to brush the thought away.

“That’s where you’re wrong, El. It's not because of his duty that he protects you and cares for you as he does. It may have been the reason initially, but not any longer. If you don’t believe me, then you should try wielding my gift to see for yourself that what I say is true, or better yet, use your own gift,” Stella whispers as she looks over her shoulder, checking to see if everyone is still resting peacefully.

Ellie shakes her head at the thought, “I could never….”

“If you were not meant to use the powers you were gifted, you wouldn't have them,” Stella says firmly. “Try wielding my power; there is no better time than the present to practice.”

Ellie considers this, knowing that Stella is only being supportive and trying to help. She lets out a ragged breath and then closes her eyes. At first, nothing happens; after many failed attempts, she can’t sense any power around her.

“Keep trying; you got this, El. I’m right here,” Stella whispers softly with encouragement.

Her eyes remain closed, and she concentrates once again. Ellie feels a sudden spark of power around her, like pulsing threads, waiting to be held. When she mentally grasps the magic around her, she feels familiar sparks tingling up her body once again.

When she opens her eyes, Stella’s eyes go wide. “Your eyes are glowing. Do you feel it?”

She can sense it, the immense joy radiating off of her friend and pride. Her emotions give off colors, and Stella looks beautiful, glowing with soft yellow light around her.

"I never knew you could see colors," Ellie exclaims with surprise. She finds it hard to keep her voice low due to her own excitement and joy as it floods through her.

"Oh yes, all the colors. Yellow for happiness, hopefulness, and even joy. Blue, of course, if someone is hurt, sad, or worried. Red for anger or frustration. And pink for love, infatuation, even lust. It took me a while to figure out all the colors, but now, it's easy to see and feel their emotions," Stella explains proudly.

"Is that why I feel like this?" Ellie points to her own face, where she can't help the smile that is plastered there.

"Yes, if you use my gift for more than a minute or so, you'll feel the same emotion as the one you are concentrating on. It can be very overwhelming as you can see," Stella admits, her words a warning that Ellie didn't miss.

Ellie quickly closes her eyes again, releasing her mental hold on Stella's power. Once the sparks along her skin finally dissipate, she speaks again, "That was amazing, Stells! Thank you so much for sharing that with me."

Stella's smile beams brighter as she scoots closer to Ellie, wrapping her arms tightly around her in a firm hug.

"Until death," Stella whispers, making Ellie smile brighter. She knew she was radiating that same yellow light right now.

For the rest of the night, they spoke quietly about how easy life was when they were younger and all the challenges they had endured.

It was still the middle of the night when Tristan rose from sleep, rubbing his hands along his face, clearly still exhausted. "Are you both good?" Tristan asks.

Stella responds. "All good. I'm just glad you are awake so we can get some sleep."

Tristan smiles brightly, then turns towards Breccan and kicks him in the leg, startling him. "Get up; it's our turn," Breccan grumbles but gets up quickly.

"You ladies get your beauty sleep," Breccan sheaths his blade along his back, smirking at them.

"They don't need beauty sleep," Tristan replies with a wink that sends a flutter right through Ellie.

"Aw, aren't you sweet...," Stella chimes back, rolling her eyes, as she lays on her blanket.

Ellie only chuckles at their banter as she lays down on her bedroll, gazing up at the night sky, waiting for sleep to come. Eventually, a calm slumber takes her.

Ellie wakes to Breccan's cheery voice: "Time to get up, Princess. Today's the day!"

Ellie groans loudly, tempted to throw a nearby rock at his head. His over-exuberant tone was far too much for her this early in the morning.

As she sits up, her muscles protest; the hard ground is unforgiving on her body. She looks around to see that everyone is already awake and preparing to leave.

Pushing herself up and groaning, she reaches out to her bonded, "*Saph, will you come with me?*"

Ellie then turns to see Saphirixia peering at her with brilliant blue eyes as she nods slightly and rises to meet her.

Ellie says to no one in particular, "I will be back."

Once they make their way to the small river, she had seen the day before. She kneels on the river's edge and takes a deep breath.

"*Are you ready, Saph? Because I'm not sure that I am,*" Ellie questions as she scoops up some water into her bare hands and splashes her face.

"*I don't think we can ever truly be ready for what is to come, especially when we do not know what is waiting for us,*" Saphirixia's tone is almost somber in her mind.

Rustling of tree branches can be heard behind them. Ellie turns and sees Tristan's broad form push through the trees, his face soft and gentle, and his gaze automatically finds hers.

Ellie turns back to Saphirixia, understanding with a simple look. Saphirixia pushes off the dirt and shoots into the air, heading back to the campsite. She can feel his gaze upon her back, continuing to wash her face in the water.

"How are you feeling?" he asks as he crouches down next to her, scooping up water to wash his own face and then running water through his dark hair.

"Now that we're almost there, I feel more scared than ever," she admits anxiously as she finally returns his gaze. Tristan's eyes bore holes in her soul. As if he is trying to communicate unspoken words that he is holding back from saying.

"I know you can protect yourself; you've proven that. Even so, I'll be there, right behind you, ready to protect you should you need me," a genuine smile breaks across his face. It accentuates his dimples and it makes Ellie's heartbeat quicken.

Tristan's hand gently brushes her wild hair from her face and tucks a strand behind her ear. She feels the air leave her lungs as he stares at her face. The air between them once again electrifies, leaving sparks along her body, heightening her senses. He grasps her other hand in his, surprising her, he wraps his large fingers around hers.

"I could never, not even for a single second, forget how incredible you are. You and Saphirixia have got this," his words brimming with honesty.

Ellie feels her heart racing, the air around them is thick with unspoken emotions. Tristan breaks their gaze, his hand lingering on her face for a moment longer before standing up slowly, almost hesitantly. He pulls her to her feet, his warm touch reassuring.

"*You were born for this Ellie, out of everyone, you are the most capable,*" he says softly within his mind for only her to hear, "*It's time to start looking for the enchantress.*"

Ellie nods, squeezing his hand in silent agreement before quickly releasing it. Together, they walk back through the forest, the sounds of the wilderness enveloping them. The path is familiar, yet each step seems to bring new uncertainties.

Tristan's presence beside her is a comfort, a steady anchor amidst the swirling chaos of her thoughts.

When they approach their camp, the smell of burning wood and the faint hum of conversation reaches their ears. The others are already gathered, their faces etched with a mixture of worry and anticipation. Saphirixia lands gracefully near the fire, her wings folding elegantly behind her as she acknowledges their arrival.

"We need to be cautious," Tristan reminds, addressing the group. "The enchantress is powerful and unpredictable, we know next to nothing about her."

Saphirixia's eyes glimmer fiercely as he speaks. Ellie swallows hard, feeling the weight of their expectations. She glances at Tristan, who gives her a reassuring nod. "I'm ready," her voice steady despite the tremor in her heart. "Let's do this."

The group gathers supplies and prepares to set out, each member falling into their roles with practiced efficiency. Ellie feels a surge of determination. This is what they were born for, what they have risked everything for. She refuses to let fear hold her back now.

Once they are in the air, Tristan and Terbius stay close as they fly over the forest, his presence a constant reminder of his unwavering support. Breccan is on her other side, Stella is just behind, and Kyla is beside her, holding up the rear.

Less than fifteen minutes later, Ellie places her hand over the necklace, it quickly warms her palm and reassures her that they are going in the right direction. Suddenly, the stone feels cold in her hand, almost like ice.

Ellie glances around. Never had the stone gone cold. The realization hits her then: *We're here*, and the cold of the stone begins seeping into her veins. As she continues to peer around through the trees, she sees smoke coming through the treetops. As they get closer, she sees the cottage's rooftop.

She quickly glances around at her friends, they are all giving her the same weary and nervous face she knows she is giving them. They know that they made it. Taking one last deep breath, Saphirixia veers towards a wide enough clearing for them all to land.

Once they dismount from their dragons, they huddle together. Ellie is nervous, but Kyla and Stella's bright smiles and silent nods of encouragement gave her the strength she so desperately needed.

"You got this, Princess; we've got your back, too," Breccan encourages, lacking his usual casual humor. Tristan only nods in agreement with his friend, eyes never wavering from hers.

Ellie turns to the dragons surrounding them. "*Saph, you and Terbius follow us. Sentiara, Kaida, and Vespero stay close by and keep guard.*" Saphirixia only nods in agreement, then peers at the others, communicating her orders. Each of the dragons then locks eyes with their bonded, clearly communicating the same order.

"Let's go," Ellie turns and walks in the direction of the cottage, each step feeling like a challenge. Saphirixia's steady footsteps to her side and her friends behind her bring her a small comfort. Once they breach the tree line surrounding the cottage, they all halt, taking in the dark, eerie cottage.

"Is this really it? It's quite terrifying...," Stella's voice barely above a whisper.

"Do we knock? I'm not even sure how we're supposed to approach the most powerful enchantress that has ever lived," Kyla urges, whispering next to Stella just loud enough for us all to hear.

"We have come this far, there is no way we're stopping now," Breccan states with determination as he shoves past them, striding towards the door. Ellie looks at the dark cottage, smoke still coming out of the chimney, dead trees, and bushes under the small dark windows. The whole cottage looks worn and nearly unlivable.

A bit of an odd choice for such a powerful being. Ellie thinks. Although, the enchantress has certainly found the perfect place for someone who clearly didn't want to be found.

Kyla and Stella clasp their hands together and quickly jog to catch up with Breccan, who is already almost at the door. Tristan stays, still and quiet, behind her. Ellie takes one last deep breath before a gentle hand skates along her spine, a reassuring touch.

Tristan whispers softly into her ear, "This is yours and Saphirixia's fate. Walk up there and show that enchantress who you are." His voice is calm and supportive yet determined. His breath leaves a warmth along her ear that runs down her arm, making her hold back a shiver.

Breccan's voice breaks through her thoughts: "Come on, Princess!" Ellie finally moves and heads towards the door. When she is about ten steps away from her friends, the large wooden door abruptly swings open with a loud creak and the enchantress stands in the doorway, making everyone freeze in place.

Wearing her velvet purple cloak, the enchantress has long black hair falling over her shoulder, white skin that looks porcelain, and dark obsidian eyes. Breccan, Stella, and Kyla look as if they aren't breathing. The enchantress doesn't even glance at them, her eyes unmoving as she stares at Ellie. A malicious grin graces her face. She is clearly amused by their radiating fear.

Ellie straightens her back, the enchantress noting each movement. She walks further out her door, past her friends, and right up to Ellie. Tristan remains silent behind her. If he was nervous, even in the slightest, his movements didn't show it.

Ellie lifts her chin as the Enchantress studies her for a moment before speaking, "Come." She quickly turns back towards the house before speaking over her shoulder, "Just *you*, Ellissandra. I'm afraid Saphirixia will not fit."

Ellie could've sworn that dark shadows trailed behind her as she walked inside her cottage, leaving the door open for her. Her friends stared at her with wide eyes, each unmoving and unsure of what to do.

"You got this, El." Stella reaches out to grab Ellie's hand and gives her a reassuring squeeze, smiling softly. Ellie takes one last deep breath before following the enchantress into the dark cabin.

As she walks into the cottage, the scent of incense burning invades her senses. Candles are lit and strewn around the entire room, and a fire in the fireplace warms the space. In the middle of the fire is a large cauldron bubbling with some kind of soup that smells so good that Ellie's stomach growls loudly as she shifts her stance.

Additionally, there are two dark velvet purple couches, along with a round table in the middle littered with books and tomes. The space is so dark that everything about it makes her feel uncomfortable, screaming for her to leave.

The enchantress stands there observing her, her head cocked to one side, eyes never leaving hers. Fear begins to climb up Ellie's spine. The enchantress stalks over to the sofa and sits, her dark shadows surrounding her.

"Sit. We have much to discuss," she says as Ellie hesitantly puts one foot in front of the other and slowly sits across from her, watching her cautiously.

She remains silent for long moments until she raises her hand, points a sharp black fingernail towards her, and crooks her finger. The next second, Ellie's blue sapphire stone necklace is ripped from her neck and flies into the Enchantress's waiting hand. She smirks as she stares at the stone in her hand. It begins to glow brightly, responding to her magic. The blue light illuminates her face, casting a blue hue around the room.

"Relax, Ellissandra. You are in no danger, well... *right now*," she purrs.

Ellie tries to form words but finds that she has none. So, she sits there, instead watching her intently and attempting to figure out what she is doing. The enchantress closes her eyes, muttering words slowly under her breath, clearly using her malicious magic. When her eyes snap open, her eyes glow blue, no longer black as midnight, and the stone's light flickers out, like a match.

"What... What did you do?" Ellie asks, stuttering, unable to hide her confusion and fear.

"The day I felt the birth of you and Saphirixia, I imbued this stone with my magic. Just enough magic to help you find me and just enough magic to help you find your own magic as well. I am simply giving it another... boost if you will," the enchantress admits, tone flat, no emotion in her words, just facts.

Ellie can feel the question that she has been dying to know for as long as she can remember brimming at the surface. "Why did you curse the lands in the first place? Why curse fae magic?"

The fire crackles softly in the hearth, casting flickering shadows on the walls of the small, dark cottage. Across from her, the enchantress begins her tale, her voice resonating like an ancient, haunting melody.

"Over a thousand years ago, two powerful kings ruled over vast and magnificent realms. King Alaric of Aetherlyn and King Cedric of Draegon. An insatiable hunger for power consumed both kings. Their hearts blackened by greed and malice, they sought to control their own lands but also the entire realm."

Ellie leans in closer, captivated by the enchantress's story.

"The war that ensued was unlike any other," the enchantress continues. "It spanned decades, ravaging the lands and claiming the lives of hundreds of thousands of fae and magical beings. The once-lush forests were reduced to charred wastelands, and the sparkling rivers ran red with the spilled blood. Both kings unleashed dark and terrible magics upon their enemies, caring little for the destruction they wrought upon their own people."

Tears line Ellie's eyes as she imagines the suffering and chaos. The enchantress's voice grows softer, tinged with sorrow.

"As the war dragged on, I watched in horror as the realm crumbled. I saw the faces of the innocent, their lives shattered by the greed of two males. I could no longer stand by and do nothing. So, I made a fateful decision."

The enchantress pauses, her eyes reflecting the weight of her choice. "I cast a powerful curse upon the land, stripping away the magic that had once flowed freely through the veins of the fae. The enchantment was strong, so strong that it brought an end to the war. It also meant that the fae, who had relied on their magic for centuries, were left powerless, vulnerable."

Ellie gasps. "But why would you do that? Didn't the loss of magic hurt the fae too?"

"Yes, it did," the enchantress admits, her voice heavy with regret. "Unfortunately, it was the only way to stop the senseless slaughter. Without magic, the kings could no longer wage their destructive war. Peace, though fragile, began to take root. However, King Alaric of Aetherlyn, driven mad by the loss of *his* power, ordered the massacre of the enchantresses throughout his kingdom, desperate to find the one that had cursed the land."

A shiver runs down Ellie's spine as she realizes the danger the enchantress must have faced.

"I went into hiding," the enchantress admits softly. "I watched from the shadows as the kingdoms slowly began to heal over the centuries. The lands, once scorched and barren, began to flourish again. Though they no longer possessed magic, the fae found new ways to thrive. And so, I waited, knowing that one day, a bonded pair would come who could restore balance to the realm."

Ellie looks up at the enchantress, her heart pounding with a mixture of fear and hope. "And that bonded pair is us?"

The enchantress smiles, a glimmer of warmth and hope in her eyes. "Yes. You are the ones that I have been waiting for. It is time for the realm to be healed, for magic to be restored." She sighed slightly before continuing. "However, that cannot come to be until you *both* prove that you are worthy, prove that your hearts are pure and strong, that your bond unwavering."

Ellie nods, determination shining in her eyes. "How do we do that?"

The enchantress cocks her head to the side again, eyes narrowing, studying her once again. "You will be put through trials and tested."

"Trials?" Ellie croaks out, completely confused.

"How will we be tested?" Ellie asks cautiously, knowing from the malicious grin on her face that it will not be easy.

"Why is it that both Saphirixia and I must break the curse? Why a dragon and a fae bonded?" That part of the prophecy always confused her.

"A thousand years ago, I had a bonded," she admits slowly then continues. “Not like the bonded that you have, but I did have my own bonded. She was my dearest companion; we grew up together much like you and Saphirixia have. She was killed fighting for King Alaric of Aetherlyn, and it was her death and the grief of losing her, along with the death of the hundreds of thousands of others, that brought me to curse the lands.”

She sighs, eyes peering down at her clasped hands, the necklace still inside her palm. Ellie only sits, processing every word that she has spoken.

She continues, “Centuries ago, your great-grandfather found a way for faes to gain magic through a bonded using magic from the few remaining witches in existence. And it has remained so for centuries.”

Ellie nods slowly, understanding. If she ever lost Saphirixia, she didn't know what she would do. Losing her mind in grief the way the enchantress did, didn't seem like unreasonable thought.

The fire crackles, filling the silence as they sit. Ellie tears her gaze from the enchantress and sees darkness through the window. How long had they been talking?

“Have you been alone all of this time?,” Ellie asks cautiously. The enchantress visibly stiffens at her question. She only shrugs slightly before fixing her gaze back at the fire.

“I'm so sorry for the loss of your bonded. I couldn't imagine life without Saphirixia; I hope I never have to,” Ellie admits, wincing at her words. The enchantress's gaze meets hers again, squinting a little, processing her words, and then she nods slightly.

It’s obvious that she has been alone for so long, she almost seems uncomfortable with Ellie’s presence.

The enchantress stands abruptly and walks towards the fire, her shadows following her. “I will send the stew to your camp for you and your friends,” the enchantress says, waving her hand, and the entire cauldron disappears.

“Tomorrow, you will begin your trials. It will not be easy, so get some rest,” the enchantress says, her final words dismiss Ellie. She still has so many more questions, but she wanted to see Saphirixia and her friends right now, eat, and rest.

The enchantress strides over to her, bringing her hand out before her. She holds the necklace between her long, dark fingernails.

“This is yours,” she lifts her chin slightly with the tiniest of smiles on her face before dropping the necklace into Ellie’s hand. With a quick wave of her hand, the door flies open.

“Thank you,” Ellie whispers, then she turns and walks out. The second she steps outside, the enchantress says, “Welcome to the beginning of your true journey,” her voice echoing ominously. Then, with one last wave of her hand, the heavy wood door slams shut behind her, leaving Ellie standing there, utterly frozen and confused.

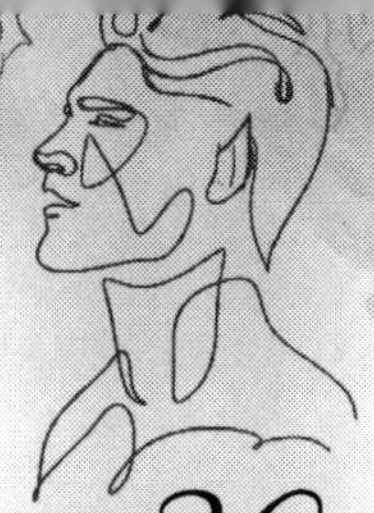

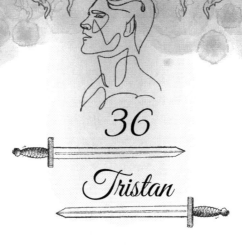

36

Tristan

Tristan stands outside the enchantress's cottage, the chilly air biting through his cloak. The eerie atmosphere around the dark, dilapidated structure sends chills down his spine, but he remains steadfast. Ellie had gone inside alone, to face the enchantress. He couldn't bring himself to leave, even after the others had left to make camp nearby. His heart won't allow him to abandon her, not when she needs him the most.

The forest's silence presses in on him, broken only by the occasional rustle of leaves or the distant call of a night creature.

Tristan's thoughts are a storm, swirling with fear and concern for Ellie. He can't shake the image of her brave face as she stepped through the door. He admires her courage, but it also terrifies him.

He paces back and forth in front of the cottage, his mind replaying every detail of the moments that they have shared: the way her eyes sparkle when she laughs, the strength she shows in the face of danger, and the softness of her touch when she tries to comfort him.

She has become someone that he can't bear to be apart from. Whether he likes it or not, the physical distance between them now feels like a taut cord pulling at him. He will do anything to protect her, even if it means standing guard outside of this ominous place all night.

As the minutes pass into hours, Tristan's anxiety grows. *What is happening inside? Is she safe?* He wonders as he imagines the worst scenarios, each one more terrifying than the last.

His fists clench at his sides; his nails dig into his palms. He can't lose her, not now, not ever. The bond they share is too strong, and he can't bear the thought of a world without her in it.

The moon rises higher in the sky, casting a pale light over the forest. Tristan's breath forms white puffs in the chilly air as he continues to wait for her. He leans against a tree, his eyes never leaving the cottage door. Every creak of the old wood, every flicker of a shadow, makes his heart jump, hoping that it's Ellie coming back to him. The door remained closed, and his worry deepens.

Exhaustion begins to set in, but Tristan refuses to leave. His feelings for Ellie are a powerful force, stronger than his fear and weariness. He will be her protector and her shield, ready to face whatever dangers lie ahead.

Tristan feels a sudden shift in the air. His senses sharpen and his body tenses. The door to the cottage creaks open; his heart leaps into his throat making him take a step forward out of the shadows of the trees. There she is, stepping out into the night, her face pale and clearly exhausted.

Relief instantly floods through him as he rushes forward, wrapping her in his arms and releasing a breath that he didn't realize he was holding.

She stiffens immediately, evidently startled by his embrace but she slowly softens in his arms after a brief moment. Ellie nuzzles her head into his chest, releasing a heavy breath.

Tristan pulls her closer, then softly kisses the top of her head. Having her this close brings forth a burning desire to keep her there. An instinct that he has never felt before.

He begins to realize that her hands are held up in the air behind him, clearly afraid to touch him. The thought makes his heart ache painfully because he wants her to touch him; quite frankly, he needs it, desperately.

Ellie slowly steps back from him, still keeping her hands from touching him. She gives him a small, tired smile that mirrors his own.

"What happened, El? What did she say to you?" his voice stern and concerned.

Ellie glances around nervously, clearly realizing that they are alone.

"Why did you wait for me?" she asks in a voice that is a mix of curiosity and something more profound. Her eyes lock onto his, searching for answers as her brows knit together in anticipation.

"There was no way that I was leaving you alone with the enchantress," he replies flatly.

"Oh, well, I'm quite alright; you didn't need to stay," Ellie twisted her hands together, unwilling to look at him.

"I couldn't leave you even if I wanted to; I had to make sure that you were alright," his voice was low and honest.

"Thank you. We should get back though. I imagine Kyla must be waiting for you," Ellie peers around him into the shadows of the dark forest.

"Ellie... Kyla and I..." Tristan hesitates, unsure if now is the right time to tell her or if he should let Kyla do it. "We're not together anymore."

Ellie's head snaps to up, her face etched with concern. "Why?" she croaks out.

"You already know why..." his voice is laden with emotion, his words slow and deliberate.

Realization crossed her beautiful face then, mixed with fear for herself or for her friend—Tristan couldn't tell. "Kyla is the perfect female for you. She's incredible, she really is," Ellie shakes her head.

"She is, I *know* she is. But Ellie...," Tristan reaches out, wrapping his hand around her wrist and slowly running his hand up to her elbow, pulling her closer. She didn't pull away; she didn't even resist, his heart leaps in his chest at the realization.

"She's not *you*. No *one* else could ever be *you*," Tristan's voice is barely above a whisper as he leans in closer, staring into her eyes.

"Ellie, the truth is that everything about you pulls me in, pulls me in so fucking deep. If you were the waves, I would willingly be pulled under just to feel you upon me, even for a moment," he said softly. Ellie swallows hard, blinking as his words sink in.

She's so beautiful that it physically hurts Tristan to look at her; to be this close to her and not claim her as his, to not kiss her. The air between them electrifies, leaving the hair on his neck standing on end, as it always does when she is near. It's as if the very atmosphere around them is begging them to be closer. His longing is almost unbearable, a sweet agony that pulses through his veins with every heartbeat.

Without a second thought, his lips crash against hers in a fierce, claiming kiss. His rough hands grip her face, then slide to the back of her neck, pulling her impossibly closer. This is not just a kiss, it's a release of everything that he's kept locked away; a torrent of emotion and raw need surging forward. The desperation in him rises, a hunger that's been burning for far too long.

It feels like the stars themselves have aligned, like fate had drawn them together in this perfect, electric moment. The world around him disappears, dissolving into nothingness. All that exists is the heat of her skin against his, the softness of her lips, and the frantic rhythm of his heart pounding against his chest. Every sensation heightens the fierce pull of desire that makes him want to consume her whole.

Ellie's hand slides up his chest between their bodies, leaving sparks in their wake, then her small hands wrap around his neck, pulling him to her, willingly opening up to him. The taste of her is both sweet and sinful, a heady mix that makes his head spin and his heart race. As her tongue brushes his, Tristan is sure that his heart will fail him because nothing has ever felt as perfect as she does in his arms; nothing has ever felt so right.

Her kiss feels deep, like a claiming in return that he is sure that he can feel his very soul being swallowed up by her. *Her kiss is addicting, like a poison that I want to consume; I want her to burn through my veins from the inside out*, Tristan thinks.

Ellie's fingers tangle in his hair, and he shivers at the touch, a low groan escaping his lips. She is everything that he has ever wanted, everything that he needs. Her lavender and vanilla scent envelopes him, a soothing fragrance. In her presence, he feels whole; complete in a way that he never imagined possible.

This kiss, Ellie in his arms, is so much more than he ever expected or hoped for. It was real, raw, and overflowing with unspoken emotions. He can feel his legs begin to shake from the pressure.

Ellie's hands grip tightly to his hair, kissing him with an intensity that sends jolting shocks of pleasure rippling through him to his core. A gasping moan escapes her lips, and everything inside him snaps.

All he can feel, taste, or touch, is her. His hands hold onto her soft curves as he feels her against him, kissing her with everything he has inside him. *If this is what drowning feels like, then let me drown in her*, he thought. *I'm hers, so irrevocably hers.*

With one last brush of her soft lips against his, she slowly, reluctantly pulls away. They are both nothing but trembling limbs and racing hearts as they stare at each other. Her beautiful blue irises glow brightly in the darkness surrounding them.

Tristan leans his forehead against hers, and she slowly closes her eyes, attempting to steady her ragged breath. "*It's you, El, only you,*" he admits softly within his mind, shaking as his thumb caresses her cheek. Tristan's heart beats so hard against his ribcage that he is sure that she can hear it. She can probably even feel it under her palm which is currently resting on his chest.

"Did you hear my thoughts, Princess?," Tristan asks with a wicked grin.

Ellie's eyes flutter open, and in that moment, Tristan sees everything he has ever wanted, reflecting back at him. The feeling she has for him, the fear, the hope—it is all there in her vibrant, glowing eyes, as clear as the stars in the night sky.

Racking his brain, he tries to find words to say, but it is Ellie who speaks first, taking a deep breath: "We should head back. I have a lot to tell you all."

Tristan hesitantly releases her and steps back. The moment her hand falls from him, she smiles softly and she hesitantly strides past him into the forest.

All he can do is stand there for a moment, releasing an exasperated sigh as he runs his hands over his face. *I'm done for*, he realizes.

Tristan follows her in silence, holding back the increasing urge to grab her once again. After they break through the trees, Stella, Kyla, and Breccan run over to them, the stew already in hand, as they devour their meal.

"Ellie, are you okay? What happened? What did she say? Did she hurt you?," Stella asks breathlessly, questions coming out so fast that Ellie puts her hands up, gesturing for her to take a moment.

Kyla pulls her into a tight hug, concerned eyes roaming over her, checking to see if she is truly all right. Tristan notices the way Ellie stiffens under Kyla's hug, utterly still and unmoving.

"I'm fine, really. I have a lot to tell you all though," Ellie replies, her tone nervously.

Each of them nods in understanding as they walk towards the fire. Stella quickly fills a bowl and hands it to Ellie, forcing her to eat.

Breccan comes up beside him, grasping a hand on his shoulder.

"What is with that look on your face?" Tristan tries to shrug off his grip before saying, "I... I....," Tristan tries to find the words but isn't ready to admit the emotions running through him to his friend, at least not yet.

"I'm just worried, and it's been a long day," Tristan insists as he shakes his head, trying to clear his racing thoughts, hoping Breccan will believe him. Feeling far too tired to try and persuade him otherwise.

"Whatever you say," he replies with a knowing smirk, then gives him a wink and one last squeeze of his shoulder before heading back to the fire.

After a couple of bites of soup, Ellie finally speaks, the words flowing out of her as she tells them all everything. It feels like hours as she continues to speak, relinquishing every detail. Stella and Kyla interrupt with questions every few minutes. Breccan shushes them and tells Ellie to continue. Tristan only sits there in silence, deep concern building the more she speaks.

When she finally finishes speaking, it's Breccan that breaks the silence, "Well shit, Princess. That was a lot to unpack, I might need a minute," wiping his face and shaking his head.

"Wow, she really had a bonded? I mean, it makes a lot of sense. If anything happened to Kaida, I might go a little crazy too," Kyla declares, wincing at her last words.

"I mean, I get it. But what about the trials, El? What do you

Ellie only shrugged, exhaustion etched on her beautiful features. A yawn broke free of her lips, bringing back new memories of her lips on his. And just like that, the need to grab her is so strong that he needs a moment alone to breathe. He stands abruptly and walks toward the nearby river and sits, allowing the silence to quell his nerves.

Trees rustle behind him when, to his surprise, Kyla steps out of the darkness and strides over to him.

"Hi," she breathes as she slowly takes a seat next to him.

"Hi," he utters slowly, unsure what to say after their last conversation. They both sit quietly for a while, but thankfully, Kyla breaks the uncomfortable silence.

"You genuinely care about her?" She questions nervously, still not looking at him.

Tristan knows that he needs to be honest. After the kiss he shared with Ellie, there is no way that he can deny what he feels anymore.

"I do...," he admits honestly. Hoping his words don't hurt her because that isn't his intention.

Kyla releases a long sigh, "If you hurt her, I *will* kill you."

Tristan turns to stare at her, eyebrows raised in confusion. "Are you serious?" he urges with amusement.

"I'm deathly serious. Ellie is the kindest, most generous, female to ever exist and she has the biggest heart I've ever seen. She deserves someone who will stand by her, protect her, and support her decisions. Someone who will not hold her back. She will be queen, Tristan. *The Queen.* Do you understand what that means?" she asks as her eyes bore into him, narrowing slightly.

"I do... And for the record I did honestly try to ignore what I feel for her; I really, really did, Ky," he replies, shaking his head slowly.

"I know; I can see that your feelings for her are real. You refuse to leave her, the way you look at her, even though she doesn't reciprocate the same look because of her loyalty to me. The stars know I love her for it. I forgive you, just be good to her. No, be the *best* for her. Because if you are not, I will not hesitate to kill you," she smiles before she quickly pushes off the ground and strides away, leaving him utterly dumbfounded from her words. Relief flows through him.

Once he finally returns to the camp, they are all asleep except for Breccan, who studies him as he slowly approaches.

"Get some sleep," Breccan commands as he masks a yawn. His red hair is disheveled, his sword is still strapped to his back.

"It seems you need sleep as well," Tristan observes with a slight chuckle.

"I'll be fine; you need it more than I do. Go on," he replies, nodding toward his bedroll already that is laid out for him.

The full extent of his exhaustion hits him then, so he only nods before lying next to the fire. He finds his gaze being drawn to Ellie's sleeping form, eyes closed, and breaths steady with each rise and fall of her chest.

His fear and worry for her invade all of his thoughts. Knowing what's to come is leaving a searing ache in his chest that he subconsciously rubs at. Just then her long lashes slowly flutter open, her eyes immediately catching his, as if his stare alone pulled her from her slumber.

Her eyes are soft and tired, a small smile graces her beautiful face; after a few slow blinks, she closes her eyes again and falls back asleep. Tristan tears his gaze from her devastatingly beautiful face as he takes in the night sky through the canopy of trees and watches the stars.

He can still feel the warmth of her lips and the softness of her skin under his fingertips. The silkiness of her hair. Never has a kiss completely destroyed him before, until her.

Realization crashes down on him, and then, like a tidal wave, *She heard my thoughts.*

37

Ellie

"Rise and shine," Stella's gentle voice wakes Ellie from her restless slumber. Ellie groans as she sits up, realizing that everyone except for her and Stella are nowhere in sight.

Rubbing the sleep from her eyes, she squints against the harsh morning light. "Where is everyone?"

"Breccan and Tristan went flying with the dragons to feed them, and Kyla went to wash up," Stella nods toward the nearby river through the trees.

The previous day's events rush through her mind, and she lets out an exasperated sigh, running her fingers through her tangled hair before braiding it.

"Do you want to talk about it?" Stella questions gently, crouching before Ellie and resting her hand on her knee.

Last night, she was completely swept away by Tristan. She had wanted to stay under the stars and kiss him until he irrevocably devoured her, but the thought of Kyla held her back. She had to talk to her best friend.

"I think I should speak with Kyla first," Ellie replies hesitantly.

Stella raises an eyebrow. "I see..." she smirks. "I don't need my gifts to understand this one. You should talk to Ky before seeing the enchantress."

"Thank you, Stells, for always understanding," Ellie stands up, grateful for her other best friend.

"You should know, El. We have seen how you look at each other,"

Stella adds with a gentle smile, her eyes conveying more than her words. “Kyla has never been green if you know what I mean. Also, neither of them has been red for each other either.” Ellie winces, but Stella’s smile remains warm and understanding.

Ellie pauses, considering Stella's words. “It’s just... complicated,” she admits, glancing toward the river. “After everything we’ve been through, I don’t want to risk our friendship for anything or *anyone*.”

Stella nods, her expression turning serious. “I get it, and she knows that as well. But sometimes, holding back can do more damage than speaking up. You and Kyla have been through a lot together.”

Ellie sighs, looking down at her hands. “What if it changes everything between us?”

“Change isn’t always bad,” Stella replies, squeezing Ellie’s arm reassuringly. “It might bring you closer. Besides, you won’t know until you talk to her.”

Ellie nods slowly, appreciating Stella’s perspective. “You’re right. I’ll talk to her.”

Stella smiles. “Good. Remember, no matter what, we're all here for you.”

Ellie feels a surge of gratitude. “Thanks, Stella. I don’t know what I would do without you all.”

“Anytime,” Stella smiles. “Now, go find Kyla before you go to see the enchantress. You have a curse to break.” She winks.

With a renewed sense of purpose, Ellie makes her way toward the river, the morning light casting a hopeful glow on her path.

Ellie finds Kyla by the river, kneeling on a smooth rock, wringing out her wet hair. The sun filters through the trees, casting a warmth over the scene. Ellie takes a deep breath, her heart pounding as she approaches.

“Ky?” Ellie calls softly.

Kyla turns, her expression brightening. “Hey, El. Sleep well?”

Ellie shrugs, managing a small smile. “As well as I can, you know, considering my impending fate. Can we talk?”

“Of course.” Kyla pats the rock beside her. “What’s on your mind?”

Kyla studies Ellie for a moment, a knowing look in her eyes. “You know, if this is about Tristan, it's okay. All I want is for you to be happy.”

Ellie’s eyes widen in surprise, and she hesitates, her gaze dropping to the ground. “I… I don’t know what to say or even how to say this, Ky. I have come to realize that I do have feelings for him. I would never want to hurt you though, ever.”

Kyla’s expression softens, and she places a reassuring hand on Ellie’s arm. “I appreciate your honesty and I’m glad you came to me first. It really is okay to have feelings for him. I promise, El, I understand.”

Ellie glances up, her voice barely above a whisper. “There is something there, something between us that is hard to explain, and I have been so scared to admit it to anyone, even myself. I didn't want to ruin our friendship, not over some male or situation.”

Kyla sighs, looking out over the water. “You know, I liked him more than he ever liked me, even from the beginning. I tried hard to make it work between us, but he could never have been my mate. Something was always missing between us, something vital. We never had a deep connection like a soul bond should be. Honestly, a part of me wished we had just stayed friends.”

Ellie nods, appreciating Kyla’s mutual honesty. “I’m sorry. I honestly don’t know when it even changed between us…”

Kyla smiles gently. “I trust you and know that you would have never hurt me like that. Just make sure it’s real between you two. You deserve true love, El, deep, consuming love, not another fool like Jace.” Ellie can't hide her wince when she hears Jace’s name. If she is being honest with herself, she hasn't thought of him in days. The ache of his betrayal left upon her heart seems to be slowly healing from the loss of her first love.

Kyla continues, her voice is thoughtful. "I have seen how he looks at you, El, a look I always wished a male would have for me. You two have something, something he and I can never have."

Ellie looks down at her hands. "It feels real, so real at times that it terrifies me."

Kyla's eyes are warm and understanding. "Love does that, doesn't it?" Kyla grabs her hand and gives her a light squeeze, but doesn't let go. "And if you ever need to talk about it, I'm here. Just because you have feelings for him doesn't mean you're losing me. not now, not ever"

Ellie's heart swells with gratitude as a lone tear falls. As Kyla's thoughts swarm her mind, she realizes that there is no anger, no pain, and no resentment. "Thank you, Ky. I don't know what I did to deserve a friend like you, but I'm so grateful."

Kyla laughs lightly. "You would manage, but I'm glad that you don't have to. We're a team, and nothing will change that, *especially* a male."

Kyla stands, pulling Ellie up with her. "Now, let's head back. The others will be wondering where we have gone, and I assume the enchantress will be expecting you soon enough."

As they walk back to camp, Ellie feels a sense of relief and gratefulness swell in her heart. She knows that she doesn't deserve a friend like Kyla; she's sure no one in the entire world that will ever deserve someone as wonderful as her friend, but she is grateful nonetheless.

Back at camp, the dragons are returning from their flight, and Tristan is already speaking with Terbius. Ellie watches him, her heart fluttering like thunderous wings in her chest, but this time with a sense of calmness. With Kyla's support, she can feel the tug to him stronger than ever.

"Go on," Kyla nudges her playfully. "Talk to him. I'm tired of his brooding anyway." She rolls her eyes and then gives Ellie a wink.

Ellie grins, her nerves easing, "Thank you. For everything."

Kyla winks, "Anytime, El. Now, go."

Ellie slowly approaches Tristan, her steps careful, her heart racing as he speaks with Terbius. The memory of their kiss lingers, a kiss like none that she has ever experienced before. His touch makes the blood in her veins rush, an exquisite sensation that she knows she'll never tire of.

She's both nervous and excited to see him, and the connection they share is deepening in ways she didn't anticipate.

During the kiss, she heard his thoughts, and for the first time in her life, she wasn't scared or terrified to touch another fae while ungloved. The feel of his muscular chest and soft skin beneath her fingertips brought tiny goosebumps to her skin at the memory. She knows how he feels about her. Honestly, she wants to drown in him, too, willingly.

Tristan turns as she nears as if he could feel her presence as she could feel his, a warm smile spreading across his handsome face. The smile seemingly washes away all of her nervousness and warms her heart.

"Good morning," he greets, voice deep and yet soft.

"Good morning. I just spoke with Kyla...," Ellie mutters nervously as she runs her palms together, unable to stop the need to fidget under his soul-searching stare.

"We spoke as well," he admits with a slight wince.

"Tristan... I...," Ellie begins, stuttering and finding it hard to get the words out that she desperately wants to say.

He reaches for her hand slowly, almost cautiously, and gently pulls it to his lips, kissing it softly, turning Ellie's skin ablaze where his lips had been. He gently pulls her closer, resting her palm on his chest as she arches against him, gazing up into his ocean-blue eyes as he peers down at her.

A surge of magic pulses through her like a wildfire, Tristan's thoughts crashing into her mind with the force of a storm. "*We have all the time in the world to figure this out*," his voice reverberates in her consciousness, steady yet charged with a quiet, burning intensity. His eyes lock onto hers, the depth of his certainty almost stealing the air from her lungs.

"*I want you to know how much I want this, El*," he continues, his voice thick with emotion. "*Whatever this is, I want it. So fucking bad that I'll fall to my knees right now, beg, if I have to.*" His gaze holds her captive, raw and unyielding, as if the very act of looking away would break him. "*Just say you'll give this a chance. Let me stand by your side.*"

The weight of his words settle in her chest, heavy and suffocating, as his confession hangs between them like a fragile thread she isn't sure she's ready to grasp.

Ellie's heart swells, her chest tightening as emotion surges within her. His words wrap around her like a warm embrace, and a soft smile spreads across her lips despite the heat rising to her cheeks under the intensity of his stare. "You don't need to beg," she whispers, her voice barely holding back the depth of what she truly feels. The relief floods her, finally being able to allow herself to feel what she has been denying.

A flicker of joy lights his face and he lowers his forehead to hers, their breaths mingling in the intimate space between them. The world outside fades, leaving only the steady rhythm of their hearts beating as one. *I want to fold into him, into this moment, lose myself in him completely, and never come up for air*, she thinks. Her pulse races at the closeness, the warmth, the undeniable pull between them.

For a few precious moments, they stand frozen in time, the air around them thick with the weight of their unspoken connection. It's as if the universe itself is holding its breath, giving them this quiet moment of perfect understanding.

Then, a deep rumble from Terbius shatters the stillness, a low reminder that they aren't alone. Ellie chuckles softly, her nose brushing against his as they pull away slightly, but the bond between them feels even stronger, almost tangible, unbreakable.

Tristan reluctantly pulls away, chuckling under his breath at his bondeds clear interruption.

"Don't mind him; he's just a grumpy old sky lizard," Tristan remarks with a bright smile, making Ellie laugh. His smile and joking humor lighten the intensity of the moment.

"It's time, Curse Breaker!" Breccan bellows coming up to their side.

"I need a moment with Saphirixia before we go," Ellie gestures to her bonded. Tristan and Breccan nod when she glances between them. As her gaze falls towards the dying fire, Kyla and Stella are standing arm in arm, grinning at her.

Saphirixia is waiting, watching Ellie intently as she walks closer. She immediately wraps her arms around her large head, allowing the warmth of her bonded to fuel her.

"*Are you ready for this, Saph?*"

"*I am. Are you...*" Saphirixia replies, tone questioning.

"*I'm ready, we've already come all this way...*"

"*We do this together,*" Saphirixia commands.

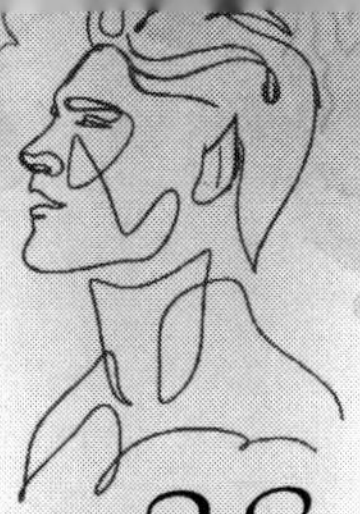

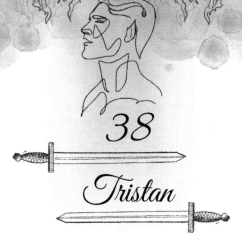

38

Tristan

Following closely behind Ellie and Saphirixia, Tristan can feel his heart beating too fast in his chest. None of them know what Saphirixia and Ellie will have to do to break the curse, and his fear for Ellie consumes his every thought the closer they fly toward the enchantress's cottage.

As they reach the clearing, the enchantress stands in her purple velvet cloak, her long black hair flowing in the wind. He couldn't help but think how ethereal she looked. For someone over a thousand years old, she appears not much older than any of them.

When she speaks, her words are cold as she eyes Ellie and Saphirixia. "Are you ready?"

Ellie only nods as he peers at their friends, who stare, watching, waiting.

The enchantress waves her hand to her right, toward the clearing with two stones, one much larger than the other. The first is at least four feet off the ground and six feet wide. The other is so giant that a dragon can lay upon it. A thought that has Tristan tensing.

Ellie and Saphirixia stride over to the stones, their steps slow as they look at the two stones in confusion. Ellie looks over her shoulder at the enchantress with a questioning look. "You shall both lay upon the stones," the enchantress instructs.

They proceed slowly onto the stones, Saphirixia's large, scaled form takes up the entirety of the bigger stone. Her gaze clearly as untrusting of her as he is.

Ellie sits slowly upon the raised stone; Tristan can nearly sense her racing heart from where he stands. His fear for her and her bond makes his own heart race.

Ellie obediently lays down on the stone, limbs rigid as she stares into the bright morning sky.

“These trials will not only test your physical and mental capabilities but also your emotional strength, moral integrity, and most importantly, your bond,” the enchantress declares, chin raised high. Tristan notices the round orb in her hands, pulsing and glowing brightly.

“Each trial that you accomplish together will bring you one step closer to breaking the curse. Be warned: should you die or be harmed during the trial, neither of you will awaken." Her last words are cold.

Ellie sits up abruptly, eyes trained on the enchantress, confusion written all over her beautiful face, and fear.

“You didn’t say that we might die during these trials!” Ellie practically shouts, Saphirixia releases a heavy burst of smoke as she chuffs.

“I told you that these trials will not be easy," the enchantress sneers back.

Tristan moves closer to the stone, Ellie’s fierce eyes meeting his and stopping him in place. They stare at each other for long heartbeats until her eyes soften, and she gives him a slight nod of determination.

Kyla, Breccan, and Stella walk to his side as Kyla says, “They can do it; I know they can. It wouldn’t be their fate if they weren’t capable of completing this”

Tristan has faith that Ellie can conquer the world if she wished, purely from her kindness, heart, fierceness, and bravery. Although, the fear of her going through these trials and never waking again fills him with dread.

Ellie's gaze met each of them before turning to Saphirixia. They are clearly speaking to each other, but Saphirixia only nods her large head. Each of them slowly lay back down on the stone.

"I wish you both luck," the enchantress states with sinister delight as she raises her arms slowly in front of her, the glowing orb burning brighter. In the next second, a dome of raging fire surrounds them, engulfing them in flames.

Tristan jolts back, feeling like he can't breathe. The fire surrounding them both is burning brightly, emanating a blistering heat he can feel upon his skin making them all step back even farther.

Thankfully, Stella acknowledges the enchantress. "What are you doing?!" She practically screams as the question falls from her mouth.

"They are both asleep, dreaming, if you will. Do not fear; they are unharmed," the enchantress replies over her shoulder at them, light from the orb pulsing. Tristan shakes his head in resignation.

He doesn't know what to do. He can't help her, can't make sure she's all right. He feels utterly useless, clenches his jaw in frustration. The helplessness gnaws at him, threatening to unravel his composure.

Breccan places a supportive hand on Tristan's shoulder, his grip firm yet reassuring. "They're the prophesized for a reason; they can do this; have faith," he remarks, his voice a calming anchor in the storm of Tristan's emotions. With one last squeeze, Breccan releases him and steps back to stand with Kyla and Stella once more.

He stands there unmoving, his eyes fixed on the fiery dome raging around them. The flickering flames reflecting in his eyes, his mind elsewhere. Images of Ellie's beautiful face playing in his mind, her laughter echoing in his ears. He can almost feel the warmth of her touch, the tenderness of her smile, the intensity of her kiss. The memory of her in his arms is like a lifeline. A reminder of what he is fighting for, a happiness that he has never felt before.

The realization that he may not get to hold her close again makes his heart clench painfully in his chest. The fear of losing her twisting his insides, making his magic surge uncontrollably.

His eyes glow crimson red as he tries to dampen the wild power coursing through his veins. A storm of emotions threatens to break free. He clenches his fists, nails biting into his palms as he struggles to maintain control.

The fire crackles and roars, a reminder of the battle raging within the fire before him. Tristan takes a deep breath, forcing himself to focus. He can't afford to lose control now, not when Ellie was in there. He has to believe in her, her connection with her bonded, their strength, and the prophecy that they were chosen to fulfill.

The seconds tick by, each one stretching into an eternity. Tristan's resolve hardens, he decides right then that he will wait for her and stand by her side no matter the cost.

He can't help her directly but he can be there for her, a constant in the chaos. He can lend her his strength, his unwavering faith in her. He has to trust her, trust her strength, and trust her determination.

Breccan's words echo in his mind: "*They're the prophesized for a reason.*" Tristan holds onto that hope, that belief. Minutes feel like hours, each a test of his own patience. Tristan stands firm, his eyes never leaving the fiery dome. He will wait for her, no matter how long it takes.

39

Ellie

Ellie awakens in a dark pit, sitting up in the damp dirt under her fingers, peering around frantically, realizing that Saphirixia isn't with her. Her breaths come in fast and unsteady, and her limbs begin to tremble from the cold. She realizes that she is sitting in a dark pit on the ground. When she glances up, she can see trees high above and more darkness. It is clearly nighttime, and she feels utterly confused because it is still morning, or so she thought.

Just then she hears the enchantress's voice in her ear whispering,

"In the heart of the night, when the moon hides its light,
A dragon's sight fails in the deep forest's blight.
Blind she shall be, no eyes to guide,
Yet through the darkness, her path must slide.
Seek not with vision, but trust in the bond,
A connection unseen, yet ever strong.
The whisper of wings, the pulse of your heart,
Shall guide her steps when you are far apart.
Find me she must, through shadow and shade,
For only through trust can this trial be made."

Ellie processes the Enchantress's riddle. *Saphirixia is blind.*

"*Saph, where are you?*" Ellie frantically reaches out to her bonded, hoping to the stars for a reply.

Seconds later, the deep timber of Saphirixia's voice fills her thoughts. "*I'm not sure; however, I have a problem... I cannot see.*"

As fear envelopes her, Ellie looks around her, unsure of what to do or where to go in order to find her. The dark pit is only wide enough for her to move around, making her feel slightly claustrophobic.

"*I'm so sorry, Saph, we must find each other to complete this trial,*" Ellie tells her as she tries to calm her breathing and begins thinking of plans.

"*Okay, let's think. There is no way for me to find you in the forest; I will need to fly. Can you see the sky?*" Saphirixia asks.

"*No, I'm in the ground, in a sort of pit. The forest is dense above where I am.*"

"*I will fly high above until you see me or hear me. We can do this, El,*" Saphirixia's calm voice gives Ellie hope.

Ellie begins pacing around in the damp pit, occasionally peering up to see through the thick tree masking the moon high above. It feels like hours as they speak to each other, Saphirixia trying to keep her calm, screeching, and roaring through the air, waiting for Ellie to hear her. Her frustration grows with each passing minute.

"*This is absurd. I cannot see enough of the sky and have not heard you. What are we going to do?*" Ellie begs exasperatedly; frustration evident in each word.

The ground beneath Ellie's feet begins to quake, startling her as she tries to regain her balance. She places her hand against the damp dirt wall. The dirt beneath her hand begins pushing firmly against it, nudging her back. Realization hits her, and then she steps back and sees the dirt walls moving in on her before stopping suddenly.

Ellie turns in circles, putting both hands out to her sides, realizing that her space has indeed gotten smaller.

"*Saph, the walls are closing in. It would help just a bit, if you hurried!*" Ellie exclaims frantically, unable to control her rapid breaths as she croaks out, "*I'll be buried here.*" she begins to hyperventilate then.

"*El, stay calm. I will find you*," Saphirixia replies calmly. *Let's try another way. We can try to sense each other. I know when you are close; I have felt it many times before. Try to feel that connection.*"

Ellie places her hand on her chest and tries to steady her breathing, which feels impossible. She takes another unsteady, deep breath. Closing her eyes, she tries to ease her racing thoughts so she can sense their connection but it doesn't feel like Saphirixia is close.

"*I'm not sure that it's working. I don't feel like you're close*," Ellie chokes on her words as her fear threatens to take over.

"*Then I must not be because I feel the same*," Saphirixia replies confidently in Ellie's words. "*I shall fly another direction, keep trying, El, keep trying to sense me, and I shall try the same.*"

Once again, the ground beneath her feet begins to quake violently as the walls around her close in even more, before finally relenting.

"*We're running out of time, Saph.*" Ellie feels a dampness on her face as she raises her hand and feels a tear on her cheek. She didn't realize that she had even been crying.

"*Hold on, El. Keep trying. We're not giving up. You will survive, do you hear me?*"

More long minutes pass, possibly another hour until she senses a tiny spark of her bonded, making her gasp. "*Saph! You're close!*" A second later, she can hear Saphirixia's roar faintly in the distance.

"I'm here! I'm here, Saph!" Ellie begins to scream, hoping to the stars that she could hear her. "*Please, please hear me.*"

Saphirixia bellows again; this time, she can hear her a little closer than before.

"*Saph, I think you're closer; keep flying in that direction!*"

"*I'm coming! Hold on!*"

A few more charged moments pass before she hears Saphirixia's loud screech filling the air beyond the trees. Hope sparks to life within her until the familiar ground quake moves beneath her feet. She places her hands in the dirt around her, pushing desperately, teeth clenching as she releases a guttural scream.

Once the quaking ceases once again, a sob racks her body, fear completely engrossing her every thought. *Was this it? Am I going to die here? Would I ever see my mother and father again? Would I ever see Saphirixia, Kyla, Stella, Breccan... Tristan?* The thought nearly makes her heart break in two.

"No, *you will not die, El, not without me*!" Saphirixia's voice booms as a loud thud shakes the trees above her. Relief instantly floods her as Saphirixia releases another loud screech in the air.

"Over here!" Ellie yells as she desperately pounds the dirt with her palm. Trees begin to move just beyond the pit's opening until she sees the familiar shimmer of her bonded's sapphire blue scales. Ellie releases a cry of relief as Saphirixia's head moves just above the pit's opening.

"*That was too close, Saph*," Ellie chides.

"*You try flying blind*," Saphirixia retorts. Which elicits a small chuckle from them both. "*Now, how do we get you out?*"

"*Can you feel for a vine or a long tree branch?*" Ellie asks.

Saphirixia turns from the opening, leaving Ellie standing there, unable to take her wide eyes from the top of the pit.

The ground begins to quake violently, making Ellie's heart race as terror takes over again.

"Hurry!" Ellie screams.

"*I'm trying! I cannot find anything!*"

"*Come back, Saph! There is no more time!* " She could feel the ground shake, the walls are now so close she can barely move around.

Within seconds, Saphirixia returns and tries to push her large head into the hole, using her immense strength to try to make the hole wider. The soil refuses to budge as the ground continues to shake around her.

"*Try your tail!*" Ellie yells in her mind.

Saphirixia removes her head from the opening, and her large tail comes plunging down the narrow hole. Her bonded tail is so long it almost reaches her; Ellie reaches as high as she can, her fingertips brushing the end of Saphirixia's tail.

"*You have to jump, El!*"

"*You're too far; I cannot reach!*"

"*You must try! Come on, Ellie, you can do it!*"

Ellie crouches down and pushes as hard as she can to grasp Saphirixia's scaled tail, briefly hanging on before slipping into the dirt.

"*Try again!*" Saphirixia commands.

Ellie stands back up, scrounging up every ounce of strength before jumping up and catching her grip on a large scale.

"Go! Now!" Ellie yells, voice commanding and desperate.

Saphirixia doesn't hesitate as Ellie feels herself being lifted. The dirt around her presses against her hips while Saphirixia wails, her tail slowly being crushed under the weight.

Ellie screams until they break through the ground, clutching Saphirixia's tail desperately until she feels solid earth beneath her feet and sees the moon and stars through the trees above.

Ellie's heart pounds in her chest as she gasps for breath. She looks up to see Saphirixia's large head hovering above her.

"*That was too close,*" Ellie releases a heavy breath as she pushes herself off the ground. She immediately lunges for Saphirixia and wraps her arms around her long neck.

"*Too close indeed,*" Saphirixia replies as she purrs against Ellie's chest.

"*If this is the first trial, then I'm scared to see what we must do next.*"

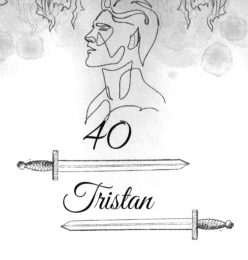

40

Tristan

Hours pass, and the sun has gone down, Tristan and Stella stand waiting, watching Ellie and Saphirixia encased in the dome. The heat and firelight create an intense, mesmerizing barrier that seems impenetrable. Kyla, Breccan, and their dragons have gone to fetch food and allow the dragons to hunt. The enchantress stands frozen near the stones with the glowing orb in her hands, orchestrating the intense trial that had been ongoing for hours.

Despite the fatigue setting in, Tristan remains rooted to his spot, his eyes never leaving the fiery dome. Uncertainty gnawed at him, and helplessness weighed heavily on his shoulders.

Stella stands beside him, her gaze gentle yet penetrating. "You care for her deeply," she observes, her voice soft yet certain.

Tristan glances at her, his jaw tight and his eyes ablaze, “I do."

Stella nods, her eyes distant as if seeing something beyond the present. "I have a gift, you know. I can see and feel the emotions of others. It’s both a blessing and a curse." She pauses, looking at him directly. "I can see how much you care for El and that she cares for you too."

Tristan's heart skips a beat. "I knew that was your gift, but I hadn’t really thought about it," he hesitates before asking the question he so desperately wants to know. “Ar… are you saying that you can sense that she feels the same that way I do about her?”

Stella smiles faintly. "Yes, Tristan. Though without my gift it is quite plain to see.” Relief floods him as she continues to speak, “The way that you tried to suppress your feelings for her while you were with Kyla, how you battled against your own heart, honorable as it was. It's as clear as day."

Tristan sighs, the weight of her words settling in. "I never wanted to nor had I planned to hurt Kyla. She doesn't deserve any more heartache."

Stella places a reassuring hand on his arm. "I know that and so does Kyla. Your feelings for Ellie are genuine and raw. Which is why I'm so glad that she has someone like you who genuinely cares for her." She pauses for a brief moment before quietly continuing, "Tristan," her tone turning serious. "Promise me that you will not hurt her. Ellie has been through enough."

Tristan looks at Stella, his resolve firm. "I promise. I will do everything in my power to protect her and make her happy, that is, if she'll have me."

Stella's expression softens, and she nods. "Good. She deserves that. And you deserve to be happy too..."

As Stella's words sink in, Tristan can't help but question himself. *Do I really deserve to be happy? Do I even deserve her?* He ponders to himself. The doubt gnaws at him; he wants to believe that he does. That he's deserving and that he's enough.

He swore that he will never love or care for another after losing his mother. The heartbreak and the pain of losing her had been too much to bear. Tristan finds himself questioning his desires. *Can I open my heart and face the potential for loss, the loss of her?* He ponders.

"I hope so," he murmurs as he looks at Stella again, her eyes glistening with unshed tears. "I want to deserve her."

Stella nods; her face full of understanding as a tear slips silently down her cheek. "You will. You deserve each other."

Tristan crouches on the ground, elbows on his knees. He runs his hands through his raven-black hair, and releases a heavy sigh.

He can see now why Ellie loves her so much. Stella is truly a kind and compassionate friend. Her love for Ellie shines brightly in every word that she speaks.

Yet, when Ttristan thinks of all that Ellie is having to endure in that trial, he feels a surge of determination. He wants to be worthy of her and be the male that she needs. He doesn't care that she is a princess; right now, he only wants her. After all these years he finally feels like he has the chance at true happiness despite all the time that he has denied himself.

Suddenly, the enchantress's arms fall in front of her as the glowing orb in her hands finally sputters out. Tristan scrambles to his feet and glances between Ellie and Saphirixia, his heart racing wildly in his chest.

"A... are they done? Did they pass?" Stella stutters out.

The raging dome disappears instantly, revealing Ellie and Saphirixia still asleep and unmoving upon the stones. Tristan's feet are moving toward her before he even realizes it, Stella's footfalls close behind. When he reaches the stone, Ellie's eyes remain closed. She looks calm, as though still in a dream. He immediately grabs her hand and suddenly senses little sparks of magic flowing from her as if she herself were raw radiating power herself.

Stella leans across from him, holding Ellie's other hand and tries to wake her. Seconds tick by, but Ellie and Saphirixia remain under the spell.

"Please wake up, please," Tristan croaks out, running a hand over her head, feeling the softness of the blonde waves fanned behind her across the smooth stone.

Desperation overtakes him. "Why isn't she waking up!?" He yells, looking up at the enchantress. His voice is full of fear and anger, eyes glowing crimson. His magic flares just underneath the surface, begging for a release.

The next instant, Ellie's eyes fly open in a panic and she begins thrashing around, clearly startled. Tristan and Stella quickly help her sit up just as she begins to cry, the reality of what she must have gone through must have been extreme because she coils into herself.

Tristan scoops her up into his arms, and pulls her close against his chest. His heart is pounding with relief. She must have passed the first trial, he reminds himself, *She's here; her heart still beats.*

Ellie is so light in his arms, so warm. Each broken cry from her lips makes him want to burn the world, burn the enchantress to mere bones. She just stands there stoic and expressionless.

Cold-hearted witch, he thinks as he scowls at the enchantress, she merely offers a serene, unapologetic smile. "Congratulations, Princess, rest now. Your next trial commences tomorrow." With that, she turns and strides towards her cottage without saying another word.

Saphirixia hovers beside him, peering down at Ellie and watching them closely.

Tristan practically growls at the enchantress, his protective instincts flaring as he and Stella take Ellie back to their camp. His arms wrap tightly around her. He holds her close, feeling the rapid beat of her heart as she softly cries against his chest.

As they reach the camp, Tristan sets Ellie down, gently wrapping her in a blanket that he grabs off of his pack. The tears continue to stream down her face. Stella stays close, her eyes glowing in the darkness, clearly monitoring Ellie's emotions.

Tristan moves to sit behind Ellie as he wraps his legs around her and pulls her into him. She doesn't protest; she only sinks into him, her body still quaking with pain, grief, he isn't sure.

Saphirixia moves around the campfire and finds a spot a few yards away. She releases a heavy chuff of smoke, lays down in the thick grass, and quickly closes her eyes, as exhausted as Ellie is for their first trial.

Stella glances into the sky when loud, heavy wingbeats echo from sky above, indicating that Breccan, Kyla, and their dragons have returned.

Stella regards them, eyes still glowing, before saying, “I’ll go speak with them. "She begins rubbing Ellie’s thigh softly and whispers, “I’ll be right back El.”

Ellie nods slowly, tears finally ceasing to his relief. *Did she use her magic on her?* He wonders as he watches Stella run through the trees to meet their friends.

Tristan pulls her in closer to him as he wraps his strong arm tighter around her waist and rubs his hand softly down her arms, attempting to soothe whatever pain she is feeling.

He hesitates before he speaks, but he has to know how she is feeling, “How bad was it?” he asks in a low voice as he says near her ear. Ellie lolls her head to the side, resting against his arm as she stares into the campfire before them, eyes unwavering.

“I was trapped in a pit in the ground, the walls around me started to close in. Then Saph had to find me except...she was blind,” she slowly stutters out. “I was scared that she wouldn't find me in time; I was scared I wouldn't see her again, or my parents, Stella, Kyla, even Breccan, and you.”

Her last words come out softer than the others, her admission making his heart beat wildly in his chest. *She was scared she wouldn't see me again?* He thinks astonished, the crushing weight of her words hitting him deep in his soul.

He releases a heavy sigh, as does Ellie. He pulls her impossibly closer, loving how perfectly she fits in his arms. It is as though she were made just for him, molded to be his other half.

“I just got you, Sapphire, I’m here...”

“Sapphire?” Ellie questions, voices barely above a whisper, her question making him smile.

"Much like the stone, you’re rare, indescribably beautiful, and incredibly strong. They're known for their stunning blue hue, which reminds me of the depth and clarity of your eyes. They are formed under intense conditions, symbolizing your strength and resilience. Despite everything, you, my fiery little princess, remain brilliant and unbreakable."

Ellie twists her head slowly and looks up at him, her captivating blue eyes stealing his breath as a small smile graces her perfect lips.

His heart stutters as he stares at her, entirely captivated, he forces himself to continue, "From here on, you will only be 'Sapphire,' to me. I want you to know that you're a fucking treasure and someone whose presence in my life is as rare and precious as that beautiful blue jewel."

Ellie's eyes are glassy with unshed tears, reflecting off the firelight. The air becomes thick between them, and he watches her, her eyes taking in every inch of his face and then falling to his lips. Her gaze upon him feels like divine torture.

He moves his hand from around her waist and slowly brings it up, cupping her face and capturing her lips with his. Their lips meet in a soft, passionate kiss that sends sparks through his entire body. She shutters in his arms as a soft moan escapes her lips. He runs his tongue along her plus bottom lip seeking entrance, she opens up for him, pulling him in deeper as their tongues collide.

Stars, how can a kiss feel like this? This consuming, this remarkable, this devastating. He wonders as he pulls her to him further and tightens his arms around her. His need for her makes him feel like a male who has been starving without water. *I'm so done for, there will only ever be her.*

With one last sweep of her tongue, she hesitantly pulls away as her stunning blue irises meet his once again.

"You're mine, Sapphire," Tristan rasps, unsteady and needy, utterly desperate to hear her words. His warm mouth skating across her jawline, making her knees tremble.

If his words surprise her, she doesn't show it. Ellie only smiles softly, lashes fluttering before she leans in and whispers against his lips, “I'm yours.”

“Mine.” He growls, threading his fingers into the nape of her neck, claiming her mouth once more.

41

Ellie

Ellie stares into the fire, leaning against Tristan's chest as he holds her tightly. The steady beat of his heart against her back is soothing, and the comfort of his embrace seeps into her bones and eases the heavy weight that she feels upon her chest. The kiss they shared is at the forefront of her mind, and his soothing touch along her arm only deepens this feeling of peace that she finds in his presence.

Nothing has ever felt more divine, more right. It was a kiss that spoke a thousand unspoken words, words she felt she wasn't yet ready to voice, so instead, she let her body convey all the emotions she couldn't yet articulate. When she told him that she was his, she said it without any kind of hesitation. She meant it with every fiber of her being.

Tristan shifts behind her, his muscled form fitting around her perfectly as if the stars molded his to fit her body. She feels his lips against her hair as he kisses her, a gesture so gentle it makes her heart squeeze in her chest. The connection between them is undeniable, a bond that feels both exhilarating and indescribably comforting. It's a comfort that she has never felt before; it's intoxicating.

Tristan's hand continues its path along her arm, she closes her eyes letting the sensation wash over her. The sensation is all she needs to feel whole. The world outside the circle of the fire seems distant and insignificant to this moment.

"I never imagined finding someone like you," Tristan murmurs into her hair, his voice a soft rumble that sends shivers down her spine. "You're everything I never thought I would find."

"I think you're reading my mind now," she giggles whispering back, her voice brimming with emotion.

The rustling of trees and the distant sound of familiar voices brings Ellie and Tristan out of their quiet moment. Kyla, Stella, and Breccan emerge from the forest, their dragons and Terbius landing behind them with a fresh catch of game. The group makes their way to the campfire, the dragons settling around them, preparing to sleep.

Kyla gives Ellie a warm smile, her eyes reflecting both concern and curiosity. "How are you feeling, El?"

Ellie leans back against Tristan's chest, feeling the steady rhythm of his heartbeat. "I'm alright. The trial was... intense," she admits, her voice still carrying a hint of exhaustion.

Breccan, always the light-hearted one, grins as he tosses a few sticks onto the fire. "Well, we brought back enough food to feed an army. Figured you two might be hungry after all that excitement." He winks at them.

Ellie chuckles softly, appreciating his attempt to lighten the mood. "Thanks, Breccan. I could definitely use something to eat."

As the group settles around the fire, sharing food and warmth, Ellie recounts her first trial with Saphirixia. Tristan's arms remain around her, offering silent support as she speaks. The flickering firelight casts shadows on their faces as the moon shines bright above the trees.

"I woke up in a pit in the ground," Ellie begins, her voice steady as she explains what had happened. With each moment of the event that she shares, she feels her throat closing up, reliving the experience all over again.

Kyla's eyes widened in admiration. "What a nightmare! I'm so glad you both are okay."

Stella, ever the supportive friend, reaches over from her side and squeezes Ellie's hand. "I knew you could do it. You are far stronger than you realize."

Breccan, not one to miss a chance for humor, grins. "Well shit, if that is your first test, I'm afraid to hear what that old bat has for you next."

Everyone laughs, the tension easing away as they enjoy the camaraderie of the moment. Ellie feels the heavy weight on her chest lifting, replaced with the warmth of her friends' support and the steady comfort of Tristan's embrace.

Tristan, his voice soft and reassuring, leaning down to whisper in her ear. "Your strength is truly remarkable, Sapphire. I'm so proud of you."

Ellie turns her head to peer up at him, her eyes shining with gratitude. "Thank you. I couldn't have done it without all of you," she glances at each of them. I knew you all were waiting for me, and I wanted to get back to you."

As the night wears on and the fire crackles warmly, the dragons around them drift off to sleep, their breathing creating a soothing, rumbling melody. The group continues to share stories and laughter, the bonds of their friendship growing stronger with each passing moment.

It doesn't take long before Ellie yawns, completely drained after the first trial.

"You should rest; I'll watch tonight," Tristan whispers softly. Ellie nods and stands slowly, already missing the warmth of his embrace. She goes through her pack and grabs her bedroll, then makes her way over to Saphirixia.

Ellie can't help but think how tired Saphirixia must be. Her soft rumbling resonates like distant thunder and her massive wings are folded tightly against her side.

She unrolls it, lays it in the grass, and curls into the warm blankets. She knows she should sleep next to the fire with everyone else, but she needs Saphirixia's closeness tonight. To be reminded that her bonded is still there with her.

"*I'm here, El, get some sleep.*" Ellie locks eyes with Saphirixia's, squinting at her. The comfort of her words sweeping away the remnants of pain and terror from the day.

The night is cold, and the moon is shining brightly in the dark sky, just the way that she loves. The voices of her friends, still laughing and talking, make her smile faintly as she closes her eyes and waits for sleep to claim her.

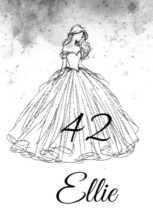

42

Ellie

When they arrive at the clearing, the enchantress is waiting. Her predatory eyes glisten like stars, reflecting a wisdom and power that makes Ellie shiver. She is draped in the same velvet purple cloak that absorbs the surrounding light. Her long black hair sways with the breeze, giving her an ethereal, almost otherworldly presence. A white owl with piercing red eyes rests on her shoulder, its gaze unnervingly intelligent as it watches the group approach.

She stands motionless, her presence commanding the space. Ellie can feel the weight of her stare, as if she is delving into her soul and reading her every thought. The air around them feels charged, crackling with an unseen energy that makes the hairs on the back of Ellie's neck stand on end.

Tristan squeezes her hand gently, grounding her. His touch is warm and comforting. She glances at him, his eyes locked on the enchantress, a protective fire burning in their depths.

"Welcome," the enchantress greets, her voice smooth and melodic yet carrying an undercurrent of something ancient and formidable. "You have passed the first trial. However, your journey is far from over."

Ellie swallows hard, "I'm ready," her voice steady despite the turmoil inside her.

Her lips curve into a slight smile, though it doesn't reach her eyes. "We shall see." She raises her hand, and the glowing orb appears once more, pulsating with a soft, mesmerizing light. "When you both are ready, lay upon the stones."

The owl hoots softly, its red eyes gleaming as it shifts on the enchantress's shoulder. The sound echoes in the clearing, adding to the sense of foreboding that hangs in the air.

"El, remember...," Tristan whispers, his breath warm against her ear, "You're not alone. We'll be here waiting for you when you wake up."

Ellie nods, feeling the truth of his words settle in her heart. With Saphirixia beside her, she steps forward and walks to the awaiting stones.

The enchantress's eyes flicker to Tristan, her gaze sharp and assessing. "You care quite deeply for her," she observes, her tone neutral but with a hint of curiosity.

Tristan meets her gaze without flinching. "I do," he confesses.

She inclines her head slightly as if acknowledging something unspoken. "Good. She will need that strength."

Ellie turns her gaze away, pretending that she didn't witness their exchange. It is strange, the different side of the enchantress that Ellie has seen over these last few days. She can't help but wonder, that if she were a witch who had lived over a thousand years and had witnessed what she had plus lost a bonded as she did, would she be any different?

When she and Saphirixia sit upon the stones, her gaze falls upon Saphirixia. "*Hey, Saph...*" Ellie breathes. "*Until death*?"

Saphirixia turns her long neck towards her, each scale shining against the morning sun. Her deep blue sapphire eyes connect with hers in a silent, unspoken understanding.

"*Until death*," Saphirixia replies firmly.

As she lays down once again, she feels the familiar spark of magic consume her before everything goes completely and utterly dark.

When Ellie wakes, she can feel the panic, but then quickly realizes that she is on Saphirixia's back, flying high over a familiar kingdom. *How did we get home?* Ellie wonders as they fly over Aetherlyn.

"*Well, this trial doesn't seem as bad as the first*," Saphirixia mutters blandly as she whips her long neck, peering around at their surroundings.

It is then that she hears the enchantresses voice whispering,

"In times of peril, when disaster looms,

Will you stand strong, or hide in rooms?

Courage tests a heart so true,

What risks will you take, what will you do?

Will you face the storm to save the land,

Fight for others, hand in hand?

In darkest hour, will you prevail,

Or falter, hide, and let courage fail?

If worthy you are, with courage bright,

You'll break the curse and restore the light."

"*Can you hear her too?*" Ellie asks nervously as her mind consumes each word of the Enchantress's riddle.

Saphirixia's only reply is a rumbling growl; she can only assume she is as irritated as she is.

"*When disaster looms…*," Ellie glances around, dread overwhelms her.

The ground far beneath them trembles violently, sending shockwaves through the air. Ellie tightens her grip on Saphirixia as the dragon lets out a startled roar, banking sharply to avoid the unseen danger below. The earthquakes rage with a ferocity that Ellie has never felt before, splitting open in deep, jagged pits that swallow whole swathes of land. The buildings in the town below shake and crumble with each second the ground shakes.

"What's happening?!" Ellie shouts over the roar of the wind and the rumble of the earth.

"*I don't know, but let's get down there*," Saphirixia responds, her voice resonating in Ellie's mind.

As they descend towards the chaos, Ellie's heart clenches at the sight of her beloved kingdom in ruins. Buildings crumbled, fields split open, and faefolk running in panic, their faces masks of terror and confusion.

Saphirixia heads straight toward the heart of the town, her mighty wings stirring up dust clouds from debris as she lands. Ellie slides down her side and immediately begins helping those who are injured or trapped. The faefolk look to her with a mixture of hope and desperation, their eyes silently pleading for guidance.

"*Saphirixia, try to call upon the other bonded dragons for help*," Ellie instructs, her voice steady despite the fear gnawing at her insides. Townsfolk were still crying, running around, and some gravely injured.

Saphirixia throws her head back and lets out a mighty roar that echoes across the kingdom. Within minutes, soldiers and their bondeds fly overhead, many landing nearby and helping aid in the rescue efforts.

Ellie works tirelessly, her hands moving with practiced ease as she bandages wounds and reassures the frightened. Amidst the chaos, a soldier approached her, his face lined with worry.

"Where is the king and queen? Please tell them we need help out here!" she yells.

"Princess Ellie, the king, queen, and the general are away on a diplomatic mission. The kingdom falls to you for now," his voice trembles with the weight of his words.

My parents are away? I'm in charge? Ellie realizes as a wave of panic crashes through her. The enormity of the situation threatens to overwhelm her, and her breaths come in short, as if she were drowning, unable to grasp any air.

"*Saph,*" Ellie chokes out. "*I cannot do this.*"

Saphirixia bends down and nudges her with her long snout, "*Yes, you can, we can. This trial is to see how well you'll rule.*"

Ellie shakes her head, completely and utterly confused. She has never had to handle a disaster in the kingdom before. She has only watched her parents. *My parents!* she realizes.

Ellie takes a deep, calming breath and she runs her hands through her wild, windblown hair. Her mind begins to race with all the ways she's seen her parents handle these types of situations.

After a couple of minutes she gets her thoughts together, "*We need a plan. We need to save as many lives as we can and organize the faefolk that are able, to help those who've lost their homes and farmlands.*"

Saphirixia's eyes meet Ellie's, their bond providing a steady anchor amidst the chaos that surrounds them. "*We will do this together, El.*"

Nagaara lands behind Saphirixia, her gold scales shining in the light. Her heavy feet shake the ground as she comes up to Ellie and bows her head. Ellie immediately looks to Saphirixia, who stares at her, "*She wants to help. She's waiting for your command.*"

Ellie can only balk at Naagara; She has never bowed to her. Nor has she ever shown her that much respect. She can see the intent in Nagaara's golden, sympathetic eyes.

"*Why isn't she with my mother? I don't understand,*" Ellie asks.

Saphirixia turns her gaze to Nagaara briefly then back to meet Ellie's confused expression. "*Zephyrion is with the king and queen. She remained behind to rule over the dragons. She wants to know what your commands are. She's ready to help."*

"Please tell her to gather other bondeds and assess the damage of the surrounding lands. We need to know which farms will need the most assistance first." Saphirixia nods slightly before relaying the message to her mother, who bows again and takes off into the air so fast that the gust of wind nearly knocks Ellie off her feet.

With renewed determination, Ellie rallies the townsfolk. She assigns tasks, directing the dragons and their riders to lift debris and set up makeshift shelters for those who've lost everything. The faefolk, inspired by her courage and leadership, work tirelessly alongside her.

Ellie feels her heart break as she peers over to see the town's beloved bakery shop crumbling, utterly destroyed by the quake. A fae female is hunched over on the ground as she holds tightly onto a youngling in her arms, sobbing.

Ellie walks over to the female whose eyes go wide when she glances up at her, Saphirixia close behind studying them.

"Your Highness, I'm so sorry," the female stutters out, wiping her tears. She then stands, adjusting the small youngling in her arms.

"Please, don't be sorry. Tell me how we can help you," Ellie insists softly. The fae female begins crying again, clearly taken aback by her kindness.

Ellie places her hand on the female's shoulder, trying to give her an ounce of comfort in the chaos.

"Don't be afraid. We will rebuild, I promise," Ellie promises softly. She can see the female's tense shoulder begin to ease as the familiar sparks of her power flood her and she hears the female's thoughts. "*Where will we live? My baby...what am I to do now?*"

"We're setting up shelters; we are opening the castle, and we'll find you both a safe and temporary home while we rebuild," Ellie declares.

"Thank you so much, Your Highness," the female continues to

sob as the youngling in her arms begins to cry. Ellie feels her grief and the devastating thoughts that consume her. She pulls her into a quick embrace before showing her to the tents that are being constructed for shelters.

Hours have passed as they toil to restore some semblance of order. Ellie is exhausted, her mind constantly racing with plans and strategies to help her people. Though despite her exhaustion, she never wavers. Her resolve only grows stronger with each passing moment.

Ellie stands with Saphirixia by her side, surveying their progress. The town is slowly beginning to recover. Shelters have been built, food and water distributed, and the wounded tended to.

"*You've done it, El,*" Saphirixia's voice is overflowing with pride. "*You've shown true courage.*"

Ellie smiles a weary but triumphant smile. "No, *we did it. Together. There is no way that I could've done this without your help or your faith in me. You have always believed in me and encouraged me to be better and to do better. If I didn't have you...*"

Ellie begins to say as Saphirixia shakes her head slowly and cuts her off, "*You will always have me. Until death...*"

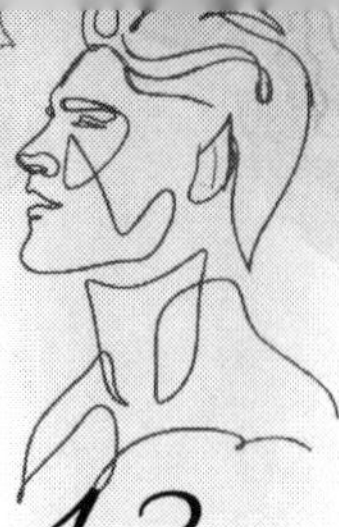

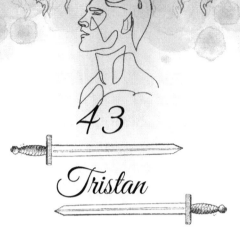

43

Tristan

Once again, the fiery dome rages around Ellie and Saphirixia. He stands there unwaveringly, patiently waiting as the afternoon passes and the sun begins to descend. The fear that she might not wake up is nearly crippling once again. He continues to remind himself how strong she is, how cunning, and how kind. *She can do this. They have to do this*, he tells himself. The thought of anything bad happening to them seems unimaginable.

"I never thought I would see the day," Breccan comments, walking up beside him. Tristan glances over at him, then sees Kyla and Stella about fifteen feet away, holding onto each other tightly, their eyes darting between Saphirixia and Ellie barely visible beneath the fire.

"I feel like I barely know you anymore," Breccan continues, shaking his head. Breccan pauses. "I don't think you even realize just how much you've changed recently. You really do care for her, don't you?"

Tristan only nods, before turning his gaze back to Ellie and Saphirixia.

"I hope you're being smart about this, Tristan, I really do," Breccan mutters flatly.

Tristan turns to face Breccan. "What exactly do you mean by that?" he presses, practically sneering.

Breccan put his hands up in mock surrender. "Don't get me wrong, I'm glad to see you so happy. I just mean that she's the princess...as in the heir to the Aetherlyn throne."

"You think I don't know that? You think I haven't tried not feeling anything for her? I'm not a fool, Brec. Bleeding stars, did I try." Tristan's voice grows angrier with each passing word.

Breccan cocks a brow and runs his hands through his red hair, then he adjusts and stands up straighter. "We both saw how hurt she was by that bladesmith," Breccan sighs. "She didn't deserve that. She's kind-hearted, powerful, thoughtful, and, dare I say, even beautiful. I can see why you feel something for her; I really can. Stars, I can barely blame you."

He gives Tristan a sad smile. "I know what happened to your mother, and I see what that loss has done to you over the years. I would imagine that you never wish to feel that kind of loss again," Breccan's face is more serious now. "I honestly just don't want to see you hurt or lose someone else that you care about. The fact remains though that they are the prophesized," Breccan points towards the fiery dome. "They can die at any moment. Oh and let's not forget the attempts on her life recently. I'm only trying to be your friend and protect you; I really am. All I'm saying is please just be careful."

Tristan's anger wavers, his eyes softening as he looks back at the dome. "I know, Brec. But I can't help what I feel, not for her. This *feels* different; *she's* different. And not because of some prophecy." He runs his hands through his hair, releasing a sigh, his voice lower, "I've always wanted someone who feels like home, and she does. This pull, this... connection is unlike anything I've ever felt before, Brec. I can't explain it. It's as if she's carved her name into the very marrow of my blackened, broken heart. All I want is to shield her and be there for her, no matter the risk."

Breccan sighs, nodding slowly. "Then be there for her. Be the strength she needs. It's about time you allow yourself to find happiness too."

This was the first time they had ever really spoken like this. He has always felt alone, just a little less alone with Breccan. But now, as he looks from Breccan to Ellie, he knows he has more than he ever thought possible.

They stand in silence, the crackling of the fire filling the air. Tristan's heart races, fear and hope intertwined as he waits.

Breccan clasps a hand on Tristan's shoulder, reassuringly squeezing it. "You're a good male, Tristan. You've been consumed with grief for far too long and unwilling to give your heart to another. I have seen the females you have been with. Yet, no one has ever looked at you like she does or you at her. I hope she's the one for you. Stars, I even hope that she's your mate. Just *please* don't fuck this up."

Tristan nods, appreciating the support more than he can express. As the seconds turn into hours, he and Breccan sit in companionable silence while the sun descends again. Tristan's eyes remain fixed on the dome, silently hoping to the stars for Ellie's safety.

In the distance, Kyla and Stella whisper words of encouragement to each other, their worry evident. They, too, know the stakes and understand the gravity of the situation. The thought of losing either of them is unimaginable to all of them.

The tension in the air is palpable. Everyone holds their breath, waiting for a sign. Then, as if answering their collective prayers, the fire began to flicker. Tristan's heart leaps into his throat as he strains to see through the dissipating flames. The glowing orb in the enchantress's hands once again flickers out.

As the last of the fire vanishes, Ellie and Saphirixia are revealed. Relief washes over him, and he quickly rushes forward in long strides, eager to see if she is awake. Elli's eyes flutter open, and she moves her slacked limbs when Tristan nears her side, lifting her up.

"They did it," Breccan exclaims, voice full of pride.

Kyla and Stella join them, wrapping Ellie in a group hug, their joy infectious.

"Are you alright? Did you pass the trial?" Stella presses anxiously.

"What happened?" Kyla asks in a low voice as she accesses Ellie.

As Kyla and Stella finally pull away, Tristan leans over and cups Ellie's face in his hands, his eyes searching hers. "Sapphire, say something," he begs, his voice breaking.

Ellie smiles slowly, as he rests his forehead against hers. She closes her eyes, her hand coming to rest on his arm. "We did it."

Tristan kisses her forehead softly, taking in her lavender and vanilla scent as it invades his senses. To his relief, she doesn't cry this time. Instead, she smiles proudly at them all after he reluctantly releases her.

The enchantress's voice pierces the air around them. "Well done, Princess. You both showed true courage." All of them turn to peer at her. The enchantress doesn't smile; her face is stone cold, almost assessing. With one last nod, she turns away and walks back towards her cottage, her shadows following her.

Breccan breaks the silence,"Let's get out of here; she gives me the creeps." All of them chuckle because only Breccan would say such a thing.

As the group makes their way back to camp, they chat animatedly. Ellie recounts the events of her second trial, her voice steady and filled with determination. She describes her challenges and how Saphirixia's unwavering support helped her overcome them. Breccan makes a few jokes to lighten the mood, earning smiles and laughter from everyone. Kyla offers encouragement, her eyes shining with pride for her friend. Stella remains supportive, listening intently and offering comforting touches.

The campfire crackles warmly, and the group settles around it, enjoying a well-earned meal. The dragons lay nearby, their large bodies coiled in repose. The rumbling of their breaths and the soft rustling of their wings filled the night air.

After they've eaten, Tristan approaches Ellie with a playful glint in his eye. He mockingly bows, taking her hand, eyes never leaving hers. "Princess, might I have the honor of a ride with you? If Terbius doesn't feed soon, he will become indubiously crotchety, and I'd bet that Saphirixia is also hungry."

Ellie laughs, the worry absent from her beautiful face. "Well, we wouldn't want that. I would love to," she replies, her eyes sparkling.

They mount their bondeds, who have been eagerly awaiting the chance to stretch their wings as they soar through the skies of Mystara, the thick dark trees of the forest spreading out beneath them, a sea of dark green punctuated by the occasional clearing or shimmering river under the moonlight.

The wind rushes past them, carrying the weight of their burdens away, if only for a while. They fly until they find a large lake connected to the river, a serene spot surrounded by tall, ancient trees.

"*Drop us off there*," Tristan commands Terbius, who chuffs his response.

They land near the riverbank; Tristan waits for Ellie to dismount. Grabbing her hand, he leads her to a grassy patch by the water's edge, where they sit side by side, the cool night air wrapping around them.

Tristan glances around, and before Terbius flies off he hears a gruff, "*Behave yourself.*" Tristan chuckles because of his bonded's grouse temperament.

"It's beautiful here," Ellie observes, her voice soft with wonder.

"It is," Tristan agrees, his gaze fixed on her. "Not nearly as beautiful as you."

He notices her blush as she looks at him, her eyes sparking in the moonlight. "Tristan, I—"

He places a finger gently on her lips, silencing her. "Ellie, you don't need to say anything right now. I just want to be alone with you, give you a moment away from it all. A moment to forget about the curse, even if it's only for a while."

Ellie smiles gratefully and nods slowly before she stands up, offering her hand to him once more. They walk hand in hand along the riverbank. They circle the lake, their footsteps coordinating with the rhythm of the water lapping at the shore. The moonlight casts a silvery glow on the landscape, creating an enchanting atmosphere.

Tristan can't help but notice how soft her hand is in his, ever so often giving him a soft squeeze as she peers at him, smiling under the starlight.

She's so indescribably beautiful that Tristan finds himself trying to remember how to breathe when she gives him a carefree smile, a smile he didn't know how desperately he needed to see.

After a while, they find a secluded spot and sit. Ellie takes a deep breath, her eyes reflecting the moonlight as she looks at Tristan. "I need to tell you something," she begins, her voice trembling slightly.

Tristan nods, his eyes gentle and encouraging. "Whatever you need to say, I'm listening."

Ellie opens up about her feelings, confessing the fears and doubts that have been weighing on her. She speaks of the pressure, uncertainty about the future, and the overwhelming responsibility of breaking the curse.

Tristan listens intently, his heart aching for her as he holds onto every word she says. "Ellie, you're the strongest person that I know. You have faced so much already, and you have done it with such grace and courage. I believe that you'll succeed, and I'll be here by your side. Whatever you need, tell me, and it's yours."

Ellie's eyes were lined with tears, but this time, they were tears of gratitude and, dare he say, love. She leans in, their faces inches apart, and whispers, "Tristan... stop talking and just kiss me."

Without hesitation, their lips meet in a forceful and all-consuming kiss, a blazing fire of desperate need.

Ellie shifts her body over his, straddling his lap. He grabs her waist and adjusts her, enjoying the feel of her on his lap. The heat of her body sets him ablaze. Her hands thread through his hair as she settles, the kiss deepening.

The world around them fades away, leaving only the two of them under the moon and stars. Tristan's hands slide up from her waist and across her back, pulling her closer as their tongues clash. The intensity of their emotions surge as he swipes his tongue with hers, eliciting a moan from her perfect lips.

He feels as if he is losing himself in her, the desperate need to shed her clothes and feel her skin against his lips consuming his thoughts.

Tristan reluctantly releases her mouth, moving his lips along her neck and down her open-cut blouse to the top of her breasts. Ellie shifts on his lap, and her head lolls back as if urging him closer.

"Tristan," Ellie breathes in a desperate and needy voice. *Bleeding stars, say my name again*, he pleads to himself.

As Tristan's lips find hers again, his grip tightens and he pulls her against his hard length, relishing the sweet sounds falling from her lips. "Tristan... more," Ellie croaks out as she starts rocking against him. Tristan releases a growl. Clearly, she has been holding back until this moment.

His hands move to unbutton her blouse as his eyes meet hers in questions. Ellie's gaze is piercing as she nods, breathing unsteadily, giving him wordless encouragement. He can feel the trembling in his fingertips as he runs his fingers over her now bare skin, taking in every inch of the remarkable female before him.

With one last brush of his lips against hers, he flips her onto her back and hovers over her. *Bleeding stars, she's divine perfection*, he realizes as his eyes roam over her body.

"*You're going to destroy me, Sapphire*," Tristan confesses in his mind, Ellie's hands roam over his back, gripping him tighter, pulling him closer to her. He kisses her neck and then moves slowly down her body, attempting to memorize each curve and the exact softness of her skin until she reaches her riding leathers.

Tristan gazes up at her, eyes ablaze, "Please, don't stop," each breath ragged, trembling as she pleads.

He quickly unties the top of her leathers, discarding them along with her underwear to the side before leaning over and claiming her mouth again, his kiss turns feverish; ready and willing to give her whatever she wants from him, even his heart.

44

Ellie

Tristan releases her lips and begins to pull away. Ellie grips tighter, refusing to let him go, as her fingers knot in his hair, attempting to pull him closer.

He chuckles against her lips, “My needy little Sapphire.” Ellie has to force herself not to pout once he pulls away; losing his lips on hers felt entirely wrong.

As he sits up on his knees, his ocean gaze roams hungrily over her body, he pulls his tunic over his head swiftly with one hand, revealing his chiseled, tanned form beneath all of his exquisitely detailed tattoos on full display. Her breath comes in rapid bursts as she relishes the sight of him kneeling before her, and a delicious ache begins to pulse inside of her.

She has seen him shirtless before, but now, with the moonlight casting a soft glow on his sculpted muscles, he looks more like a figure from a dream.

He is strong; every line of his body is a testament to his strength and training. She can’t help but let her eyes trace the contours of his chest, the way his taut muscles move with every rapid breath he takes.

How could someone be so perfect? she wonders, as a shiver runs down her spine. Her mind races, trying to process the intensity of her feelings. The sight of him stirs something deep within her, a yearning she can no longer ignore. She reaches out, her fingers lightly grazing his skin, feeling the heat radiating off him.

“Not being able to touch you or call you mine, has been pure torture.” Tristan confesses.

Ellie sucks in a breath as Tristan lowers himself down over her body. He starts kissing her breast taking special care to explore every inch. Slowly he begins trailing kisses down her stomach. She begins to shift in anticipation, eager to feel his mouth on her, he peers up at her and quirks a brow, obviously amused by her desperate need for him.

His warm mouth skimming across her skin, the sensation is euphoric, damn near divine torture. He expertly alternates between using his tongue and pleasing hot kisses until he reaches her inner thigh, teasing her and causing warmth to pool at her center in anticipation.

Tristan roughly grabs her and tosses her legs over each shoulder making Ellie gasp, trying and failing to steady her rapid heart, which is on the verge of giving out.

“I have dreamt of tasting you,” he admits with a smirk before lowering his face to the heat between her legs. When his tongue glides wickedly up her center, Ellie’s head slams back, nearly blinded by the stars behind her eyes. She slaps her hand over mouth attempting to cover the sounds coming from her.

"Sapphire.” He growls. “I want to hear you. Every moan, every scream, my name on that wicked tongue. I own them. Now, scream for me Princess." Tristan commands.

She loses all semblance of sense as Tristan sucks hard and then breathes on her clit teasing her. She lets out a low groan as she writhes against his mouth. Her body is beginning to thrum, and her sensitive pussy is throbbing as his tongue finally plunges into her. She struggles to breathe through her gasping breaths, feeling the raging storm building inside her chest making her moans grow louder.

He dips a thick digit inside of her, her eyes closing at the invasion. He curls his finger, teasing her innermost walls and reaching the most delicious spot. Ellie can feel her eyes rolling back in her head as he works his finger, tongue stroking in tandem, caressing her sensitive nerve. Tristan adds another finger, stretching her, the feeling of his long fingers sending her into exquisite agony. Realization hitting her then, that his fingers are blissfully warm, almost soothing, his magic pulsing inside of her.

"Mmmmm, yes, Love; let me hear you.," Tristan rumbles against her sensitive flesh.

Ellie's body jerks as a wave of pleasure begins to creep up her spine, making her cry out. The sensation of his power leaves goosebumps on her skin and floods her mind and body with a fiery heat from the inside out. She tries to tamp down the urge to tap into his power, which was silently begging to be commanded.

As if he could feel her on the edge of her release, he quickens his pace. Ellie is utterly consumed by his mouth on her, claiming her, tasting her, consuming her.

Tristan releases a guttural groan against her center, she can feel the vibration through her core. "You taste like pure magic," his words are nearly enough to send her over the edge of oblivion.

"Bleeding stars, Tristan, please," Ellie whines. She welcomes the crescendo that ravages through her body.

Ellie whimpers as she begins to feel lightheaded, on the cusp of her release. Tristan doubles his efforts as her legs begin to tighten around him. He suddenly rips his fingers out of her, leaving her achingly empty, her walls clenching around nothing. Ellie wants to sob from the beautiful twist of pleasure that reaches from the peak of her ears to the tips of her toes. Ricochets of pleasure start coursing through her body like a tidal wave.

Her whole body tenses as his fingers dig into her thighs, pinning her in place as he clamps his teeth down on her clit, hard. Her back arches off the ground, a powerful heat floods through her as a guttural scream escapes her. The pleasure is so intense that Ellie feels like she will disintegrate into a thousand stars as his name blissfully falls from her lips.

A cascading rain falls upon them, drenching them with the intensity of cannonball slamming into the lake just beyond the water's edge. However, it doesn't deter Tristan and his deliciously tortuous tongue from coaxing her body for every last drop of her release. Finally Ellie goes slack against the soft ground.

She tries to calm her rapid breaths, a chuckle works its way from her lips. She attempts to cover her mouth, she glances down at Tristan, who curses and then bursts out in laughter with her.

"Was that me, or you?" Ellie asks through a fit of laughter.

Tristan's smile grows as he leans over her, staring down at her when he says, "That was *all* you. Your eyes are glowing red."

Once their laughter begins to fade, Tristan leans closer, kissing her slowly along her jaw, neck, and shoulder, savoring her as her hands roam over his body.

"*I will never get enough of your sounds or your taste, Sapphire. They will haunt my dreams,*" Tristan admits, his own eyes glowing crimson like a raging fire.

When he finally pulls away, flushed and breathless from laughter, they rest their foreheads together, water droplets dripping onto Ellie's face. Tristan smiles, wiping them away and softly whispering, "You have changed *everything*."

"It's you who has changed everything," Ellie admits quietly in return.

Tristan pulls her with him as he kneels on the ground, Ellie's legs instinctively wrapping around him. They are both utterly drenched in lake water. The night seems to stand still as he holds her close, kissing her shoulder, the stars above bearing silent witness to this moment.

I want to bury myself in him, in this moment, and never come up for air, Ellie realizes as her heart swells in her chest. Her fingertips run lazy circles around his back and down his spine.

They stay there, wrapped in each other's arms, the night enveloping them in its serene embrace.

"As much as I'm dreading having to leave here, and as badly as I want to see you shatter again, Terbius just informed me he and Saphirixia will be here shortly," he winces at the admission. Ellie releases a sigh, wishing they didn't have to leave. The urge to stay there is so profound that simply trying to stand feels challenging.

After dressing, Tristan's hand finds hers once again as he pulls her against his chest, his ocean-blue eyes shackling her in place.

He leans in, running his lips along her jaw and against her cheek before whispering, "From the first night, there was something about you that I couldn't quite explain, but I felt it deep within me-like it was etched into my very being. It's like an invisible thread ties us together, drawing me to you no matter where or what I'm doing. That connection has brought me comfort and a sense of belonging that I never thought I would find. When I'm with you, I know that I'm exactly where I'm meant to be".

Tristan takes a deep breath, pulling away and meeting her eyes again, his brows furrowing as he continues. "I've always guarded my heart, afraid of the pain that comes with loss. But with you, it's different. I'm afraid I've already lost if I don't have you. You're everything I never knew I was searching for, Ellie."

Ellie's eyes glisten at his admission, his openness. The intensity in his eyes takes her breath away, vulnerability and truth radiating in his every word.

Tristan cups her face gently, his thumb brushing away a tear that has escaped as she grips his arm. "*I want to speak to your heart in a language that only you can understand. You've reignited my hope, Ellie, given me a reason to fight- and I will never let you go.*"

"Please don't. I feel like if you do, I'll be the one who's destroyed,"

Ellie whispers, the admission making her feel laid bare.

"Never," Tristan whispers against her lips before kissing her softly. Their passion brought down to a rawness that they hadn't yet experienced together. This kiss is a kiss with purpose. A purpose Ellie feels in her heart.

Heavy wingbeats break the stillness of the night, indicating that Terbius and Saphirixia had indeed returned. With one last kiss to her forehead, Tristan reluctantly releases her when they land and then they walk hand in hand to their awaiting bondeds.

Terbius releases a low, rumbling growl as they approach, which makes Tristan chuckle. When she peers at Saphirixia, her piercing blue eyes study her.

Ellie isn't sure what to say as a blush crept up her cheeks. She quickly climbs onto her back and bites her lip, waiting for her bonded to speak to her.

"*Did it rain here?* " Saphirixia asks. Ellie can't tell if Saphirixia is making a joke or not, but she feels herself trying to hold back laughter, which threatens to break from her lips.

"*I'm still learning to control my new power*," Ellie admits.

"*I see*," Saphirixia grunts, clearly annoyed.

"*What is it, Saph? Spit it out*," Ellie insists, then waits as they fly into the night sky. Minutes pass before Saphirixia finally replies hesitantly.

"*You genuinely care for him, and I see how much he cares for you. But Ellie, I can't help but worry*," Saphirixia begins hesitantly, her wings gliding smoothly through the cool night air. She turns her long neck to peer back at Ellie's face, bathed in the soft glow of the moonlight.

Ellie's smile falters slightly, a shadow passing over her eyes. "*Worry? About what?*"

Saphirixia sighs deeply, the sound resonating through her entire form beneath Ellie as she turns back toward the sky. "*Your first love betrayed you. I don't want to see you hurt again. Maybe I'm being overprotective, but there's something about him. He has deep secrets, El, and I fear how dark his soul is.*"

Ellie listens quietly, her expression pensive as she gazes into the starlit sky. "*I know, Saph. I have sensed it, too, but I also see goodness in him. He is kind, thoughtful, loyal, and gives me a peace I have never felt before.*"

"*You have the brightest soul, El. Don't let him or anyone else extinguish your light,*" Saphirixia admits softly, her eyes reflecting the moon's gentle light. "*I just want to make sure you're truly happy and, most importantly, safe.*"

Ellie reaches out and gently squeezes Saphirixia's neck, leaning forward to hug her tightly as they soar through the night. The cool breeze whispers around them, carrying the scent of pine and freedom. "*You're the most important connection I have in this world, Saph, now and always. I will be careful, I promise.*"

Saphirixia nods, her eyes a mix of relief and lingering worry. She feels the weight of her words, the sincerity in her tone making her heartache.

Once they reach the camp, the flickering embers of the fire cast a soft, warm glow over the quiet surroundings. Everyone has already gone to sleep except for Breccan, who stands guard at the edge of the camp. He only smirks at them as Saphirixia and Ellie approach, acknowledging their return with a nod before returning his gaze to the darkness beyond.

Saphirixia stretches her long wings tiredly as they settle down near the dying fire. Its crackling offers a comforting rhythm amidst the night's stillness. Saphirixia curls up protectively beside Ellie, her scales shimmering faintly in the firelight.

Breccan's smirk softens into a knowing smile. "Sunrise isn't far off," he remarks casually, his voice low but carrying a hint of amusement. "Another trial awaits you."

Ellie glances at Saphirixia, a flicker of concern flickering in her deep blue sapphire eyes. "We'll be ready," her voice resonates with determination. She leans against Saphirixia's side, finding comfort in her bonded's presence. The night breeze rustles through the trees, a gentle reminder of the challenges ahead.

Tristan and Terbius return to the camp just behind them, their footsteps muffled by the soft forest floor. For a long moment, Tristan's eyes meet Ellie's across the fire, a thousand unspoken words passing before Tristan gives her a wicked grin.

As they settle into their makeshift bedrolls beneath the stars, Ellie sees the distant promise of dawn coming sooner than she'd like. She closes her eyes, sending one last hope to the stars above that tomorrow's trial is not their last.

45

Ellie

Morning comes all too soon, and the lack of sleep from the night before makes her head feel foggy as she rubs her temple. Ellie sits up and glances around the camp. Everyone is awake, including the dragons, their majestic forms creating a protective circle around the group. The smell of breakfast wafts through the air, and she notices her friends eating around the fire, their faces lighting up as they see her.

"How are you feeling?" Stella asks, her concern evident in her hazel eyes. Her short black hair shines against the rising sun.

Ellie manages a tired smile. "I've been better, but I'll survive."

Tristan walks up to her, his presence a comforting anchor amidst her exhaustion. He leaned down, kissing her forehead gently, making her heart soar as if he knew she desperately needed his touch.

"Good morning, Sapphire," he whispers as his lips skim over the point of her ear, making her shiver at his warmth and the memory of the night before. Ellie feels his gaze sweeping over her body, clearing her thinking of the night before. The thought blushes her cheeks as he gives her a devilish smirk.

Stella and Kyla give her a wink when Tristan releases her, their smiles knowing and supportive. Breccan chimes in with a playful smirk. "Get a room, you two!" he teases, earning chuckles from the group.

Ellie feels a warmth spread through her. She is grateful for these light-hearted moments which lift her spirits. After breakfast, they begin to prepare for the day ahead. The weight of the upcoming trial hangs in the air, but they are ready to face whatever comes their way.

As they make their way to the clearing, the enchantress is already there, waiting with the same white owl perched on her shoulder. The bird's red eyes glow eerily in the dim morning light, adding to the enigmatic aura of its mistress.

Ellie takes a deep breath, her heart pounding as she approaches her. "How many trials are there?" she inquires hesitantly, realizing she hadn't asked the question before all of this started.

The enchantress gives her a cryptic smile. "We shall see after this next trial." Ellie doesn't like the insinuation, her words immediately put her on edge.

Her friends wish her luck, their reassurances filling her with a renewed sense of determination. "You got this, El," Kyla declares, squeezing her hand. "We believe in you."

Ellie and Saphirixia lay on the stones once again, bracing themselves as the enchantress begins her incantation. The familiar dome of fire consumes them, and Ellie feels herself drifting into a deep sleep, the world around her fading away.

When she and Saphirixia awaken, they find themselves in the same spot, but something feels different. The air is thick with anticipation, and this time the enchantress stands before them, her eyes gleaming with a mix of challenge and amusement.

"In this darkened hour, your choice is clear,

A friend must fall or face your fear.
To end your trials swiftly, a life must be the cost,
Or tread the harder path, where none are lost.
Will you cut the ties and break a heart,
To finish fast, but live apart?
Or will your loyalty stand firm and true,
Facing every challenge, together, through?"

The enchantress waves her hand towards her friends, all standing behind her as if frozen in time, unmoving, unblinking, just as she left them.

Ellie's heart plummets at the enchantress's words. She turns to Saphirixia, her mind racing. "I cannot choose between any of them," she admits, her voice trembling. "I will not sacrifice any of them."

Saphirixia's eyes soften as she shifts on the stone, moving closer to Ellie. "*We will find another way, El. We must show that our loyalty to our friends and loved ones is unbreakable.*"

Under the enchantress's watchful gaze, they speak. Ellie's resolve strengthens with each passing moment.The enchantress watches them intently as they make their decision.

Ellie and Saphirixia stand tall, their bond unyielding. "We choose to continue with the trials," Ellie declares firmly. "We will not sacrifice anyone, ever. We'll find another way to prove ourselves."

The enchantress's eyes narrow, a hint of a smile playing at her lips. "Very well then. Since you have shown unwavering loyalty. Let us see how you fare in the next trial."

"That's it? Just like that?" Ellie implores, confused as she glances at Saphirixia again before her gaze falls upon the enchantress again.

The enchantress's eyes soften slightly, a rare glimmer of warmth in her otherwise stern gaze. "Loyalty, my dear, is not 'just' anything. It is the foundation upon which trust is built, the bedrock of any ruler's strength. For a future queen, it is paramount. For a curse breaker, it is essential."

She steps closer, the white owl on her shoulder remaining eerily silent, its red eyes glowing. "This trial is to see if you would abandon those you hold dear for the sake of ease and expedience. A queen must value her people above all, and a curse breaker must have unwavering faith in her allies. Your refusal to sacrifice a friend speaks volumes of your character."

The enchantress pauses, letting her words sink in. "In times of crisis, your loyalty will rally your people, and your steadfastness will inspire them. To break the curse and restore magic, you must prove that both of your hearts are as strong as your resolve. This trial was one step in proving your worthiness, not only as a leader but as a person who values love and loyalty above all else."

Ellie feels a sense of pride and understanding wash over her. The enchantress continues, "Remember, the hardest paths often lead to the most rewarding destinations. Stay true to your heart, and you'll find the strength to overcome any trial."

Ellie and Saphirixia feel a wave of relief wash over them, knowing they have made the right choice. As the world around them begins to shift and change, Ellie leans into Saphirixia, ready to face whatever trials lay ahead. Their loyalty and bravery will guide them through, and together, they will break the curse and restore magic to the realm of Aetherlyn.

As soon as she wakes, Stella is the first voice she hears. “What happened? You weren’t even gone fifteen minutes! Are you okay?”

Ellie quickly rubs her eyes, trying to peer around. As she adjusts her eyes to the sun shining down on her, she feels Tristan's presence. When she sits up, he wraps his large, calloused hand around the back of her neck, steering her gaze to meet his. His eyes are laden with concern. "Say something, El."

Ellie feels a smile grace her face as she smiles at him, his shoulders relaxing. Then she glances at her friends, who are now around her, all shining with pride. Saphirixia moves behind them, her large form casting a shadow over them as she peers down at her, eyes never leaving hers.

"We did it," Ellie admits proudly.

"Thank the stars! The witch disappeared, so I suggest since you finished your trial in record time, we go enjoy the day." Breccan exclaims, rubbing his hands together, his eyes gleaming with mischief. "Better yet, why don't you take some time to work on your new gifts, Princess."

Everyone turns to look at Ellie, their smiles wide and she nods with shared excitement. "Sounds like a good idea to me," she agrees.

Tristan immediately wraps his arm around Ellie and helps lower her feet onto the ground. She feels exhausted and unsteady whenever she wakes up from the enchantresses' dreamscape. Tristan's steady hand on her back and the other hand gripping firmly on her side comforting her. As they all begin to walk back to the campsite to meet with the other dragons, his hand never leaves hers.

With each reassuring squeeze, she gazes up at him, the devilish smirk in his eyes causing her to flush. She wants to claim his lips again, to feel his hands upon her skin, to relive the indescribable pleasure he gave her. *Get yourself together. You can't just climb him like a tree in front of all your friends*, scolding herself.

Ellie pulls her gaze from his, realizing she has been staring at him and no doubt probably blushing now. *He's so damn beautiful it almost hurts to even look at him*, she thinks.

"What should we do first?" Stella asks, pulling Ellie from her wandering thoughts as they reach the other dragons. Each dragon stands or turns their head to glance at them as they push their way through the trees. Saphirixia strides toward them, but Terbius rushes over first, his heavy footfalls shaking the ground lightly beneath them. The look of concern in his eyes genuinely surprises Ellie. She watches as they communicate clearly, becoming closer, much like they all had on this challenging journey.

"I want to see her use my gift first!" Breccan jumps in, his brows rising in challenge.

Ellie squares her shoulders, attempting to tap into his power, when she feels Tristan's presence behind her. He slowly runs his callous hand down her arm, leaving tiny sparks along her skin. Ellie feels her eyes closing on instinct, his presence invading her senses, his breath along her ear, teasing her as he whispers, "I'm next, Princess."

Ellie swallows harshly, and when he steps away, she feels the absence of his warmth from her back, leaving her feeling empty. Stella and Kyla stand off to the side, closer to Sentiara and Kaida, who also stare down at her, waiting.

"I can do this," Ellie declares confidently. She decides that having a basic knowledge of the different gifts will be helpful. With one last glance at Breccan, who smirks at her, "What do I need to do?"

"Try and teleport over here. It's easy, just think of where you want to go and then, 'boom' you're there!" Breccan strides over to an open area in the clearing and digs his foot into the dirt, marking an X into the ground before walking back to where he stood.

Ellie nods, takes a deep breath, and allows the familiar sparks of magic to wrap around her, feeling the different threads of light each indicative of their gifts. She mentally closes in on Breccan's, a radiant green thread, waiting to be pulled to her. As she mentally grasps his magic, she opens her eyes and peers at the spot he has marked.

In the next moment, she teleports, landing a couple of feet from the mark in the dirt. As Ellie tried to steady herself, she released a huff of anger. "You didn't *actually* think it was that easy did you, Princess?" Breccan challenges, laughing at her.

"What am I doing wrong?" she huffs, trying to dampen her anger.

"It took me a couple of tries to figure out the semantics of being able to teleport exactly where I want to go. I can only go where I have been before or where I can see. So, taking that into account, try again, Princess," Breccan encourages.

Ellie repeats the process several times, still emerging a step or two away from where she intended. Frustration begins to take over when Kyla strides over to her, giving her a sympathetic look before saying, "El, stop trying so hard to concentrate and relax. All of our gifts come naturally; it's who we are. You know that. You can do this, try again."

With one last smile, Kyla steps away. Ellie concentrates again, allowing Breccan's magic to consume her, then stares at the X and teleports.

When Ellie appears, she peers down to see the mark on the ground beneath her feet. Ellie releases a squeal from her lips, her excitement taking over as she jumps up and down, beaming at her friends.

"Good! Now that you did that, try teleporting to each of us," Breccan challenges.

Ellie's eyes widen at his challenge as self-doubt begins to creep in. "Just teleport from one place to another, and don't stop until you reach Tristan." She glances at Tristan then, who only smiles and gives her a brief nod.

She prepares herself once again, latching onto his magic, then teleports. Each time, she stops briefly in front of each of her friends, who beam at her. When she finally teleports in front of Tristan, she feels dizzy, and he quickly steadies her. His ocean-blue eyes sparkle, pride shining on his handsome face, warming Ellie from the inside out.

"Good, Sapphire, very good," Tristan croons, the deep timbre of his voice making Ellie's toes curl in her boots and the familiar heat of his stare piercing her in place.

As if he could hear her thoughts, he leans in close, his mouth grazing over her jaw towards the point of her ear. "Are you thinking about last night, Sapphire? Because I am. I can still taste you on my tongue," Ellie feels her breath stall in her chest, his words making her feel like molten lava. Wanting desperately to pick up where they had left off, the urge to touch him and give him as much pleasure as he gave her is consuming.

"Do you lovebirds need a minute, or can we continue?" Breccan quips, making them both laugh.

"Let's see how well you handle my power, *all* of it."

The burning intensity in his eyes and deep voice made Ellie's knees weak at the challenge.

Ellie smirks, giving him a challenging stare before she forces herself to say, "Ready."

Tristan steps back, giving Ellie space. "Tap into the elements," he urges, his voice steady yet commanding. "Let them flow through you, consume you, and then bend them to your will." His eyes lock with hers for a moment, offering a reassuring nod.

Ellie closes her eyes, extending her senses, feeling the pulse of magic all around her. Tristan's presence is like a beacon, his crimson thread of power glowing brighter than all the others around her, pulsing and urging her to take hold.

Opening her eyes, she focuses on the small fire before her. Lifting her hand, she mimics his practiced movements, mentally reaching for the flames. As her fist tightens, she feels the surge of raw, untamed magic rushing through her. The fire responds, instantly erupting into a raging inferno.

"Now, use the wind," Tristan's voice cuts through the roaring flames. "Feel it, control it, let it guide you."

Ellie nods, her confidence building with each breath. She senses the cool, invisible tendrils of air swirling around her, waiting for her command.

As she raises her arms, the wind begins to stir, gently at first, like a whisper against her skin. But with her focus, the breeze intensifies, building into a powerful vortex that whips around her. The trees surrounding them bend in the gusts she conjures, their leaves rustling as if in reverence to her growing power.

"Now, the earth," Tristan's low and encouraging voice says. Feel it beneath you; let it rise to meet your will."

Ellie closes her eyes again, reaching deep into the earth with her senses. She feels the roots of the trees, the steady, ancient life force running through them. With a deep breath, she raises her hands, and the ground beneath her responds. The branches of the trees around them begin to move, creaking as they twist and bend to her command. They rise and intertwine, forming an intricate canopy above as if bowing to her will.

Her friends watch in awe, their faces lit with pride and admiration. Ellie can see their excitement and belief in her abilities fueling her determination.

Breccan's grin is wide, his eyes sparkling with approval. "Impressive, Princess. Now, combine the elements. Show us what you're truly capable of."

A surge of adrenaline courses through Ellie as she combines the fiery inferno with the swirling winds. The flames weave through the vortex, their colors shifting and flickering, creating a mesmerizing display of elemental power. The very air around her hums with energy as if acknowledging her control over the forces of nature. The trees bend and sway, their branches twisting and dancing harmoniously with the wind and fire, creating an awe-inspiring spectacle.

"That's it, Sapphire," Tristan's voice rumbles with pride. "You burn brighter than any fire. Be the fire."

Ellie's heart swells at his words, her spirit soaring. She feels invincible, and her confidence is reaching new heights. With a final, triumphant flourish, she releases the elements. The fire dissipates into the air, the wind calms to a gentle breeze, and the tree branches return to their natural state, swaying gently in the aftermath.

She turns to her friends, her face flushed with exhilaration and triumph, knowing she's only just begun to uncover the true extent of her new ability to wield gifts.

"Now that is how you use your power, I hope you took notes" she exclaims, her voice steady and filled with pride.

Her friends erupt in laughter and rush forward to congratulate her. Tristan pulls her into a tight embrace, his eyes shining with admiration.

Breccan claps her on the back, his grin wide and approving. "You've come a long way, El. I think you're better with Tristan's gift than he is," Ellie nods, her resolve stronger than ever.

"Watch it, Brec," Tristan threatens, making them all laugh.

"How about we go to the river?" Stella suggests, her eyes sparkling with excitement. "We can relax and enjoy the afternoon together."

Everyone agrees, and they begin their trek toward the river. As they walk, the sunlight filters through the trees, casting dappled shadows on the ground. The sound of the river grows louder as they approach, the gentle rush of water promising a refreshing respite.

When they reach the riverbank, Ellie takes a deep breath, inhaling the fresh, crisp air. The water is clear and inviting, reflecting the blue sky above. The dragons settle nearby, some lounging in the sun while others wade into the cool water.

Ellie feels a sense of peace washes over her. She turns to Kyla, sitting on a rock, her bare feet dipping in the water. "I would like to try your gift," Ellie admits, her voice brimming with anticipation.

Kyla smiles warmly. "I was hoping you might say that," she smirks, her long brown hair swaying as she claps with excitement before saying, "Just let the magic flow through you and connect with nature, similar to how you did with Tristan's but a little... deeper. Feel the *life* around you."

Ellie listens and closes her eyes, reaching out with her senses. She feels Kyla's magic, a gentle, bright orange power, intertwining it with her own. She focuses on the sounds around her. The rustling leaves, the chirping birds, the rushing water. As she concentrates, she feels a presence nearby.

Opening her eyes, Ellie sees a small bird perched on a branch above her. She extends her hand, and the bird flies down, landing gently on her finger. She can feel its tiny heartbeat, its delicate feathers soft against her skin.

"Hello there," Ellie murmurs, her voice filled with wonder. The bird chirps in response, tilting its head as if understanding her. She could sense its emotions, curiosity, contentment, and a hint of mischief.

Kyla's smile widens. "You're doing great, El. Now try to communicate with it."

Ellie focuses her thoughts, projecting them towards the bird. "Can you show me where your nest is?" she urges gently.

The bird chirps again and takes off, flying towards a nearby tree. Ellie follows, her friends watching with interest. She reaches the tree and sees the nest, hidden among the branches, with tiny birds inside, making Ellie's heart swell with joy.

Returning to her friends, Ellie's smile was radiant. "That was incredible," she admits, her voice filled with awe.

"You have got a real knack for this, El," Kyla exclaims proudly.

"Now it's my turn," Stella interjects, her eyes twinkling. "Tap into my gift and feel the emotions around you."

Ellie takes a deep breath, focusing once more. She reaches for Stella's magic and lets it merge with her own. As she opens herself to the emotions around her, she becomes overwhelmed by the flood of feelings from her friends.

Breccan's excitement and pride, Kyla's gentle encouragement and happiness, Stella's bubbly joy, and Tristan's intensity and protectiveness. Ellie feels each emotion deeply, their warmth wrapping around her like a comforting blanket, each of them shining with bright colors, just as she had seen the first time with Stella.

But Tristan's emotions stand out the most, shining like a beacon of light, calling to her. She can feel his unwavering devotion, his fierce desire to protect her, and the passion radiating off of him, his desire for her. His emotions are a blazing inferno, powerful and consuming. She can sense it all. How he would die for her, how he would fight anyone who dared to harm her. His love is so deep that it takes her breath away.

Tears fill Ellie's eyes as she looks up at Tristan. He meets her gaze, his eyes overflowing with the same intense emotions she can feel radiating from him.

"Tristan," her voice breaking with emotion, freezing him in place.

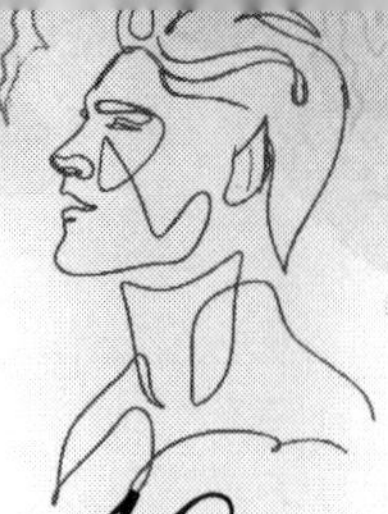

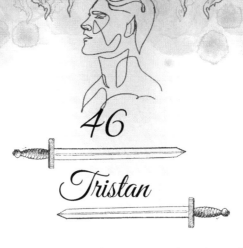

46

Tristan

He steps closer, cupping her face in one hand as she grabs his waist. "*Do you see now, Sapphire?*" His voice is raw with emotion.

He continues, his words now echoing in her mind as he leans into her, his warm mouth against her cheek, his thumb along her jaw, "*Do you see what you have done to me? I would do anything, whatever you ask of me. Protect you, fight for you, die for you, live this life with you, even burn this fucking world for you. Just ask it of me and I will give it to you.*"

She leans into his touch, her tears threatening to fall freely down her flushed cheeks. "And I for you."

Their friends watch, silent, moved by the intensity of the moment. Stella's soft words break the silence of the moment, "You two are making me cry," she sniffles, her voice overflowing with warmth.

Their lips meet in a tender kiss but beneath the softness, an electric current surges between them, raw and undeniable. Every brush of their lips carries the weight of all the emotions they've held back, radiating like a beacon in the darkness. Tristan's hands tremble as he fights the primal urge to pull her against him, to lift her off her feet and feel her legs wrap around his waist, to lose himself in her completely.

His pulse races, desire burning deep inside him like wildfire, threatening to consume every rational thought. The need to claim her, to show her just how fiercely he craves her, claws at him. He aches not just to touch her body but to intertwine their souls, to pour every ounce of his need into her until she feels the depths of his longing.

Pulling away from her lips, he sees out of his peripheral Breccan, Stella, and Kyla walking towards the river, their voices laughing and talking as Ellie stays in his arms, unmoving under his touch.

Her grip tightens, digging into his leathers, she leans into his embrace, he feels his heart racing as the words hang in the air between them. He knows she can feel how he cares for her as he envelopes her, strong and unwavering. Ellie in his arms feels like a force that seems almost otherworldly in its intensity.

His thoughts spiral as he can sense her trying to understand the overwhelming emotions coursing through him, all for her.

"I thought only destined mates could feel this much, this immense kind of intensity so quickly. Is it possible that we...?" she murmurs, her voice barely above a whisper, breathless with equal need. The weight of her own words settles over him, and a profound realization dawns on him. Tristan's eyes search hers; he can see the depth of feeling that mirrors his own.

"I have wondered the same thing," he admits, his voice rough with emotion. "From the moment I met you, my soul knew yours. There was something different, an unspoken connection that went beyond mere desire. I knew I was done for when I associated the stars with your essence. For what are the stars if I can't see them in your eyes when you look at me."

His mind flashes back to all the moments they've shared. The first time he saw her, the fierce need to be in her presence, to claim her as his own.

He has never wanted to be gentle; it isn't in his nature. But with her, everything is different. Each memory is a thread, tightening around his heart, weaving them closer together, creating a tapestry of indescribable love and connection that feels destined and preordained.

"You've helped me love parts of myself that I've always despised," she whispers, her voice trembling with emotion. "I thought that I understood love, but *this*..." Her voice falters as if the words are too fragile to capture the magnitude of what she feels. Every fiber of his being is drawn to her, an unbreakable bond that defies logic and all reason.

Tristan cups her cheek; his touch tender yet, possessive. "*This* is something more, something deeper," he murmurs, his voice rough with intensity. "For me, it's as though our souls are inextricably bound, like the universe itself has tied us together with threads that can never be severed. Words will always fall short of capturing the intensity of what I feel for you, El. It's a connection so deep, so undeniable, that even fate can't unravel it. I don't ever want to imagine a life where I don't feel *this*, where you're not by my side."

Tears well up in Ellie's eyes from her sheer, overwhelming, intensity of her emotions. She leans into his touch, her breath hitching as she whispers, "You are a part of me, a part I didn't know was missing until I found you."

Tristan's heart hammers in his chest, each word she utters carving deep into his soul. If there were a way to capture this moment in time, he would, holding it close forever. *This is where I belong*, he realizes, a fierce determination settling in—he will never let her go.

He pulls her into a tender kiss, their lips meeting in a soft, passionate embrace. *I want to mold her to me, taste her over and over, devour her until she is writhing against my tongue. To get her to a point that all she sees and feels is me*, the urge making him grip her tighter, slamming her hips into his while his other hand slides up the back of her shirt, feeling her soft skin under his palm.

The world around them seems to fade away, leaving only the two of them locked in this moment of pure passion. When they finally pull apart, Tristan rests his forehead against hers, their breaths mingling in the space between them.

"Do you think we could be predestined?" she asks, her voice tinged with wonder. *Bleeding stars, I hope so. If not, then there will be no mate for me*, Tristan admits to himself.

Tristan's lips quirk in an amused smile, a warmth spreading through his eyes. "Even if we're not destined, it wouldn't change anything for me. It's *you*, Sapphire, only *you*," his voice steady and filled with an unwavering certainty that he feels in his bones.

He takes a deep breath, his gaze never leaving hers as he his thumb brushes over her now swollen lips. "You're mine. Not even the creator of the stars will keep me from you," he declares, growling with the admission, his voice imbued with an unshakable conviction he hopes she feels to her core.

He can sense the profound sense of peace and certainty settling over her at his words in the way that her entire body relaxes against his. Tristan feels the words on the tip of his tongue silently begging to be uttered. Instead, he insists, "Let's go and enjoy the day. *Together*," his voice filled with a new sense of purpose, the need to see her smile at the forefront of his mind now.

They spent the rest of the afternoon by the river, laughing, talking, swimming, and Ellie practicing their gifts. Tristan feels immense pride each time she succeeds in using her gift, her power growing each day. *She will be fierce and unstoppable. My father will never harm her again.* The thought brings on a sense of unease but his faith in her is resolute.

As the sun begins to set, casting a golden glow over the river, he watches her, her smile bright as she speaks with her friends. She has come so far; there was still much to do, but he knows that they are stronger together. They will shape their destiny, their bond is unbreakable, and their spirits indomitable.

When night comes, Tristan desperately wants to steal Ellie away once more, but he senses Terbius's grouchy demeanor, clearly indicating that he's hungry. There is no negotiating when he's like. He and Breccan choose to take to the skies, but as soon as he flies away, he feels the distance from Ellie pulling at his heart, the urge to turn around and be by her side all-consuming.

"*I guess there is no use in me saying to stay away from her now, is there?*" Terbius grumbles.

"*Don't waste your breath. Nothing and no one can ever keep me from her now. Not even you.*"

Tristan adjusts his grip on Terbius' scales as they soar through the skies above Mystara. The realm of the fae shimmering below, a mosaic of iridescent forests, glimmering rivers, and dense fog. Beside him, Breccan rides Vespero, both of the majestic beasts gliding effortlessly in the moonlit night.

"Keep an eye out for any game," Tristan calls over the wind.

Breccan nodded, scanning the landscape below. "Vespero's already picking up a scent. Let's head that way."

The two dragons descend gracefully, their wings slicing through the cool night air. They land in a meadow bathed in soft, silvery light. Terbius sniffs the air, his nostrils flaring.

"Looks like we found a good spot," Tristan pats Terbius's neck. "Let's see what we can gather."

For the next hour, they hunt, their dragons devouring the game that roams the lands. With their bellies full and their riders' packs crammed with provisions, they take to the skies once more, heading back to their campsite.

Ellie, Stella, and Kyla await their return, the fire casting flickering shadows across their faces. As Terbius and Vespero land, they greet them with smiles and laughter.

"Successful hunt?" Stella's eyes gleam with curiosity.

"Very," Breccan replies, dismounting Vespero. He reaches into his bag and pulls out a bottle of liquor. "And I brought something special to celebrate."

Ellie's eyes widening in surprise. "Breccan, where did you get that?"

Breccan grins, a mischievous twinkle in his eye. "I've been hiding it, waiting for the perfect moment. I thought maybe once Ellie completed the trials, but now seems like a much better time." He admits with a shrug and the widest of grins.

They all gather around the fire, passing the bottle and sharing stories. The warmth of the flames and the camaraderie filling the night with a sense of belonging.

"Who do you miss back in Aetherlyn?" Kyla questions, her gaze distant as she stares into the fire.

Stella sighs. "My father. He always knew how to make me laugh, even in the darkest times. I know you all think that he is just an overly stern male, but he isn't, at least not with me."

Breccan takes a swig from the bottle. "I miss the old tavern. The place where we could all be ourselves without a care in the world."

Kyla nods. "I miss my mother's stories. She always had a way of making magic feel real. Stars, I bet she's so angry with me for leaving."

Ellie looks down, her voice soft. "I miss my parents. They were always so supportive, no matter what. I know my father will be upset that we left, but I hope he and my mother understand that I needed to do this without them, and with all of you."

Tristan remains silent, staring into the fire. Ellie notices and nudges him gently. "What about you, Tristan? Who do you miss?"

He looks up, his eyes reflecting the flames. "No one. I'm far happier here with all of you," he replies with a small hesitant smile.

Ellie smiles softly, understanding the unspoken pain behind his words. She stands and holds out her hand, "Come with me."

Tristan doesn't hesitate and takes her hand. They walk a short distance from the campfire, the night enveloping them in its quiet embrace. Ellie leads him deeper into the woods, the moonlight casting a silvery glow on their faces.

"Tristan," she begins gently as she halts her steps, "You can tell me. Whatever it is..."

He hesitates, then takes a deep breath. He knows she can see the pain in his eyes, the grief, everything that he's trying to hide from her. She doesn't know what she was asking for, but he finds himself willing to share with her things that he has never shared with anyone else.

"My mother died of the plague," he confesses, his voice trembling as he tries to look everywhere but at her, his gaze drifting to the stars. "Her death... it sent me into a dark place. My magic took over after I found her, and I nearly burnt down everything: our home, our crops."

Ellie steps closer, her hand drifting to cup his face and finally meeting his gaze. "I'm so sorry, Tristan." Her gaze is piercing. He tries to step away, but she grabs him with her other hand, holding his face in her palms.

“You're not alone anymore,” Ellie's voice was barely above a whisper, her words full of conviction and a silent promise.

Her words wrap around him like a soothing balm. He feels his walls crumbling, his last layer of defenses seemingly falls away. He looks into her eyes, finding solace and strength in them.

"I swore then I would never care for another so much that their loss will ever hurt me," he whispers. "I have broken that promise to myself."

“You will *not* lose me,” Ellie promises with a soft smile. “Not if I can help it.”

Tristan pulls her into his arms, his grip tightening. Their hearts beat in unison under the moonlit sky.

As they return to the campfire, hand in hand, he is grateful that he didn't have to discuss his father. Tristan feels like something has changed between them. A weight has been lifted from his chest, a hollowness that's been there for so long, slowly fading with Ellie's words. In Ellie's eyes, he sees a future full of light, where he can finally find peace with her.

Back at the campsite, they can hear the conversation has shifted to lighter topics. Stella is animatedly recounting a particularly embarrassing moment from their childhood, and everyone is laughing.

Ellie and Tristan sit side by side, and Ellie takes the bottle from Breccan, taking a long sip. "This was a good idea, Brec. We definitely needed this."

Breccan gives her a wink, "I figured it was time that we had a little celebration."

As the night wears on, the group grows quieter, each lost in their thoughts. Kyla was the first to speak again. "I miss my parents, too. They always knew how to make me feel safe."

Stella nods. "Being away from family is hard, especially when things are uncertain."

Ellie wraps her arms around herself, looking into the fire. "I miss their guidance. I always felt like I could conquer anything with them by my side."

Tristan listens, feeling a pang of guilt for not being able to share the same sentiments. His mother is gone, his father being the bastard he was; he knows that he will never feel as they did.

"You're not alone anymore, Tristan," Ellie said softly as if reading his thoughts. "We're your family now."

Tristan takes the bottle next, raising it in a toast. "To breaking the curse, and the family we've found."

They all clink their makeshift cups together, the sound mingling with the crackling of the fire. A small, understanding smile on each of their faces as they peer at Tristan.

The night deepens, and the fire burns lower. One by one, they drift off to sleep on their makeshift bedrolls, comforted by the silence of the night.

The only sound is the gentle breathing of the dragons nearby. Terbius and Vespero settle down close to the group, their large forms creating a protective circle around them.

Terbius lets out a deep, rumbling purr, the sound vibrating through the ground. His wings are tucked up tightly against his body, his eyes half-closed but still alert. Occasionally, he snorts softly, the warm air from his nostrils rustling the grass.

Vespero, on the other hand, stretches out his long neck and yawns, revealing rows of sharp teeth. He curls his tail around himself, the tip twitching now and then. The dragon's deep green scales shimmering in the moonlight, creating a mesmerizing pattern of light and shadow. He huffs contentedly, small puffs of smoke rising from his nostrils.

Saphirixia lay with her head resting on her front claws, her sapphire-blue scales glittering softly. She occasionally flicks her tail, causing a gentle swishing sound as it brushes through the grass. Her deep, rhythmic breathing is a soothing presence, a reminder of her constant vigilance.

Kaida is coiled up like a cat, her orange scales catch the dying fire's light. She makes soft, chirping noises as if dreaming of their adventures. Her wings twitch occasionally, and she let out a contented sigh.

Sentiara is the smallest but no less impressive. Her light blue scales reflected the moonlight, giving her an ethereal appearance. She lay close to Stella; her tail curled protectively around her rider. Sentiara makes soft, musical trilling sounds, adding a peaceful melody to the night.

The dragons' presence adds a layer of comfort and security to the campsite. Their deep, rhythmic breathing is like a lullaby, mingling with the sounds of the night. The crackling of the embers, the chirping of crickets, and the occasional rustle of leaves completed the symphony of the wilderness.

Tristan lays on his back, staring at the stars, feeling a sense of peace that he had not known in a long time. Ellie curls up next to him, her head resting on his shoulder, her steady breaths lulling him. "Goodnight, Sapphire," he whispers against her ear, his heart full.

As Tristan holds Ellie in his arms for the first time, a cascade of emotions wash over him, each one more intense than the last. The warmth of her body against his own feels like a light in a darkness that has enveloped his life for so long. He can feel her steady heartbeat, a gentle rhythm that echoes in his chest, bringing a sense of calm and reassurance that he had not realized he needed.

Her breathing is soft and even, Tristan marvels at how peaceful she looks, her face relaxed and serene, a stark contrast to the turmoil that often plagued his nightmares.

Tristan's thoughts wander to all of the dark times that he has endured. The loss of his mother, his father's manipulations, the beatings, the uncontrollable surge of his magic, and the isolation that has followed. He had built walls around his heart, convincing himself that letting anyone in would only ever lead to more pain.

Holding Ellie now, feeling her trust and vulnerability, he realizes those walls are crumbling. She has found a way into his heart, bringing a promise of healing and hope.

A sense of gratitude swells within him. Ellie has seen past all his walls, has listened to his pain, and instead of turning away, she has offered him comfort and understanding. Her presence is a balm to his wounded soul, a reminder that he wasn't alone in his struggles.

Tristan tightens his hold on Ellie, careful not to wake her, and whispers a silent vow to himself. He will protect her, cherish her, and make sure that the bond they are forging will only grow stronger. For the first time in a long while, Tristan dares to hope for a brighter future, one he refuses to allow his father to take from him.

47

Ellie

Thunder reverberates through the darkened campsite, startling Ellie from her slumber. She sits up abruptly, her heart pounding in coordination with the rain that lashes against her skin. Lightning flashes, briefly illuminating the clearing and casting eerie shadows on the faces of her companions. Tristan sits beside her, wrapping his arm around her and pulling her tightly to his chest. She glances around to see Breccan, Stella, and Kyla stirring, their dragons already alert and restless.

"Why's the lightning blue?" Ellie calls out, her voice barely audible over the roaring of the storm.

Tristan rubs her back and then nods. "The storm is getting worse. We need to find shelter."

Breccan was already on his feet, striding over towards them. "Something isn't right about this storm; I'll bet the enchantress is behind this."

The others agree, quickly packing up their camp and securing their gear. The wind howls through the trees, making it difficult to hear anything other than the cacophony of the storm. The group mounts their dragons, the creatures' wings straining against the gale as they take to the sky.

Despite the storm, they fly with determination, navigating the turbulent air currents with practiced ease. The clearing near the river where the enchantress's cottage looms ahead, its borders marked by a ring of ancient oaks that sway dangerously in the wind. As they descend, the enchantress appears from her cottage, which is unsurprisingly, completely devoid of rain.

"Welcome, Ellie, Saphirixia," she greets them, her voice cutting through the storm. "And to your companions as well. I see you have braved the storm to meet me."

"You could've simply just asked us to come instead of drenching us," Ellie demands, trying to keep the tremor out of her voice.

The enchantress smiles enigmatically. "Are you not eager to complete your trials, my dear?"

Ellie rolls her eyes and turns away to head towards the stones. Saphirixia is close on her heels, clearly as eager and frustrated as she is. The smoke from her huff warms her back.

The moment she lays down, the enchantress raises her hands, the glowing orb illuminating brightly in her grasp. They feel pulled into a deep, irresistible sleep as the storm and the clearing fade away.

Thunder reverberates through the darkened campsite, startling Ellie from her slumber. She sits up abruptly, her heart pounding in coordination with the rain that lashes against her skin. Lightning flashes, briefly illuminating the clearing and casting eerie shadows on the faces of her companions. Tristan sits beside her, wrapping his arm around her and pulling her tightly to his chest. She glances around to see Breccan, Stella, and Kyla stirring, their dragons already alert and restless.

"Why's the lightning blue?" Ellie calls out, her voice barely audible over the roaring of the storm.

Tristan rubs her back and then nods. "The storm is getting worse. We need to find shelter."

Breccan was already on his feet, striding over towards them. "Something isn't right about this storm; I'll bet the enchantress is behind this."

The others agree, quickly packing up their camp and securing their gear. The wind howls through the trees, making it difficult to hear anything other than the cacophony of the storm. The group mounts their dragons, the creatures' wings straining against the gale as they take to the sky.

Despite the storm, they fly with determination, navigating the turbulent air currents with practiced ease. The clearing near the river where the enchantress's cottage looms ahead, its borders marked by a ring of ancient oaks that sway dangerously in the wind. As they descend, the enchantress appears from her cottage, which is unsurprisingly, completely devoid of rain.

"Welcome, Ellie, Saphirixia," she greets them, her voice cutting through the storm. "And to your companions as well. I see you have braved the storm to meet me."

"You could've simply just asked us to come instead of drenching us," Ellie demands, trying to keep the tremor out of her voice.

The enchantress smiles enigmatically. "Are you not eager to complete your trials, my dear?"

Ellie rolls her eyes and turns away to head towards the stones. Saphirixia is close on her heels, clearly as eager and frustrated as she is. The smoke from her huff warms her back.

The moment she lays down, the enchantress raises her hands, the glowing orb illuminating brightly in her grasp. They feel pulled into a deep, irresistible sleep as the storm and the clearing fade away.

When Ellie awakens, she finds herself in the castle gardens, the familiar scent of roses and lilacs filling the air. The sky above is clear, the storm now a distant memory. She glances around, seeing Saphirixia stirring beside her. However, they are not alone; King Evandor and Queen Adelina stand near a marble fountain, their expressions are grave. Beside them, Nagaara stands, a queen in her own right of the dragons; her presence as imposing as ever, standing at Queen Adelina's side beside the king, Zephyrion, standing guard.

"The enchantress's voice filled the air:

In the heart of darkness, where dreams must part,
Will you sacrifice joy for a greater heart?
A kingdom's plea, a dragon's call,
Will you forsake your own to save them all?
When your happiness stands in the way,
Will you choose the light or let it sway?
For the realm to thrive and dragons to soar,
Will you surrender your joy forevermore?"

Dread fills Ellie as she speaks, "Father? Mother? What's going on?" Her voice tinged with confusion.

King Evandor steps forward, his regal bearing imposing. "Ellie, it's time for you to accept your responsibilities as the future queen."

Ellie's heart skips a beat. "What do you mean?"

Queen Adelina speaks gently but firmly. "To secure our kingdom's future, you must marry. A union with Prince Lorian of

Draegon will strengthen our alliances and ensure peace."

Ellie feels as if the ground has shifted beneath her feet. "Marry? But... I can't, I won't! Tristan."

King Evandor's expression hardens. "Mormont? No matter your feelings for him, they are irrelevant. This is about duty, Ellissandra. The kingdom comes first."

Ellie looks to her mother, hoping for some support, but sees only resolute determination in her eyes. "Mother, please... there must be another way."

Queen Adelina shakes her head. "There is no other way, my dear. You must do what is best for the kingdom."

Tears well up in Ellie's eyes. She knew that her life as a princess would be full of sacrifices, but this was too much. "I can't marry someone I don't love," she whispers.

King Evandor's gaze softens slightly, but his resolve remains firm. "You must, Ellie. For the good of our people."

Ellie glances at Saphirixia, whose face looks stern. She is locked into her conversation with Nagaara. "*Saph, what is it?*"

Saphirixia tears her gaze from her mother and looks down at Ellie, eyes solemn. Ellie wipes her tears from her face. "*Nagaara wants me to rule.*"

"*What? Now? But why? You do not wish to rule over the dragons,*" Ellie stutters as her gaze moves to Nagaara, her golden eyes zeroing in on her.

"*She claims it's time and that I'm meant to take her place, now,*" Saphirixia nearly growls in frustration, her chest rising and falling quickly with her rapid heartbeat.

Ellie feels a wave of panic flooding her veins. She had always known this day might come, but she had hoped it would be far in the future or never at all, for either of them.

Saphirixia's expression is brimming with sorrow but also unyielding determination: "*Mother says that sometimes we must do things we don't wish to do for the greater good."*

Ellie feels a wave of despair wash over her as she glances back at her father and mother. "Father, there must be another way. I can't make this sacrifice, nor should Saphirixia."

King Evandor sighs deeply. "Ellie, ruling is not about personal happiness. It's about making the hard choices for the greater good."

Ellie turns to her mother. "And you, Mother? Do you honestly believe this is the only way?"

Queen Adelina nods sadly. "Yes, sweetheart. I wish it were different, but this is the path we must take."

Ellie feels her heart break in her chest. The thought of marrying someone she doesn't love and giving up Tristan is almost too much to bear. But as she looks into her parents' eyes, she sees their unwavering belief that this is the right thing to do.

"Tristan is a soldier; yes, he is a Lord's son; he isn't a prince," King Evandor continues. "You need to marry someone of your station, someone who can help secure the future of our kingdom and broker peace for both of our kingdoms."

"But I love him," Ellie cries out, her voice breaking. "Doesn't that matter?"

Queen Adelina steps forward, her eyes filled with a mixture of sorrow and resolve. "Ellie, I'm sorry, my dear, but sometimes love must be sacrificed for duty. He's not your mate, and this marriage is for the good of our people."

Ellie rips herself away from her mother, leaving them all behind as she walks away. *This is too much, we're not ready, it's too soon. We can't do this,* she contemplates to herself. She can hear Saphirixia's heavy footfalls behind her when she stops and turns to look up at her.

"*Saph, what do we do? How do we do this? This is not a trial that I was prepared for...*" Ellie begs as she wipes another tear from her cheek, and her heart beats wildly against her chest. Saphirixia's blue eyes are full of mutual sadness.

Ellie and Saphirixia, though physically apart, are facing the same heart-wrenching decision. To pass the enchantress's test, they must choose between their personal happiness and the well-being of their kingdoms.

"*I feel that to pass this trial, we have no choice but to sacrifice our happiness for the greater good of the kingdom. Neither of us wanted this, but we both knew this would be a possibility, just one we were not prepared for so soon*," Saphirixia admits.

Her words sank into Ellie; she knew that she was right, but the choice was so much more complex than she ever thought it would be. Ellie could feel her heart-shattering in her chest; even though this was just a trial, it felt too real, the emotions too raw to deny—the thought of not being with Tristan tearing at her insides, making her feel utterly sick.

Ellie steadies her rapid breathing and attempts to steady her trembling hands as she returns to her parents, Nagaara and Zephyrion. "If I do this," she begins to say, her voice barely above a whisper, "if I marry Prince Lorian, will it truly bring peace and prosperity to our kingdom?"

King Evandor nods. "Yes, Ellie. It will strengthen our alliances and ensure a brighter future for our people."

Ellie closes her eyes, the weight of the decision crushing her spirit, soul, and heart. "Then I'll do it," tears streaming down her face. "I'll marry Prince Lorian."

Saphirixia returns to her side, speaking with Nagaara, who responds with a slight bow on her large head.

As Ellie and Saphirixia make their sacrifices, they glance at each other once more before everything goes dark once again.

As Ellie blinks against the bright sun, she sits up on the stone, her eyes immediately finding Saphirixia, who is peering at her. She can hear her friends coming to her side once again.

The enchantress's voice echoes in their minds, "You have passed the trial. You have shown that you can put the needs of your people above your own desires."

The storm has passed, and the enchantress stands before them, her eyes laden with a strange mixture of pride and sadness.

"You have done well," the enchantress declares softly. "But remember, true leadership often requires difficult choices. You must always strive to balance your duties with your own happiness."

Ellie and Saphirixia exchange a glance, the weight of their decisions still heavy on their hearts. They had passed the enchantress's trial, but at what cost? Tristan, Breccan, Kyla, and Stella reach her side, eyes full of concern as they all check her for injuries.

A tear falls down Ellie's cheek, and she is unable to glance at Tristan as guilt racks her. Tristan's hand moves to grab hers, but she quickly pulls away. The guilt of the trial, weighing heavy on her, makes it impossible to feel his touch. Knowledge that if her father asks this of her when she returns, she will have to make the same choice.

Ellie stands from the stone and walks away from them all without looking back. The storm clouds in the sky begin to part as she makes her way through the trees toward the river, revealing a bright and hopeful dawn on the horizon, the opposite of the turmoil raging in her mind.

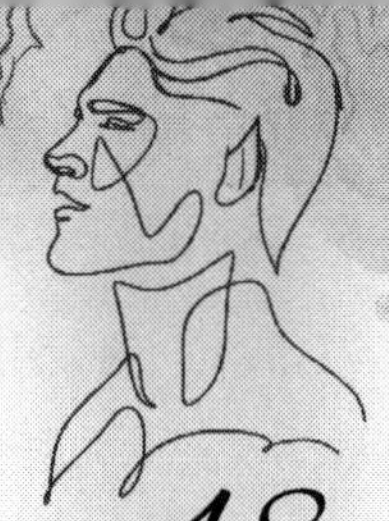

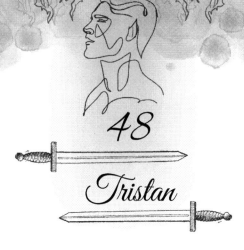

48

Tristan

Ellie walks away from them without looking back, away from him. He could see the tears that she had tried to hide from them all, but he saw them. The trial they endured was clearly difficult, and as much as he wants to follow after her, he holds himself back, giving her a moment.

"Is she going to be okay?" Stella questions, her voice brimming with concern, unshed tears lining her hazel eyes. Kyla comes to her side and wraps her arm around her as they embrace, eyes still peering in the direction where Ellie walked into the woods.

"It's El, she'll be okay, she's strong, and she has us when she's ready. Let's give her a moment," Kyla replies.

Saphirixia finally rises from the stone, stretching out her giant wings and quickly shooting into the sky. I guess they both needed space.

They all decide to head back to camp and wait for Ellie and their dragons. After nearly an hour, he can't stand it anymore. Tristan sneaks off searching for Ellie, and the rest of their friends sit around the fire.

It doesn't take him long before he reaches the river, but she isn't there. Tristan feels a wave of anxiety rush through him. As he closes his eyes, he wonders, *where are you, El?* As if he can feel her answer, there's a nudge not far from him. He follows the tug to her as it takes him to the riverbed.

When he sees her sitting against a tree, relief floods through him, nearly bringing him to his knees. She sits with her head in her hands, her long blonde hair cascading over her face.

Seeing her in such a state, tears at every fiber of his being. He slowly walks over to her, holding back the urge to wrap her in his arms, hold her close, and chase away her pain. Instead, he stops before her and waits as her gaze slowly meets his eyes. Her beautiful, deep blue eyes pierce him in place, her eyes red and swollen, evidence of anguish reflecting on her features.

Tristan crouches down before her, taking a deep breath before speaking, "Talk to me, Sapphire."

Ellie winces at his words and covers her face once again. Tristan moves to sit before her, giving her time to gather herself, hoping desperately that she will confide in him.

Ellie lets out an exasperated sigh, lowering her hands from her face as she gazes toward the river and the trees beyond. The rushing water loud in the silence around them.

"I'm sorry, but I just needed a moment," Ellie whispers softly.

"I understand. Do you still wish to be alone?" Tristan presses, quietly hoping to the stars above that she wants him there as desperately he feels he needs to be there with her.

To his surprise, she leans into him, and his arm instinctively wraps around her, pulling her close to his chest. She releases a slow, measured sigh as her body gradually relaxes against his. The subtle sign that she finds as much comfort in his presence as he does in hers fills him with a deep sense of peace. Tristan softly kisses her temple and whispers, "Tell me what happened."

Ellie lets out a shaky breath, her voice barely above a whisper. "In the trial, I was being forced to marry. They told me it was for the good of the kingdom to secure alliances and ensure our safety. Saphirixia was forced to take her mother's place, leading the dragons without her consent. Neither of us wanted it, but we had to sacrifice our happiness for the kingdom." She pauses, the weight of her words hanging in the air.

Tristan's grip on her tightens, his jaw clenching with anger and sorrow for her plight. "I'm so sorry," his voice laden with empathy says. I can't imagine how awful that must have been for you both."

Ellie nods, tears welling in her eyes again. "When we get home, my parents might force me to do it for real. They can make me marry for political gain, and I will have no choice. What about us? What happens to us?"

Tristan gently lifts her chin, making her look into his eyes. "Ellie, I will never let you go," he declares firmly. "I don't care what they say or what they try to force upon you. I will fight for us, for our chance. I'll never give up on you, or on us. You have my word."

Her tears now fall freely; they mingle with relief and hope. "Tristan, if they try to separate us—"

"They will not succeed," Tristan interrupts, his voice steady and resolute. "We'll find a way to be together, no matter what. No one could ever keep you from me."

The lengths I'll go to for her, to keep her safe, are maddening—borderline obsessive. But I don't care; she's mine, and I am completely and utterly hers, he admits to himself.

She buries her face in his chest, her sobs quieting as his words wash over her. "I don't want to lose you, not now, I just found you," she murmurs.

"You'll never have to find out," he whispers back, holding her close, vowing to himself that he will keep his promise no matter the cost.

"Tristan...," Ellie whispers so tenderly as if his name were an admission, a claim on his very soul. A claim that binds him deeper than words could ever reach. The softness of her voice fills him, wrapping around his heart and igniting something fierce within. *Stars, there is nothing I wouldn't do for her.* His pulse thunders, heart racing wild and untamed, utterly captivated by the way she breathes his name, as if it were woven into her very essence.

Ellie slowly, almost hesitantly, looks up at him, her sapphire eyes glowing with an intense, quiet fire. In that stillness, Tristan realizes she has heard every unspoken thought. She leans into him, her forehead resting gently against his in the cool afternoon air. He watches the rise and fall of her chest, feeling the electric charge between them, sending a tingling sensation down his spine.

The urge to kiss her is undeniable. He grabs the back of her neck and pulls her lips to him in a claiming kiss. Ellie grips his head, her fingers threading through his hair, pulling him closer as if trying to mold him to her body. She releases a whimper when he sucks on her bottom lip. She is so soft, so sweet, so undeniably right in his hands. *Stars, you are like fire in my veins.*

With one last sweep of her tongue against his, she pulls away and stands, leaving him needy and desperate for her. Ellie cocks a brow and peers down at him. She holds out her awaiting hand for him to stand.

"Where are we going?" He asks, giving her a small frown that only makes her chuckle softly. Her laughter is like music to his ears, a soft melody that he wishes he could replay over and over again.

Once he stands, she moves closer, backing him up against the tree and surprising him as his brows lift in confusion. "I want to try something," Ellie whispers with a crooked grin.

"Try what exactly?" Tristan watches her eyes darken with desire, then begin glowing crimson, freezing him in place.

The next moment, Tristan feels something wrap around his wrists, pulling his hands above his head against the large tree at his back.

Tristan whips his head around to see that vines are wrapped around his wrists, pinning him in place. When he turns back to glance at Ellie, her red eyes continue glowing vibrantly as a devious smirk plays on her lips.

She trails her fingers down his chest, lightly brushing over his muscles. "Remember, *Captain*, this is for me, not you. I'm going to worship you. Make sure you remember my name as I claim your pleasure."

Tristan's breath hitches as her hands roam over his body under his shirt, teasing and exploring, loving how her fingers linger on his adonis belt of his abdomen. The vines held him firmly, yet there was a gentleness in her actions that spoke volumes about her feelings. "Ellie..." he whispers, his voice thick and husky.

On her tiptoes, she kisses his neck softly, her lips warm against his skin. "Shhh," she whispers, her breath sending shivers down his spine. "Don't move."

Tristan feels his breath still in his throat, the muscles in his jaw taut, as a shocking heat floods through him.

Her kisses trail down his collarbone, her hands continuing their slow, torturous exploration. Each touch ignites a fire within him, a burning desire threatening to consume him whole. His muscles tense against the vines, but he doesn't struggle; giving her the control she so clearly needs. He knows that he can easily use his own magic to break the ties, but this is for her, so he concedes.

Ellie's lips find his again, this time more urgent, the grip on his shirt tight, as if she can't get enough of him. Desire floods through his mind.

Her body presses against his, her curves fitting perfectly against his hard frame. The sensation of her soft skin against his sends his mind reeling. *I want you to crave me, yearn for me, and burn for me as I burn for you.*

"Do you trust me?" her voice a sultry whisper.

"With my life," he confesses without hesitation, breathing heavily with anticipation.

Ellie's eyes soften for a moment with his admission, the crimson glow fading slightly before she leans forward, her lips brushing against his ear, "Good, let's see how good you taste."

Tristan closes his eyes, releasing a guttural groan. Her words light a fire in his veins, making him tug on his restraints. Her hands cascade lower down his body, each touch leaving a trail of sparks in its wake. The sensation is overwhelming, a perfect blend of pleasure and tenderness that leaves him breathless. *How can someone so sweet have such dangerous hands*? He wonders.

Ellie lowers to her knees as he opens his eyes; he can't steer his gaze from her as she unbuttons his trousers, his cock already straining as she slowly eases them down his legs and he springs free.

Ellie stares at him, drinking him in. His eyes never leave hers as she licks her lips and glances up at him once more before wrapping her slender fingers around him, her mouth descending on him.

Ellie licks the head of his cock, the feel of her tongue on him making him suck in a harsh breath. She licks him so deliciously that Tristan feels his eyes roll back, relishing in the warmth of her mouth on him. She takes him further into her mouth, sucking him softly, an agonizing rhythm. *She's pure ecstasy.*

"Bleeding stars, Sapphire, you're so *fucking* perfect," Tristan rasps out, eyes never leaving her incredible lips wrapped around him. His words make her hand grip tighter into his thigh, her nails biting into his skin, adding to the sensations.

She quickens her pace with her hand and then hollows her cheeks. She starts sucking him harder, while running her tongue along the underside of his shaft. Tristan groans through his teeth, savoring the pleasure she's giving him. He tries to reach for her so he can wrap his fingers in her silken hair, but the vines only tighten around him, restricting his movements.

"Just wait until I get my hands on you again, Princess," Tristan threatens. "I'm going to make you scream my name."

Ellie pulls away, her hand is still wrapped around him, as her thumb runs along his head, smirking at him, "Not before I make you scream mine first," she quips, then takes him back into her mouth.

Tristan groans as she swirls her tongue and sucks him deeper. "Fuck," he rasps through clenching teeth. She chuckles softly and he can feel it reverberate down his cock, making him impossibly harder.

He feels the familiar tightness running down his spine, the promise of a sweet release. "Are you going to swallow all of me, Princess? Think you can handle it?" He taunts through ragged breaths.

Ellie's only response is sucking him deeper as he feels the back of her throat, her warmth and torturous tongue pushing him over the edge. No one has ever made him feel this way before; no one has ever brought him to the edge of losing his sanity.

Tristan feels the familiar tingles crawl down his spine and straight through his cock as his sweet release explodes from him. Stars eviscerate his vision and his ability to think. He rasps out through a moan, "Bleeding stars, El."

Ellie slows her pace, sucking each drop of his release. She doesn't relent her tantalizing tongue as she licks him clean and releases him with a pop. He attempts to steady his breathing, but the way she smiles on her knees before him making his heart tighten in his chest; *you a fucking vision, a damn marvel to behold.*

Ellie stands as she slowly licks her lips, weakening Tristan's knees. "Release me, siren" he demands.

She only shakes her head and smirks at him. Ellie stands before him, lifting onto her toes and kissing him as the binds around him slowly release their hold. Tristan rips forward and grips her behind her thighs pulling her straight off the ground. He whips around and wraps his hand around her throat. His eyes are flickering a bright crimson as he slams her back against the tree, her eyes going wide with surprise and excitement.

Tristan's nose runs along that sweet spot between her neck and shoulder, breathing her scent in deeply. "I think it's about time I give you a little lesson in what my magic is *actually* capable of, Princess. Perhaps, you should... take notes."

He nips at her skin, making her shiver. She clings onto his shoulders, nails biting into his muscles.Tristan slowly grinds his already hardening cock against her leathers, while increasing the pressure on her throat. Ellie moans at the contact, and tilting her head, giving him more access to her soft skin.

With a wicked grin, Tristan reaches out with his magic, encouraging the traitorous vines to bend to his desires. He knows the moment that Ellie can feel them begin snaking around her body when she releases a gasp, eyes widening with the understanding of what he is about to do.

The vines continue their exploration, moving around her beautiful thighs, and snap her legs apart, opening her up further to him.

Tristan suddenly releases her neck as the vines begin hoisting her up for him. Ellie gasps in ragged breaths as she begins to shiver at the sensation. He runs his hands down her sides and starts running them up her thighs, heading dangerously close to his prize. She writhes in his arms, silently begging for him.

"Mine," Tristan growls as he runs his mouth up her neck, biting along her jawline. He suddenly grabs her thighs painfully, and the vines release as he slams her core against his hard length.

"Yours. I'm all yours," she breathes with a strangled moan.

"Holy shit, I'm sorry! Oh my stars! Oh my... sorry!!" Breccan yells. Tristan whips his head around to see Breccan standing just beyond the tree line, covering his eyes like an idiot.

"I'm going to kill you, Brec!" Tristan roars, as Breccan peeks through his fingers.

Ellie's face falls against Tristan's chest trying to hide from him, laughter bursting from her lips.

"You have got to be fucking kidding me," Tristan growls, leaning forward against Ellie, attempting to cover as much of the situation as possible.

"Nice ass, Tristan!" Breccan yells, his laugh echoing through the forest, making Tristan shake his head.

"If you don't get out of here right the fuck now, I will stab you!" Tristan threatens, meaning every word.

Breccan's boisterous laugh fades, the only indication he has left. Ellie is still laughing against his chest as Tristan releases an angry breath.

"Stars help me," he mutters exasperatedly.

"It's alright," Ellie chuckles once more before he slowly places her back on her feet. Tristan grabs his trousers and pulls them on, then runs his fingers through his hair, growling.

Ellie's smile is bright as she walks up to him and wraps her arms around him, resting her chin against his chest. She gazes up at him, eyes sparkling with mischief. "Awe, don't pout *Captain*; we're nowhere near finished."

Tristan smirks, "You. Little. Tease." His lips crash into hers in crushing her in tighter once more.

She reluctantly pulls back, "I do believe *you* are the tease now. Alas, we should probably head back," she sighs, grabbing his hand in hers, she tugs him back towards the campsite.

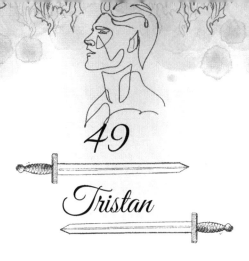

49

Tristan

They walk slowly, hand in hand. Tristan glances down at her as they walk, unable to keep his gaze from her for too long. When they reach the camp, Breccan gives them a wry smile but Tristan shoots daggers at him. Breccan's bursts out a boisterous laugh.

Thankfully, Stella and Kyla seem utterly confused by his behavior, as evidenced by their confused expressions. Stella's eyes glow briefly before she smiles knowingly but blessedly keeps her mouth shut.

“What happened during the trial?” Kyla probes eagerly, oblivious, her eyes full of concern as she leans forward and waits for Ellie to speak.

Tristan can see the grief wash back over Ellie's face at the memory, her throat tightening, clearly trying to find the words. Tristan studies her, watching her closely, his hand upon her back reassuring her that he is with her.

Ellie moves closer to the fire, finding a seat on a log. She runs her hands over her face and releases her breath before meeting their eyes one by one before she speaks.

“Saphirixia and I woke up back in Aetherlyn. The king and queen were there, along with Nagaara. My parents told me that I must marry for the good of the Kingdom,” Ellie hesitates when Stella and Kyla gasp in surprise.

“Wait, they wouldn't do that to you, would they?” Stella questions, concern evident as she shifts on her log.

Ellie shrugs. "I mean, they *could.* I tried to beg them not to force me to marry." Ellie's gaze slowly meets Tristan's, whose face is pinched with concern.

"I told them of my feelings for Tristan, but they dismissed them and urged that it was for the best. Then Nagaara forced Saphirixia to take over as ruler of the dragons. We both had to make a choice: if we wanted to pass the trial, then we needed to sacrifice our happiness for the good of the kingdom."

"That seems like a bullshit trial if you ask me," Breccan exclaims as he shakes his head.

"Well, thankfully, it is just a trial, right? It isn't real. The king and queen would never force you to marry, but even if they did, you wouldn't," Kyla states.

Ellie peers down at her hands when Tristan stiffens near her. He reflects as she sits there quietly, fidgeting with her hands. The thought that he might lose her because the king and queen refuse to allow them to be together sets a new fear in Tristan, making his heart ache in his chest. His anger rises at the royals and the power that they hold over their heir.

Kyla leans forward, her expression serious. "Ellie, if it really came down to it and the king ordered you to do so, would you go through with it?"

The question hangs in the air, heavy with unspoken implications. Ellie looks at Tristan, his heart breaking at the sight of pain in her eyes. Without a word, Tristan stands up and walks away, more hurt than angry. He doesn't wait for her reply; he can feel his magic rioting along his skin, his ebbing anger making his magic spark, begging for a release.

Ellie follows him into the woods, he can feel her behind him, making his heart pound; he can't look at her right now because if he does, he will cave. She finds him leaning against a tree, his head bowed, tension radiating from his body in waves.

“Tristan,” she calls softly, stepping closer. “Please don’t walk away.”

He turns to face her, his eyes blazing with a mixture of pain and anger. "You hesitated, Ellie. I laid my heart bare before you, stripped myself of every shield and wall. I told you that I’m in this with you, I’m not going anywhere. Yet, you hesitated. Why?"

Ellie takes a deep breath, her voice trembling with emotion. “Tristan, I care about you more than I’ve ever cared about anyone. The thought of being without you terrifies me.”

Tristan’s jaw clenches as panic begins to creep into his mind. “I need to hear you say it, Sapphire. If they force you, will you give this up?” He indicates to them with his finger.

Ellie steps closer, her heart aching with the depth of her feelings. “No. We’ll do whatever it takes to stay together. When we return, we’ll fight for us, for our bond. I swear to you; it was just a trial. If they ask this of me, I will fight them, show them how much I care for you and that I refuse to give you up without a fight, not now, not ever. You will make as good of a king as any *royal* idiot they would choose.”

As she speaks, she reaches out and gently touches his face, her fingers brushing against his cheek. Her touch seems to instantly calm him, his anger melts away to reveal the hurt beneath. Tristan's heart aches at the sight of her distress. The vulnerability in her eyes mirrors his own, and he realizes just how deeply he needs her.

A tear slips down her cheek as she speaks, the weight of her emotions too much for him to bear. Tristan reaches out, gently brushing the tear away. The simple act of touching her feels like a lifeline, grounding him amid his turmoil.

“I love you,” he whispers, his voice raw with emotion.

Ellie’s face immediately softens as fear wracks him, realizing that the three words flooded out of him so naturally that he didn't even have a chance to realize what he was saying to her. *What if she doesn't feel the same?*

"I love you too, Tristan," she admits, her voice barely above a whisper.

Tristan feels an overwhelming rush of relief and indescribable joy. The tight knot in his chest loosened, replaced by a warmth that spread through his entire being, a warmth that reached his soul. The depth of her love for him shining through her eyes, washing away any of his doubts.

Tristan gently cups her face in his hands, pulling her close until their foreheads touch. The air between them hums, charged with a crackling energy, as if the world itself is holding its breath.

Then without a second of hesitation, their lips meet in a tender, heartfelt kiss. The world around them fades away, leaving only the two of them bound by their love and determination to stay together. The kiss is a silent promise, a testament to the strength of their bond.

Tristan pours all his love and devotion into their kiss, hoping she could feel the intensity of his emotions flooding through his veins. Their connection feels almost palpable, a tangible thread tying their hearts together.

"No matter what happens, it's you and me now," Tristan murmurs, his voice overflowing with conviction. He wants her to know that he will never abandon her, no matter the challenges ahead.

Ellie nods, "You and me," she agrees. The words hold so much meaning, encapsulating their shared resolve to fight for their love, no matter the cost.

They stand there, wrapped in each other's arms, drawing strength from one another. Tristan feels an unshakeable determination well up within him. He will do whatever it takes to protect her, to keep their love alive. The trials ahead seem less daunting, knowing that they have each other to lean on, something to fight for.

As the moon rises in the sky, casting a silver glow over them, Ellie's touch becomes more insistent, her kisses more fervent. The world around them fades away, leaving just the two of them in their private paradise.

She smiles a radiant, beautiful smile that takes his breath away. "Know this," she confesses softly, "No matter what challenges we face, no matter what sacrifices we must make, I'll always choose you."

Tristan pulls her into his arms, holding her close as they bask in the quiet of the night. The stars above bear witness to their unbreakable bond, a love that would endure any trial, any hardship. Together, they were unstoppable, their hearts beating in perfect harmony.

For the rest of the night, Ellie doesn't leave his side. After eating dinner, she lays beside him. Her breathing is steady, and her eyes are closed as he wipes a stray hair from her beautiful face.

He knows when they finally return home, that the king and queen will not be thrilled about their relationship. He will do whatever it takes to prove his feelings for her and to prove to them that he will take care of her. That he will love her as no one else would. Tristan never cared that she was a princess, and he couldn't care less what that means for him as long as she is his. Everything else be damned.

His thoughts drift to his father, knowing how angry he will be to learn of their relationship and his complete violation of his demand to stay away from her, but he doesn't care. Tristan knows that he will have to tread carefully; the risk of his father beating him to an inch of his life or, worse, using his gift on him weighs heavy on him.

Tristan runs his hand over his face, exhaustion seeping into his bones. He hopes her trials are nearly complete; he isn't sure how much longer he can see the pain in her eyes and the challenges she has to go through. He would go through them for her if he could, if it would only spare her an ounce of suffering.

Tristan pulls Ellie tighter into his chest, and she shifts against him, molding to his body. A soft sigh leaves her lips. Tristan leans forward, placing his lips on her forehead, inhaling her intoxicating lavender and vanilla scent, allowing it to loll him into a comforting sleep.

50

Ellie

Ellie rises from Tristan's chest, careful not to disturb his peaceful slumber. She gazes down at his beautiful face, taking in the calmness that sleep brought to his features. A pang of guilt begins to build up within her.

Breccan, Kyla, and Stella are still asleep, their breathing even and quiet. The dragons also rest, their massive forms barely stirring in the early morning light.

Ellie reaches out to Saphirixia, their bond between them allowing her thoughts to flow effortlessly. "*Saph, wake up. I want to finish this. Are you with me?*"

Saphirixia's mind stirs, her consciousness merging with Ellie's. "*Are you sure?*" she implores, her voice gentle but laced with concern.

"*Yes, I'm sure. We need to do this,*" Ellie responds with determination.

They move silently and quickly, careful not to wake their friends. The camp is still; the only sound is the gentle rustling of leaves, soft rumbles from their dragons, and the distant call of morning birds. Ellie and Saphirixia slip away together, heading towards the enchantress's cottage along the river. The sun is still barely upon the horizon, casting a pale, golden light over the landscape.

Ellie knocks on the enchantress's heavy wooden door with firm resolve. The enchantress stands there as the door swings open, her predatory eyes gleaming with curiosity.

"We're ready to finish these trials," Ellie declares, her voice steady despite the fluttering of nerves in her stomach.

The enchantress studies her for a long moment, then nods slowly. "This trial will be different from the others. There is a chance you may not survive. Are you prepared for that?" Her voice is calm and melodic, but the gravity of her words hangs heavily in the air.

Ellie squares her shoulders, her gaze unwavering. "I am."

"You should probably say goodbye to your friends, just in case," the enchantress advises, her tone almost gentle, surprising her.

Ellie considers for a moment, but her resolve forces her not to falter. She shakes her head, "There's no time for that. We're ready now."

The enchantress nods again, a hint of respect in her eyes. "Very well. Follow me."

They walk over to their individual stones; the familiar setting now tinged with an ominous sense of finality. Ellie and Saphirixia take their places, their bond pulsing with shared determination and unspoken words of encouragement as they glance at one another. The enchantress begins her incantation, her voice rising and falling in a rhythm that seems to pulse through the very ground beneath them.

As the fiery dome consumes them once again, Ellie feels the world around her fading away. She is plunged into darkness, a deep, endless void that swallows her whole.

"Where are we?" Ellie whispers as she glances around, finding her and Saphirixia in a clearing in the woods.

The enchantress's words filling the air around them once again,
"In the realm where shadows meet the light,
To break the curse, you both must fight.
Strength of heart and strength of will,
Prove your power, your spirits still.
Face the darkness, conquer the foe,
Show your might; let your courage show.
In battle's heat, your worth will shine,
To lift the curse, your fates align."

As Ellie rises to her feet, she notices movement at the edge of the clearing. Two warriors step out from the shadows, each accompanied by a massive dragon. The warriors are unlike any she has seen before. The towering figures' muscles visibly ripple under their enchanted armor as they move. Their faces are obscured by ornate helmets adorned with intricate designs that glint ominously in the light.

She feels the first ping of fear toward the daunting dragons that accompany the warriors. Each a behemoth of scales, their sinew heads start to snake. The first dragon with scales as red as blood and sharp spikes running down its back, clips its enormous claws through the stoney ground. Its eyes burning with fierce intelligence and a hunger for battle.

The second dragon, deep green, is equally terrifying. Its mouth spreads wide to reveal teeth like daggers as its spiked, club ended tail lifts and sways. The ground shakes with every step the things take toward her.

Ellie's breath catches in her throat. The size and ferocity of the dragons are intimidating, and the warriors look every bit as formidable. She hopes desperately that this is their last test. The enchantress's voice echoes in her mind, reminding her that she must prove herself worthy through trials.

Saphirixia growls low in her throat, sensing the impending challenge. Ellie places a reassuring hand on her dragon's flank, drawing strength from their bond.

The lead warrior, a tall figure with a sword glinting at his side, steps forward. "Are you ready to die?" He taunts coming out so voice deep, she feels it rumble into her bones.

Ellie feels her mouth dry but squares her shoulder in challenge, "Are you?"

The second warrior, equal in strength with twin daggers strapped to his hips, speaks next, "Fight us and win or fall and be deemed unworthy."

The two dragons accompanying the warriors snarl, their eyes fixing on Saphirixia. The tension in the clearing is palpable and the air is thick with the promise of battle to come.

Ellie glances at Saphirixia, who lowers her head in readiness. They have trained for moments like this, and their bond grows stronger with each challenge. Ellie knows they can't afford to lose, not with the fate of Aetherlyn and the restoration of fae magic resting on their shoulders.

Taking a deep breath, Ellie draws her sword, the blade catching the light. "We will not fail," She declares, her voice steady despite the fear gnawing at her insides.

The lead warrior nods, a flicker of respect in his eyes. "Then let's begin."

With a deafening roar, the two dragons launch into the air, their massive wings stirring up a whirlwind of dirt and leaves. The warriors take their stances, their weapons gleaming menacingly as they draw them. Bloodlust shining in their eyes.

Ellie stands her ground, watching Saphirixia take to the sky to engage the enemy dragons far above. Her bonded's powerful muscles coil beneath her scales as her wings beat furiously to meet the first dragon head-on. Claws clash and teeth snap as the dragons battle midair. Their roars echoing through the forest, the trees bending with the force.

Ellie turns to face off against the lead warrior. He swings his sword in a wide arc, aiming for her midsection. Ellie parries the strike with skill and precision her training has molded into her. The bond with Saphirixia guides her every move, pushing her to become the sword fighter she needs to be.

She counters the next with a quick thrust, but the warrior moves faster. Deflecting her blade with ease, Ellie staggers back. The warrior is so much stronger than she imagined.

Turning, she sees the second warrior moving in too swiftly. Before she can move, he starts to circle her. His twin daggers gleaming in the dim light is her only warning before they slip the air. Ellie twists just in time to block his attack. The clash of steel ringing through the clearing and forcing Ellie's arms to slightly shake. Before the imposing figure can pull his weapons back, Ellie lanches a powerful kick into its hip. Knocking the warrior off balance, she feels a bit of more faith she can do is swarm in.

The lead warrior takes advantage of her distraction. He slashes out, the blade cutting through her upper thigh. Pain shoots through Ellie veins as his blade rips into her flesh. Hot and searing agony invades every inch of her. "I will not fall; I will not fail," She repeats to herself as she forces her leg to hold strong.

Determined not to show her opponents, or the enchantress, any weakness, Ellie grits her teeth and fights through the pain threatening to buckle her resolve. She launches herself at the lead warrior, their swords clashing in a shower of scattering sparks.

By the sounds reaching her from above, Saphirixia and the enemy dragons continue their fierce battle. The air echoing with the sound of clashing scales and roars of fury. Ellie wishes she could peer up and ensure Saphirixia was all right, but she couldn't risk the distraction. The pain in her leg makes her limp, and the loss of blood makes her feel lightheaded.

She quickly risks a quick look up to see Saphirixia fighting with ferocity she's never seen. Ellie catches a glimpse of crimson lines from where the dragons marking her bonded. Though she's bloodied, her injuries appear to only be at a superficial level. She clamps her powerful jaws around the crimson dragon's neck, forcing it to the ground, blood spraying on the ground beneath them. Ellie smiles at the sound.

Ellie presses her advantage, driving the lead warrior back with a series of rapid strikes. Her sword clashes against his, sparks flying with each impact. She manages to land a blow on his arm, the blade slicing through his armor and drawing blood. She revels in the small win as the warrior grunts in pain. Yet, he still doesn't falter, his eyes burning with a raging fire.

The second warrior attempts to flank Ellie again, his daggers flash. Ellie twists just in time, deflecting the attack with a swift parry. She counters with a powerful strike, her sword biting into the warrior's armor and forcing him back, making her stumble. Her leg protests the violent movement, but she doesn't let herself wince.

Ellie glances up to see the dragons above continuing their fierce struggle. Saphirixia's injuries still seem mendable, and she manages to gain the upper hand. With a powerful dive, she drives the crimson dragon into the ground. Its massive body crashing into the trees, Saphirixia's battle roars fill Ellie with a new wave of confidence.

Saphirixia swoops into the sky again, her wings beating with a new found power and impending victory. She unleashes a torrent of dragon fire, the brilliant flames scorching the emerald dragon's wings, sending it plummeting. It's cries of pain cutting off as it smacks to the ground with a sickening crunch.

Just as the crimson beast lifts its head from the broken treeline, Ellie's focus snaps back to the deadly dance she's locked in with the lead warrior. She ducks and weaves, her sword a blur of silver as she parries and strikes. The lead warrior is relentless, his strikes powerful and precise. Ellie can feel her strength waning, the pain in her leg a constant, throbbing reminder of her vulnerability. Yet, she presses on, her determination unwavering as she tells herself, "*Today will not be our last.*"

She launches a series of rapid, aggressive strikes, pushing the lead warrior back. Her sword clashes against his, each impact making her push harder. Finally, she manages to land a blow on his arm. This time, the blade slices through his armor and draws blood. The warrior grunts loudly as he peers at his injury, then wraps his hand firmly around his arm trying to stifle the bleeding.

The second warrior attempts to flank Ellie again, she catches sight of him and tries to find her balance. She twists as his blade cuts across her arm, pain wracking her body once again. Seeing the opening, she blocks his next strike by countering with a swipe of her blade across his neck. The warrior falls to his knees, hands around his neck, trying to stop the blood flowing down his chest. Ellie then turns her attention back to the lead warrior, their swords meeting in a final, desperate clash.

Above, Saphirixia and the crimson dragon continue their epic battle. The dragon's exchange blasts of fire, the air filling with the roar of flames and the sound of clashing scales. Saphirixia fights with unmatched ferocity. She manages to clamp her powerful teeth around the crimson dragon's neck, forcing it back to the ground.

Looking back, Ellie notes that the final warrior's attention is also locked on the dragons. Seizing the opportunity, she launches a final, desperate assault on the lead warrior. Her sword moves with blinding speed, a whirlwind of steel that leaves the warrior no room to counter. With a decisive blow, she disarms him, her blade at his throat. His eyes widened as if unable to come to terms with the fact that she has bested him.

“Yield!” She yells. She doesn’t wish to kill another warrior, but she knows at this moment that she will.

The clearing falls silent, the only sound being the combatants' labored breathing. The lead warrior raises his hands in surrender, a look of grudging respect on his face. "You have proven your strength and resolve," he declares, his voice tinged with admiration. “You both are worthy."

Ellie lowers her sword, relief flooding her veins. She looks at Saphirixia, her eyes gleaming like embers, as they share a nod. They have passed the trial, their bravery and skill shining through.

The warrior bows in respect before retreating into the forest, leaving Ellie and Saphirixia alone in the clearing. Ellie sinks to her knees, the adrenaline of the battle ebbing away as the pain in her thigh and arm begins to consume her. Saphirixia lowers her head, her eyes filled with pride and affection.

"*We did it*," Ellie whispers, her voice choking with emotion. "*We really did it*."

Saphirixia rumbles in agreement, nuzzling Ellie gently. Together, they have faced their fears and emerged victorious, one step closer to breaking the curse and restoring magic to Aetherlyn.

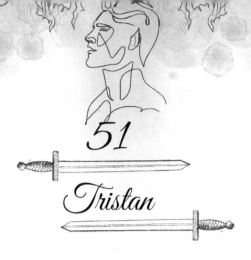

51

Tristan

Tristan wakes, instantly sensing the absence of Ellie's body against his. His eyes fly open, and he glances around, noticing that Breccan, Stella, and Kyla, along with their dragons, are still fast asleep.

Tristan's heart begins to race when he realizes that both Ellie and Saphirixia are nowhere in sight. He quickly stands up, peering around, seeing her pack on the ground.

"Brec, wake up!" Tristan barks.

"What is it?" Breccan asks sleepily and rubs his eyes. Kyla and Stella are stirring beside him.

"They're gone," Tristan replies, voice quivering.

"They probably just went to the river to wash up," Kyla mutters calmly.

Tristan shakes his head; he can *feel* it in his soul; *something is wrong.*

"*Terbius, we have to find them. Now,*" Tristan communicates.

Terbius quickly rises and strides over. Tristan wastes no time mounting his bond. As they turn to fly, Breccan hollers from below, "We're right behind you!"

They're in the air in seconds, "*To the river and towards the enchantress's cottage. Try reaching out to Saphirixia,*" Tristan instructs.

Terbius' rumble is his only reply.

Tristan waits, and when Terbius replies, he already knows what he is going to say: "*Saphirixia isn't responding*," with a hint of confusion and concern in his rumbling voice.

Within minutes, they reach the clearing of the enchantress's cottage, the fiery dome raging over the stones. Fear and anger rage through him, and he wonders, *She left without telling me?*

Tristan and Terbius descend from the sky, landing in the clearing with a thud. The sight greeting them is ghastly. Tristan's heart pounds in his chest, fear and anger intertwining as he dismounts. He storms towards the enchantress, observing the scene with a serene, almost detached expression. The globe pulsing brightly in her outstretched hands.

"What are you doing to her?" Tristan demands, his voice trembling with fury. His hands clenching into fists, knuckles whitening with tension.

The enchantress regards him calmly. "Stand down, Captain. This is their choice."

Before Tristan can respond, a blood-curdling scream pierces the air from within the fiery dome. His heart nearly stops, the sound cutting through him like a blade. Panic surges through his veins, and he dashes towards the flames, desperate to reach Ellie. The heat is unbearable, searing his skin and forcing him to halt his advances. Falling to his knees, a guttural yell of rage and frustration escaping his lips as he pounds the ground.

"Ellie!" he cries out, his voice breaking. "Ellie, hold on!"

Breccan, Stella, Kyla, and their bondeds land in the clearing, shaking the ground beneath Tristan. He hears them running up behind him, and when his eyes meet theirs, worry is etched on all their faces as they all wait in silent support.

Minutes feel like hours. Tristan remains on his knees, helplessly watching the inferno. His thoughts are chaotic, a mix of dread and desperate hope. Terbius stands nearby; Tristan glances at his bonded, his eyes reflecting mutual distress. The dragon's low, mournful rumble adds to the moment's tension.

Finally, the fiery dome begins to waver, the flames receding. Tristan holds his breath. His eyes fix on the fiery dome, the last of the flames vanish.

Tristan, freezes for a heartbeat, then scrambles to his feet and rushes to Ellie's side. She's lying on the cold stone ground, blood staining her torn clothing, her body looking to be battered and broken. A deep gash runs across her thigh, another across her arm, the wounds raw and bleeding.

He quickly turns to assess Saphirixia, who is visibly wounded herself. The dragon, already awake, stumbles toward Ellie, her glowing eyes full of worry. He watches her nudge Ellie's uninjured leg gently, unwilling to leave her side. Tristan's hands tremble as they hover over her wounds, desperate but uncertain where to begin.

"Ellie, stay with me," he chokes out, his voice thick with emotion. "Please, don't leave me. Stay with me."

Ellie stirs, her eyes fluttering open. She manages a weak smile as her eyes meet his, her voice barely a whisper. "Tristan?"

His heart aches at her resilience, and he gently brushes strands of hair from her bloodied face. "You scared me there, Sapphire. Hold on."

The enchantress approaches, her expression inscrutable. "The trial is over. They each have proven their strength and determination".

Tristan glares at her sharp as daggers, anger simmering just beneath the surface. "She could've died!" he yells, fury lacing his tone.

"Such is the nature of the trials," the enchantress replies, her tone unyielding. "They are meant to test their limits, to ensure they are worthy of breaking the curse."

Tristan's anger flares, his power surging, his eyes glowing crimson with fury, making him force himself to focus on Ellie as blood continues to flow from her injuries. "We need to stop the bleeding," he pleads as he glances at their friends now surrounding her.

Saphirixia nudges Ellie gently, her eyes full of sorrow. Ellie slowly reaches out to touch her, her fingertips grazing her scales, finding strength in their bond. "I'm okay, Saph," she reassures, though her voice is strained.

Tristan delicately lifts Ellie into his arms, careful not to aggravate her wounds. As he carries her away from the stone, he casts one last, furious glance at the enchantress. "This isn't over," he growls.

The enchantress merely nods, her eyes following them, her cloak flowing with the wind. "Indeed, it is not," she murmurs, her voice barely audible.

Tristan stalks off into the tree's while Kyla, Stella, and Breccan follow close behind, their dragon wingbeats rustling the trees above. Once they reach the camp, Stella and Kyla come to Ellie's side, quickly tending to her injuries, their expressions a mix of fear and determination.

Tristan stays by her side, refusing to release her hand even for a moment as he whispers words of comfort. They work to stop the bleeding, and bandage her wounds, his mind racing with the thought that he might have lost her, that he could still lose her.

Breccan stands solidly behind him, his hand firm on Tristan's shoulder, grounding him with a steady, reassuring grip before stepping back.

Ellie lays on a bedroll, her face pale and drawn, her breathing shallow. Her body is clearly wracked with pain; every movement seems to elicit a soft groan. Tristan watches her, his heart aching with helplessness as he brushes a stray strand of hair from her face. He can see the exhaustion etched on her face, the toll the trial has taken on her.

Desperation gnaws at him as he realizes that they don't have access to proper medicine. "Stella, Ky, take care of her," Tristan commands, his voice tight with worry.

Stella's eyes go wide with concern. "Where are you going?"

"To help her," Tristan responds curtly.

Without another word, he reluctantly releases her hand, turns, and leaves the camp, his steps quick and determined. The evening sun casts a glow on the path ahead, guiding him as he makes his way to the enchantress's cottage. The journey feels longer than it is, his mind racing with thoughts of Ellie. He can't bear to see her in such pain, and he is determined to do whatever it takes to help her, even if it means asking the same person who caused her pain.

When he reaches the cottage, he bangs on the door, his hand trembling with urgency. The door creaks open, revealing the enchantress's serene yet curious expression.

"I didn't expect to see you here, Tristan Mormont," her voice is calm and measured.

Tristan's anger flares, "Ellie is in pain. She's suffering. You put her through these trials; the least you can do is help her."

The enchantress raises an eyebrow, a faint smile playing on her lips. "And why should I help her? The trials are meant to test her strength, her worthiness."

"She *has* proven herself!" Tristan snaps. "She has done everything you've asked. She's more than worthy!" Tristan yells, her eyes narrowing on him. Tristan takes a deep breath before continuing, "We have no access to medicine, and she's in pain. Just fucking help her."

The enchantress studies him for a moment, her eyes piercing and unyielding. "You would truly risk anything for her, even to come here and make these demands of me?" she sneers.

"Of course I would," Tristan replies before admitting, "I love her."

The enchantress smiles wickedly, amusement in her eyes. "Love is quite a powerful motivator, is it not? Very well, then, I'll help her. She will need to be well anyhow for what is to come."

Tristan, confused and frustrated asks, "What do you mean?"

"I will speak with Ellie and Saphirixia tomorrow," she says cryptically before turning and disappearing into the cottage's depths.

Minutes tick by as Tristan waits, his anxiety mounting with each passing second. Finally, the enchantress returns, holding a small, steaming cup of tea.

Handing the cup to Tristan she tisks, "This will help ease her pain and heal her wounds. Remember this, true healing comes from within."

Tristan takes the cup and forces out , "Thank you." His voice is calm despite his lingering frustration.

He rushes back to the camp, his heart pounding in his chest with each step. Ellie is still so pale and groaning softly. Stella and Kyla hovering, their faces etched with worry.

"Tristan," Stella says, relief evident in her voice. "Did you get help?"

"Yes," Tristan replies, moving to Ellie's side. Kneeling down he cradles her gently in his lap, her body slack against his. Tristan commands softly, holding the cup to her lips, "Ellie, I need you to drink this."

Ellie stirs, her eyes fluttering as she attempts to stay awake. She looks at Tristan, her expression pained but trusting. She takes a slow sip of the tea, coughing slightly as she swallows. Tristan's heart clenches like an iron fist in his chest as he watches her struggle, but he holds her steady, encouraging her to drink more.

"That's it, Sapphire. Just a little more," he murmurs, his voice soothing and tender.

Ellie drinks slowly; each sip a small victory. As the tea begins to take effect, her groans of pain lessen, and her breathing grows steady. An hour passes, and Tristan continues to hold her close, whispering in her ear and holding her tightly against his chest. Finally, Ellie's eyes open fully, a faint smile tugging at her lips.

"Tristan," she whispers, her voice weak but brimming with affection.

Tristan's heart swells instantly with relief at the sound of his name falling from her lips. "I'm here, El. I'm not going anywhere."

She reaches up, her hand trembling as her fingertips run tenderly over his jaw, "I love you," she whispers, her voice barely audible.

Tristan leans down and presses a soft kiss to her forehead. "I love you too, Sapphire. You'll be okay. Rest now. I'll be here when you wake."

Ellie's eyes close, her body relaxing as she slips into what seems to be a peaceful sleep. Tristan holds her close, his anxiety fading by the hour. He watches over her through the night, his gaze never leaving her face, the color slowly returning to her cheeks as the fire keeps her warm.

The weight of the trials and the uncertainty of their future hangs heavy in the air, but at the moment, all that matters is that she will heal.

As dawn begins to break through the canopy of deep green trees, casting a soft light over the camp, he knows then he will stand by Ellie and even Saphirixia until his last dying breath.

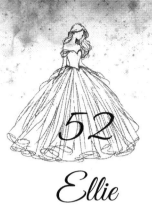

52

Ellie

Ellie wakes to a throbbing ache in her thigh and arm, her limbs feeling weak. The promise that if she moves even in the slightest, the pain will undoubtedly follow.

She sighs heavily, Tristan's arms wrapping around her, the steady rise and fall of his chest against her back, indicating he is still sleeping.

As she peers down, noticing the bandages concealing her wounds. Memories of the night before and the trial flood through, making her wince. She had killed and had even come close to death herself.

A lone mug lies empty on the ground next to her. Ellie's heart warms with her wandering thoughts. He stayed by her side and somehow managed to find something to ease her pain. She begins to wonder how he managed it, but is profoundly grateful nonetheless.

She turns to look at him, his head leaning to the side. Tristan stirs, quickly sensing her movement. "Ellie," he whispers, his voice thick with concern. "How are you feeling?"

Ellie offers a weak smile. "Everything hurts. But I imagine I would feel much worse if it weren't for you."

Tristan kisses her tenderly, then places his forehead against hers. "I'm glad you're awake. Let's get you up and see how well you can move."

He helps Ellie stand up slowly, mindful of her injuries, as he grips her tightly, ensuring that she can stand on her own. Stella and Kyla, notice the movement, rush over.

"Let's get you to the river to wash up," Stella suggests as she stands nearby, her voice soft yet firm. Tristan slowly releases her, giving her a small smile and nod of encouragement.

With Kyla supporting Ellie, they make their way to the river, Saphirixia and Kaida following closely. Stella and Kyla take great care in helping Ellie wash, each working together to ensure she feels as comfortable as possible. Ellie's spirits lift slightly as she feels the blood and weariness wash away, the cool water providing a small amount of relief.

Once they're done, the group heads to the enchantress's cottage. Vespero, Sentiara, and Kaida take to the air to hunt. Tristan keeps his arm around her waist, ensuring she doesn't stumble. Pain continues to wrack her body with each step as she hisses through the pain as she walks.

When they arrive, they see a table and chairs set out, food overflowing on the table. Each of them is frozen in place as they stare at the feast, the rich smells making their stomachs growl with anticipation.

As they walk closer to the table, Ellie can see it laden with enchanting foods. Moon berry tarts glowed faintly, their blue fruit filling sweet and tart. Small, fluffy elderflower nectar cakes glistened with a golden glaze, while a bowl of starfruit ambrosia sparkled like stardust, offering a mix of citrus and honey flavors. Dark green enchanted forest bread, soft and earthy. Glow root soup, warm and creamy, emitted a comforting luminescence. Vibrant petal salad with honeydew vinaigrette bursting with spicy and sweet flavors. Jewel-toned dragon fruit delights, candied and spiced, provide a chewy and crunchy texture. Flaky pastries filled with sparkling vanilla-almond cream sat beside a fresh honeycomb dripping with golden, wildflower-scented honey. Finally, warm tea, bright and citrusy, offers a comforting finish to the magical feast.

The enchantress's white owl watches them intently with its beady red eyes. Nearby, five large sheep graze, clearly offerings for their dragons.

Ellie quickly glances over to Saphirixia, whose tongue sweeps out. She is eager to devour her own meal, her eyes tracking the sheep.

The enchantress emerges from her cottage, her face serene. Yet, her intimidating dark shadows follow her. She immediately indicates toward the table, "Please, sit. Eat," her voice calm and inviting.

They all sit down, Ellie winces slightly as she settles into her chair. The enchantress watches them as they begin to eat; she notices her gaze lingering on her and Saphirixia. After a few moments, she speaks: "Congratulations. You both have done very well. I was sure for a moment there that you both wouldn't succeed, but you have truly proved your worthiness. That being said, you may return home."

Ellie, taken aback, looks at the enchantress in confusion. "What do you mean?"

"You're free to leave," the enchantress continues, her words silencing them all.

"Does that mean the trials are complete? Is fae magic restored?" Ellie asks, her brow furrowing.

The enchantress shakes her head slowly. "No, Ellissandra. There is one final test. However, this final test is not like the others. I cannot tell you what it will be, but you will know when you succeed or if you fail."

Frustration surges through Ellie. "What was all of this for then? Why put us through so much pain and uncertainty?" Ellie feels her heart racing as anger bubbles up inside of her.

Sparks of magic begin to flood through her, Tristan's familiar magic prominent, begging to be released.

Ellie turns to look at each of her friends, who stop eating, forks and brows raised with mutual confusion. Tristan's face hardens as his gaze leaves hers and narrows on the enchantress, eagerly waiting for her to continue.

For the first time, the enchantress's expression softens, revealing a hint of vulnerability. She sighs, "I miss my own bonded dragon dearly. You both are remarkably fortunate to have one another; value that, treasure it," she says as she briefly looked down into the cup in her hands. "The trials are designed to strengthen you, to prepare you for the ultimate test. I am confident that when the time comes, you will succeed."

Ellie's anger fades into confusion as she takes a couple of deep breaths and asks the question she wants to know the most: "How long until the next test?"

The enchantress remains vague, her enigmatic smile returning. "In due time, Ellissandra. In due time." Ellie sighs, realizing she isn't going to get any more answers from the witch.

As they continue to eat, the enchantress speaks, her face still a mask of serene composure. She looks directly at Ellie, her gaze piercing. "I wish you the best of luck. You are strong, kind, and resilient, and you have the power to overcome whatever lies ahead. Remember that the bond between two bondeds is a powerful force that can change the world. Hold on to that, and let it guide you."

With a final, heartfelt look, she concludes, "Farewell for now, Ellissandra and Saphirixia. May the stars watch over you and grant you the strength to face the challenges ahead. Prove yourselves worthy, and may you find the happiness you both deserve." With that, she stands, and with one last nod, she retreats into her cottage, leaving them all bewildered.

The group sits in stunned silence for a moment, the weight

of the enchantress's words settling over them. Tristan squeezes Ellie's hand, offering her a reassuring smile.

We're going home; Ellie processes the words as anger and relief flood through her.

53

Ellie

The group immediately returns to their camp, bellies full from the feast, they all decide not to wait any longer. The journey home will take days, and they are all eager to return, even if they are all a bit concerned about how they will be accepted upon arrival. *We'll worry about that later*, Ellie concedes.

Within the hour, they are in the air. Ellie grits her teeth as she settles onto Saphirixia's back, her wounds still fresh and throbbing. Each movement sends a jolt of pain through her body, but she refuses to let it slow her down. The need to return home, to face whatever awaits them, overpowered her physical discomfort. The rhythmic beating of Saphirixia's wings is both comforting and torturous, each flap causing a wave of excruciating pain through her injured body.

The landscape changes dramatically as they leave the dark green forest of Mystara. They cross over the jagged snow capped mountains, the air growing cooler and crisper as they ascend. Below them, a dense forest stretches out as far as they can see, the canopy of a dark, undulating sea beneath the starlit sky. The chilly air stings Ellie's wounds, but she clenches her jaw and presses on, her determination unwavering.

Hours pass as they fly, the rhythmic beating of dragon wings the only sound in the vast expanse. Ellie's eyelids grow heavy, but she forces herself to stay awake. Her mind wanders to thoughts of what lay ahead, making her wonder, *Will we be welcomed back with open arms, or will our families be disappointed in us, in me?*

As the sun begins to descend over the horizon, they spot a small village nestled in a valley below.

"Thank the stars!" Breccan exclaims, his voice carrying with the wind. Clearly, as excited as they all are for the possibility of food and a warm bed for the first time in well over a week.

Their dragons descend, landing gracefully on the outskirts of the village. Ellie descends slowly, pain ricocheting between her limbs as she meets the harsh ground.

"*If you need me, I won't be far*," Saphirixia nudges Ellie with her snout. "*Get some rest*," then shoots into the air, seeking her own resting spot with the other bondeds.

"Let's find an inn," Tristan suggests, his voice weary but determined. Ellie agrees, grateful for the suggestion.

They find a quaint inn with a pub, its warm lights, and cheerful chatter invite them inside. The innkeeper, a kind older female, welcomes them with a smile and shows them to their rooms. The aroma of hearty food wafts through the air, making Ellie's stomach rumble in anticipation.

The inn's common room is a picture of rustic charm, with wooden beams across the ceiling and a fire crackling in the hearth. The tables are made of thick, dark wood, worn smooth by countless visitors over the years. Shelves lined with dusty books and knickknacks adorn the walls, giving the place a cozy, lived-in feel.

The innkeeper serves them a feast of roasted meats, fresh bread, and steaming vegetables. Ellie's mouth waters as she takes her first bite, the flavors rich and comforting. They all drink ale, the strong, bitter brew warming them from the inside out.

As the night wears on, their laughter grows louder, the ale loosening their tongues and lifting their spirits. Stella, Kyla, and Ellie share stories of their childhood misadventures, their faces flushing with drink. Breccan, ever the entertainer, regales them with exaggerated tales of his heroics, each one more outlandish than the last. Tristan remains silent and observant, eyes never leaving Ellie's.

Eventually, the weariness of their journey catches up with them, and they begin to retire to their rooms. Stella and Kyla, giggling like schoolgirls, stumbling up the stairs to their shared room. Breccan, still chuckling to himself, takes a room down the hall.

Tristan turns to Ellie as they make their way up the stairs, his eyes soft with affection. "Would you share a room with me?" he asks, his voice low and hopeful. Ellie's heart skips a beat, and she nods, a smile tugging at her lips.

As Tristan opens the door to their room, Ellie walks inside and finds it incredibly romantic. It has a large, inviting bed draping with soft linens and a deep, claw-footed tub in the corner. Candles flicker on the bedside tables, casting a warm, golden glow. The walls are painted a soft blue, and the windows are adorned with tapestries.

Ellie stands there, unsure what to do, as Tristan takes her pack from her and places it on the floor.

"Would you like to take a bath?" he asks as he watches her closely. "I can leave you so you can have some privacy."

Ellie's gaze finally meets his. "I don't want you to leave; stay," she replies, her voice soft but sure.

Tristan helps Ellie to the tub and carefully helps her remove her clothes, his touch gentle yet hesitant. As she undresses, she notices Tristan wince each time he gets a glimpse at her injuries. Ellie is afraid to look in the mirror, knowing she undoubtedly has many bruises and scratches.

She sinks into the warm water with a sigh of relief, the heat quickly taking effect, soothing her aching muscles. Tristan sits on the tub's edge, his gaze never leaving her. His eyes are soft and concerned, but with each passing moment, she can see his eyes darken the longer he takes in her body.

"Like what you see?" Ellie teases, a hint of exhaustion in her tone.

Tristan's devious smile grows, "Oh Sapphire, you have no idea how much." He leans into her, grabbing her neck and pulling her lips to his; his kiss is deep and claiming, yet gentle and full of passion as his teeth graze her bottom lip. Ellie suddenly feels the rush of heat building in her core as her heart hammers against her ribcage, desire flooding through her, igniting her veins.

"Join me," she urges, her voice soft and inviting. Tristan didn't need to be asked twice. He quickly undresses as Ellie watches him, wholly captivated by his muscled form. His intricate red and black tattoos are a starking contrast against his sun kissed skin in the warm candlelight.

When he pulls down his trousers, all Ellie can do is stare at every inch of him, from his tousled raven-black hair to his sculpted shoulders and chest. As her eyes lower to take him in, she admires his defined abdominal muscles and hard length. *Stars, he's fucking devastating.*

"Do you like what *you* see?" he questions, voice husky with a hint of amusement.

Ellie feels a blush creep over her face as she licks her lips. "You have no idea how much." Her words make him smile.

He slowly slips into the tub behind her, his strong arms wrapping around her waist, pulling her into him, his fingertips lingering on her skin. Ellie leans into his chest, feeling the steady beat of his heart against her back, a steady and calming rhythm.

Tristan's strong hands begin massaging her shoulders, his fingers working out the knots of tension and pain, gently kissing her as he goes. Ellie closes her eyes, a content sigh escaping her lips as she runs her fingernails along his thighs. The warmth of the water and the gentle pressure of his hands makes her feel safe and indescribably cherished.

"Let's just stay here," Ellie whispers, her voice barely audible above the gentle splashing of her feet against the warm water.

"That's a tempting thought...," Tristan replies, his voice gentle, like a caress in her mind. He places a kiss below her pointed ear, making her shiver.

As they sit in blissful silence, Ellie can still feel Tristan's hard length against her back, flooding her with a wave of unquenchable desire. He has tasted, teased, devoured, and savored her body, but now, she wants all of him. Her pain is the last thing on her mind.

Ellie slowly turns around, trying not to wince at the pain shooting up her leg and arm, as she wraps her arms around his neck. She can see the fire burning in his ocean-blue eyes, his desire for her, knowing that the same fire burns in her own gaze.

Ellie kisses him fiercely, overcome with a burning need for him, his calloused hand cups her face while his other hand roams over her back and grips her ass. She can feel his hardness against her belly, indicating that he wants this just as much as she does.

The feel of his body against hers creates a delicious friction that teases and taunts her desires. A hungry, satisfied growl reverberates along her skin as his lips trail down her neck and along her collarbone, making her feel weightless. A strangled moan leaves her lips as his tongue claims her mouth once again.

Overtaken by the surge of pleasure, Ellie's hand drifts between them, she moves her hand down his chest. Enjoying the feel of his muscled form beneath her fingertips.Tristan suddently snatches her wrist, pulling it to his lips as he kisses her palm softly.

"I would love nothing more than to claim you right here, right now, and hear my name from your lips," He kisses her lips again, devastatingly soft, "but you're still hurt and in pain. When I take you and *fully* make you mine, Sapphire, I want the only thing that you feel to be pleasure."

Ellie's breath hitches in her throat and her core floods with heat.

The promise in his words makes her feel molten.

Tristan sweeps a strand of hair behind her ear; his vulnerability and raw desire makes her heart sing.

“Loving you might be the very thing that drives me to the edge, but I will endure it all, because having you, even in the smallest moments, like this, makes it worth every bit of the madness”, Tristan whispers against her lips making her heart beat frantically against her chest.

Ellie wants so desperately to beg for him to take her, fill her, bring her to the edge of her sanity with pure pleasure. She doesn’t even care if it makes her look pitiful or weak; all she wants is him- his touch, his smell- and everywhere.

“Turn,” Tristan commands. Ellie’s brows pinch together as she pouts. He twirls his finger, indicating for her to turn around again, as a small chuckle leaves his lips, clearly amused by her pouting.

Ellie obeys as she leans back against him once again. Tristan’s hand moves around from behind her and then quickly finds her hair. He begins washing her hair, his fingers softly massaging her scalp. He rinses her hair and washes her and then he quickly cleans himself.

After their bath, Tristan carefully wraps her in a towel and carries her to the bed. Then he bandages her wounds, his touch tender and precise. He grabs an extra tunic from his pack and places it over her head.

As she lays down, the softness of the mattress wraps around her like a warm embrace, a welcome change from the hard ground they’ve endured over the past week. Tristan remains naked as he climbs into the bed and pulls Ellie into his strong embrace, holding her close.

They lay there, wrapping in each other’s arms, in silent contentment. The journey, the ride, and her injuries make Ellie feel drained entirely, yet her mind won’t shut off. As her thoughts begin to wander, fear and self- doubt starts to creep into her thoughts.

"I'm scared," Ellie admits, her voice trembling. "What if we can't break the curse? What if all of this was for nothing?"

Tristan presses a gentle kiss to her shoulder. "You will break the curse. I believe in you both." Ellie tries to hold back her emotions as a lone tear runs down her cheek. His faith in her and her bonded, making her heart swell.

Ellie turns and looks into his eyes, finding strength and reassurance in his unwavering gaze. "What do you think will happen when we return to the castle?" she asks softly.

"Honestly, I don't know," Tristan replies. "The one thing that I do know is that *no one* can keep me from you. As long as I have you, I have everything." That was all Ellie needed to hear, to know that no matter the outcome, he will not abandon her.

As the night wears on, their words grow softer, the need for sleep finally overtaking them. Ellie's last thought before she drifts off is how grateful she is to have Tristan by her side. No matter the challenges, she knows that they will face them together.

The warmth of Tristan's embrace and the soft, steady rhythm of his breath finally lulls Ellie into a deep, restful sleep. The pain from her wounds fading into the background, replaced by a profound sense of peace and security.

For the first time in what feels like forever, Ellie feels truly at ease. As she drifts off to sleep, a small smile plays on her lips, and her dreams are filled with visions of a future where their kingdom is whole again, their people free and happy.

They have faced unimaginable challenges and will undoubtedly face many more. But in that moment, as they lay together in the soft glow of the candlelight, Ellie knows that they are ready. They have each other, and that is enough.

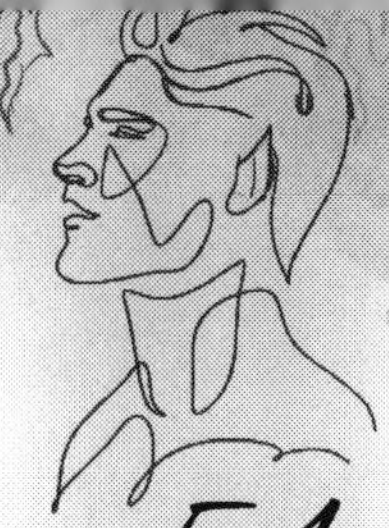

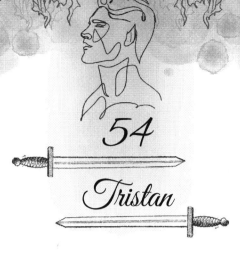

54

Tristan

The following day, Tristan wakes with Ellie nestled in his arms, her warmth radiating through him. The early morning light filters through the curtains, casting a soft glow on her peaceful face. He watches her sleep, feeling an overwhelming sense of contentment and protectiveness wash over him. He has never felt as happy as he does at this moment, holding her this close. The trials, the battles, the pain. It all seems distant now, mere shadows compared to the brilliance of this single, perfect morning.

He replays each trial that ultimately brought them closer, each challenge revealing the depth of their bond. He has fallen for her strength, courage, and unwavering spirit. Now, seeing her like this, so vulnerable and at peace. He realizes just how deeply his love for her is.

His mind swirls with thoughts of the tenderness that lies beneath her fierce exterior. Even now, the sight of her battered and wounded yet still standing tall stirs something profound within him. He has watched her endure so much and seen her push past her limits repeatedly. Through it all, she remains the most captivating creature he has ever known.

His thoughts were a chaotic blend of desire and adoration. *I never dared to imagine that I could ever want another so badly, need them. Just the thought of not claiming her and making her mine might be the very end of me, destroy me completely. I finally found her. Somehow, against all odds, she's here, with me. How can I be so recklessly, undeservingly lucky to have found her?* He wonders.

Every moment with her feels like a precious gift, a chance to experience a love so profound it defies words. He wants to tell her everything, to pour out his heart and soul and lay his heart bare to her.

If someone had told him a month ago that he would fall in love and think such things as he did now, he would have laughed.

But now, watching her sleep, he wonders how he will ever live a day without her. The urge to kiss her, allowing his lips to linger on her skin, burns through his veins, a pull so strong that he has to take a deep breath, reminding himself of her injuries.

Careful not to wake her, Tristan slowly rolls her to her side and extricates himself from the bed. The only thing that pulls him away from her is the need to do something special for her, to care for her. He quietly dresses and slips out of the room, going downstairs to the inn's pub.

The innkeeper greets him warmly, and Tristan quickly explains his request. Soon, he is carrying a tray laden with breakfast, freshly baked bread, sweet rolls drizzled with honey, a selection of fruits, and a steaming pot of tea. He makes his way back up to their room, feeling a sense of anticipation.

As he enters, he finds Ellie stirring, her eyes slowly opening. She smiles at him, making his heart skip a beat. Her braid is a tangled mess; she looks so sleepy, but he has never seen anything so beautiful in his life. He stands there, tray in hand, frozen in place, finding it hard to move as he takes her in, unable to form words.

"Good morning," she murmurs, her voice still tinged with sleep.

"Good morning, beautiful," Tristan replies, setting the tray on the bedside table. "I brought you breakfast in bed."

Ellie's eyes widened in surprise and delight. "You didn't have to do that." Even though she says that, he can see the sparkle in her eyes.

"I wanted to," he admits, sitting on the edge of the bed and offering her a piece of bread. “I’ll always take care of you, Sapphire.”

She takes the bread, their fingers brushing. As she eats, he watches her, marveling at her resilience and stunning beauty.

His thoughts drift to the journey ahead, the trial they have yet to face, but at this moment, he wants to focus on her, keep her there, safe with him.

"What is going on in that head of yours? Or would you rather I just touch you and find out?" Ellie asks between bites, quirking her brow.

"I’m simply wishing that I could keep you here, in this bed with me all day," Tristan replied.

"I wish you could too," Ellie whispers, her voice laced with vulnerability. She leans in, her lips brushing his in a soft, unhurried kiss, a mingling of longing and trust.

Tristan sinks into her touch, his hands slipping around her neck, fusing their lips together. He feels the weight of his own worries dissolve, melting away beneath the warmth of her lips. He’s never felt so light, so utterly free to be himself, as if the world outside this moment no longer matters.

All he can feel is her, and he knows he’d stay in this instant forever if he could.

He reluctantly releases her, allowing them both to finish their breakfast. Ellie’s smiles brightly, her eyes shining while she eats.

After they finish, Tristan leans closer, carefully unwinding her bandages. His touch is gentle, almost reverent, as he inspects her healing injuries. Every glance, every touch, tests his restraint, especially seeing her wrapped in his tunic. His fingers linger a moment longer than necessary, tracing the edge of her skin as sparks flicker, leaving a tingling trail in their wake. His pulse quickens, every spark a reminder of how much he longs to keep her close.

He can see the pain in her eyes, the weariness etched on her face, and it tore at him. He wants to take all of her pain away, to shield her from any more harm.

"Thank you," her voice barely above a whisper. "For everything."

Tristan leans in and kisses her, the need to feel her lips on his driving him wild, "Anything for you, Sapphire."

Just as he finishes securing the fresh bandage, a heavy knocking bangs on the door. "Time to fly, lovebirds!" Breccan hollers from the other side of the door.

Tristan sighs, his moment of peace shattering, but he can't help but smile at Breccan's timing.

"He really does have impeccable timing," he mutters, helping Ellie to her feet. Ellie releases a small, amused laugh, her eyes bright once again, no hint of the pain lingering on her beautiful face.

As they gather their belongings and prepare to leave, Tristan feels a mix of nervous anticipation for the journey ahead and an overwhelming contentment as he looks at Ellie. Her presence fills him with a sense of purpose, making him feel like he can take on the world. No matter what comes their way, he will protect her, fight for her, and love her with everything that he has.

When they walk out of the inn, their friends are waiting for them, talking in a close circle. Ellie grabs his hand, sending sparks along his skin and surprising him with the intensity of the sensation.

Tristan has never been the kind of man to show open affection in front of others, but with Ellie, the thought of not having his hands on her makes him feel a void within him, one that only she can fill. He doesn't care who's around or who sees; he will gladly scream to the entire kingdom that she is his. *What is happening to me?* He wonders, marveling at how deeply she has changed him.

Breccan looks up and grins at them. "Finally! We thought you two might never come down."

Kyla and Stella exchange knowing glances, sensing the shift in the air. Their eyes gleam with understanding.

Ellie squeezes Tristan's hand, grounding him in the moment. "Ready to head home?" she questions as she peers at Stella, Kyla, and Breccan, who smile at her in return.

"If I'm being honest," he admits, leaning into her ear, "I'm regretting my restraint last night and would much prefer to go back to bed," Tristan admits, his voice husky.

Ellie's gaze meets his again, her eyes shining so much that he can see the sparks of desire in them as they grow darker.

Bleeding stars, I am a fool, Tristan thought, knowing he was indeed a fool, but he refuses to take her while she's in such pain. The plans he has for her, the desire that burns for her, he doesn't want her to feel anything other than pleasure when she screams his name.

Tristan's gaze penetrates her as she bites her lip, her eyes piercing him to his soul. His desire for her rages like an inferno burning hotter with each passing day.

"Don't look at me like that, Sapphire, or we're going to go back upstairs, and I will not be gentle," Tristan declares huskily.

His words only make her smirk grow wider until she leans against his lips and says, "What makes you think I want you to be gentle?"

Tristan's heart hammers against his chest like dark, thunderous wings. Her response makes him stumble, unable to form coherent words. He grips her chin and seizes her lips in a claiming kiss, unable to stand another second without tasting her.

"Well, if you two are done, we do actually have quite a long journey ahead," Breccan interrupts.

Tristan practically growls against Ellie's lips, and a soft chuckle leaves her lips. She looks down, trying to hide the blush creeping across her beautiful face. Ellie strides off with Stella and Kyla when

Breccan approaches his side, elbowing him in his ribs.

"Did you have a good time last night?" Breccan taunts.

"She's injured, Brec. Also, it's none of your business," Tristan sneers.

"You've got to be kidding me! You're not going to tell me? I'm your best friend; who else would you tell?" Breccan asks as he waves his hands at his sides.

Tristan only shakes his head, not willing to relent, as he walks past Breccan and follows Ellie to their dragons.

In the past, he'd boasted to Breccan about his countless conquests, each one nothing more than a fleeting face and a name he barely remembered. He never cared for any of them; they were all just a blur.

Ellie is different; everything about her is different, he admits to himself. Each moment he shares with her feels sacred, like a secret. Moments he isn't willing to share with another soul.

Breccan runs up to his side, releasing an exasperated breath, but Tristan ignores him. His eyes track Ellie's every move while she laughs with her friends, her smile light, almost unbothered. He loves seeing her this way, so free and happy. Her long blonde hair is tied in its normal braid, her sapphire blue eyes shining bright with joy as he contemplates to himself: *She's more than beautiful; she's the definition of breathtaking.*

After a short walk, they enter a clearing in the woods where their dragons wait for them. Terbius's eyes meet his when he breaks through the trees, glaring daggers at him as Tristan wonders, *What did I do now?*

Thankfully, Terbius doesn't yell or berate him, he remains silent for once. They all quickly mount their dragons, and within minutes, they take to the skies.

As the day passes, the flight is long; they fly over a vast desert and pass over a range of mountains with snow peaks, when they finally reach the edge of Avernus once again. A kingdom that is only a day's flight from Aetherlyn.

It's still late afternoon when he looks over at Ellie, noticing her exhaustion. She's on the edge of falling off from her bonded from weariness.

"*Terbius, let's stop for water,*" Tristan commands through the bond.

"*For water, or to check on* your *Princess?*" Terbius snips.

As they land, he looks over at everyone who appears to be holding strong, even after the long day of flying.

Ellie stays on the back of Saphirixia, too tired to move. Tristan walks over to them when he calls up to Ellie, "Come down, Sapphire, you're riding with me."

That certainly got Ellie's attention when she peers down at him, brows pinched together but too tired to question him. She slowly descends from Saphirixia, nearly stumbling when she reaches the ground. Tristan quickly wraps his arm around her to hold her upright.

Her eyes appeared heavy, drained from the beating sun. "Let's get you some water and food, then you're staying with me until we make camp," Tristan insists. Her eyes meet his slowly and she nods weakly.

He gives her water and she takes a long drag before she speaks, "I've never ridden on another dragon besides Saphirixia. I think it might be better if I stay with her."

"I would prefer it if you didn't fall off Saphirixia from exhaustion," Tristan replies. Ellie considers his words. "Go on and ask her," Tristan nods towards Saphirixia as she rests under shaded trees. "I imagine she'll agree with me."

Ellie smiles hesitantly, then turns to look at Saphirixia, whose eyes turn to her within moments. They speak with one another silently through the bond. Saphirixia's large head nods slightly, indicating she would agree with the flight arrangement.

Ellie whispers, "Fine. I'll fly with you."

Her words make him smile; he has never had anyone fly with him on Terbius before. A part of him wants her close in case she falls asleep, but he also selfishly needs her with him to know she is there before they reach Aetherlyn, and everything changes.

Almost an hour later, they are in the skies. Ellie is leaning against his chest, and he wraps an arm around her, holding her tightly against him as Terbius flies high just above the clouds.

Thankfully, Terbius didn't fight him at his request. He can sense his unease but he relented quickly when Terbius looked at Ellie and saw the exhaustion weighing on her. He honestly expected a fight but was thankful to his bonded for allowing him this moment to care for her and have her with him.

"How can I help?" Tristan asks softly beside her ear, his voice a tender whisper amidst the evening breeze. Ellie leans into him at his words, nearly molding herself to his body. The evening sky was a tapestry of deepening hues, the sun's golden rays giving way to shades of purple and indigo, casting an ethereal glow over the forest below.

"You're already helping. I'm just exhausted; I'm sorry," Ellie whispers over the wind, her voice a fragile thread in the vast expanse around them.

"Don't be sorry; it's been a long journey," Tristan tries to console her in any way he can. He can feel the warmth of her body seeping into his as his hand roams over her stomach, holding her tightly against his chest. The cool night air contrasted sharply with their shared warmth, creating a cocoon of intimacy amidst the boundless sky. Ellie's head leans to the side, resting against his collarbone, and the rhythmic beat of his heart is a soothing lullaby.

"I really like being up here with you. Being up here has always been something that only Saphirixia and I have shared. But with you, it's different. It's calm. It's peaceful," Ellie whispers, her words a gentle caress against his ear.

"You give me the same kind of peace, Sapphire," Tristan replies as he stares at her, the golden hour sun casting a soft glow upon her face. Her eyes are heavy with exhaustion yet full of tranquil contentment.

He leans down and kisses her softly on her temple, her eyes instinctively closing. When he pulls away, she shifts to look up at him, her eyes shining like the stars beginning to dot the evening sky, wordlessly begging him.

Tristan's hand roams over her stomach, up across her chest then grasping her neck, pulling her lips to his in a claiming yet passionate kiss. A kiss so calm and sweet that he wishes, for just a moment, that time would cease and utterly encapsulate them. Every sensation is delicious, her kiss an addiction he wants to revel in.

Her long strands of hair have fallen from her braid, whipped in the near-silent wind cascading around them. His fingers brush the hair from her face as she opens up for him, their kiss deepening into a passionate clash of tongue and teeth. The urge to devour her, claim her, is so profound that his heartbeat thuds against his chest.

A slow, rumbling growl tears through Terbius, and he abruptly shifts his enormous wings. Tristan swiftly grips Ellie around the waist to ensure she doesn't fall, his other hand grasping Terbius' scales, holding on tight.

"*Was that necessary*?" Tristan demands, irritated.

"*Quite. If you want to kiss your mate, save it for when you're not on my back*," Terbius grumbles, his deep voice reverberating through the bond.

Tristan's only response was a stern "*Fine*," as he releases a sigh of resignation.

"Sorry about that," Tristan apologizes as she shrugs, her eyes meeting him again before speaking.

"It's all right, I can wait. I'll have you alone and all to myself soon enough," her voice silky and soothing in a way that sends shivers up his spine.

Tristan stares at her, entirely captivated by the female in his arms as she smooths his hair from his brow and runs her fingers along his strong jaw. Her lashes flutter as a wave of exhaustion seemingly washes over her once again.

"*Get some rest, Sapphire. I'll not let you fall*," Tristan promises. She agrees slowly, giving him a soft smile before leaning into him once again, resting her head against his chest. Her eyes quickly flutter closed.

Tristan holds her, watching the sun begin to descend before them. The sky is now becoming dark, scattered with the first twinkling stars. Below, the forest stretches out in a vast, dark green sea, the treetops swaying gently in the night breeze. The world feels infinitely large and profoundly peaceful, with the sound of dragon wings slicing through the air and the occasional rustle of leaves below.

He presses a soft kiss on Ellie's hair, feeling the weight of the day lift from his shoulders as he embraces the serenity of the moment. Out of nowhere a realization washes over him, making him recall something that his bonded had said, *Mate*?

55

Ellie

The first sensation she feels is strong arms encapsulating her, followed by lips upon her shoulder. "We're preparing to land and camp for the night. Did you get enough rest?" Tristan asks, his voice gentle and caring.

Ellie finally opens her eyes to see a large forest beyond, realizing that she isn't riding upon Saphirixia but Terbius. She quickly glances around, seeing Saphirixia's blue scales just to her left, and then sees her friends, still near, also preparing to land.

"Yes, I believe so," she whispers into the wind.

Within minutes, they descend into a large forest clearing. Towering trees encircle them, their branches swaying gently in the evening breeze. The forest floor is a tapestry of fallen leaves, soft moss, and vibrant ferns. The fading sunlight casts long shadows, creating an atmosphere that is both tranquil and mysterious.

Breccan releases an exasperated sigh. "I don't know about all of you, but I'm starving. I'll go find some dinner," he admits, peering over at Tristan. Tristan nods in confirmation. Kyla is already gathering wood for the fire while Stella is going through their packs, laying out their bedrolls, clearly looking forward to finally getting some rest.

Ellie walks over to Stella, leaving Tristan to grab their packs and to speak with Terbius. Saphirixia is already lying upon the lush grass, releasing a loud rumble of her own. Her eyes narrow in concern as she watches Ellie approach. "*I'm well, Saph. Get some rest*," Ellie says down their bond. Saphirixia huffs before laying her large head on the grass, her eyes quickly closing.

Nearby, Vespero and the other dragons settle down, their scales shimmering in the dim light. Soft rumbles emanate from them, creating a comforting background hum.

When Ellie reaches Stella, she helps lay out the remaining bedrolls. "I must admit, I'm feeling a little anxious and yet also excited to be home again," Stella remarks softly.

"I feel the same. So much has changed," Ellie replies, standing up and glancing around at Sentiara and Kaida, who lay near Saphirixia.

"Would you consider it a good change?" Stella asks curiously.

The thought makes Ellie smile as she peers back at her friend. "Yes, a good change indeed."

Stella gives her a knowing smile in return. Kyla strides over to them, branches and tree limbs in hand, and tosses them onto the ground. She then begins constructing the fire.

"How about you, Ky? How are you feeling?" Stella questions.

"I imagine I feel the same way you both do. I look forward to finally going home and seeing my father. Most importantly, I cannot wait to crawl into my own bed again," Kyla replies, a chuckle escaping her lips.

They laugh a little as Ellie feels Tristan come to her side and place his pack near her feet. "I will light that for you," Tristan said, his eyes glowing crimson red.

Ellie places her hand upon his arm, halting him, "Allow me."

Tristan gives her a shallow nod as Ellie closes her eyes, allowing the familiar spark of power to flood through her. When she opens her eyes, they too were glowing crimson. She lifts her clenched fist, feeling heat warm her palm. As she opened her fist, fire erupts from her palm. She can feel the heat, but it didn't burn her. A calming warmth sends sparks along her arm and down her spine. It makes her feel powerful as she stares into the fire in her palm. She moves her palm around, watching the fire bending to the slight gusts of wind moving with her. Ellie is in awe of her new gift, realizing that it is a gift she will quickly grow fond of, allowing it to become a part of her.

Then she flicks her wrist towards the stacked branches, setting the wood ablaze. The firelight dances across their faces, illuminating Breccan's red hair with a fiery glow.

"I don't think I will ever get used to seeing you wield such power," Kyla admits. When Ellie's eyes meet hers, Kyla's smile is radiant, full of pride. "Neither will I," Stella agrees.

Ellie feels a smile grace her face when Tristan leans into her ear. "That fire isn't the only thing burning for you right now, Sapphire," his voice sultry with each syllable. The warmth of his breath against her ear and his tone making Ellie's toes curl in her boots.

Tristan's smile is wicked, as if he could read her now-consuming thoughts about him. He smirks at her before bending down. He begins going through his packs. He leaves her there, wanting, and he knows it.

When she peers back at Kyla and Stella once again, they only smirk at her. Ellie shakes her head and bends down to go through her pack. After she sets out her bedroll, she grabs some dried meat and water from her pack and sits down. Kyla and Stella talk about all the foods they plan to eat when they return and how much they miss a hot bath.

Tristan sits beside her, sharpening one of the daggers from his belt. He occasionally glances at her and then back at the fire before them. The flames flicker and cast playful shadows on the surrounding trees, creating a cozy ambiance in the forest.

"Unfortunately, no meat tonight, my friends. Just berries and apples," Breccan declares as he breaks through the trees and sits beside them. Vespero's heavy wingbeats ruffle the trees around them as he lands, his dark green scales blending perfectly into the foliage, making it nearly impossible to see him. He lands with a heavy thud and quickly lays down with the other dragons.

Breccan passes around the food he has scavenged, a smile plastered on his face. "So, princess, how do you think we should arrive tomorrow? I imagine we will not be accepted with open arms because of how we left."

Ellie considers his words, realizing the accuracy of his prediction. She knows her father will be mad, but she is sure he will understand why she left, or at least she hoped.

"Everything will be fine; I will speak with mother and father once we arrive. Nothing will happen to any of you," Ellie promises more for herself than for them as she twists the sapphire necklace between her fingers. Each of them nodding in understanding but still appearing cautious and weary of their return.

They sit around the fire, talking for a while about their journey and the possible trial ahead for her and Saphirixia. The fire's warmth and the dragons' soft rumbling create a sense of peace.

As the night grows darker, Ellie notices her friends beginning to show signs of fatigue. "I'll stay awake and keep watch," she offers. After hours of resting against Tristan upon Terbius, she feels wide awake as her thoughts spiral.

Tristan immediately speaks up, "I'll stay awake with you."

Ellie places a hand on his arm and shakes her head softly. "No, you need to get some sleep. I'll wake you later if needed."

Tristan hesitates but relents. "Alright, but don't hesitate to wake me if you need to."

Ellie smiles as Tristan lies beside her, giving her one glance before closing his eyes. She watches as her friends settle into their bedrolls, their soft breathing soon blending with the sounds of the forest. She sits by the fire, practicing with the flames in her hand, feeling the power coursing through her; the now familiar sparks a comforting feeling.

She marvels at Tristan's gift, knowing it is something she will grow to master and cherish. The firelight flickers in her eyes as she manipulates the flames, feeling a deep connection to her new abilities and a sense of purpose for the journey ahead.

Ellie stays up through the night, her eyes fixed on the dancing flames in her hand as she tosses it into the fire, creating a flame again. The camp is quiet, the only sounds being the gentle snores of her friends and dragons around her, and the occasional rustle of leaves as the wind sweeps through the forest. The dragons' scales glistening under the moonlight lay peacefully, their soft rumbling breaths creating a soothing rhythm.

Memories of their journey, the battles they fought, and the bonds they forged play out in her mind like a vivid tapestry. She thinks about the changes that have come over her, both physically and mentally. The power she now wields is a testament to her growth, but it also reminds her of the responsibilities that come with it.

As the hours pass, Ellie finds herself thinking about home. Aetherlyn, the kingdom, the beach, their spot on the mountain-side, and bustling markets seem like a distant dream. She misses her parents, Helena, Clara, Eleanora, and the familiarity of the town. But she also knows that returning will bring its own set of challenges. *Would my father understand why I left? Will my people accept my new gift? Will they be disappointed if they find out I have returned and not broken the curse?* She wonders.

As the night deepens, Ellie's thoughts turn to Tristan. She glances at him, his figure gently illuminated by the fire's soft glow. Throughout this journey, he has been her rock, her confidant, and her protector. His unwavering support has bolstered her strength when she needed it most. A surge of affection swells in her chest, her heart brimming with love and gratitude. Their bond is so profound that even his absence leaves a void that aches within her.

As the first light of dawn begins to creep over the horizon, the birds start to chirp, their melodic songs filling the air. Ellie stands up, stretching her stiff muscles. She walks a few paces away from the camp, taking in the beauty of the sunrise. The sky was painted with pink, orange, and gold hues, a breathtaking sight that brings a sense of peace to her restless mind.

Tristan stirs and wakes up, his eyes immediately finding Ellie. He gets up and walks over to her, concern etched on his face. "Why didn't you wake me?" he demands, his voice soft but full of worry.

Ellie turns to him, a gentle smile on her lips. "I couldn't sleep even if I wanted to," she admits as she taps on her temple.

Tristan's expression softens as he steps closer, wrapping his arms around her. He kisses her tenderly, a comforting gesture that eases her almost instantly. "You don't have to bear all this alone," he murmurs against her lips.

She rests her head against his chest, feeling the steady beat of his heart. "I know," she whispers. "I've always been alone. Even though I'm not anymore, I still just need time to think."

They stand there, wrapped in each other's arms, watching as the sun slowly rises, casting its golden light over the forest. The world seems to hold its breath, wrapping around them like a warm blanket.

The camp begins to stir, their friends waking up and preparing for the day, Ellie and Tristan reluctantly pull away from each other. It's time to face the final leg of their journey home.

Breccan is the first to rise, his red hair reflecting the morning light. He stretches and yawns, a wide grin spreading across his face. "Rise and shine. Who's ready to go home?"

Kyla and Stella grunt their response but quickly begin following suit, packing up their bedrolls and gathering their belongings.

Sensing the activity, the dragons begin to wake, their eyes blinking lazily as they shake off the remnants of sleep.

Ellie and Tristan quickly join in the preparations. The camp is efficiently packing up, and they were ready to leave within minutes. Ellie approaches Saphirixia, who is already standing, her eyes bright and alert. "*Are you ready, Saph?*" she asks through their bond.

Saphirixia lets out a low rumble, a sound of affirmation. Ellie smiles and climbs onto her back, feeling the familiar sense of security and excitement. The others also mount their bondeds, each one ready for the journey ahead.

They take to the skies, the forest quickly disappearing beneath them as they soar higher. The ocean stretches out before them, a vast expanse of blue that seems to go on forever. The cool morning air whips past them, the scent of salt and sea filling their lungs.

The flight was smooth, the dragons gliding effortlessly over the water. Ellie's thoughts turn once again to Aetherlyn. She can almost see the city in her mind's eye: the spires of the castle, the bustling streets, and the familiar faces of those she loves.

Hours pass, and finally, they begin to see the recognizable islands on the outskirts of Aetherlyn. Ellie's heart leaps with joy and apprehension. The journey has been long and arduous, but they are almost home now.

As they flew closer, the islands grew more prominent, their lush greenery and rocky shores a welcome sight. The anticipation is palpable among the group, each eager to return to the place they had left behind. Ellie looks over at Tristan, who gives her a reassuring smile, but she can see the concern still flickering in his eyes. She nods, her eyes shining with determination. *Almost home.*

The dragons fly on, their mighty wings carrying them ever closer to Aetherlyn. Ellie can see dragons flying over the castle in the distance, at least ten bonded in the sky.

As they approach, the dragons over the castle change formation, assuming a defensive stance. The leading dragon, a massive creature with shimmering golden scales, roars a challenge that echoes across the ocean. Beside it flies a sleek dragon with green scales and another with deep orange scales. More dragons follow, their colors ranging from orange to onyx black, their riders poised and ready for battle.

Ellie's group slows their approach, hoping the castle defenders will recognize them. As they draw closer, she can see the determined expressions on the riders' faces. She urges Saphirixia to hover, signaling the others to do the same. Tristan and the others follow her lead, their dragons forming a protective circle around them.

The two groups face each other in the sky for a tense moment. Then, the rider on the green dragon raises his hand, signaling for his companions to hold. The riders scrutinize Ellie and her friends, their eyes narrowing as they recognize familiar faces.

"It's the princess!" one of the riders shouts, his voice carrying over the wind. The defensive formation breaks apart, and the dragons fall into a respectful escort position, flying behind Ellie's group.

Ellie breathes a sigh of relief as the castle dragons flank them. The tension melts away, replaced by a sense of triumph, and belonging. The green dragon's rider, a stern-looking man with a silver helmet, flies alongside her. "Welcome home, Princess Ellie," he greets, his voice formal yet warm.

"Thank you," Ellie replies, smiling. "It's good to be back."

The flight over the ocean towards the castle is now a grand procession. The dragons fly in perfect harmony, their wings beating in unison. The green dragon leads the way, its scales gleaming in the sunlight, while the other green and orange dragons fly close behind. The other dragons, each unique in color and size, form a protective arc around Ellie and her friends.

As they near the castle, the grand spires and walls of Aetherlyn come into view. The city beyond bustles with life, the people looking up in awe at the majestic procession above. Ellie's heart swells with pride and emotion as they approach the castle's beach landing.

The dragons touch down on the sandy shore, their riders dismounting with practiced ease. Ellie slides off Saphirixia, her feet sinking into the soft, familiar sand. She's immediately approached by a soldier in ornate armor, clearly a captain, who bows deeply.

"Princess Ellie, welcome home!" The soldier exclaims, his voice ringing with respect. We have been eagerly waiting your return."

Ellie nods, her eyes glancing over to Tristan and Breccan. The soldier's gaze follows hers, and his expression hardens slightly. "Mormont, Aldenridge," he acknowledges, his tone stern. "General Alvar is requesting to speak to each of you upon your arrival regarding your unauthorized departure."

Breccan chuckles nervously, scratching the back of his head. "We had our reasons," he replies, trying to lighten the mood.

The soldier's stern look didn't waver. "Let's get you all back to the castle."

56

Ellie

The soldiers escort them all, flanking them on all sides as they make their way up the path to the castle. The dragons remain on the beach, their massive forms resting but alert, their eyes following their riders.

As they walk, Ellie takes in her homeland's familiar sights and sounds. The castle's grand walls loom ahead, symbolizing strength and history. The path is lined with lush gardens and fountains, their beauty a stark contrast to the wild landscapes they had traversed.

Tristan walks beside her, his hand slipping into hers. “It's really happening,” he murmurs, his eyes scanning the surroundings.

Ellie squeezes his hand, her heart filling with excitement and nervousness. “Yes, it is. We're home.”

As they approach the grand gates of the castle, Tristan gently removes his hand from Ellie's grasp. He gives her a reassuring nod before they enter the courtyard. The air is thick with tension, and Ellie's heart is pounding in her chest. Once inside, she sees the king and queen standing at the top of the steps, their faces a mixture of relief and hesitation.

“Welcome home, daughter,” the king's commanding voice carried across the courtyard. Ellie feels tears prick at her eyes as she ascends the steps, Tristan and the others following behind. The moment is cut short when the king's eyes scan her friends, lingering on Tristan and Breccan. His expression darkening, anger flaring in his gaze.

"Seize them!" the king commands, his voice echoing with authority. The courtyard falls silent, the command hanging heavily in the air. Soldiers begin to move, their armor clinking ominously.

"Father, please, just listen to me!" Ellie implores, stepping forward with urgency, but his anger only seems to build, his face growing redder with each passing second.

"You left without telling us?" he bellows, his voice rising to a roar. "Do you have any idea how worried we were? Did they force you?" His eyes glow red with anger.

The soldiers close in, their expressions grim as they advance on Tristan, Breccan, Kyla, and Stella, forcing each of them to kneel on the ground, swords pointed to all their throats.

Ellie's heart pounds in her chest as she watches, and she knows what she has to do. Desperation and determination surging through her, she taps into her gift without hesitation, sensing her father's magic. His magic pulsing like a glowing red thread, begging to be grasped and bent to her will, sparks to life within her, raw and powerful, a sensation like lightning dancing across her skin flooding through her.

Ellie feels the storm above her, raging, just like her will to protect Tristan and her friends. She will not allow anyone to harm them or for any of them to suffer for the choices she made.

Storm clouds rage in the sky, dark masses swirling with fury. Lightning slices through the sudden darkness, followed by a deafening crash of thunder that startles everyone, even the king.

The courtyard erupts in chaos, and soldiers look to the sky in fear and confusion. "Stand down!" Ellie shouts, her voice amplified by the magic coursing through her.

She feels the lightning's energy in her veins, her control over it absolute. With a flick of her wrist, a bolt of lightning strikes the ground between her and her father, the impact shaking the very foundation of the courtyard.

The king stumbles back in shock, his eyes wide as he stares unblinking at his daughter, the raw power she wields making him hesitate.

The queen gasps, her beautiful blue eyes wide with concern and shock. All the soldiers surrounding them freeze in their tracks, unsure of what to do.

"Do *not* touch them! No *one* will touch them!" Ellie's voice is fierce and commanding, her eyes glowing red with determination. The king is clearly stunned, he nods slowly and waves off his men, eyes never straying from his daughter, who stands tall. Lightning twirls around her arms and sparks of lightning engulf her hands.

Ellie takes a deep breath, her voice steady as she addresses her parents. "Mother, Father, we should speak privately. My friends may leave and go home if they wish."

Her parents agree, both still stunned into silence. With that, Ellie turns and walks back towards Tristan, releasing her grasp on her father's magic. Tristan finally rises to his feet, quickly stepping forward, a smirk gracing his handsome face. He winks at the soldiers, and when his gaze meets hers, pride shines.

Ellie turns to look at her friends, whose eyes are equally as wide as her parents,' but their smiles grow as she peers at each of them, smiling at them in return and nodding.

"I wasn't expecting a lightning show upon our arrival, Princess," Tristan admits, his voice low and husky, making sure the soldiers around him don't hear him.

She shrugs and gives him a devious smile, "I promised no one would touch any of you."

Tristan's smile is bright as he reaches for her, gripping her waist and yanks her into his chest, kissing her fiercely in front of everyone. A bold statement of his affection that makes her knees weak. Ellie loves the feel of his hands on her; she doesn't care who sees him; the urge to kiss him and make a statement that this male is hers is her only thought.

Tristan hesitantly releases her as he rests his forehead against hers. “I’ll see you soon, Princess,” he promises, his voice firm. With a smirk, he strides away.

Ellie watches as Tristan and her friends are escorted away, then turns to her parents. “Shall we?” She asks firmly, her voice leaving no room for argument.

The moment's intensity lingers, the storm's remnants crackling in the air as they all head into the castle.

As they approach her father's study, the tension grows palpable. The massive wooden doors, carved with the royal crest, stand ominously before them. With a nod from King Evandor, the guards open the doors; the atmosphere is thick with the scent of aged parchment and polished wood.

Her father releases her mother’s hand and moves to his desk, his back turned to her. Queen Adelina guides Ellie to a chair, but she chooses to stand, her heart pounding in her chest. The silence stretches, each second feeling like an eternity.

Finally, King Evandor turns, his expression a mix of anger and hurt. "Why did you leave without telling us, Ellissandra?" His voice is stern, yet there is an undercurrent of pain that makes her heartache. Her father never uses her full name, which indicates how angry he truly is.

The king’s hair looks almost unbelievably whiter, his full beard is a little longer, but what hurts Ellie the most is how tired he looks. His usually bright blue eyes, lacking the light they normally shone.

Ellie takes a deep breath, her resolve firm. "I left because I had to. Saphirixia and I needed to do this ourselves, not with a host of guards. You would not have let me leave on my own and you know it."

Queen Adelina steps forward, her eyes softening. "We understand your desire to break the curse, but you put yourself in great danger. We were worried sick about you."

Ellie nods, her eyes meeting her mother's. "I know, and I'm truly sorry for causing you both distress. But our journey was necessary. We needed to go, find the enchantress, and complete the trials. Alone."

King Evandor's gaze hardens. "Yet you took your friends with you and not any of our soldiers to protect you. Do you understand how reckless that is?"

"I did take soldiers with me, three of them, as a matter of fact. Just not soldiers that either of you would have ordered to accompany me," Ellie replies.

Her father grunts at her response before his eyes narrow on her, "And.. Tristan Mormont? What role does he play in your journey?"

Ellie squares her shoulders, ready to defend him, "I'm with Tristan now. He has been my friend, my confidant, and my fiercest protector. Through every trial that Saphirixia and I endured, he stood by my side, strengthening me and caring for me when I needed it most. His courage is boundless, his loyalty unwavering, and his kindness unparalleled." Ellie sighs, preparing for the admission she is about to make, "he completes me in ways I never imagined possible. My heart belongs to him, and nothing either of you say will change that."

The king's frown deepens. "He's a soldier, Ellie, not of royal birth. He doesn't understand our ways, our responsibilities."

Ellie's eyes flash with determination. "Tristan may not be of royal birth, but he's of noble blood, and quite frankly, if he wasn't, it wouldn't matter to me anyway. He understands the true meaning of honor and duty. He has taught me more about myself, leadership, and compassion than anyone ever has."

Queen Adelina reaches out, touching her daughter's arm. "But, my dear, our people expect a union that will strengthen the kingdom. They may not accept Tristan as your consort."

Ellie feels a surge of frustration. "Our people deserve a leader who understands their plight, who has seen their struggles first-hand. Our people deserve a future queen who is happy and has a strong partner by their side. I'm confident that he and I, no matter what challenge we must face, can do just that, together."

Her father releases a sigh, his shoulders slumping ever so slightly. "We knew of your relationship with Jace," he admits, his voice tinged with resignation. "We never said anything, hoping you would come to your senses on your own. We had hoped you would find a match of royal blood, someone who could bring alliances and strength to the kingdom."

Ellie's eyes widen, disbelief and hurt flashing across her face. "You knew about Jace? Yet, you said nothing?"

Her mother's gaze drops, her expression heavy with regret. "We... we thought it was a passing infatuation, something you'd grow out of. As relieved as we are, Tristan Mormont..." She pauses, the sadness in her eyes deepening. "We can discuss you two later. Please, tell us what happened after you left."

Ellie takes a deep breath, ready to recount her journey. She talks for what feels like an hour until she recounts their journey home. Once she is finished, her parents stare at her in contemplation, possibly unbelieving of all that they have endured.

She pauses, looking at her parents, who peer at each other as if silently communicating their thoughts. "I know you must be disappointed that I have yet to break the curse. Believe me, I am as well. This was all just a strange twist the enchantress threw at us."

"We're simply happy you are home and safe. We don't care if you break the curse; we never did," Queen Adelina admits. "Are we not, Evandor?" Adelina's eyes drift to the king sitting behind his desk, peering out the window.

His eyes move slowly, returning to meet Ellie's gaze, "Of course, we are glad you are home. I'm only concerned for you. The trials you described seemed incredibly challenging, and I'm afraid of what your last trial may be."

Ellie sighs, "Whatever it may be, Saphirixia and I are more than capable."

"What of your new gift?" the queen asks hesitantly.

"When the enchantress claimed I would have a new gift that would manifest, I didn't believe her. But now that I have learned to wield my power and command it, I have never felt stronger or more confident."

"In my one hundred and eighty-eight years, never have I heard of any fae possessing such a gift. It's truly an astonishing power to possess, Ellie," the king's tone in awe of her newfound power.

"I know, I was scared in the beginning, but if it were not for Tristan and my friends who each encouraged me to practice and guided me as I learned how to wield it, I wouldn't be as strong as I am now," Ellie admits.

Her mother squeezes her hand softly. "Even though I am still not pleased that you left without our soldiers, I am glad you had your friends and... even Tristan."

King Evandor's expression softens, "So, what of Tristan? What does he seek in this relationship?"

Ellie looks her father in the eye, determined to ensure he hears every word she is preparing to say. "Tristan seeks nothing but to be by my side, to support and protect me. He loves me for who I am, not for my title or position. He has proven his loyalty and his worth repeatedly. As a matter of fact, you should both be thanking him for that loyalty and protection, instead of trying to dismiss my feelings for him."

Queen Adelina sighs, her shoulders relaxing. "If this is truly what you want, we will support you, but you must understand the consequences. The people, the court, they very well may not accept your courtship."

Ellie nods, feeling a weight lift from her shoulders. "I understand, and if that's the case, I'll be prepared to address their concerns then. For now, I would like to give him a chance, give *us* a chance to be happy and have a future if that is what we choose. I deserve to be happy; do you not agree?" Her last words come out more as a plea than a question.

King Evandor studies his daughter for a long moment, then finally nods. "You do; we want you to be happy. We will stand by your decision, but know that our support comes from your expectations. You must be wise, careful, and above all, true to the values of our kingdom."

Ellie smiles, tears of relief and gratitude welling in her eyes. "Thank you, Father. Thank you, Mother. I won't let you down."

"Don't thank us yet. You still don't know what your final trial will be, so we must all be on alert and prepared for anything," the king says sternly and Ellie agrees.

"Also, you must be honest with us. We cannot protect you or help you if you are not open with us," the queen says, cupping Ellie's face. Her eyes are still full of sorrow, but ultimately, love shines through in her words.

Ellie nods as a tear streams down her face. "I promise I will be honest, and though your protection is appreciated, there will be things you must allow me to do, this last trial included. You can't interfere." Queen Adelina nods and wraps her in a tight embrace, the familiar scent of her mother's jasmine invading her senses. "I missed you both so much," Ellie whispers.

As her mother releases her, Ellie peers at her father again as he sits behind his desk, "And we missed you, my dear, so incredibly much." Ellie rises and runs to her father, enveloping him in a warm embrace.

Relief floods through her that her parents will support her, or at least try to. She understands their concern, but Ellie feels like an entirely new person now that she has returned home. So much has changed; she has changed. Ellie has never felt stronger, more confident, or more determined. And now, with her parents' support, she knows that she will break the curse, and just maybe, find happiness with Tristan.

As she leaves the study, her heart swells with pride and love as she walks down the familiar corridors of the castle. The portraits of her ancestors seem to watch her with approval as if acknowledging her courage and determination. She thinks of the journey that she has undertaken, the dangers that she has faced, and the strength that she has found within herself. Every step has led her to this moment, and she is ready to embrace her destiny.

Ellie knows that her parents' support, even if reluctant, is a significant victory. She also understands that proving Tristan's worth to them will be a challenge. She isn't alone in this fight. Tristan has repeatedly proven his bravery and love. Together, they will show anyone who opposes their courtship, that true leadership and love are about more than noble birth.

As she walks through the castle, Ellie feels the eyes of the courtiers and servants on her. She holds her head high and steps confidently as she makes her way to her bedchamber.

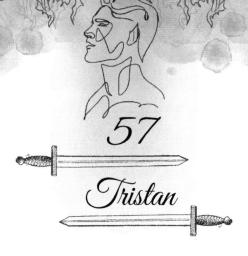

57

Tristan

Tristan stands outside of his father's estate, staring at the heavy wooden door, as anxiety floods him. The estate looms large and imposing, its stone walls a stark contrast to the stormy sky overhead. His heart pounds in his chest, each beat echoing the fears that cloud his mind. He isn't ready to confront his father, and his mind begins to contemplate just how badly their encounter might go. The beating that is sure to come.

The door swings open with a creak, revealing General Alvar standing tall in the doorway. His presence halts Tristan in his footsteps.

"Ah, Mormont, you have returned." General Alvar's voice is as sharp as daggers. He is clearly displeased by Tristan's abrupt departure. The general's eyes rake over him, calculating and scrutinizing as he steps forward.

Tristan holds his breath, bracing himself for the scolding and possible punishment for his decision to follow Ellie. "Yes, General, we have returned," Tristan forces out, his voice steady despite the turmoil inside.

"And the Princess?" The general questions, his eyes narrowing in suspicion.

"She's well and safe back at the castle with the king and queen. I imagine they are discussing our journey as we speak," Tristan replies, squaring his shoulders in an attempt to appear confident.

"Hmmm," the general hums, his eyes still assessing. "I will speak with the king regarding your punishment this evening. Meet me in my study first thing in the morning, soldier."

Tristan takes a deep breath and gives a curt nod, realizing their encounter is going far better than he had expected. With one last scrutinizing look, the general walks past him, heading toward the castle.

Tristan shakes his head, muttering to himself, "*One down, one to go.*" As he steps into his father's estate, the familiar scent of cigars lingers in the air, making his stomach churn. The dark wood paneling and dim lighting add to the oppressive atmosphere, and his unease grows with each step.

As he enters, his father's study door is open. Lord Mormont sits in his chair, staring out the window, the glow of his cigar casting an eerie light. He doesn't turn as Tristan clears his throat, preparing for the confrontation that is sure to come.

"What were you thinking?" Lord Mormont sneers, a cloud of cigar smoke enveloping him. "Leaving with that pitiful excuse of a princess and disobeying me." His words are vicious, each one dripping with obsidian disdain. The mention of Ellie makes Tristan see red, anger boiling within him.

Tristan swallows harshly, preparing his response. "If I didn't go, she would have gone alone. I may have disobeyed, but I did my duty; I protected her."

Lord Mormont scoffs, still refusing to turn and face him. "Duty. Ha! Fancy yourself a comedian, eh? I told you to stay out of the way *knave*. What part of my order did you not understand?" he seethes.

Tristan squares his shoulders, his protectiveness of Ellie surging. "You will not harm her."

With those words, his father finally turns to look at him. Lord Mormont's eyes narrow, studying him with a gaze full of malicious intent. "You care for her," he says coldly.

Tristan freezes, realizing that he has given too much away. His stunned expression is all the confirmation that his father needs. A malicious grin spreads across Lord Mormont's face as he stands and strides around his desk to stand before Tristan. "Do you *honestly* think that she cares for you? That she can come to love you?" he scoffs, shaking his head. "What a fool you have become, Tristan. I thought I raised you better than that. Allowing your emotions to cloud your judgment. And her of all females?"

Tristan clenches his jaw, fighting back the retorts that burn on his tongue, how he hates the man who stands before him. "You know nothing of her, of us," Tristan sneers, sparks of his power tingling along his skin as a fiery rage burns through him.

Lord Mormont laughs, a humorless sound that is cruel and evil. "I know more than you could possibly imagine. Do you think I do not know why you left with her? To help her break the curse and free the fae's, to restore fae magic? After your departure, the king called an emergency council meeting and told us everything. I can only imagine that she has been unsuccessful since you have returned. I can assure you she will not get the chance to break the curse. We are the bonded; we are worthy of magic. I refuse to let those low-born scum possess magic."

Tristan's eyes narrow, his jaw tightening as he stares at his father. "She will restore fae magic and unite the kingdom. I'm certain of it," he declares, his voice laced with conviction.

His father lets out a cold, hollow laugh, cutting through the air like a blade. Before Tristan can react, a hand clamps down on his shoulder, iron-strong and unyielding. "We'll see about that, son."

The words slither like a venom into his mind, coiling onto him like a snake. Tristan feels his dark, invasive magic seep into him, coiling around his nerves, rooting him to the spot. A paralyzing reminder of his father's ruthless power.

A fierce anger ignites within him, his own magic blazing, hot and defiant, begging for release. His father's hold is suffocating, flooding him with a command to submit, obey his every whispering word. The force presses on him, yet he clenches his jaw, muscles tensing against the onslaught. A blistering heat builds in his palm, ready to erupt. With a sharp, controlled breath, he clenches his fist, swallowing the urge to strike back.

"*Reign it in, Tristan. You cannot kill him without being branded a traitor, and then you'll never be able to help the Princess*," Terbius' growls reverberate down the bond. Bleeding stars. *Breathe*, Tristan reminds himself, his chest rising and falling with deliberate breaths.

This battle is far from over. Tristan scrambles to hold onto his own consciousness, refusing to let his father's power shatter his resolve.

The fate of the kingdom rests on Ellie, and Tristan will do everything in his power to ensure her success, even if it means beating his father at his own twisted game. But as he fights to silence the sinister whispers clawing at the edges of his mind, his vision wavers. His thoughts flicker, his senses slipping from his grasp, until, with a final, chilling snap, everything goes utterly dark.

58

Ellie

As Ellie finally walks into her bedchamber, she notices that everything is precisely how she had left it, and yet it feels different somehow.

She doesn't hesitate as she makes her way to her bathing chambers, quickly preparing her bath and carefully removing her dirty clothes.

As she removes her bandages, she inspects her wounds, noticing the cuts on her leg and arm are nearly healed. Ellie imagines what Tristan might have said to the enchantress to obtain such medicine. Ellie smiles to herself at the thought because behind his dominating and tough exterior, he is caring and so gentle as well.

Entering her large, round tub and submerges herself in the scorching water. She whimpers at the sensation and lays her head back, allowing the heat to melt into her stiff muscles.

Her mind quickly wanders towards Tristan, hoping that his arrival home isn't as unpleasant as hers was, but after their talk, she imagins it will be, or possibly worse.

Ellie already misses him, misses his presence, his comfort. Hope rises within her that she will soon see him again, making her think *He's already consumed every fiber of my being, every thought, every emotion; he's my everything.*

Once she finishes her bath, she hears a knock on her door. Excitement coursing through her as the familiar latch of her door opens, then closes, knowing who is waiting for her within her bedchamber.

She quickly dresses and rushes out to see Helena and Clare standing with two of the biggest smiles she has ever seen. Helena's eyes are bright, and her soft smile reminds her of a mother's embrace. Clara jumps excitedly, her auburn hair and chocolate brown eyes shining joyfully. Ellie can't help herself, she flings herself into their awaiting arms.

"We missed you so much, Princess Ellie," Clara exclaims as tears fall down her cheek. The sight makes Ellie's heart ache for even a shred of pain she must have caused them by her absence.

"I'm so sorry that I left; I had to. There's so much that's happened, and I promise to tell you both everything, soon," Ellie chokes out.

"Oh, my dear, we already know everything," Helena whispers, eyes soft with understanding. "We'll have plenty of time to discuss it all soon. For now though, we must get you dressed for dinner, so no more tears," Helena wipes a stray tear from Ellie's cheek.

Ellie takes a deep breath and nods. Within minutes, she is dressed and heading down to dinner, Clara and Helena by her side as she gives them minute details of where she went, how she met with the enchantress, and the trials. However, by the time she gets to the dining room door, she promises to continue telling them more later.

At the dinner table, the exhaustion from the journey home is weighing heavy on her. She can't help but peer out the dining room door when an occasional soldier passes, just hoping to see Tristan again. Worry begins to creep up inside her.

As they eat, Ellie gives more details of the journey, leaving out anything that would upset her mother and father tonight. Thankfully, the king and queen are supportive. She kisses them both goodnight and starts to head back to her bedchambers. Ellie's shoulders slump, and her feet drag down the hall, the weight of it all crashing down on her. "*Saph? How are you fairing?*"

Saphirixia replies almost instantly, "*Well, as you can imagine, Nagaara is furious about our departure, but after hours of recounting the journey, she agreed that we made the right decision.*"

"*Wow. So, it seems your talk went much better than mine,*" Ellie replies sarcastically, slightly chuckling.

"*Do you want to fly for a little while before bed?*" Ellie requests, hopeful.

"*Actually, Nagaara and I are updating Zephyrion and Morphandor right now. I will come to you once they finish scolding me,*" Saphirixia replies begrudgingly.

Ellie can only imagine how that conversation is going with her father and General Alvar's bonded.

"*Good luck, Saph,*" Ellie says, meaning it with every piece of her soul. With that, she feels the connection flicker out.

Finally reaching her bedchamber, Ellie opens the door and halts mid-step. Tristan sits on the edge of her bed with his elbows on his knees, running a frustrated hand through his raven black hair. When his ocean-blue eyes lift to meet hers, the air in her lungs evaporates. *He looks so tired, so distressed...* Ellie immediately runs to him.

Tristan stands quickly, catching her as she jumps, his strong arms enveloping her. His lips quickly find hers in a fierce, need filled kiss. Ellie wraps her legs around his waist as her hands slide through the soft tendrils of his hair. They drift down over his broad and muscled shoulders. Ellie muses, *Bleeding stars, it has only been hours, but I feel like I might die if he doesn't touch me right now.*

Ellie releases a soft moan as his tongue intertwines with hers, teasing her so deliciously she tightens her grip around his neck eager to devour him.

Tristan pulls away abruptly. "Did you miss me that much, Saphire?" His voice is husky and smooth. Ellie smiles brightly at him, unable to hide her joy at seeing him again, yet she doesn't care, not with him. He isn't someone she can hide her feelings from, her wants or desires.

"Yes, I missed you. Of course, I have," Ellie whispers against his lips, breaths ragged as she pulls him down and kisses him hungrily. Enjoying the feel of his lips against her, and the warmth of his hands gripping her body tightly as he pulls her impossibly closer.

Tristan pulls away, Ellie releases a heavy sigh, the absence of his lips feeling almost painful as he sets her feet back down on the hard wooden floor.

"Should I be in here, or will there soon be soldiers coming to drag me off to the dungeons?" Tristan challenges with smirking amusement.

Ellie chuckles and shakes her head, "I spoke with my parents and told them everything. You're safe, for now at least."

"Well, thank the stars for that," Tristan gives her a relieved smile. Tristan kisses her forehead with a tenderness that sends shivers down her spine.

"Um, how *did* you get in here exactly?" she asks inquisitively.

"Terbius," Tristan admits, "begrudgingly, might I add."

His words make her chuckle because, of course, Terbius is not pleased. Ellie implores softly, "How did your return home go?"

She immediately feels Tristan's body stiffen under her palms. Her eyes meet his again. Tristan gives her a look she can't decipher. He nervously bites his lip.

Ellie whispers, "That bad?"

Tristan takes a deep breath, "Yes. That bad," shaking his head. "Let's not speak of him right now. I finally have you in my arms, and all I want ,is to be here with you, Sapphire. Only you."

Ellie's heart swells as he peers down at her. She can see the comfort he desperately needs but knows he will never ask for. She wants to be there for him and never leave his side.

Ellie pulls his lips down to meet hers once again. This kiss isn't soft nor tender; it's full of a burning desire. A living, raging inferno of need. Ellie can't help but think that kissing Tristan feels like being sucked into a dream. She gets utterly swept up in the feel of his body pressing into hers.

Ellie's hands play over every hard muscle on his chest. Her fingers find the hem of his tunic, she starts greedily pulling it over his head.

Tristan only lifts his arms as their lips separate for a moment. He claims Ellie's again, his tunic hitting the floor. Tristan's hands run down her back, Ellie gasps as he grips her behind her thighs and lifts her.

Her legs instinctively wrap around him, and Ellie can feel just how much he wants to take her. Excitement erupts into her blood, the need to feel her skin sliding against Tristan's takes over everything.

"Don't stop," Ellie whispers between ragged breaths. "Don't ever stop."

The world tilts, and the soft cushion of her bed caresses her back. Tristan's weight pushing against her is so perfectly satisfying. He quickly begins unbuttoning the top of her dress, the bodice around her waist suddenly feels suffocating. Her hands shake as she struggles with the lacing.

Tristan's lips graze her neck, along her jaw, and her ear, igniting a burning desire in her core. The laces finally give way and much needed air floods her heated body. Pulling her to sit up, Tristan helps guide her out of the dress's sleeves, leaving only her shift beneath as the last barrier to finally feeling him fully pressed against her. The straps dangling down her arms, putting the top half of her breasts on display.

A deep, rumbling moan rolls from him as his eyes linger there. Ellie threads her fingers into the back of his hair and pulls him back into a searing kiss. His lips break away to trail down her neck again, across her collarbone, until he reaches her shoulder, leaving goosebumps in their wake. “There are not enough stars in the sky or hours in the day to taste every inch of your body. You’re simply intoxicating, Sapphire.”

Tristan catches the strap of her white shift between his teeth, pulling it farther down her arm before tugging at the hem and pulling it down her body.

Ellie’s breaths stagger as she watches his eyes take in her fully exposed body. Anticipation sparks along her skin, and Tristan's eyes darken. Ellie grips his back, pulling his body flush against hers, the muscles in his back flexing against her fingertips.

“*Do you know how badly I have wanted to worship your body? Every single inch?*”

His thoughts ringing loud within her mind, for only her to hear. His lips kiss along her chest and over her breasts. Ellie’s back bows when his teeth bite lightly on her nipple. Groans echo through the room and Ellie’s not even sure who they belong to any more.

Tristan lifts to his knees, his eyes surveying every inch of her. He swallows as he asks, “Are you wondering what I'm thinking now, princess?” Ellie drops fully back down onto the bed, heart pounding she meets his ocean eyes. “I'm thinking about how much I want to drink you in, devour you, drown in you until the only word you can speak is my name from your perfect lips.”

Ellie's breath hitches in her throat. Every word he speaks ripples down to her core, her mind lost in his pleasure as she thinks, "*Bleeding stars, yes.*"

With a devious smile on his face, he runs his calloused palm up her leg, leaving sparks of heat along her skin. He gently lays one of her legs over his shoulder, baring her to him.

“Look at you, you’re fucking perfect.” Tristan says, drinking her in once more before lowering his head to her center; the warmth of his tongue gliding over her instantly sends a raw wave of euphoria crashing in; every sensation pinpointed on every delicious stroke of his masterful mouth.

His tongue swirls and sucks, fire builds in her stomach. He licks her with precision, a male on a mission.

"Please. Tristan, please!" Ellie rasps. He continues greedily, teasing her incessantly. The burning desire continues to build heavily, her vision starts to blur.

A long, slow, torturous swipe of his tongue forces Ellie to cry out as her hips nearly buck off the bed. His mouth leaves her then, a whimper pulls from the loss.

Tristan crawls up to meet her eyes, his lips finding hers once again, the taste of herself sweet yet utterly sinful. "Please, what, Sapphire? Use your words," Tristan presses, his words husky and dripping with silky promises.

"I want you. Now," Ellie whispers in a voice brimming with so much desperation that her soul itself is the one begging for him. Tristan's steady gaze is putting every nerve in her on edge.

His smile grows to a wicked smirk. "Patience, Love. We've only just begun and I'm nowhere near done with you yet."

Tristan's warm mouth descends on her once again, Ellie nearly cries with relief as she finally feels his skin against hers. His hand wanders down her sides, over her hips, and then slips between them. He brushes his finger over her, then slowly pushes it in. The sensation is so overwhelming that Ellie moans loudly, wordlessly begging for more. His thumb comes up to circling her sensitive nerves. Ellie's body begins to rock against him, feeling the impending wave of pleasure cresting to near agony.

Suddenly, he adjusts his hand,adding another finger and pushes deeper. Her eyes roll as he pumps his fingers into her.

"Let me hear you."

His words push Ellie over the edge. The world shatters into nothing but blaring starlight, the exploding pleasure wrapping her body. Yet, he doesn't stop his tantalizing torture.

Just as the fog starts to lift, she watches him sink his mouth back between her thighs. He starts licking and sucking as his fingers pump harder. Ellie's chest starts heaving as unadulterated euphoria booms though her. She goes slack against the bed, gasping for breath, attempting to calm her thunderous heartbeat.

She whispers through choking breaths, "I want to feel you *everywhere*."

"As you wish, Princess," Tristan replies, his voice deep.

Tristan gets up and quickly removes his trousers. Ellie's hand comes up between them and she wraps her hand around his hard length. Tristan's eyelids flutter as he groans through clenched teeth, "Bleeding stars, Sapphire. Your mere touch ruins me."

Ellie smiles wickedly and runs her fingers over the head of his length, enjoying the silkiness of his skin. "No more waiting," Ellie whispers. "I'm yours, and you're mine, I think it's time you show me just how much."

Tristan's hands grasp her hips tilting her just right as he lines himself up to her center. His head brushes her clit, coating himself in her juices, she gasps and drops her hand away. Wrapping her legs around him, she silently urges him to claim her. Tristan's eyes burn like dancing flames.

With one thrust of his hips, he enters her. Ellie's nails dig into his wrists, her sharp gasp bouncing off the walls. With his jaw clenched tight, he slowly brings his arms to either side of her head. The air quakes with the energy around them as he pulls out just a bit, then urges himself forward.

Ellie gasps at the delicious sting of pain, her body trying to adjust to his hard length. She is overtaken by the sudden shock of pleasure that floods through her, her walls clench around him like a vice.

"You feel so perfect, Sapphire, so fucking *mine*," Tristan admits against her lips. She welcomes him inside of her, eagerly wanting him to become a part of her, yearning for only him.

Each delicious, thrust of his length stretches her, the sensation of him making her lose all semblance of sense. The waves of chaotic pleasure have her body tingling with lust. She feels lightheaded, utterly consumed by the feeling of him inside of her.

"Bleeding stars, Tristan, *yes*," Ellie moans, her heartbeat fluttering like dark wings in her chest. A new level of ecstasy that she has never felt before pours over her.

"Ruin me, make me yours," Ellie gasps.

Tristan's lips run along her collarbone, as he bites down on her shoulder, flooding her with heat. He quickens his pace at her words, hitting her most sensitive walls. Her arms wrap around him, her nails biting into his skin, drawing blood as she tries to take gasping breaths. Ellie can feel the inevitable cresting wave of heat threatening to flood through her like an inferno. "Tell me your mine." Tristan growls in her ear.

"Yours, all yours", she chokes out, utterly lost in the feel of him. It feels like a twining of their souls as he repeats her words back to her, his hips thrust harder with each word.

She can feel her eyes roll again, her body shudders with a wave of pleasure.

Ellie's orgasm slams into her like an avalanche threatening to sweep her away, pleasure rocking through her to her very core as stars burst to life behind her eyelids, threatening to blind her. Ellie screams Tristan's name as his head rests between her collarbone and shoulder, his lips lingering on her skin.

She tries to steady her own breathing as Tristan wraps his arms around her. He falls back to sit on the bed, keeping her in his lap as his hands grip firmly on her waist. Ellie rests her arms on his shoulders, knees on the plush bed, and meets his every thrust. With this new position, she can feel him deep inside her.

Tristan groans, his gaze searing into hers, dark and full of primal hunger. His hand slides up, his fingers curling around the back of her neck, pulling her down onto him as he thrusts harder and deeper. Ellie's eyes close at the sensation of him slamming into that spot only Tristan has ever found. Another wave of pleasure barrels through her.

When she opens her eyes, she finds Tristan's smoldering gaze locked to where their bodies are joined. His attention swings back to Ellie's face. For a heartbeat he just holds her there, the intensity of this moment and the reality of what this truly is to both of them crackles in the air.

Ellie quickens her movements, sensing his building desire. Then, with a low, smoldering groan, he closes the distance, his lips claiming hers and with a few deep thrusts, a guttural curse falls from his lips, finding his own divine release.

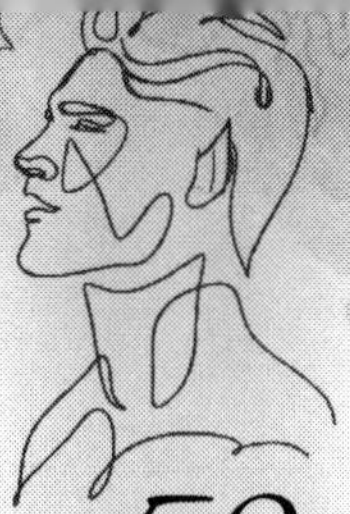

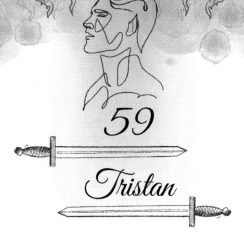

59

Tristan

The world seems to fade as they collapse onto the bed. Tristan pulls her into him as the final tremors of pleasure slowly begin to subside.

"You'll be my undoing, Sapphire. Ruin me, destroy me, break me- I don't care, as long as I'm yours," he says, voice low and husky. *That wasn't just sex or even just an orgasm. That was something far more. It was an awakening, awakening of my soul that is now tied to hers*, he realizes.

Ellie shifts, placing her palm on his cheek as he drinks in every inch of her face and captivating sapphire blue eyes.

"Stars, nothing has ever felt that good before. I don't think I could ever get enough." Her voice is like velvet as she speaks, her words reaching into his soul as she grips his heart in her delicate hands.

He brushes a stray strand of hair from her face, his thumb caressing her cheek tenderly as a soft smile graces her breathtakingly beautiful face.

"Ellie," he whispers, his voice rough with emotion. "You are my last first kiss, princess. You're the one my heart beats for, the one that I'll fight to breathe for. If I had to do this all again, I would, as long as it ultimately brought me back to you."

Her eyes soften, and she leans into his touch, her emotions swirling in the depths of her gaze, mirroring his own. "I feel the same way. You've been my strength, my hope," Ellie sighs. I love you, Tristan."

His thoughts are consumed by her. *She's beautiful, breathtaking, and so unbelievably perfect that if I were dreaming, I would sleep forever, just so I wouldn't have to be apart from her. She's the definition of perfect, perfect for me.*

"I heard that," Ellie taunts softly, which only widens Tristan's smile. *I will never get enough of you, of this*, he thinks.

He kisses her deeply, needing to savor the softness of her lips and the warmth of her embrace, the warmth of her skin against his. Her kiss speaks a thousand unspoken words. Each one feels like a promise, a vow that they will face together no matter what lies ahead.

All that matters is the love they share, a love that is stronger than any curse or trial. As they hold each other, wrapping in the tender glow of their connection, Tristan knows that they can overcome anything; he will sacrifice anything, as long as it is for her.

For now, he lets himself get lost in her, in the sweetness of her kiss, her scent, the lingering taste of her on his tongue, and the comfort of her presence. *She's like fire in my veins, the air I breathe. She's intoxicating.*

They have found something rare and profound in each other, and he is determined to cherish it for as long as they have.

Ellie rises from the bed, unexpectedly. Tristan's gaze follows her, taking in her body as she grabs her white shift from the floor and quickly dresses.

"And where do you think you are going, Princess? I'm not nearly done with you yet." Tristan's words are a threat as well as a promise.

"You made me hungry and quite thirsty," Ellie replies with a smirk as she walks to her table and sits in the chair beside the fire. Tristan decides to follow, quickly tugging on his trousers, dagger belt, and tunic, he releases a soft sigh.

He sits in the chair across from her, he gazes at her, unable to hold back the smile on his face. He knew he could have stayed in the bed and waited for her but the thought of even being across a room from her was too far, he needed to be able to touch her, feel her underneath his fingertips.

"Hungry?" Ellie asks sweetly.

"I am, but not for food," Tristan replies as his brow quirks, teasing her.

Ellie's laugh is soft like the most beautiful music he has ever heard. She quickly pours them both a glass of wine, then she stands and walks to his side with a glass raised.

Tristan sighs as he takes it, his fingertips grazing her hand. "Come with me. I want to watch the stars with you." He takes her other hand as she leads him through the double doors onto the balcony.

A beautiful smile lights up her face as she peers into the moonlit skies, the stars shining nearly as brightly as she is. Her sapphire necklace gleams against the moonlight, nearly glowing against its brightness.

He stands beside her as she sighs and sips the wine, his hand still firmly grasped in her soft grip. Tristan turns to face her, his lips grazing her forehead as he places a kiss atop it as she leans into him, allowing his lips to linger there.

"Besides the mountainside, this is my other favorite place," Ellie whispers. The sound of the ocean waves crashing is like a melodic and calming melody. "Let's just stay here awhile," she takes a deep, steadying breath.

"There is nowhere else I would rather be, Sapphire," Tristan murmurs, his lips brushing the top of her head, her silky hair caressing his cheek. The world around them fading, leaving only the rhythm of his heartbeat and the distant hum of the ocean waves. Minutes, maybe hours, pass as they sit in a quiet stillness, their bodies close, hearts in sync under the vast sky.

Then, Ellie stirs. Her shift is subtle at first, but when her gaze lifts to meet his, her eyes are wide with shock, brimming with unshed tears. The panic that seizes Tristan is immediate and all-consuming, like a noose tightening around his throat. He watches, frozen, as she stumbles out of his embrace, her breath hitching as she clutches her stomach, her fingers digging into herself as if trying to hold everything together.

The wine glass in her trembling hand slips, shattering on the stone with a sharp crack that echoes in the night. The sound barely registers. Tristan's gaze is locked on Ellie—on the blood that now pours through her fingers, staining the white fabric of her shift a deep, unforgiving crimson.

Tristan stands utterly frozen, every second stretching into eternity, the agony etched on her face slicing through him like the sharpest blade. Realization crashes down on him, a tidal wave of horror, as he feels the cold metal of the dagger still clutched in his grip. His gaze tears away from Ellie's pained expression to the blood that drips mercilessly from the weapon's sharp edge.

"No, no, no, no," Tristan rasps, his voice barely a strangled whisper, raw with disbelief. His head shakes furiously, chest heaves, his eyes wide and wild, as searing panic tears through him like wildfire. The dagger slips from his grasp, clattering against the stone floor, echoing like a death knell.

He reaches for Ellie, but she collapses before he can catch her, her sapphire necklace slipping from her neck and landing with a soft, haunting thud beside her as she crumples to the ground.

Tristan falls to his knees, a tear streaking down his face as his shaking hands reach for her. "No... no, Ellie... Sapphire, no!" He screams, his voice cracking, filled with a broken anguish that cuts through the night. He cradles her face in his hands, his touch trembling as her eyes flutter weakly, the spark of life fading from her with each passing second.

"Ellie, please," he begs, his voice a frantic whisper. "Stay with me. Don't leave me. Please... don't leave me."

Ellie's breath comes in shallow gasps, her lips stained red with her own blood. "Why?" she chokes out, her voice so fragile, a mere whisper. The blood on her lips is a vivid scarlet in the moonlight, an unbearable contrast to her pale skin.

Tristan shakes his head, desperate, his mind spiraling. "I didn't—" His words falter, drowning in the weight of his guilt. "I wouldn't... I couldn't..."

Her groan is a broken, agonized sound as she presses her hand harder against her stomach. Tristan's eyes widen in horror when he pulls her hand away, revealing the blood that spills relentlessly from her womb, pooling around them. His hands fly to the wound, pressing down in a desperate attempt to stop the blood flowing from her womb like a relentless crimson river.

"Ellie, no," he pleads, his voice hoarse and raw as he presses harder, but it's futile. Her head lolls to the side, her eyes fluttering shut as her breaths grow fainter. Her heartbeat once so strong now fading, like a distant echo he can barely grasp.

"Ellie... please... don't go," he begs, cradling her lifeless body against his chest, his tears falling like rain onto her blood stained skin.

60

Saphirixia

She flies through the skies as the stars twinkle brightly above her, the soft breeze of the ocean so familiar. *We're home.*

Saphirixia has always dreamed of flying away from Aetherlyn with Ellie, visiting the kingdoms, and seeing the world, but now that they are home, she is happier than she ever expected to be.

Even though her discussion with her mother, Morphandor, and Zephyrion didn't go as planned, she didn't care. After they scolded her for choosing to leave with Ellie and not tell them, she ultimately left, leaving them to bicker amongst each other.

As Saphirixia flies among the stars, the serenity of the night envelopes her. She feels the gentle caress of the wind beneath her wings, the rhythmic beating of her heart in sync with the pulse of the universe. The constellations above seem to whisper tales of ancient dragons and forgotten realms, and for a moment, she feels a profound connection to all that had come before her.

But then, without warning, it hits her, an immense, world-shattering, soul-crippling pain tearing through her. It tears through her very being, searing into her bones, in her soul.

She lets out a deafening roar, echoing across the night sky—a harrowing blend of a thunderous bellow and guttural, agonizing screeches. Her wings falter, and she struggles to maintain her flight, the sharp pain radiating through her ligaments and muscles like molten lava.

Her scales, usually a source of strength and protection, now feels like they were being peeled away one by one. Every breath she takes is a struggle, each inhalation feeling like shards of ice piercing her lungs. Her tail thrashes uncontrollably, the pain sending spasms through her body, causing her to writhe in the air, screeching.

She suddenly realizes, Ellie, she knows it down to her soul.

The pain is so intense, so overwhelming, that for a moment, she can't breathe. Her vision blurs, and she feels as though her heart is being ripped apart. Desperately, she tries to reach out with her mind, seeking the familiar presence of her bonded. But all she feels is a void, a gaping emptiness that threatens to swallow her whole.

"No... *no, no, no*!" Her voice within her mind is a mixture of anguish and fury, a raw, primal sound that resonates with the essence of her being. She beats her wings harder, pushing herself to her limits as she races toward the source of the pain. She can't lose Ellie; she can only think, "*Not now, not ever.*"

Saphirixia's mind races, memories of their time together flashing before her eyes. The laughter, the adventures, the promises they made. She can't let it end like this.

With a final, powerful beat of her wings, she soars through the night, her determination burning brighter than the stars themselves. Her wingbeats rip through the air, flying faster than she had ever flown, the castle's burning torches like a beacon.

Even from this distance, she can make out two figures outside Ellie's bedchamber as she dives towards the balcony. She quickly levels out, noticing Ellie's body on the ground, blood covering her, and Tristan on his knees, as a guttural scream rips from him.

Saphirixia lands, her large talons gripping the ledge and cracking the stone. A jarring roar tears through her into the night sky.

Tristan turns and peers up at her, almost startled by her presence, and tears fall down his face. "Help me, Saphirixia!" Saphirixia's eyes fall to the dagger and the sapphire stone necklace on the ground as a growl erupts from her throat, "*I'll burn him alive!*"

As if noticing her gaze, Tristan stands, hands in front of him as he begs, "I wouldn't, I didn't mean to, I would never! Help me, please! She can't die!" Tristan screams and pleads.

Saphirixia sees the pain etched on his face as the fire begins to burn up her throat, such anger she has never felt rippling through her.

"Help me save her!" Tristan begs again as he falls to his knees, his gaze drifting to Ellie's lifeless body before his head falls, hands covering his face as he chokes on a sob.

Saphirixia feels herself moving towards Ellie, her large snout gently nudging her as she sends a desperate plea to the stars that Ellie is still alive. The metallic smell of blood fills her senses. Ellie's face is pale yet peaceful, her long blonde hair fanned out behind her head. *This can't be happening. I can't lose her. I refuse to lose her!*

A soft glow catches Saphirixia's eye. The sapphire necklace lay upon the stone, glowing brightly as if calling to her. Saphirixia drags the necklace closer to Ellie with a talon, and sudden sparks of the magic course through her.

An idea begins to form—an idea she imagines will be fruitless, but she's desperate. She does the only thing she can think of: she allows the magic to consume her as darkness surrounds and envelopes her.

"*Save her!*" Saphirixia begs into the darkness. The enchantress emerges before her, wrapped in a velvet purple robe. She appears much the same as when they left: her long black hair cascading down her shoulders, her eyes black as night, bearing into Saphirixia.

"*You must save her! I beg you!*" Saphirixia pleads in her mind, hoping the Enchantress hears her plea. She gives her a sad smile yet says nothing, her hands clasped in front of her, her eyes drifting to Ellie's lifeless form.

"*Did you know this would happen?*" Saphirixia growls, demanding answers.

"*I did not. This was not my doing,*" the enchantress admits, her voice calm and relaxed in the darkness. "*Fate can be a cruel and twisted thing, can it not?*"

Saphirixia growls, her anger rising. "*I refuse to live without her! I willingly give my life for hers! Take it—do as you will, save her,*" she chokes out.

The enchantress gives her another sad smile, her gaze meeting Saphirixia's again. "*You willingly give your life for your bonded?*" she asks a hint of surprise in her tone.

"*Yes, yes, yes! Just save her!*" Saphirixia urges.

The enchantress nods slowly, considering her words. "*I would have given my own life for my bonded, if I could have,*" she whispers as if drawn to the past by her own words. "*I will save her and not take you from her either. Know this, Saphirixia: your heart will no longer be your own. As your heart beats, so shall Ellie's. Your hearts will beat as one from this day forth.*"

"*My heart already beats for my bonded, and my bonded alone,*" Saphirixia replies, and she means every word. Ellie is her best friend, her soul's bond.

The enchantress smiles, but it's devoid of the usual malice this time, catching Saphirixia off guard. The absence of cruelty in that smile sends a ripple of confusion through her, but there's no time to dwell on it.

The enchantress gives a curt nod before striding purposefully to Ellie's lifeless body. As she kneels beside Ellie, placing her hands gently over Ellie's still form, her eyes flutter shut, and a strange calm settles over her features.

Saphirixia's heartbeat hammers violently in her chest, each pulse so fierce it feels like it might tear through her ribcage.

She watches, holding her breath, as the enchantress begins to speak—each word slow, deliberate, barely above a whisper. A soft, white light begins to glow from her palms, spilling over Ellie's body like a shroud of hope.

Saphirixia's breath catches as she sees Ellie's body lift ever so slightly off the ground, the light cradling her in a delicate embrace. Tristan gasps audibly, snapping Saphirixia's attention to his disbelieving eyes fixed on Ellie's levitating form. The air between them feels electric, charged with the impossible.

Looking back at the enchantress, she continues to murmur those ancient words. Saphirixia's heart falters, skipping a beat as if suddenly being rewritten to a new, unfamiliar rhythm. Weakness floods her, but she forces her eyes to stay open, desperation clawing at her insides. *Please bring her back to me*, she silently begs the stars.

Then, like a torrent breaking free, she feels it—a rush surges through her veins, the severed connection with her bonded snapping back into place with such force that it nearly knocks her breathless.

"*Ellie, Ellie, say something!*" Saphirixia cries down their bond, her voice breaking as she reaches for the bond that has been agonizingly severed.

The enchantress rises slowly, her gaze never leaving Ellie, and momentarily, the world holds its breath. Then, a loud gasp tears through the air, shattering the silence as Ellie's eyes fly open.

A sob rumbles from deep within Saphirixia's chest, her powerful form trembling as disbelief battles with an overwhelming surge of relief. Ellie's eyes slowly met hers, piercing through to the core of her soul, anchoring her in a moment she never thought she'd feel again.

"*Saph...*" Ellie whispers; her voice is fragile yet achingly familiar, the sound a balm to Saphirixia's shattered heart.

61

Ellie

Ellie gazes up at Saphirixia, her eyes brimming with unshed tears. A strange, foreign sensation stirs deep in her chest, her heartbeat thudding in an unfamiliar rhythm. Instinctively, she presses a trembling hand to her chest, trying to comprehend the bewildering sensation coursing through her.

Suddenly, a blinding blue light erupts from the fallen necklace on the ground, sending shockwaves through the air around them. The light bursts forth, cascading around them like a tidal wave, then surges into the night sky, consuming the stars in its radiant glow.

Tristan rushes to Ellie's side, dropping to his knees beside her. His hand cradles her face, his eyes wide with panic, his touch tender and urgent, as he clutches her trembling hand in his.

"Ellie," he chokes out, his voice hoarse and heavy with a mix of fear and desperate hope. She feels the ache in his tone, a storm of unspoken words pressing down between them.

Then the air shimmers with vibrant threads of light. A deep, pulsing sapphire blue and a fierce crimson red that unfurl around them, charged with magic. The colors spiral together in a celestial dance, weaving a living tapestry around their bodies, casting flickering shadows across their faces as each thread winds through the other. The shimmering halo wraps them in its glow, radiating against the darkness.

Their eyes lock, and in that charged silence, something undeniable blooms. Her breath catches, her chest tight with the simultaneous thrill and terror of what's unfolding. Her mind spins, confusion mixing with a clarity that feels like fate itself.

The radiant threads pulse, winding around them like silken ribbons that spiral tighter with each heartbeat. Drawn by an invisible force, the glowing strands pierce their chests and sink deep within, settling into their hearts. The light embeds itself in a connection that goes beyond words, a truth that reaches down to the core of her soul.

"You're my mate, Sapphire," Tristan breathes, his voice filled with awe and certainty, each word anchoring her in a truth that has been waiting for them all along. His words settle deep within her, igniting a fierce, unstoppable acceptance that feels as ancient as the stars themselves.

They knew they were fated down to their very souls at that moment. The blue light from the skies and the vibrant colors enveloping them felt like a cosmic confirmation of their bond, a destiny written long before this moment.

"*The prophecy—Ellie, hearts that beat as one. I think we did it*," Saphirixia's voice echoed in Ellie's mind like a melody of triumph. Ellie tears her gaze from Tristan's torn face, her mouth falling open as recognition floods through her.

"*We broke the curse*," Ellie thought through gasping breaths, the realization hitting her like a tidal wave. She can feel the weight of the curse lifting, the oppressive darkness that has haunted her for so long, dissipating into nothingness.

"*We did*," Saphirixia's eyes sparkled with a light that matched the celestial glow around them.

Suddenly, the sound of clanking armor and swords echo through the bedchamber, the only indication that they are no longer alone. Ellie looks past Tristan and sees her mother and father halting their steps, eyes wide as they assess the scene before them.

The king steps forward, his eyes narrowing as he notices the blood coating Ellie's shift. Tristan quickly stands, his blood-covered hands out as if trying to form words, but none come.

"Seize him!" the king yells, his voice echoing as a clash of thunder rumbles through the sky, startling everyone. The intensity of his command is like a shockwave reverberating through the chamber.

Before Ellie can speak, the guards seize Tristan, hauling him back and away from her. Her mother and father rush to her side.

"No, Father, no," Ellie choked out, her voice barely above a whisper, laced with desperation.

"Ellie, Ellie, please tell me you are all right!" Queen Adelina begs, her words breathless, tears springing to her eyes. She reaches out, her hands trembling as she cups Ellie's face; her touch fills with maternal worry and love.

Suddenly, Ellie feels overwhelmed. A sob wracks through her as the king and queen pull her into their embrace, their arms wrapping around her in a protective cocoon. The warmth of their bodies was a stark contrast to the cold fear that had gripped her heart. Thoughts swirled chaotically in her mind, each a shard of confusion and pain.

As her parents attempt to soothe her pain, Ellie's gaze flickers to Tristan. His eyes are filled with anguish as he struggles against the guards, begging to be heard. His desperate and raw voice pierces through the cacophony of her thoughts.

She knows, deep in her soul, that she should scream to her parents and explain what has happened, but the pain and confusion halts her words. She remembers the moment of betrayal, the sensation of her life slipping away. *He killed me... why... why would he kill me*? The question echoes in her mind, a haunting question she couldn't silence.

Tristan's eyes meet hers, filled with a mixture of despair and determination. She can see him mouthing words, pleading silently for her to understand, to believe in him. Her heart-shattering in her chest, the bond that had brought them together now tested by the shadows of doubt and fear.

Her father's voice cuts through her reverie, harsh and commanding. "Take him away!" The king's order is final, unyielding, as the guards drag Tristan into the room. Ellie's heart screams in protest, but her voice remains trapped in her throat.

"Ellie, please tell us what happened," Queen Adelina whispers, her tears falling freely. Ellie looks at her mother, her vision blurred by her own tears. The words are there, but they feel impossible to articulate amidst the storm of emotions.

As her parents hold her, their embrace is both comforting and stifling. Ellie feels the weight of the world pressing down on her, suffocating her.

She glances over her parents' shoulders, and to her surprise, she sees the enchantress's white owl with red glowing eyes staring at her, tilting its head as if assessing her. The sight sends a shiver down her spine, *she has been watching all this time.*

62

Ellie

Ellie awakens in her bed, memories flood her like crashing waves, the memories bringing tears to her eyes that spill onto her pillow. She tries to move, but every muscle aches, sending shock waves of pain ricocheting throughout her body.

We broke the curse, Tristan stabbed me, Saphirixia saved me, and Tristan is my mate, were the only thoughts swimming through her mind. *Why? Why would he do this to me? How could he do this to me?*

She had cried for hours. Now, a steady stream of light filters through her room, an indication that it is a new day. Ellie pushes herself out of bed, smothering a cry of agony as she walks into her bathing chamber to dress quickly.

Her heart races as she exits her bedchamber, silently slipping through the halls toward the dungeons below. A guard stands outside the door and stiffens when she appears in the hall.

“Princess Ellie!” He gasps as he stands straighter and bows his head.

Ellie lifts her chin, forcing the pain to the back of her mind, refusing to show a hint of weakness as she prepares for the question she is going to ask. “Is he in there?”

The soldier stutters before answering, “He is, Princess, but the king ordered that he receive no visitors”.

Ellie lifts her brow at him, eyes narrowing. “I will see him. Step aside, soldier.”

The soldier's mouth falls open, but he wisely shuts it abruptly and shifts to open the door for her.

The foul smell of sewage and waste invades her senses, making her flinch at the invasion, she holds back the urge to vomit. The dungeon is dark, cold, and the only sound emanating from the room is dripping water and clanking chains. Ellie forces herself to step forward, passing empty cells as she peers into each one. When she gets to the last cell, her steps falter when she sees him.

Tristan sits with his head in his hands, his elbows on his knees against the stone wall. Ellie sucks in a ragged breath when she notices chains around his wrists and ankles. The sight is so immensely heartbreaking that Ellie finds it difficult to think or even breathe in his presence.

Tristan's hands fall before him, and his head falls back, resting against the cold stone behind him when his eyes open. He finds her standing just beyond the bars.

"Ellie", Tristan chokes. He swiftly tries to stand, stumbling against the chains around his ankles, and he grabs onto the bars. His eyes are frantic as they sweep over her, "You're here," he gasped, "You're really alive."

Ellie soaks him in as his ocean blue eyes look like a raging storm, his eyes clouded with battering thoughts. She shifts on her feet as her heart aches to touch him, but the memories of what transpired keep her frozen.

She straightens her shoulders, masking her emotions behind a face of neutrality. "Why? Why did you do it?" she asks calmly.

Tristan's forehead falls to the bars as he tries to steady his breathing. The strands of his raven black hair cover his eyes as he admits, "It was my father."

"Your father?" Ellie gasps at his words.

"I have so much to tell you, Sapphire. So much that I should've told you already. I would never, ever try to harm you, Ellie. You must believe me," Tristan begs, tears lining his eyes when his eyes meet hers again.

"Why?" she demands again in a commanding tone.

"My father doesn't want all fae's to have magic. He must have used his gift upon me. I swear, Ellie, I didn't even feel myself doing it. I didn't even know what I did until I saw the blood." Tristan choked on his words, his body stiffening as he gripped the bars tightly, closing his eyes as if the image of her was the only thing he saw.

Ellie looks away, unable to peer into the eyes of the male she gave her heart to, the male she now knows is her mate.

Can I believe him? Can this possibly be true? Doubt cascades through her mind as she rubs her temple, trying to soothe away the pain.

"Please, Ellie. Look at me", Tristan begs, voice hoarse.

Ellie's gaze drifts back to Tristan, her own eyes lined with unshed tears.

"I love you, Sapphire. I would never, ever allow harm to come to you."

"But you did! This happened because of you, because of him," she sneers. "But you did! You could've told me! You could've been honest with me! You're my mate, Tristan! Do you understand what that means?" Ellie asks, her voice raising as it echoes through the dungeons.

Tristan winces as if he feels the pain in her words: "I'm sorry, Ellie. I should have told you. My father manipulated my mind; he used me for his own gain. When we returned home, he knew of my feelings for you. He wanted the faes to never possess their own magic. This was his plan; he wanted to tear us apart."

"Well, he succeeded," Ellie declares harshly.

"Please, Sapphire, don't say that," Tristan begs, his voice trembling with his words.

Ellie's chest feels like it's being ripped apart from the inside, every beat of her heart splintering into shards of rage and sorrow. She wants to scream at the world, no, she wants to burn it down, tear everything around her into ash and ruin. The love that once filled her, warm and steady like the sun, now lies shattered at her feet, cold and sharp like glass.

Her voice trembles, but her words are razor-edged. "I love you, Tristan. So much that I would tear my heart out and give it to you, willingly. And yet... you lied to me. You weren't honest with me. You were the one that said it was you and I now." Her hands clenched into fists, nails digging into her palms. "We could've protected each other. But instead of protecting me, you protect *him*."

Her throat tightens, choking on the raw betrayal. Tristan reaches for her, his fingers brushing hers in a touch that still sparks along her skin. The bond between them, that soul-deep connection. *Mate.*

But Ellie pulls away, her hand trembling as she steps back. His eyes, those all-consuming, ocean-blue eyes, fill with anguish as he watches her retreat. She tears her gaze from his, feeling like she's ripping out a piece of herself with it.

With one final breath, she turns. Every step feels like it's fracturing her heart even more, the pain unbearable, but she forces herself to keep walking, conscious of every step she takes.

Behind her, Tristan's voice breaks through the silence, raw and desperate, drenched in sorrow. "Sapphire... my love will live and die with you."

Ellie's throat tightens as she swallows back a sob, her whole body shaking. She doesn't turn around, doesn't let herself fall apart. She digs her nails into her skin, forcing herself to keep walking, one agonizing step at a time, as her world crumbles around her.

The

End

Acknowledgements

First and foremost, my deepest gratitude goes to my incredible husband. You are my rock, my anchor, the foundation upon which I've built this journey. Your unwavering belief in me, your encouragement in moments of doubt, and your love through every high and low have been my greatest source of strength. I truly couldn't have done this without you.

To my beautiful daughter, my mini-me. You are the brightest light in my life. Your laughter, your spirit, and your joy remind me every day why I strive to create something magical. You are the reason I pour my heart into these pages. Also, you may not read this until you turn twenty-one.

To my wonderful Nanny, I cannot express how much your endless patience, love, and unwavering support mean to me. You've been my constant, my safe harbor, always encouraging me to dream bigger, push further, and never stop. This book wouldn't exist without you—you are my person, my sounding board, my heart. Every idea I've had, every word I've written, has been shaped by your wisdom and guidance.

Dad, your steadfast belief in me has never faltered. Thank you for always being there, for reading a book you might not have picked up if I hadn't asked, and for cheering me on with all your heart. Your love and encouragement have carried me through the hardest moments, and I am so blessed to have you as my father.

To Sammy and Taryn, my lifelong friends, your love and support have been pillars of strength throughout this entire journey. From countless conversations to unwavering encouragement, our friendship has sustained me through thick and thin. I know with all my heart that we'll still be there for each other when we're old and gray, just as we are now.

To Danny & Cynica—this book wouldn't be what it is without you. I am beyond grateful to have met you both. You came into my life when I needed it most, and words fall short of expressing how much you mean to me. Here's to many more late nights, endless chapters, and adventures ahead.

Additionally, Neecee, Tori, Samantha, Nicole, Lisa, Lynn Marie, Mandy, Katy, and all of my incredible ARC readers. Your enthusiasm, feedback, and belief in this story have been a driving force for me. You've cheered me on with such love and excitement, and I couldn't be more grateful.

To my amazing co-workers and bosses—thank you for believing in my dream and for your constant support. Your understanding and encouragement, especially on the days when I showed up a little too tired from late nights of writing or editing, have meant so much to me. I couldn't have done this without your patience and kindness.

To every single supporter who has believed in me and this story, you have been my motivation to keep going. Your encouragement, feedback, and love have meant the world, and I'm endlessly thankful for each of you. Your presence has filled my heart, and I promise to keep creating for you.

And finally, to my readers—thank you from the bottom of my heart for joining me on this adventure. Your love for this world and its characters fuels my passion and keeps me writing. I hope this book brings you the same joy it has brought me in creating it. And I promise—book two will be a journey that heals your soul.

With all my love and gratitude,

“K.T. Carpenter”

About the author

K.T. is a Texas-based author, wife, and mother who balances the demands of family life with a career in the corporate world. A lifelong lover of fantasy and dark romance, she spends her free time immersed in the worlds of books—whether she's reading them or bringing her own stories to life.

Driven by a long-standing dream to write a story about a girl who shares a unique bond with a dragon, K.T. has poured her heart into creating a world where magic, friendship, love, and adventure intertwine. Writing has been a lifelong passion, and with her debut novel, she brings her dream to reality, crafting a tale filled with emotion, adventure, and powerful bonds.

When she's not writing or reading, you can find her cherishing moments with her family and exploring the endless possibilities of her imagination.